More Praise for *THE LIST*

"Breezy, dishy . . . a witty and caffeinated glimpse into a world few of us ever see. But underneath is a surprisingly moving coming of age story about a young woman navigating the bumpy terrain between ambition and ethics, between her hunger for professional success and the quiet truth of her own heart."

—LAUREN FOX, author of *Still Life with Husband*

"An energetic, humorous debut that perfectly captures the frenetic, all-consuming pace of political reporting, with a healthy dose of scandal, glamour and intrigue thrown in."

—SARAH PEKKANEN, author of *These Girls*

"Part coming of age, part political thriller, with the most irresistible heroine since Bridget Jones at its center. This is Evelyn Waugh's *Scoop* for the 21st century."

—SUSAN FALES-HILL, author of *Imperfect Bliss*

"A wonderfully witty insider's romp through Washington. Tanabe has as sharp a tongue as she does an eye for detail."

—CRISTINA ALGER, author of *The Darlings*

"A gorgeous book—I loved it. Funny, intriguing, and utterly unputdownable."

—PENNY VINCENZI, internationally bestselling author

THE LIST

THE LIST

A NOVEL

Karin Tanabe

WASHINGTON SQUARE PRESS

New York   London   Toronto   Sydney   New Delhi

WASHINGTON SQUARE PRESS
A Division of Simon & Schuster, Inc.
1230 Avenue of the Americas
New York, NY 10020

First Washington Square Press trade paperback edition February 2013

WASHINGTON SQUARE PRESS and colophon are registered trademarks of Simon & Schuster, Inc.

For information about special discounts for bulk purchases, please contact Simon & Schuster Special Sales at 1-866-506-1949 or business@simonandschuster.com.

The Simon & Schuster Speakers Bureau can bring authors to your live event. For more information or to book an event contact the Simon & Schuster Speakers Bureau at 1-866-248-3049 or visit our website at www.simonspeakers.com.

Designed by Akasha Archer

Manufactured in the United States of America

10 9 8 7 6 5 4 3 2 1

Library of Congress Cataloging-in-Publication Data

Tanabe, Karin.
  The list : a novel / Karin Tanabe.—1st Washington Square Press trade pbk. ed.
    p. cm.
  1. Women journalists—Fiction. 2. Legislators—United States—Fiction.
  3. Adultery—Fiction. 4. Washington (D.C.)—Fiction. 5. Political fiction. I. Title.
  PS3620.A6837L57 2013
  813'.6—dc23   2012022076

ISBN 978-1-4516-9559-5
ISBN 978-1-4516-9560-1 (ebook)

For my mom and dad

THE LIST

CHAPTER 1

Isabelle Norman's skin was the color of uncooked meat, and her green eyes glistened with panic. She ran toward me, a Usain Bolt in heels.

She had just sprinted out of a closed-door meeting with our newspaper's editor in chief, Mark Upton, and she looked about as happy as the fat girl picked last in gym class.

When she stopped at our group of plastic desks in the very back of the newsroom, I saw the lines of tears covering her pretty oval face.

"I'm going to get fired. Immediately," she bleated, grabbing my arm, leading me toward a bank of glossy white elevators and collapsing onto a bench. "I'm—I'm a—I'm going to get fired for being an incompetent fool on CNN! Of all the networks out there, I had to be an absolute dimwitted idiot on CNN!" Her tears started to fall faster. She put her head between her knees and let her wavy blond hair fall into the pleats of her magenta silk skirt.

I wanted to wrap her up and take her directly to the Four Seasons for a large tequila and a shiatsu massage. But instead, I just watched her sob in a building with the privacy of a maximum-security prison.

What was she doing on CNN again? Wasn't she doing a hit

with that scary White House reporter Olivia Campo? A woman so pompous she made Hosni Mubarak look humble.

"Were you on with Olivia?" I asked, smoothing her sweaty hair down. I tried to speak in a buttery, soothing voice.

"Yes, I was on with that little termite," shrieked Isabelle, clearly not responding to my lullaby tones. "And guess what? She stole everything! She stole all of my talking points! I sat silent on CNN for twenty entire minutes. A third of an hour. Someone called the network and asked if I had facial paralysis!"

That last part had to be made up.

She looked me square in the eyes and said, "That last part is not made up."

Eek.

"It could not have been that bad," I lied. I tried to sound calming and nurturing. The Mother Teresa of colleagues. "You are so charismatic. And smart!" I offered up. "I'm sure the majority of it went swimmingly."

She looked up at me with the pain of an abandoned child. "Swimmingly?" she repeated. "No. Not even a little. Not even a dog paddle. I drowned, and I'm going to get fired. It was a quiet death, at least. I was mute," she said, wiping away her tears. She took a coffee filter from the side table and patted her face with it.

"My mother texted me and said she's praying for both my sanity and continued employment. She said she's overnighting my white Confirmation dress, because it made me look so innocent. I'm going to wear it to work tomorrow."

Confirmation? Wasn't that a rite of Catholic passage dedicated to tweens?

"But didn't you wear that like thirteen years ago? It might be a little tight," I advised.

"Adrienne! Be realistic! Drastic measures must be taken."

"No one watches stupid CNN anyway. Their ratings are way

down," I said. "Think about it. The only time I tune in is to see the rise and fall of the Asian markets. But that's all. I bet like five thousand people were watching, tops."

Isabelle shook her head no. She motioned for my mohair cardigan. I placed it in her shaky hand, and she rubbed it on her cheek and clutched it like a security blanket.

"This wasn't some Washington-only program," she assured me. "It was CNN. Hundreds of thousands of people saw me. Maybe millions!" she wailed, sounding muffled through the fabric. "And it was the international edition. I'm going to kill myself."

That sounded bad. Had people from other time zones called in? Was the woman who asked if Isabelle had a mummified face ringing up the CNN hotline in New Delhi?

"How could Olivia have possibly stolen all your notes?" I asked. "Did she write them all on her palm? Can we have her ejected for verbal plagiarism?"

"There are no rules in television!" Isabelle screamed. Her voice bounced off the glass walls surrounding the bank of elevators and the smoky gray marble floors. "Plus," she said, cracking all her knuckles one after the other, "it was all my fault. I should know that every single person at the *Capitolist* is a self-serving, self-righteous prick."

After she had soaked two coffee filters with her saliva and tears, she balled them up, handed them to me, and explained what had led to her anguish.

"It was around eight P.M. last night. We were just sitting in the greenroom at the CNN headquarters in Northeast before our segment on the president's upcoming vacation to the Gulf Coast. I was fact-checking a few things online and making small talk with Olivia. I've known the troll for a year, after all. And for some reason, I was pretty nervous. You know, I do a lot of

TV, but it was a forty-minute segment, twenty minutes each. That's a hell of a long time to be live. But I was prepared. I spent all weekend writing notes, everything organized and written in black and red fountain pen."

I nodded encouragingly. It was always a good idea to have executive-looking pens.

"And then in the greenroom, while I drank a triple espresso so that I would be extra peppy, Olivia asked me what I was going to talk about, so we wouldn't overlap. I viewed it as a perfectly normal team-player kind of question, so I let her look at my notes."

At this point, she started to cry again, as if her puppy had just been microwaved.

"Adrienne, I swear, I didn't know that red-haired narcissist would steal everything! I mean, who has a memory like that! If she's so smart, why didn't she just make her own multicolored notes!"

Her facial paralysis seemed to have been cured: she had dropped the cardigan and was scrunching up her button nose like a Shih Tzu.

"Well, you should say something," I suggested. "Rat her out. Tell Upton that you were more prepped than the president but Benedict Arnold swiped your notes!"

Isabelle sighed. "They won't believe me. Or care."

"Show them your talking points," I urged. "Give them irrefutable proof."

Isabelle reached for another coffee filter. "You know how this place works, Adrienne. No missteps. No mercy! They'll just say I'm totally stupid for having to prep that much. You know them. They think you should be able to recite the entire history of American politics on cue, like a dancing monkey. I just don't think that way. I have to prep."

She was right. I had only been at the paper for three weeks, but I knew that. You walked in the door, and they gave you a phone and a computer and said "go." That was it. From that moment on, you had to get everything right.

"You should talk to Upton anyway," I said. "That's so morally wrong. Maybe they'll actually listen to you and fire her." I knew they wouldn't. They didn't care how you got your info, as long as you didn't plagiarize it and you presented it with Napoleonic confidence. But I had to say it anyway.

"Fire her? They love her," said Isabelle through her sniffles. "God, I wish she would just disappear to the mountains of Papua New Guinea. Are there mountains in Papua New Guinea?"

I shrugged and looked at her blankly.

"Maybe someone would eat her. Or maybe she would contract a horrific case of syphilis like Paul Gauguin and die a slow and painful death."

"I think that happened in Tahiti." I was standing in front of her, trying to shield her from curious colleagues who might suddenly jump out of the elevators.

"Whatever. Tropical island teeming with germs, STDs, and cannibals," said Isabelle. "That's where the little thief deserves to be."

I was ready to share a hearty laugh and invent a few more ways for our amoral colleague to die, but Isabelle had succumbed to further crying.

"You must have answered a few questions. I don't believe it was all that bad," I said. I had seen Isabelle do plenty of TV, and she was photogenic and great on camera. That's why our media bookers had dared to put her on CNN for twenty long minutes.

"I didn't answer a thing," said Isabelle. "I sat there, frozen, like those ice people they found perfectly pickled in Nova Scotia. Whiskers and everything."

"I think you mean preserved."

"Whatever! I looked like I was born without the ability to smile," she said, sniffling. "Oh, and as a bonus, those horrific media training girls marched right in to my Upton meeting. That girl Gretchen, the one who always eats papayas with a steak knife, she analyzed the footage for our dear editor and guided him on a master plan of damage control. She watched it ten times!"

Wow. Ten times. That seemed excessive. The only videos I had seen ten times were *Love Actually* and this night-vision sex tape I made with a Parisian bartender in college. Both did get better after multiple viewings but I doubted the same rule applied to Isabelle on CNN.

"What did Gretchen say?" I asked cautiously.

"Oh, well she was an absolute dear. A real chum. She said I was too thin and mannish and not meant for the screen." Isabelle's eyes started to tear up in a soap opera kind of way. "She brought the video into the meeting and forced us all to watch it together. While I was making this terrible blank face, she smacked the pause button and sucked in her breath through her teeth. It made this sound: *ahhzzzzz*. Then she looked at me and said, 'Isabelle. Let me say something to you woman to woman.' I thought she was going to compliment me on my skin-care regime or something equally chickish, but she didn't. Oh and of course Upton was right there. Woman to woman, my ass. So while I sat on my hands to keep from punching her in the jaw, she said, 'I look at that video, and I just can't stop thinking, Ron Paul. Ron Paul. I'm looking at the female Ron Paul.' Can you believe it? Ron fucking Paul!"

"Wait, what?!" I exclaimed. "He's like eight hundred years old."

Isabelle shook her head. "Well then that's what I look like, too. Because according to the media witch, I am the spitting image of United States representative Ron Paul. Never mind that he's very old and a man."

"He is a doctor and a committed Libertarian!" I pointed out. "And a Texan."

"Gretchen said that if I was going to put on this big California glamour act of mine, I needed more pigment in my face and more meat on my bones. It's like she wants me to be a Maori rugby player! And male. Do you know how hard people work to be thin? Has she never seen Giuliana Rancic? People are supposed to want to be thin. I'm an athlete. I've been thin and muscular all my life! Since birth. I weighed five and a half pounds and was the only baby in the hospital with a six-pack."

Looking from glass door to glass door to make sure no one was coming, Isabelle put her head between her knees again and said, "It's too much. Please fetch me my pistols."

"How about I just get us some lunch?" I asked, trying to sound upbeat.

"Fine, suit yourself. I might as well accept your charity since I'll be out of work in the next twenty-four hours. They'll probably choose lethal injection as my going-away present."

Isabelle was afraid her CNN clip was going to go viral. That every reporter on earth would forward it to each other as what not to do when given a great television opportunity. Luckily, that didn't happen. It racked up a couple thousand hits on YouTube and Upton joked about it in the next company-wide meeting, which had Isabelle eating Xanax for a week. But the wave never swelled into a tsunami. Of course, CNN stopped requesting her and the *Capitolist*'s media bookers struck her name from their telegenic reporters list—you didn't get to make the same mistake twice at the paper. When Isabelle got her next television assignment, it was talking about presidential pets on a Maryland public access station.

CHAPTER 2

I once had a dream that I was backstroking naked with John Edwards in a murky swimming pool in Washington, D.C. It was a bit like a swimming pool mated with a pot of soup. We were splashing around together, and every so often I would duck my head under and take a look at his baby maker. Besides us and the lobster bisque water, there was only one other thing in the pool: a huge inflatable football that we batted around like it was the size of a grapefruit rather than a Clydesdale. We just swatted and splashed, all naked and flirty, until I was woken up by the piercing death machine commonly known as the alarm clock.

While my trusty dream analysis book told me that my vision meant I would be pregnant within a year and could expect a large raise, I interpreted it to mean that John Edwards was going to be the 2008 Democratic nominee for president. Turns out I have the intuition of someone with stage 6 Alzheimer's. John Edwards was not made of the stuff presidents are made of. He was a man whore. The whole disaster was a bit of a blow to my romance with politics, but it was more like a slingshot to the heart than a semiautomatic to the head.

I quickly forgot about baby daddy Edwards and gave all my spare change to Hillary Clinton. I could throw all my egg whites in one basket for Hillary and not worry that she was going to get knocked up.

It didn't work out. As we all know, the chosen one from Honolulu did the hula all the way into the White House, Hillary Clinton got her consolation prize, and John Edwards became everyone's favorite voodoo doll. I wouldn't have written history that way, but I was happy to be a tiny part of it. I donated, I voted, I embraced my born-and-bred-in-the-Washington-area status and went to handfuls of political events in duplex apartments in Manhattan. One time, I dressed as a donkey and casually ate a bunch of carrots at a debate night party. At twenty-five, I was proud to be more politically involved than your average American.

Fast-forward three years and my life revolves around politicians, all of whom seem to think that laws are as flexible as gymnasts. Before the sun is up, I start reading about politics. A few minutes later, I start writing about politics. And three hours after that, I start physically stalking the people who write our incomprehensible laws. Why? Because I work in Washington, a town where you don't set up shop unless you're ready to let politics control your life. It's like *1984* without the overalls and mind control torture.

I didn't succumb to Washington's marble fist immediately. When I became the proud owner of a two-hundred-thousand-dollar college diploma, I knew I had to move to Manhattan, have casual sex, and spend my rent money on Italian-made clothing and the Hampton Jitney for a few years. So I did. I said goodbye to the sisterhood of Wellesley College and moved to a minuscule apartment in a really nice neighborhood with a view of Central Park. For a handful of years, I did what my Gen Y English major peers did and worked my way up at glossy publications in

Manhattan. It was very glamorous and terribly paid. It was also fun. (Really fun. Especially that one Dutch banker named Fritz who had hands like Sharper Image back massagers.) But even as my apartments and paychecks got bigger, I never thought I'd stay forever. I grew up in Middleburg, Virginia, a historic town just outside Washington. I canvassed for a congressman in college up north and always thought politics would be part of my future. After so many years in New York's luxury media world, I realized that I missed breaking affordable bread with people who loved Capitol Hill.

When I was ready to bite the bullet and say goodbye to heiresses with the last name Getty and say a stern hello to hard-hitting news, I put out some feelers.

At the end of July, when New York was in its summer slow-down, I started reaching out to my Washington contacts and was told that *the* place to be was the *Capitolist*. Both the fast-moving website and the daily print publication were dominating the Hill, an editor friend at the *Washington Post* told me. As soon as her contract ended, she was applying there and I should, too. I asked her for her *Capitolist* contact, sent my résumé to the hiring manager for a Style reporter position, and a month of interviews and writing tests later, I had an offer.

The *Capitolist*. I considered it for about a nanosecond, and then I said yes.

"You've gone insane," said my boss at *Town & Country* magazine in New York when I gave notice in September. "Do you know what happens to people who work at the *Capitolist*? Immediate varicose veins. All over. Even in your face. You'll gain ten to fifteen pounds, your hair will dull, your teeth will yellow, you'll forget all foreign languages, and you'll start eating entire cakes for breakfast."

"Entire cakes?" I asked.

"Yes, entire cakes," he said.

He sighed and looked at me as if I had just declared that I was donating all my working limbs to science. "But yes," he conceded, "you will know a hell of a lot about politics and those ugly, sad people who call themselves leaders." He walked right up to me, gave me a kiss on each cheek, and said, "If that's what you want, go on." He took my official, typed two-weeks notice and told human resources to open the job I had worked so hard to get.

After deciding to trade in Manhattan's money and eccentricity for Washington's power and traditions, I called my only childhood friend who had stayed home rather than running north. Twenty years ago, we had eaten live starfish together while on a church group vacation and had ended the jaunt as two very ill best friends. She was working at the single cool art gallery in D.C. and had taken to wearing origami shapes instead of clothing with archaic things like sleeves.

Elsa's take on the offer was that if I said anything but yes, I was as good as lobotomized. Forget that it paid Starbucks wages. "You got a job at the *Capitolist*? That's huge!" she shouted into her iPhone. "Everyone wants to work there. Seriously. People have been leaving the *Washington Post* in droves to work there. I read an article that said as much in the *New York Times*. Of course they're probably biased, but whatever. It's the place to be right now. It wins awards daily. It's filled with geniuses. People are obsessed." In the back I could hear a strange harmonica sound mixed with the clanging of dishes.

Elsa yelled at her interns to keep it down. "By the way, did I tell you I was pregnant? Not actually pregnant, but metaphorically so. It's all part of this performance art piece we're putting on next weekend. Will you be down here by then? We could use another metaphorically pregnant person. Plus, you have to take that job."

"Eh, no. Next week, no. No time to be metaphorically pregnant until October," I replied. Forget performance art; I was still a touch skeptical about the job. I liked to get my politics the old-fashioned way: from long-form articles, public radio, or drunks at cocktail parties. I wasn't totally sold on taking over Capitol Hill one tweetable sentence at a time. But Elsa was right about the *Capitolist*'s reputation. The paper had its wonky tentacles stretched all over the country.

"Who are the obsessive people who read the *Capitolist*?" I asked. "Do you know any of them? Or are they all incarcerated? Because I had a gig in college that required a pair of latex gloves and tweezers to read the packets of mail delivered from the penitentiary."

This was actually true. My first job in journalism was at a religious magazine in Boston that I believe was the most popular rag at America's maximum-security prisons. Besides porn, obviously.

"No! Like everyone on the Hill," Elsa assured me. "Everyone. And plus, their reporters are on TV all the time. You'll definitely be on Larry King."

"He retired."

"Whatever. Take the job."

I already had.

When I first arrived at *Town & Country* after slogging at a regional magazine for two years, I would have tattooed "I heart *T&C*" on a number of different body parts, not that the esteemed magazine would have approved such a tacky move. But I would have. It was such a fascinating place. The women were like smart, polished, walking, talking Barneys mannequins. They knew how to set a table for a ten-course meal, traded stories about summers in Cap d'Antibes and winters in Cape Town, but could also write delightful articles comparing Gilbert and

Sullivan to Lil Wayne without breaking a sweat. Not that anyone at *T&C* ever broke a sweat—that's why God invented arm-
pit Botox. I was in awe and the awe lasted for years.

I can't pinpoint the exact time when my devotion started
to crack, but I think it was while dating a PhD student named
Ilya who was obsessed with Russian literature. His name wasn't
actually Ilya, it was Brett Olney, but he made everyone call him
Ilya for obvious reasons.

On our first date we sat in Central Park and he read to
me from a book called *The Master and Margarita*, which I said
sounded like a smutty Mexican telenovela. He stopped reading
after I made that comment but I was so hot for him that I faked
an obsession with Russian literature to try to get in his pants.
The downside of this BS obsession was that I agreed to go to a
lecture on the Russian Revolution of 1917, which I had stupidly
said changed my perspective on history, never mind the fact that
my knowledge of Russian history extended to ballet and caviar.
The weekend before the daunting lecture I locked myself in my
apartment with a five-hundred-page tome on that pesky war, a
Rachmaninov playlist, and a bottle of Smirnoff, and had my own
little holiday in St. Petersburg, or Petrograd as I soon started
calling it. I only got halfway through the book, but I remember
putting the thing down and thinking, *Wowyzowy, I'm insanely
wasted.* After I ate a loaf of bread to sober up, my next thought
was, *I haven't penned anything of substance since college.*

I wanted to write about something other than luxury vaca-
tions and eccentric heiresses. Maybe history. Maybe politics. I
soon realized that only senior citizens who can spell the word
Smithsonian backward read history publications. Plus, the only
part of that big book that held my attention was the description
of Nicholas II's lavish palace, complete with a hydraulic lift and
a movie theater.

Politics won.

The first thing I had to do after I decided to ditch New York living was make a really depressing phone call to my parents asking if I could squat with them in Middleburg, Virginia, until I figured out how to maneuver a D.C. that had become far more expensive than the one I left behind in high school. I was taking a 25 percent pay cut to become one of those reporters who was on TV all the time. I had thought about alternatives: living in a houseboat on the Potomac River, living with a bunch of unknown roommates who ate cat for dinner, or dwelling in Washington's seedy Ward 8, where I could afford an apartment with an actual bedroom. On my budget, it turned out the houseboat would be an inflatable raft, the Craigslist apartment ad I answered had the words "Wiccan witch circle" in tiny print at the bottom, and when I looked at the number of violent crimes in Ward 8, I decided that as exciting as a drive-by shooting might sound on my résumé, it was probably not something I wanted to endure.

My twenty-eight-year-old fingers dialed the first phone number I ever knew, and I prepared myself for a little humiliation. That morning I had been writing copy about why tiaras weren't at all out of fashion, and just twelve hours later I had to grovel for room and board in the commonwealth of Virginia.

"Let Dad answer, let Dad answer," I chanted out loud as the phone rang. "Helloo, helloo, Caroline Cleves Brown here!" my mother shouted into the receiver after three rings.

This was going to be a very belittling experience.

"Adrienne Brown here!" I shouted back. "Your favorite child. The one who didn't pour scalding water on your feet when she was a teen." This was true. When she was fifteen, my very dexterous and evil-spirited sister, Payton, "spilled" a large pot of boiling water on my mother's toes. I don't think my mother or her pedicurist ever truly forgave her.

After I yapped out some small talk, spouting lines about how much I appreciated her continued love and affection and how I would be a shred of an ugly little person if it weren't for her wisdom, grace, and guidance, I made my request.

My mother huffed and puffed like someone at the summit of Everest, paused, and then declared, "Of course you can live with us! It will be just like old times. Except that spoiled sister of yours now lives in Argentina and your father has turned her bedroom into some sort of *Hoarders* den. I'm sure the housekeeper is thinking of reporting us to A&E. And did I tell you we had to fix the Tuscan shingled roof because of a hurricane and that the insurance company claimed it was 'an act of God.'" She stopped to catch her breath, muttered something about the pains of seasonal affective disorder, and then added, "Oh, and you. Sorry. Yes, it will be great to have you home. The barn apartment happens to be empty right now."

I looked at my feet to make sure I hadn't sprouted hooves. "I have to live in the barn?"

"Sweetheart. You make it sound like we're treating you like a donkey! It's the barn *apartment.* The horse trainers used to live there, but their kids just shot right up into giants and they outgrew it. You'll feel more independent there, anyway. You're just a touch o-l-d to be living in your parents' actual house, don't you think?"

No, I didn't think. I thought it might be nice not to dwell twelve feet above piles of horse manure. I knew just what to say to my gentlemen callers: "Keep walking until you're almost floored by the smell of animal feces. Then look up! I'll be waving from the barn window!"

But free rent was free rent, so I sucked it up and agreed to live in the barn at my horse-loving parents' house. Who cared if the first floor of my residence was full of dung? I was going

to be a reporter for one of the country's most prestigious newspapers. Writing careers were made at the *Capitolist*. There was
more blood, sweat, and tears within those walls than in an Am-
sterdam brothel. Or that's what I was told, anyway. All I really
knew about the gig was that it would allow me to go back home,
hobnob with politicians, and write breaking news. And everyone
would pay attention.

I had been hired to work at the *Capitolist* (or the *List*, as the
employees called it) by a very intense woman from L.A. named
Rachel Monsoon. She had been a music critic for *Rolling Stone*,
a book critic for the *Los Angeles Times*, and then media editor
for the *San Francisco Chronicle*. Basically, nothing like the usual
Capitolist employee. But, to the delight of her conservative
mother, she fell in love with a preppy East Coaster who made
hand-carved wooden boats for a living and took the gig with the
D.C.-based paper to avoid a life of air travel and conjugal visits.
She had been there for three months when she hired me. There
was an opening on the Style section because one of the reporters
had left to "reclaim her soul in the blue waters of Goa," according to Rachel. I didn't ask how this girl had lost her soul, and
instead babbled enthusiastically about how right I was for the
job. What I liked best about Rachel was her claim that my piles
of prose and action-packed résumé had won her over. She didn't
even mention the fact that my mother was once the scariest gossip columnist Washington had ever known.

For a couple of decades, my parents had been raising horses
in Virginia, but in her former life my mom had penned the *Washington Post*'s scandal sheet. She ruled the rumor roost even when
she was dragged to Middleburg, but she grew out of it when
people became "sober and boring." Somehow she had managed
to keep a friend or two in town, but her enemies probably out-
numbered the allies. Once, when I was twelve, a woman poured

two gallons of milk on my mother's head in a supermarket while screaming that she was a fat bitch who had ruined her marriage. It was extremely awesome and the exact moment I decided to become a writer.

But I still appreciated the fact that Rachel was not explicitly hiring me for my mother's golden Rolodex. Our interview was interesting. I was completely overdressed, even though I was interviewing for the Style section, but Rachel and her quick-draw mind seemed to like me anyway. And I liked her. She had a white streak in her hair and laughed at my nervously rehearsed jokes. She had me take a two-day writing test and meet with the higher-ups; she then called me to say, "Okay, welcome to Style. You start in three weeks."

Three weeks? Fantastic. I spent what would have been next month's rent on a case of really good champagne, boarded a friend's chopper to Sag Harbor, and did the naked lambada with a man named Dan (Stan, was it? Okay, Stan) for seventy-two hours. And then my time ran out. My New York years were over. After I had packed seven years of East Side living into boxes, I opened an email that read, "Why don't you come in at 11 A.M. on October 15 and we'll take it from there." Eleven sounded perfectly civilized. I had worked 10 A.M. to 7 P.M. during my days at *Town & Country* and was happy to cut that down a smidge. A girl needs time to do glamorous things like groom her parents' horses for pocket money and meet someone to have sex with.

In a rented Chevy van packed to the brim with my shabby chic furniture and the free luxury goods I had amassed working in fashion journalism, I drove Beverly Hillbilly style behind the moving truck I had soundly rented. The pollution of Elizabeth, New Jersey, turned into the concrete skyways of the New Jersey Turnpike and then, finally, the cold, glistening water under the Delaware Bridge. When I crossed into Maryland and the Dixie side of the Mason-Dixon Line, I blew a goodbye kiss to the northern lights. And when my rented moving truck squished a raccoon three blocks from my parents' house, I knew I was really home.

In the twilight I could see my mother rushing out of the big wooden front door with the brass pineapple knocker to open the white gate onto the driveway. She had blond hair like mine, but hers had a hint of red in it thanks to the miracles of modern hair dye. It was perfectly straight at the top, curled under at the bottom and swishing across the thick roll neck of her white cashmere sweater. Both Payton and I were a little taller than her, having inherited our height from my father, Winston Brown's side of the family, but my mother had the same pale—though slightly freckled—skin and lean limbs. She often liked to point out that at my age she weighed 114 pounds and didn't I want to think about giving up my addiction to carbohydrates? I could hear her green Hunter boots crunching on fallen leaves and she waved energetically in my direction. That's when it hit me. I was going to live with my parents.

"Here you are! You penniless, squatting ingrate," my mother said as she walked toward me with open arms. She smelled like home and French perfume. Inside her sprawling white and green house most of the lights were on and three English setters barked just outside the door. She gave me a hug and whispered, "You know I'm happy, really," in my pink ear.

Relaxation and motherly love didn't last long.

The Monday after I moved home, I was ready to walk into the *List*'s Capitol Hill newsroom and become the wonkiest of wonks; the kind of person who chided others for not knowing every single member of the United States Senate and House of Representatives. "What?" I would say. "There are only five hundred thirty-five members of Congress. Is it too much for you to get to know your government? What do you think the Constitution is, anyway? An advice column?" I was going to be so brilliant and so annoying.

In my navy blue 2002 Volvo station wagon, the clunker I had driven home and abandoned after college, I drove to the glass and steel office building on Constitution Avenue that held the new media empire to which I now belonged. I had been inside for my interviews and to drop off monogrammed thank-you notes, but walking in as an employee felt different. Sure, I had to sign an ethics agreement that required me to just say no to the free trips to Malaga I had grown so accustomed to at *Town & Country*, and there was no closet overflowing with feathered frocks for me to don at my leisure, but I was about to become a brilliant Washington mind, digging up fraud—gossip fraud—for the greater good.

Having been trained by the most primped and preened people in America, I had begun getting ready for my first day on the job weeks in advance. My hair, usually bleached a very expensive girl-from-the-fjords blond, was toned down with lowlights. I also got my angular bangs straightened so I looked more *Good Housekeeping* than *Interview* magazine. At five foot eight I was tall enough to scare short girls and short enough not to scare shorter men, and that was something I really couldn't change in Washington. So I didn't. I bought a new pair of Louboutin heels, very high, very shiny. I also bought an Hermès scarf that I could fashion into a cape, a headscarf, or even a chic winter sarong of sorts. It also came in handy as a blanket if I needed to take a quick nap. As it was both unique and expensive, I deemed it perfect to wrap myself in for day one.

"First impressions are lasting impressions," I sang out, quoting my old *Town & Country* editor Kevin St. Clair. He wore Finnish reindeer hide slippers, even when out for a jog. Really.

You might have seen him running the New York City Marathon one year in these slippers while simultaneously smoking a massive Cuban cigar. It was quite a sight.

Seven years of working at glossy magazines in New York had given me a really great wardrobe. I had no money at all, but even my underwear was Miu Miu. That was the way of the New York world: Everyone who worked at a fashion magazine had Ivanka Trump's wardrobe, but free. (The downside is that we were paid in air kisses and comped meals, but it all balanced out. The only things I ever paid for in New York were rent, cabs, and medicine.) Perhaps my wardrobe was a little zany for Washington, but wouldn't some originality help me get a leg up? Anything to build a name for myself in a town dominated by massive egos.

Flying into the office, as my wonderful new 11 A.M. start time meant no rush hour traffic, I left my old car with the valet, failing to see the sign for the restaurant next door that read, "Valet for restaurant patrons only." I opened the *Capitolist*'s glass doors and got ready to become smarter just by breathing the same air as those celebrated scribes.

"Umm, humm, just sign, here, here, here, here, and here. And initial here. And here. Oh, and there," said the receptionist as she gave me my secure pass and building access codes. I was about to ask her if *Capitolist* headquarters also doubled as our country's uranium plant, but I was distracted by the sight of Nathaniel Heard, a Congress reporter I saw on TV all the time. He was shorter in person, and his hair looked like he washed it with chlorine. But he had the sheen of someone very busy and important. That, I decided, was what I would radiate in less than a week, even if I had to donate all my Kérastase hair products to an animal shelter.

The receptionist motioned to me to follow Nathaniel through

the door. But first I had to put my thumb on some sort of soul-stealing reader. Two frosted doors, etched with the company logo, slid open at my thumb's command. I felt like I was about to open the Christian Dior couture show. "Think authority! Think girl genius!" I whispered to myself as I walked down the navy blue carpeted hall roughly the length of an airplane runway.

Not one person looked up at me or the coif I had just paid Nancy Pelosi's stylist several hundred dollars to create. All I could hear besides my overactive heartbeat were the murmur of dozens of massive televisions tuned to CNN, MSNBC, Fox News, and C-SPAN, an occasional serious-sounding phone conversation, and the frenetic pitter-patter of calloused fingers on keyboards.

On every wall THE CAPITOLIST was printed in huge, navy blue block letters. Some of the letters were painted on; others floated slightly above the wall. But they were everywhere, just in case someone had a bout of dementia and forgot where they worked. The walls were gray, the desks were gray, the ceilings were gray, and the faces that hovered semipossessed behind computers looked a touch ashen, too. But heck! It was probably just the lighting. This was the place to be right now. So they hired people with a lack of skin pigment. Pish posh. History was being changed by these waxen beings, and I was lucky to join them.

I learned very soon that people who were important had two desks. People who were less important had one. And people of the least importance, like me and the other Style section girls, had one small desk in the very back of the office in a corner with no windows.

I found Rachel sitting at her desk, her dark, angular haircut swooshing like a sail as she typed. She welcomed me with a smile, gave me a hug, and put a BlackBerry, two backup batteries, and a headset into my sweaty hand.

"This is your BlackBerry," she declared. She pointed to the device, gripped tightly by my navy blue *Capitolist*-pride manicured nails, and said, "Keep it with you at all times. It helps if you imagine that it's Velcroed to your hand. Feel free to do that if it makes it easier."

I looked down at the phone and saw that it was already turned on and had the phrase "Write to Live, Live to Write" as a screen saver. That would have to be changed at once.

"We've disabled the off buttons on all the phones, so just keep charging it when the battery is low. If it breaks from overuse— which it will—no problem, we'll get you a new one immediately. And it's configured to work in every country in the world. Even East Timor." I expected us to share a hearty laugh right about then, but Rachel was silent.

She reached across the desk and wrapped my fingers around the device a little tighter.

"If you don't reply to an email within three minutes, I will be calling you. The pace is frenetic here, to put it mildly. We write seven to ten articles a day. It sounds like a lot, and it is. If you're re-reporting a story, get fresh quotes. Don't start paragraphs with questions; I hate that. Speed is more important than grammatical accuracy. You can always change a comma, not a time stamp. Have a good kicker, but don't take ten minutes to write it. You don't have to come up with your own headlines, but I will like you more if you do. So do. And they have to stay under one hundred and sixty-five characters and be written with search engines in mind. So keep them boring, but fun. Be creative, but not edgy. Always use a neutral voice, but try not to make it a total yawn. Inspire, but never with bias. Remember, you can't do or say anything politically charged outside the office. You can't campaign, you can't donate, and you can't wear any T-shirts or buttons printed with political slogans." She looked at my outfit, made almost entirely of Mongolian cashmere, and added, "not that you look like the Newt Gingrich T-shirt type . . . Oh! and I'll expect you to file at least one thing today. Two would be better. Three would be best. Sound good?"

I smiled and nodded, trying to look like this was exactly what I'd expected. Like it was perfectly normal to rig a BlackBerry so it never turned off. And who didn't want to write ten articles a day? I was clearly going to thrive at this place. I mentally revised my list of prepared questions, dropping the ones about whether the paper had a car service or a cappuccino machine.

Keeping her eyes not on me but on her computer, where she was simultaneously editing a short piece on Senator Kirsten Gillibrand's remarkable weight loss, Rachel kept talking. "I don't know if I told you already, but we start at five A.M. every day. This means you're writing at five A.M., not waking up or looking for things to write about. And you're on email and on your phone and able to do interviews in different time zones if you have to. If you need time to find news, get up earlier. And you have to be on call on Sundays. You'll get used to it, don't worry."

She finally looked up at me, smiled sincerely, and pointed to the far wall. Like all the others, it said THE CAPITOLIST and had two short rows of flat-screen TVs hanging on it. "Your desk is at the end of the hall. The one under the TV that always plays CNN. Don't even think about changing the channel. You'll ignite a revolution. The IT guys should be there in a few minutes to set you up. Three minutes, actually." She turned back to her monitor, away from my bright, shiny, confused face, and said, "Better get walking. Oh . . . and good luck." I scurried off lest I miss the punctual IT patrol.

Although my heart was toying with the possibility of cardiac arrest, my mind had grown surprisingly calm. I could definitely do this. I could be the kind of person who never slept, drank

venti espressos, and stalked politicians for sport. Why not! I
went to Wellesley College, a school that produced Hillary frig-
ging Clinton. I was up to the task. I was not intimidated at all.
And no, she hadn't told me about the 5 A.M. start time. Must
have slipped her dazzlingly acute mind.

As I sprinted to the back of the newsroom, a man with a
safari hat stuck to his sweaty head ran past my empty desk.
He clutched a tape recorder playing something and two Black-
Berrys. His round tortoiseshell glasses bounced around on his
nose like a cowboy atop a bronco.

I must have stared for an unnaturally long time, because a
girl with hair the color of India ink felt free to look me over
rather unsubtly. Then, like an actual human being, she smiled
and spoke. I almost kissed the hem of her dress; she might as
well have been the Dalai Lama, as far as I was concerned.

"That's David Bush. No relation. He always wears a safari
hat, unless he's on TV, which is often," she said, crossing her
muscular legs.

Naturally. Like Bindi the Jungle Girl.

I smiled and started to introduce myself, but she interrupted
me with a wave of her thin hand. "He's quirky, but he's nice
and he's a genius and they love him. Worship him. He writes
the *Morning List.* It's like the Bible, but with bullet points. You
better read it every single day the second it goes to print. We
get it five minutes before the rest of the world, so read it then.
He writes it three hundred sixty-five days a year. Even Christmas morning. When it's his birthday we have an actual carnival.
There was a real penguin you could pose for pictures with last
year. When it's your birthday, no one will remember and you'll
probably have to work late."

"Cool."

"You're Adrienne Brown, right?" She extended her hand.

"I'm Julia Kincaid. We thought you were starting today. You're going to be the sixth on the section. I don't mean to be rude, but I'm the one worth knowing."

I was about to thank her for conversing with me, when I saw three gangly young men holding wires and laptops heading in our direction: the IT team. But before they made it to us, the sound of a dull cake knife tapping the side of a drinking glass filled the vast room. The IT men turned on their rubber heels, computer parts in hand, and went the other way.

"Get up. It's time for awkward cake," said my raven-haired colleague. Never mind that I was already standing at attention like a Navy SEAL.

"What's awkward cake?" I asked her.

"It's just cake. We have two cakes every time someone leaves. And that's pretty often, almost weekly in the summer. One is always chocolate, and the other is a fruit tart. Unless they liked you, and then you get expensive cupcakes. Georgetown Cupcakes. There's a speech or two that goes along with the cakes. They always wish the person good luck and then smugly assure them that they'll come to their senses and return soon. Of course, if they really hate you, then you don't get awkward cake at all. You'll see, it's incredibly awkward."

She was right. It was incredibly awkward. Before the paper's tow-haired editor in chief, Mark Upton, tapped his long knife against a *Capitolist* glass and started speaking, all the office lights brightened to a level Dr. Sanjay Gupta would describe as just right for brain surgery. The reporters and editors all gathered around in neat concentric circles and plastered on huge smiles like they were being handed Oprah's favorite things. I backed into a corner with my colleague and sat on a stapler.

"It's with heavy hearts that we say goodbye to our prized defense reporter Roger Roche," Upton declared. His speaking pattern was soothing and rhythmic. "Roger has given so much to the paper over his eight months here. He covered the president's trip to Iraq and the changing of the guard at the Pentagon. He even disguised himself as a corpse and slept in Arlington Cemetery for a piece on grave robbing."

Wait, it was okay to pretend to be dead? I looked around to see if anyone else thought this last anecdote was odd. Julia grabbed my shoulder and whispered very loudly, "Don't believe that shit. They fucking hate him. And they made him wake up at *three* every morning to write the 'Good Morning Military' tip sheet, so he hates them, too. See? No cupcakes." She motioned to the table: two fruit tarts and nothing else.

The short but saccharine speeches had every person in the room laughing and clapping at things that weren't at all funny. When the speeches were over, the staff leapt toward the cakes like prisoners of war, and Julia, who knew how to handle the scrum, brought me back a slice.

"You should eat this. That way you can get used to the weight you will inevitably put on while working here," she said, handing me a piece without candied fruit. "Just don't drop any crumbs. We have mice. So don't leave food on your desk. But if you do see a mouse, don't say anything, and don't tweet about it. They'll be pissed. If anything ever goes wrong at the office, don't mention it outside the office, because if they find out you did, they'll start thinking about ways to demote or fire you."

Eating with our plates right under our chins, Julia and I watched as Upton approached the paper's managing editor, Justin Cushing. Cushing had Groton, Yale, and over a decade breaking news at the *Wall Street Journal* stamped on his résumé. His aura sang, "Trust me! I'm always right." And people usually did.

"Justin Cushing once hit a reporter with his umbrella. Like a thwack below the knee," said Julia, making a Babe Ruth batting gesture and flinging her empty plate into the garbage can.

"Really?"

"Yeah. But they didn't report it to the HR department or anything. One, we don't have HR, and two, the reporter was flattered that Cushing actually knew who he was. You should have seen him. He was glowing like he ate a flashlight. Just because you work here doesn't mean the important people have to learn your name."

And that, I realized, was what the *Capitolist* was all about: not sleeping, working around the clock, and fighting so that Upton and Cushing not only knew who you were but also cared enough about you to occasionally put your stories on the front page, maybe even to shoot the shit with you every couple of weeks. That meant coming by your desk and asking about your life. The right answer to that question was always "What do you mean? This *is* my life."

The *Capitolist* was three years old. Four young Silicon Valley investors had founded it when all the other little papers were dying, but it had skyrocketed. From the beginning, the *Capitolist* had what other papers didn't: money and intensely dedicated labor. They bought reporters away from other publications, they made the paper they printed on thicker than a book jacket, and they threw more parties than *Vogue*.

The paper and its equally prestigious website were still flying high, and so were its employees. A place obsessed with breaking news, the *List* was launched as print and online because there was no way any *List* story worth its ink was going to wait until the next day's paper. The daily print edition and the site appealed to different readers, but they both brought in nearly equal dollar amounts and equally stressed out the employees. We Style girls had to file two Web stories in the morning, then a paper story, then *more* Web stories. Meaning that when we were breaking news, we were also writing long-form pieces for the paper. It was a little like the decathlon without the bonus calorie burn. If you lasted a year, you deserved to be knighted. Small nervous breakdowns requiring prescription drugs and Skype counseling (to save time) were commonplace. Sick days were never taken. If you had a mix of bubonic plague and shingles you might be allowed to work from home. The paper chewed employees up and spat them out in a matter of months, sometimes weeks. But the ones who made it past the breaking point loved it beyond all reason. The only other jobs they would ever consider were United States senator or dictator of planet earth and outlying galaxies. Or, if they had to, host of *Meet the Press.* The newsroom was filled with extremely young reporters, all rabidly desperate to make a name for themselves. If they played their cards right, they definitely would. One year at the *Capitolist* could save you five years somewhere else, but you had to get through that year without doubling your body weight and tripling your blood pressure.

Most people took their cues from Robert Redford in *All the President's Men:* they dressed like farsighted intellectuals, called each other by last names, and shouted to sound important. They spoke almost entirely in acronyms, and each one quickly adopted a signature sartorial quirk. This quirk was never wearing father's vintage Rolex: it was sporting a skunk hat once owned by Ronald Reagan's press secretary or a stain-covered tie handed down from Senator Boring.

The Style section was free of the typical *Capitolist* type because the typical *Capitolist* type viewed Style reporting as the ninth circle of hell.

But I saw the Style girls as enviable, attractive geniuses.

Instead of deciding I was the competition and freezing up,

Julia called a source in the office of the Speaker of the House, introduced me on a conference call, and helped me type out my first article. Rachel didn't edit it to pieces, and seven minutes after I turned it in, it was live on the *Capitolist* website. I emailed my parents a screen shot.

Not sure what to write about next—though Julia told me we'd better figure it out quick, so I wouldn't be fired immediately—I headed to the front of the building, to the photography department, to have my picture taken for the staff page. Before I reached it, though, a gangly man leapt out of his desk chair, planted himself in my path, and started shaking my hand up and down like a water pump. "Welcome to the *Capitolist*. I'm Mason Swisher. Congress reporter. Also elections. Sometimes business and lobbying. We're thrilled to have you," he said loudly.

"It's really exciting to be here," I said, introducing myself.

"Adrienne Brown, Adrienne Brown." He said my name twice and then sat back down at his desk. "I've heard of your mother. Obviously. Did she get you this gig?"

After giving Mason a firm "no, but thanks so much for asking," I escaped, had my quick portrait session with our staff photographers, and walked back to tell Julia about my encounter. She laughed as if the entire cast of *Saturday Night Live* were tickling her with feathers.

"Don't even worry about him. He will probably take over the world in five to seven years, but that doesn't mean you're required to speak to him now. I'll show you who you should waste your breath on." She was touch-typing an email on her phone while speaking to me. "There's me, of course. And the other Style girls, because in the grand scheme of things they're kind of normal. The design team, the photographers, the cartoonists, a few energy reporters, the two cute lobbying reporters, and Rachel. That's it."

I was twisting around, trying to identify the cute people, but Julia kept talking about our shared boss.

"Rachel's our third editor in a year," she explained. "She's the best one we've had. The last one had a mild nervous breakdown and went to Crossroads rehab center in Antigua, where she met Colin Farrell. Now she works at the *New York Times*."

"Really? That's pretty cool."

"Well, that's what this place gets you eventually. A great new job, ten extra pounds, a brush with celebrity, and deep mental scars."

"Got it." I pressed my fingers together as hard as I could until I noticed they were stuck in the American Sign Language hand gesture for "camp." I gave them a shake and tried to position them nonchalantly on my waist, but I still looked nervous. And like I was about to clog dance. I had to calm down. Julia wasn't exactly painting the paper out to be Disneyland for adults, but I was still high on the power of the place. Everyone looked busy and important. At *Town & Country*, everyone looked rich and hungry. Why not embrace change?

I hadn't spotted one single male I would consider swapping DNA with, but the three chairs around Julia and me were still empty.

"Who sits here?" I asked, giving one a swirl.

"Chicks. All three. This is Style," replied Julia, pointing to the nameplates I'd missed.

She gestured toward the first desk. "That's where Libby Barnesworth sits. She's from Kennebunkport, Maine, and went to Dartmouth, as you can tell from the mug." Julia pointed to a large green coffee cup. "She always smells like cinnamon. I think she has one of those pine tree air fresheners sewn into her pants. She came here two years ago from *Washingtonian* and has a vocabulary like John McEnroe, but she's not so bad if you're nice to her. She's very Georgetown. Hangs out with those preppy types, like Jenna Bush."

"She knows Jenna Bush? Cool."

"I didn't say Jenna Bush. I said *like* Jenna Bush. Same hair color. Different fathers."

She pointed to the even smaller desk next to Libby's. It had a huge snow globe of Aspen and a picture of very attractive blond people on it. "That's Isabelle." She looked, clearly expecting some sign of recognition, but all I gave her was the look of someone whose mind has just been erased with a magnet. "Everyone knows Isabelle. She was in the Olympics. For the slalom."

"You're kidding."

"I am not. I can't believe you don't know her."

I couldn't believe it, either. I was going to work with an Olympian? I needed to know every single detail starting with the Olympic trials and ending with the closing ceremonies. Was it Vancouver? Or maybe Turin? Nagano? I was crossing my fingers for Nagano. That was my favorite. All those picturesque Japanese villages covered in snow and fiery Olympic rings.

Before I started singing the national anthem, I caught myself and replied coolly, "I'm more a summer Olympics type." This was true. I still had a balance beam in my parents' basement and had grand plans to get my backflip back now that I was pushing thirty. I mean, Jackie Chan could do, like, eight, and he was nearly sixty.

I looked at the stacks of papers and notepads on Isabelle's desk. I didn't see one single medal or trophy. If I were an elite athlete, even a retired one, I would tie my medal to my head and never ever take it off, even when going through airport security. Those pirates at TSA would just have to give me a CAT scan.

"What is she doing at the *Capitolist* if she's an Olympian?" I asked. "Shouldn't she be coaching our next generation of champions?"

She shrugged and gave one of Isabelle's plastic bobbleheads a pat. "I have no idea. I think they just liked the fact that she was a tall, blond Olympian from Aspen. She came in tenth, but whatever. The Olympics is still kind of big-time. And she knows everyone. Except you, apparently."

Julia looked at her watch and logged onto her RSS reader. It showed 157 new stories since we'd started talking.

"Crap," she said, opening a new document. "I haven't filed something in over an hour. I need a piece or I'm going to get bitch-slapped."

I assumed "bitch-slapped" was reporter speak for "lightly chided with a friendly hug" and kept asking her questions.

"Wait, what about that one," I asked, pointing to the last desk. Julia turned around and looked at the third, mostly empty, desk.

"Oh, right. That's Alison Lee. She's sweet. Kind of down-homey. She's from North Carolina, like from a dune. And she wears a lot of pinstripes. Why does she wear all these pinstripes? I've never had the heart to ask. Is she trying to tell someone that she's a prisoner in this office? Because I get that. Or is it because she watches too much *Law & Order*? I don't know. But she wears them almost every day. She doesn't reveal much about herself, though—she's the Mona Lisa of colleagues. And she's pretty young, twenty-three, I think. Basically, when I was driving, she was in the third grade."

"Why is everyone in here so young?" I asked, looking around at the sea of intense twenty-somethings.

"Because old people are not stupid enough to do these jobs," replied Julia. "Nor do they have enough energy. Think of us like sled dogs. They use the young ones who can go the distance and take the crack of a whip and when we're tired they trade us out. But you can't be too resentful because everyone knows this is the best launching pad in journalism."

Right. Launching pad. Perhaps my grand visions of being a *Capitolist* lifer were a little ridiculous. But if I had to go from *Capitolist* reporter to senior features writer at the *New York Times* in a handful of years, I could deal.

I wouldn't meet the rest of my inner circle of colleagues that day. All three of them were working from the Capitol, so all I saw was their bylines, magically appearing again and again on the site. Meanwhile Julia and I looked for news and wrote it up as fast as our fingers could move. It kind of made my eyes cross. I would have to adapt.

After turning around two articles by the grace of my high society connections and Julia's charity, I understood what she meant by deep mental scars. There was clearly only one thing to do: start spending all spare waking hours hobnobbing with the Hill power players—or the people who kept their schedules.

"Chiefs of staff and press secretaries are like bouncers in the Meatpacking District in New York," explained Julia. "If you don't win them over, you'll get nothing."

"Nothing" sounded bad. "Nothing" sounded like I would have to spend the rest of my days reshelving books at Barnes & Noble. I resolved to woo these staffers like a playmate in a crowd of sailors.

As the day wound down for the rest of the world, but just kept chugging along at the *Capitolist*, I convinced myself that, with a deep commitment to kissing political ass and a complete annihilation of my personal life, I could succeed at the *List*. Then I received my first reader comment. It was on the Speaker article Julia had helped me write.

I scrolled to the notification and clicked on it.

It came through our awkwardly formatted email system in small bold type.

Adrienne Brown has received a reader's comment:

"Eat dick you fat Commi bitch whore!!!!!!!!"

Thank you,
The Capitolist

Trying not to cry, I showed it to Julia. Maybe this was just some sort of first-day joke, like secret society hazing. In college I had to pluck a live chicken once. I was sure that as soon as Julia read it, she would start laughing and hand me a pink hair ribbon with my name on it.

She skimmed it over, smiled, and turned around in her ergonomic chair. I waited for my hair ribbon, or for her to pick up the phone and report the inappropriate comment to a higher power.

But nothing happened. When she could feel my eyes on her, she turned back around and looked at my screen.

"That part is all formatted," she said, pointing to the top and bottom of the email with a bored finger. Dragging her thumb over the body of the email, she said, "The only part the reader wrote was 'Eat dick you fat Commi bitch whore.'"

"Right, understood," I said shakily. "And a thank-you from the *Capitolist* to me for reading the comment. How thoughtful."

"Be prepared," Julia said as she shot her seventh story of the day to Rachel. "I get them all the time. Some are so racist. They call Michelle Obama MoMo the gorilla. They write things I thought only Klan members would dare type out. I have a folder with over five hundred comments that I keep, just in case one of these people ever tries to shoot the president or something."

How wonderful. I had never corresponded with a band of

racists before. Now I would learn what it was like to have my soul eat itself.

"Should I write back when this happens? I mean, I have their email address, right? Can I just write 'thank you for your time, you depraved, racist lunatic. I look forward to our future correspondence the way I look forward to a spinal tap'?"

Julia shook her head no. "No, no, never write back. You don't want to anger the crazy racists. They know your name, where you work. They could come over here and shoot you with their homemade weapons. Better to just file them away to hand over to the police one day. Plus, we signed neutrality agreements. Can't express an opinion one way or the other."

Neutral. I could do that. I was the queen of neutrality. My mother might disagree, based on an incident in 1998 when I tried to have my sister arrested for un-American activities, but I had grown since then. I had skimmed the company policy demanding that we just "shrug off the crazies and keep on typing" and clearly I had to obey. I would just ignore these lunatics who took time out of their days to type me offensive emails. I would stay the course. The quiet course.

For the next two hours, I ignored my hate mail and personally called every single press secretary I could find outside of working hours on Capitol Hill. I made small talk, I tried to arrange meet-and-greets, I grilled them about the stylish things their bosses were doing. Then I reached out to three old socialites who still kind of liked my mother and asked if I could take them to lunch. I figured that jumping on the rich, arthritic crowd was a good place to start.

When I put down the phone and reclined in my chair, people looked at me like I was sitting there enjoying a paid vacation. And when I got up to go to the bathroom, a Web editor asked if I was lost.

Work was the only thing you were supposed to do inside the *Capitolist* walls, and if that meant typing while dehydrated, so be it. You only got ahead one way in life, and that was working harder, longer, faster, and with less water than everyone else.

At 8 P.M., I was happy to head back to Virginia and the "home" I shared with apolitical animals. They were actual animals, but whatever. They weren't going to tell me I had five minutes to get two fresh quotes and twelve minutes to turn them into "something palatable." Before I left, I printed out the three articles I had written as well as my first comment. My mother hadn't added to my scrapbook since I broke an opponent's nose at field hockey camp in the late nineties, but I thought it might be time.

The drive home took an hour and a half. I thought about all the places I could have flown in that time: Boston. Lexington. Charleston. Cleveland, perhaps? Instead I was listening to the German-language CD I had purchased for my commute and was reciting words related to the home.

At the end of my parents' long stone driveway, I parked my car, changed into my Tod's loafers to save my shiny pin heels from the dirt of country living, passed the barn, and went in search of human contact.

My mom was busy ruining store-bought beef bourguignon, but she paused in her destruction to cluck at my appearance.

"Oh, good. You're home. I thought for a second you'd either flown back to New York or been abducted. I could think of no other options besides those two." She gave me a hug, fastened her arm around me, and pulled my face into the light that illuminated the cooktop. "You look really pale . . . green, almost. Like a frog with streaky blond hair and eyebrows," she said.

"Yeah, well, I didn't get out much today," I said. She pinched my dry, pale skin and swabbed at my face with olive oil.

"Your father can't wait to see you," she said, going back to her stirring. "He's busy spending a fortune on some prize horse in Argentina with your sister. I knew I should never have let him watch *Secretariat*. But he'll be back in a few weeks. They've got the best horse movers in that crazy country driving the poor thing up here, but you know your dad, he's along for the ride."

"Better him than me," I said while my mother fluttered her blue eyes at me and bopped me on the nose with a wooden spoon.

"Well, Payton and your father, they're happiest when they're riding. We're the wordsmiths, they're the true horse people."

That night, my mother gave me a free dinner, a heavy pour of Rémy Martin, and a speech about the good old days of journalism. She asked why the *Capitolist* demanded so much work. Three stories on day one, she noted—did I want to lose the ability to bend my hands in my later years?

"We used to have so much fun in the newsroom. Smoking pot in the stairwells before staff meetings. It was like a big celebration of grass and words," she said, sliding a bowl of Kalamata olives toward me across the smooth wooden kitchen table.

"Sounds swell, Mom," I answered, declining the pitted snack. "Like Woodstock with pencils."

She ignored me and kept telling her stories about the old days, more for her own benefit than mine. As much as she appreciated not getting milk spilled on her head by crazed housewives, I knew she missed the pace and the bylines sometimes.

"I'll never forget the time when I stayed incredibly late, like eleven or something, and I walked into the book room to grab the new Social Registry, and there were Clyde and Sharon—you remember Sharon, she was the old food editor. She gave you that *Pasta Making for Kids* book you liked so much?"

I had no idea. But I clearly should hate this Sharon for making me a carb addict so early on.

My mother was still talking. "Anyway. She and Clyde were

going at it like wild animals. Naked in the stacks. She was married at the time, of course. I think her husband was a professor at Johns Hopkins. Ethnobotany, to be precise." Placing a pit into a monogrammed cocktail napkin, she said, "I saw them doing it in the newsroom once, too, but that was after her second divorce. They didn't give a hoot who saw once it was kosher."

I thought I would rather shave my eyebrows off and eat them than have sex in our newsroom. I had to get away from her old-lady reminiscing. I made my excuses and skulked in my loafers out to the barn, where I cracked one of the windows and listened to the sounds of early fall. When the turning leaves all fell in a few weeks, I would be able to see the Blue Ridge Mountains. Now I could see the moon shining down on the manicured fields.

I threw myself onto my cashmere-blanket-covered bed and looked at the black-and-white pictures hanging on the wall. Before I came home, my mother asked her interior designer to spruce up the joint a little. To most people, that would mean add a bed, maybe a simple Shaker-inspired chair, a fresh towel or two, and voilà! But not my mother. She had removed the word *simple* from her vocabulary decades ago. The barn apartment, though nothing more than a few small rooms and a poor excuse for a kitchen and a bathroom, now looked ready to host Ralph Lauren and his entire sun-kissed family. There was a queen-size bed with a mahogany wood frame covered in down comforters and navy and cream blankets, an oversize farm table with hand-carved benches, a navy velvet couch with ten equestrian-themed throw pillows, thick braided rugs, a wall covered in brown velvet riding hats, a candle-burning chandelier, two fire extinguishers for said candle-burning chandelier, and a wall of family photos. The last part sounds awfully quaint and sentimental, but it was mostly glamour shots of my mother with slightly lifted eyes that screamed, "I'm watching you!," pictures of my dad making judgmental faces, my Wellesley graduation photo, and a few snaps from high school of me looking gangly and awkward while my sister Payton posed like a Swedish supermodel. Those would have to go.

It's not that I wasn't well-rounded in high school; I was. I was yearbook editor, co-captain of the field hockey team, took difficult classes, and had a series of cute boyfriends with good abs, dreamy eyes, and SUVs. It's just that Payton had already done all that, but better, and by the time I got there, my golden sister had set an impossibly high standard.

Payton was incredibly popular, in part because she was so pretty and mostly because she was so scary. She was fantastic at sports, got great grades without trying, always had a tan, and dated a very popular lacrosse player named Dean McLaughlin, who looked like a man at seventeen and called her babe. He used to bench press Payton during their lacrosse practices and even modeled for the Abercrombie & Fitch catalog his summer between high school and college. I loved him. I made a collage of his Abercrombie pictures and hid it behind my desk but Payton found it and presented it to Dean right in front of me. I laughed it off, excused myself from the table, and cried until my eyes looked like two fireballs stuck in my face.

At an age when most girls just wanted to be liked and asked out on a date or two, Payton was running high school like a Fortune 500 company. Her senior year, she even had a stalker. He was a junior on the wrestling team named Leo and chased Payton around in a white Bronco very similar to O. J. Simpson's. My father had to call his parents and threaten legal action. It was the coolest thing ever.

The last summer before Payton left for college we both worked as counselors at a riding camp in the Blue Ridge Mountains. It was 80 percent girls but there was one rather cute stable hand named Trevor Mariani whom I ended up making out with behind the barn a few times. When I refused to go skinny-dipping in the lake with him after a particularly hot and heavy smooch fest, he told every other counselor that we'd had sex in the hayloft "thoroughbred style." I wanted to die. I was still rather petrified of male genitalia at that stage and I was being accused of acts outlawed in much of the American South.

Naturally, I didn't do anything but cry alone in the bathroom, but when the rumor kept on growing after a few days, Payton walked up to him after our daily flag-raising ceremony and, in front of everyone, slapped him across the face, paused for a few seconds, and then muttered "loser," for everyone to hear. She was kindly asked to leave and stay far away from children, but for the rest of the summer, she was my hero. When I awkwardly thanked her before she left for Columbia, she didn't crack a smile and said she did it because she was sick of spending her summer toiling in Appalachia when all her friends were backpacking through Europe. I didn't care. Payton was happy to push my head under water, but she wouldn't sit around and watch anyone else do it.

Fine. I would keep the photos up there for now. I walked up to the wall and straightened one of me flashing a particularly heinous set of turquoise braces.

I had an hour before I had to be asleep, so I lay back on my sleigh bed, picked up my landline, called Elsa, and begged her to leave the District Saturday night and spend the weekend with me in Middleburg. "I hate you," she replied. "And I'll see you Saturday. You better buy me a present."

Free of computers but with my BlackBerry nestled right next to my pillow, I got ready to rack up six hours of sleep. But Julia woke me up with a text at midnight to see if I was going to come back for day two. I told her I'd had an hour-and-a-half commute back to my Middleburg barn to think about it and had decided yes. Definitely, yes. It was the place to be right now. They—no, *we*—were leading political journalism and the new media empire. I was lucky to work there.

"Good," Julia texted back. She added a P.S. two minutes later.

"You're 28. It might be time to kiss the commute goodbye and move into the city. Living with your parents is quaint and all, but you're not a girl from Saudi Arabia waiting for someone to propose."

"That sounds racist," I wrote.

"Well, living in a barn that your parents own sounds inbred."

It kind of did.

CHAPTER 3

It wasn't that I didn't like my job. It was just a whole lot of job. A month in, there was no time for anything besides being a *Capitolist* reporter and getting a few hours of sleep. I never had sex, I never drank, and I now communicated with my friends through short, impersonal, spam-like emails. They probably thought I was trying to sell them cheap Viagra and steal their Social Security numbers.

But I did get to interview a lot of celebrities. Perfect, glossy celebrities.

On a particularly cold Thursday in mid-November, when the oak and maple trees around the city were losing their color, I had four do-gooder celebrities to trail on Capitol Hill. Two were pretty B-list, so I had no interest in talking to them, but their crazy communications directors called me with the persistence of my eighth-grade boyfriend and gave me no choice but to say yes. The third was Chevy Chase, and the fourth was January Jones, the woman who made wearing a pointy bra acceptable again. The morning would be long. I would have to do a lot of fake smiling, but I was happy to escape the newsroom and the mystical sounds of C-SPAN that filled it.

On the drive in from northern Virginia, I pulled up the

parking brake at a red light and began searching the car floor for my very serious media credentials. They identified me, Adrienne Brown, as a hard-boiled reporter for the *Capitolist*. I found them affixed with chewing gum to what looked like animal fur. Since I never locked my car, I figured it must have been taken for a joyride by taxidermists. I also found part of yesterday's Chop't salad, three empty cans of Diet Coke, a Canadian penny, tiny red underwear printed with the words "thong-tha-thong-thong-thong," and enough Bobbi Brown bronzer to turn a family of Swedes into vacationing Brazilians.

Fascinated by the results of my excavation, at the next red light, I dug a little more. I still had to find my House of Representatives and Senate credentials, which should have been attached to each other but were more likely attached to a discarded sandwich.

Many years before I started my gig at the *Capitolist*, I read an article in the *New York Post* about a woman who had gotten arrested for smoking a cigarette, making a call, and shaving her bikini line while driving. I was hysterical. I folded myself into the fetal position and laughed until my appendix hurt. I mean, who in their right mind would shave their moneymaker while driving? But now that I was basically a serf, I knew better. She probably didn't have time to schedule a Brazilian wax because her boss wanted her to work until her eyes popped out and shriveled up like raisins.

In Washington, fall meant Congress was still in session and a horrendous number of school groups arrived with their history classes in hyperactive packs on the Mall. It also meant there was a month left of crazy traffic before the holiday slowdown, but I appreciated it. It was my only downtime. I flipped through e-books, sat in on conference calls, spastically checked

my BlackBerry, tweeted, and read the style sections of two
newspapers as I waited for the mind-numbing rush hour traffic
to carry me to the epicenter of the American wonk.

I mopped some sticky caffeinated substance off the laminated
ID passes I finally found, popped them all around my neck, and
looked for semilegal parking. It was time to head to one of the
marble House offices and act important. Or at least not lost.

My first three interviews were taking place in Cannon, one
of the seven almost identical House and Senate buildings flanking the Capitol. I sprayed my hair with hundred-dollar hair glue,
threw on a practical yet stylish Louis Vuitton capelet, and gal-
loped toward the building.

I put my bag through the X-ray machine, explained to the
baby-faced security guards why I had three cucumbers in my
purse (South Beach diet, not perversion), and headed down a
hall lined by the heavy wooden doors that guard congressional
offices. Girls wearing sensible shoes raced toward their sensible
jobs, and young men with good heads of hair and a fondness for
the missionary position looked at me as if I were a space alien
who had just ambled in.

Once I was in the building's dramatic two-story rotunda
complete with Corinthian columns and a coffered dome, I
waited around and watched the B-list celebs eagerly do Fox and
MSNBC interviews. I saw two girls, both from our print competition, both with video crews, and closed my eyes. If they were
here, it meant I had to file my articles immediately because they
would be trying to beat my time stamp.

I took out my second BlackBerry and texted Isabelle, "Jaycee
Burke is here with a fucking camera crew!!" My new BlackBerry
was called the Torch and the tech department promised me it
would outlast BlackBerry number one, which lost half the keyboard keys after two weeks of overuse.

"She has back hair," Isabelle replied. "Not just fuzz, like genuine long fur." Isabelle was the most talented smack talker on the Style team, and the girl you wanted around when spouting out insults about other Washington journalists. She was also the second newest on the section, having only been at the *List* for a year, and still seemed to have a grasp on the outside world. Julia was my guide at the paper, but Isabelle was my guide to the rest of the city.

"Did you know she's leaving?" she added. "It sounds like you don't. She got a job with the *Wall Street Journal*. She's going to be part of their election team. Can you believe it?" Isabelle wrote.

I guess the *Journal* didn't discriminate against back hair.

"Who else is there?" asked Isabelle.

"Some girl with really short hair. Like Justin Bieber," I wrote.

"Krista Gabriel. She's with *Roll Call*," Isabelle wrote back. "You don't know her because no one pays attention to them. They have a pay wall. Can you imagine? She once came up to me, kissed me on each check, and said, 'Oh, the competition's here.' I mean really? We're national, she's local, and that's really all that needs to be said. Don't bother talking to her."

"That nice guy from the *Daily Caller* is here, too," I wrote. "The one with the shaved head."

"Did you hear that the *Daily Caller* has a keg? Can you imagine Upton ever letting us have a keg? He would fill it with liquid speed," Isabelle wrote back. I liked Isabelle. And not just because she was friends with Apolo Ohno. She was one of the only ones at the paper who dared to have a life. Everyone else just sacrificed their friends and family to live permanently in a *Capitolist* world.

Isabelle excused herself from BBM to go file an article, and I started eavesdropping on two reporters I didn't know.

"I heard you can't even expense coffee with a source at the *Post* anymore," said one of them, looking down at her hot Starbucks. "Can you imagine? Who wants to talk to you if you can't even buy them a latte?"

"It's true," said her friend. "An all-staff memo went out about it. It was forwarded to me within five minutes. Why does anyone ever send out all-staff emails anymore? They are made public immediately. It's so stupid. Old people really don't understand how this world works. Nothing is private, especially not a staff-wide email that basically reads, 'we're bleeding money, get out while you can.'"

I was very caught up in their conversation when the first almost-famous person approached me. I shook her hand, grabbed a pen, and lobbed a handful of softballs at her. "If you could dine with the president or John Boehner, who would you choose? Which dog would you rather own—Champ Biden, a well-bred German shepherd, or Bo Obama, a Portuguese water dog descended from the Kennedy family canine? And do you think Michele Bachmann would rather guest star on *Teen Mom*, *Glee*, or *MTV Cribs*?"

Next up, Chevy Chase. He was in town because his wife was getting some sort of green hippie award for eating only cardboard. Her actions were certainly noble, but of course everyone wanted to interview her much more famous, much funnier husband.

I asked him about the delicate dance between comedy and politics, and he said the words *fuck* and *George Bush* a lot. His affable wife chided him for speaking to a reporter that way. "He meant all that off the record," she offered, a last-ditch attempt to scrub my story of Republican bashing and f-bombs.

By the time I wrapped with Chevy, I had eight minutes to get to the Dirksen Senate Office Building to interview January

Jones. I would no doubt have to fight my way through a pack of male staffers with dreams of dry-humping her, but that was not my biggest problem. Eight minutes: I had eight minutes to go a mile.

I hustled to the underground train that runs between the House and Senate buildings. It's a little like Epcot Center, but instead of sitting next to chubby children wearing mouse ears, you sit behind our country's anointed ones. I say behind, because they have reserved seating and you get to stare at the backs of their heads from steerage.

Darting around like a Senate page, I finally made it to Dirksen and to the front of the line for press interviews with the blond actress.

"Oh, the *Capitolist*," an eager PR gal in lots of J. Crew knitwear said after eyeing the pack of shiny credentials hanging around my neck. "You're Adrienne Brown, and I'm Kate Bonneville," she said, offering her hand.

We walked around a mess of TV crew wires. Kate gripped my elbow. "We don't have the press packets ready yet as my idiot intern printed them in red ink. Don't worry, I fired her, but you read the release I sent yesterday, right?" she asked. "It had all the information you need. Info about Miss Jones's current work with the group, her recent PSAs, even a lengthy piece about the historical significance of her current hairdo."

"Of course," I replied unconvincingly. In truth, I had glanced at it while robotically reciting my morning Starbucks order. I took some shoddy notes, but January Jones could be in town to promote atomic bombs for all I knew.

I nodded to the cameramen, photographers, and other gossipy writers—all the people I was used to seeing in Hill rooms—and scanned January's Wikipedia entry and some Google news hits on my phone before I entered her holding room. I wasn't prepping for *Celebrity Jeopardy* against Stephen Hawking. I was sure I could gather enough from IMDb to do a decent job with my quick-hit interview of a doe-eyed actress. January's hair was glossy, her hemline long, her neckline high. She looked like a very attractive person playing the part of an erudite Washingtonian. I sat down next to her at a slick mahogany conference table, pushed my bangs out of my face, got out my *Capitolist*-stamped pen and notepad, and gave my notes a glance. It seemed, according to the nonsense I had jotted down this morning, that the actress had descended on our city to lend her voice to the plight of the snail. I looked at my scrawl again. It was written in a kind of exhausted hieroglyphics, but it definitely said "Jan Jones. Snails." Weird, but I had seen far stranger. Like those PETA girls who stand in public parks, slather their bodies in egg-free mayonnaise, throw some iceberg lettuce on their privates, and scream the day away about animal rights.

After shaking January's slender, scented hand, I said, with far too much excitement, "How wonderful that you're in Washington advocating on behalf of the endangered snail. Ah, the woe of a snail!" I flashed a smile in response to hers, feeling sure that my teeth were the color of mud compared to her snow-white chompers. I quickly wrote "Schedule Zoom! whitening" on my reporter's pad right under the scrawl about snails.

Her press flack, sitting to her left, glared and mouthed something at me, which I ignored.

"Tell me then, how did your passion for protecting snails come about?" I asked January. "Years spent in the region around Burgundy perhaps? Les escargots de Bourgogne are my absolute favorite . . . to save, that is! My favorite snails to protect in the wild."

Phew! Brilliant recovery on my part.

Snapping her fingers and then rapping the table with her

nails, January's assistant mouthed something at me again. She looked very much like a monkey eating chewing gum. What was she saying . . . inhale? Curtail? No . . . no . . . what was it. Whale? Oh! Of course. Whales. Shit. "I mean whales!" I blurted out. "The endangered whales. Right! Who cares about saving snails. They're delicious!"

January didn't seem to notice that I thought she was on the Hill to defend a slug with a house on its back. We talked about whales. It was beautiful. She really seemed to care about the huge, frightening things. She even showed me a public service announcement on her iPad: there she was in a wet suit, swimming with whales and only kind of showing off her famous rack. She then deflected all my personal questions, but considering she also ignored my snail gaffe, I let it go and we went our separate ways. She, to do the things famous people do, and me to file the story and then trudge back to the newsroom so I could try to wrap up my fourteen-hour day.

The article filing process at the *List* was very simple. As soon as you finished your interviews, you typed them up on whatever writing device was readily accessible. This usually meant your BlackBerry. You could walk a few feet, maybe move to a pressroom or an empty hallway, but you never moved much because that was just a waste of time. You tried to avoid all factual errors and typos but what really mattered was speed. Much better to break the news that Cher was yelling at Michele Bachmann over Twitter than to spell the name Bachmann correctly. As soon as you sent your piece to your editor, he or she wrote you an email that said, "Got it, hold for edits." You then sat there and pinched a stress ball or started your next article and then five minutes later, your article was back to you and ready for your approval. You were allowed to go back and forth on breaking news pieces twice and no more. If you didn't like the edits, it was not worth your time to speak up because there was no time. And five minutes after you wrote the words, "Okay, let's go live," to your editor, your piece was on the site and in design for the next day's paper.

At *Town & Country*, we filed three months in advance.

After exiting the conference room, and in the hope of staving off arthritis for a few more months, I took two small rubber stress balls out of my suitcase-sized purse and began trying to turn my extremities back into hands. Since I had gotten the stress balls at some Sally Field event for Boniva, they were stamped with inspirational phrases about bone health.

Four minutes had gone by and I was just starting to regain feeling in my thumbs when my BlackBerry started buzzing. It was an email from Rachel. "Where are you? Are you done? How were the interviews? Did they talk about Boehner? Did they talk about who they're voting for in the primaries and can you file the stories from your phone or do you absolutely have to take the extra time to come in?"

I dropped the stress balls into the nearest trash can. "Yes on Boehner, no on primaries, Chase was funny, Jones was less funny but prettier. And yes. I can definitely file from my phone," I wrote back.

I found an empty marble bench in a quiet Dirksen hallway. With my purse strapped to me like an Eagle Scout's day pack, I hunkered down and started punching out back-to-back six-hundred-word pieces on a phone keyboard, Hill staffers darting past me all the while. During those twenty minutes, I shared my bench first with Senator Al Franken, then a painfully smelly woman, and then a young Hill intern screaming on the phone in a *Gone with the Wind* drawl. (I also checked the word *whale* every time I typed it, worried I would name the garlic-friendly mollusk instead of the mammal the size of a submarine.) It was nice to have a brush with senators, malodorous people, Scarlett O'Hara's offspring, and January Jones in the same day. But what I was really savoring was a rare moment in the sun. I had almost forgotten what heat generated by something other than stress felt like.

I paused for the first time on my "Celebs who love promoting causes" pieces, walked out the heavy bronze doors into the cold November air, and typed out my kicker. As I pushed send, I looked at the long list of messages I had missed during my type-fest: fifty-five emails, including one from Rachel that just read, "No rush, but when do you think you'll file? The next two minutes would be best."

I had missed her deadline by a minute and a half.

I couldn't get to sleep that night. I was so wired that even the thought of changing into my pajamas and lying down gave me anxiety. I had reached the point that Isabelle described as Listintoxication. It's when the paper got so deep in your brain that every part of your life overlapped with work.

Still mad at myself for filing my Jones story late, I turned off my "sounds of the Amazon" noise machine and walked to my closet. I put on a coat and old riding boots and headed outside. The downsides of living out in the country were plenty, but sometimes when I stood on the neatly mown lawn in the silence and moonlight, looking out at the horse fields and their white fences, it seemed worth it. Especially since I was paying for none of it.

From the barn, I strolled out into a long meadow and sat on the top slat of one of the fences. It was made for girls to sit serenely on while their Palomino horse grazed in front of them. I had used the same exact slab of fence as a balance beam once when I was ten; I fell off and basically broke my face. For two years afterward, my sister had me convinced that they had replaced the cartilage in my broken nose with wood. She called me Pinocchio and threatened me with matches.

I really don't miss her very much.

It was incredibly quiet, after-midnight quiet. I was happy to pick silence over sleep for a few hours, if it meant time without my BlackBerry or a screen covered in Twitter babble.

I always left the keys in my Volvo, just in case I had to drive into the city with my taillights on fire, but this time, I got in slowly. I knew my hours of sleep were ticking away, but I couldn't help it. I just wanted to drive without feeling like I had to get anywhere—no traffic, no deadline.

A repeat of that day's Diane Rehm show was crackling on NPR, but I turned it off in favor of a little Waylon Jennings. Being an outlaw country star with a guitar and a drinking problem sounded like a really good job right now. Maybe I could start guzzling Kentucky bourbon in the morning and carry a banjo everywhere I went. I would certainly get fired then. Sometimes I wanted to get fired. But then I remembered how hard I had worked in New York to get to the *List*, and I decided against it. I was at one of the best publications in the country and I shouldn't take that lightly. Yes, the pace was ridiculous, but I had great access, interviewed interesting people, and liked all the Style girls. I knew I was going to do something amazing with my journalism serfdom; I just wasn't sure what yet.

I drove down my parents' winding drive. There were no lights, but there were lots of trees trimmed to look miniature and a broad iron gate that opened as you approached it. I crept out of our patch of land and headed to East Washington Street.

There weren't many places to go in the sleepy town at such a late hour, but there was one store open round the clock in Middleburg and that's where I was headed. I didn't need anything, I just felt like seeing the inside of a building that wasn't my office or my house. The small twenty-four-hour store probably grossed about thirty dollars from midnight to 6 A.M., but it stayed open anyway. I figured they got a few extra bucks from the tourism board to do it, just to prove that Middleburg was more than a haven for moneyed geriatrics.

I drove twenty miles per hour past the English clothiers, the riding supply store, a café with a picture of a garden snake on it, and the restaurant that John F. Kennedy had once graced with his good looks, assuring it local fame for all eternity.

Over the slow rumble of my motor, I could hear a red fox groaning a few feet away. If you've never heard one before, let me tell you that they sound like a person in the throes of an ice-pick attack. When my parents first moved to Middleburg, my mother continuously called the police because she thought women were being slaughtered all around her. Not so. Just the song of a bourgeois hunting animal.

There wasn't another car on the dark roads. The lampposts were out in an effort to go green, and the storefronts' dim lights did only enough so you didn't trip on your own feet. The inn where Liz Taylor and John Warner used to lock their blue eyes on each other was pitch black, though inside, you knew, all the tables were set, tall tapered candles waiting to be lit.

I parked my car in front of Baker's, the twenty-four-hour store. The bell on the door rang for safety when I walked in, and I started to slowly walk the aisles of processed food. I reached for five products, all containing caffeine. Richard Baker, the owner of the store, had his oldest son working the graveyard shift, and in my daze I was happy that I remembered to ask after his family. Decades ago, his grandmother had been a great source for Jackie Kennedy in hunt country sightings.

Back in my car, I cracked open the passenger side window and started to drink some lukewarm hazelnut coffee without turning on the ignition. In front of me were the lights of the store; behind me, you couldn't see a thing.

I finished my drink without hearing the rumble of a single motor. That's just the way it is out in the country. And then, when I was about to head home for four hours of sleep, I heard the purr of an engine, a white BMW 650i Coupe creeping down the road. Elsa had the same one in silver. She bought it after she sold an entire Kara Walker show to a widow in Palm Beach.

The car slowed down across from the little market and parked in front of the closed stores on the other side of the wide, dark street. The headlights dimmed but stayed on, the door opened, and a woman who looked upset emerged in a thick red down coat and perched on the hood. The light from Baker's store was faint, but even in the darkness, she seemed a little familiar.

I reached for my wool riding jacket. I could have just closed the window, but I liked the feeling of the cold night wind on my tired face. By the time I slipped it on and turned around in the worn leather seat again, the woman had turned her face to the left and was looking at Baker's old-fashioned sign.

I did know her—Olivia Campo. She worked at the *Capitolist* and sat within my line of sight in the newsroom. She had a big title and covered the White House—the very top on the *List*'s pyramid of importance. We had never spoken, because I was in my Style section bubble, and she didn't waste her breath on anyone except the editors she was sucking up to. But based on office layout, I did a lot of staring at the side of her head. And of course, I also knew her as the girl who ruined Isabelle's future in television. It was definitely her. Her flame-colored hair and aggravated expression were visible even in the dark.

I could only see her because her headlights were on, and what did I care if she saw me? But my heart seemed to care; I thought if I looked down I'd be able to see it bumping around underneath my sweater.

I rolled up my driver's side window and slumped down in my seat. When my nose was the same height as the steering wheel, I dared to turn around in the driver's seat and peek in her direction. She didn't exactly look like she was trying to keep a low profile, but in Middleburg at 1 A.M., there was no need to try.

Why was she out here in the middle of the night? I knew why I was out so late. I lived here, and I was restless. I had no idea where Olivia lived, but my guess was that it wasn't Middleburg, Virginia. And if her parents lived in Middleburg, I would have known. It was that kind of town. Unless they had a different name? Was it possible that I was not the only *Capitolist* reporter crashing with her parents in the country? But no. No girl as hungry to get ahead as Olivia would dare live outside the city. In Washington, after people looked you up and down to determine if you were fat, smelly, or unimportant, they always asked you the following three questions: what do you do, where did you go to college, and where do you live. Based on your answers, they might ask your name.

Isabelle had mentioned that all the senior Congress and White House reporters made twice our salaries, so Olivia probably lived in a town house in Georgetown or Capitol Hill, not out here in hunt country. Maybe she had a country house? It was possible. The real estate was sinfully expensive in Middleburg, but if she was married to someone with money, she could.

I wanted to drive away and stop awkwardly staring at her, but I also didn't want to draw her attention. She was still reclining on her car, her arms crossed to stay warm, looking out of place but strangely at home.

After five idle minutes, she took her phone out of her coat

pocket. If the *Capitolist* had taught me anything, it was how to drive and dial at the same time. But she didn't actually make a call. She just looked at her phone. Maybe she was reading a text?

Finally, Olivia got back into her expensive car. She looked at the phone again and put her seat belt on. She then let out a groan, hit her steering wheel, and drove off in the direction she had come.

I didn't know what to think, except that it was weird for someone in their twenties to be alone in Middleburg on a weekday. Someone besides me.

When I finally did collapse into bed, the soothing frog noises I turned on failed to soothe me. I tossed around, wondering what to do the next day. Should I mention to Olivia that I had seen her? I had never uttered a word to her, so it might be odd to open with "Oh hey, I saw you casually kicking around horse country last night. Were you lost? Or just in need of some fresh air fifty miles away from home?"

But the next day was Friday, and the president was traveling. She was probably escaping the city, and I told myself it was unlikely she would even be in the office. And I was right. Friday came without one Olivia sighting and I never mentioned seeing her to Libby or Isabelle or anyone else.

Days at the paper went by at a gallop. Some days you worked every waking moment; others allowed you an hour or two of downtime to frantically research future story ideas for the paper. But all had you spinning at a pace that sitting world leaders would look at and mutter, "You can't be serious. No one can keep that schedule." And some people couldn't. Like Rachel.

CHAPTER 4

In most offices, there were employees who sprinted from task to task, happy to bring their blood pressure up to heart attack levels, while others kicked back at their desks like their cubicle was a tropical island. At the *List*, there was only one kind of employee, the kind that never stopped working. When a person decided that they didn't want to devote every brain cell to the *Capitolist* or they started overdosing on Washington, they left and left quickly.

One sunny Tuesday morning, after our section meeting, Rachel announced to us that she had given her two weeks' notice to Upton and was ready to say goodbye to 5 A.M. wake-up calls and wall-to-wall C-SPAN. She had only been my editor for forty-five days.

I wanted to hug her ankles the way I did Mrs. Van Hollen's on my last day of kindergarten, but my pencil skirt really compromised my range of motion. So instead I nodded my head encouragingly, trying to look brave but feeling the way I did just before my sister shoved me off a ski lift in Gstaad. I had known her mitten-covered hand was going for the small of my back before I felt the firm shove and heard the cackle of joy, but there was nothing I could do about it. I flew through the crisp Swiss air in my pink snowsuit complete with rabbit ears and crash-landed onto a family of five frightened Germans. Unless

I drugged Rachel and shoved her in a filing cabinet, there was probably nothing I could do about her departure, either.

Deep in mourning about the loss of Rachel, we stayed mum for much of the afternoon, only looking up when someone stopped in front of our bank of desks in the very back. Though there were five of us seated in the corner that I had dubbed the Outback, Upton liked to use the space just in front of our desks as a little conference area, oblivious that we were sitting there with working ears. There were plenty of glass-walled conference rooms in the newsroom, but if given the chance, staffers preferred to have desk-side chats with Upton to show their close personal relationships off to the rest of us.

A few hours after Rachel dropped her "ta-ta suckers!" bomb on us, Upton, Cushing, two of the deputy editors, and Olivia Campo all gathered in front of our desks holding *Capitolist* coffee mugs. I hadn't seen very much of Olivia since the night I spotted her in Middleburg. I'd learned she was a senior White House reporter who spent most of her time on Pennsylvania Avenue— and I had never been this close to her. I lifted my head, trying to look like a girl casually engrossed in *The Situation Room,* playing on the TV closest to them.

"I think we go big with Hu Jintao," Olivia said, getting into details about the Chinese president's imminent visit. She really was very thin, and her skin was kind of magical looking. It was so pale that I was pretty convinced that with the help of a flashlight and some reading glasses, I could actually see the blood coursing through her veins.

"Olivia's right," said Cushing. "That should be tomorrow's lead. Olivia, their meeting is open press?"

"It's not," she replied, shifting her thin legs to lean in closer to Cushing. "But Kelson will give me ten minutes."

"Are you sure?" asked Clark, the deputy managing editor for

online. "Why would POTUS's press sec give you ten minutes on such a busy day?" Upton and Olivia both smirked and looked at each other knowingly.

Gross. Was Olivia lap-dancing for the president's press flack or was she really that much better of a reporter than everyone else? I looked at her, all thin and pale with her limp red hair and gray wool pantsuit, and didn't see anything so extraordinary about her. She didn't look like she could bend kryptonite with her teeth; she just looked like a girl who liked frowning. In a few months, I had learned that part of making it big at the *List* was acting like you owned the building. Few had the temerity to do it, especially the women and definitely not me. But Olivia did and it was kind of amazing to watch.

When it was all sorted that Olivia would save the day with her close, nearly familial connection to the president's press secretary, the little group broke up, leaving only Upton and Olivia to finish their coffee and pretend the Style section didn't exist.

"Olivia, I'm sending Mike to follow the president and his delegation to India next week. I know I've had you in a holding pattern for pool duty, so I wanted you to know you can clear your schedule," Upton said, draining his coffee and shifting his tall slender frame.

Olivia's pale face was suddenly not so pale anymore.

"Upton! You can't put Mike on that trip. He doesn't have the foreign policy experience," she replied at a perfectly audible level. "The only trip he's been on for the paper was with POTUS to Toronto, which is basically like going to upstate New York. He's not going to be able to cover."

"Does she know Mike is sitting right behind her?" asked Alison quietly from her desk.

"Of course she knows! It's all part of her warped power game," hissed Julia, the resident expert on analyzing Machiavellian behavior at the *List*. It was true. Mike Bowles sat at the bank of desks just in front of us. There was a wide hallway and a pillar between them, but from the expression on his face, he could definitely hear her.

"Let's talk about it at lunch," said Upton in a low, quiet voice before rapping his fingers on the top of a water cooler and walking back to his office.

Mike looked like he had just been told he had testicular cancer.

Standing alone by our back area, I saw Olivia's face light up, not with a smile exactly, but with a confident, satisfied expression. She must have finally realized that instead of a wall next to her, there were actual people with eardrums and the ability to write disparaging emails. She turned toward our group, looked directly at my terrified face, and said, "Don't you have something to do?" Too frozen to respond, I looked down at my keyboard and Julia waved her away with an annoyed flick of the wrist.

"She's having lunch with Upton?" hissed Libby when Olivia had left our area. "No way. I could never eat lunch with him. I would be so nervous. I would spill everything and probably start crying and call my mother." Alison nodded in nervous agreement and I tried to bring my pulse down, still shaken by my very first verbal interaction with Olivia. Well, verbal on her part.

"You two would not cry," said Isabelle, calmly fluffing her perky blond ponytail. "I had lunch with him and Apolo once. It wasn't that big a deal."

Apolo Ohno! I loved when Isabelle talked about Apolo. It made me feel like his best friend once removed.

"But you're trained to handle stress," Alison shot back. "You skied in front of like ten million people. You probably had a stress coach and a team of sports psychiatrists."

"I didn't," said Isabelle. "I had confidence in my craft and so should you. We're not idiots. Just because Olivia and people like Olivia treat us like we're the Dallas Cowboy Cheerleaders who happened to have gotten hold of some laptops and press credentials does not mean we're bad at our jobs. All our badges around our necks say *Capitolist* reporter, just like Olivia's." Isabelle was right, but I bet that if I talked back to Upton in the middle of the newsroom I would have been asked to give notice.

Though I hated to admit it to myself, the way I hated to admit that I listened to Josh Groban's *Noël* album in July, part of me was in awe of Olivia. What she said in earshot of Mike was terribly mean, but she was so confident in her work, so vocal in her demands, while I still felt guilty and unworthy when I took a *Capitolist* stamped envelope from the supply room. How, I wondered, did she learn to act like that?

Seeing my puzzled face, Julia frowned and said, "Olivia Campo is actually the devil. If her red hair doesn't tip you off, then her egomaniacal personality and her ability to shove her face up Upton's ass will." I nodded my understanding and got back to writing a piece on football players with political aspirations.

After Rachel left, one of the older Congress editors stepped in for a few weeks. Our copy was rewritten to sound like breaking legislation news. We got morning emails written in all caps and were chided for not getting direct quotes from every lawmaker we referenced. It was like having a gymnastics squad led by the curling coach. But we knew it was temporary.

Just before Christmas, I woke up to a company-wide email announcing new hires. At the top was a new tech reporter to replace the one who had smashed his computer and moved to New Mexico. There was also a copy editor who came from *USA Today*, and then, listed last, was the new Style section editor. You would think we Style reporters might have learned about our new boss before the mass email went out, but no. After all,

Libby and Isabelle had once overheard Upton saying, "Honestly, I never read the Style section."

"We are very pleased to welcome Hardy Hamm, who will serve as our new Style editor," the email nod to him began. "Hardy, a 2010 graduate of Yale, was editor of the *Yale Daily News*, completed internships at the *Herald Tribune* in London and *Le Monde* in Paris and worked for the *New York Times* business section before coming to the *Capitolist*. He is the recipient of a William Randolph Hearst Foundation journalism award, the College Press Freedom Award, and a Poynter award. A native of Minot, North Dakota, he graduated from Yale in three years. In his spare time, he enjoys bass fishing, following the stock market, coin collecting, and writing to the editors of *Bloomberg* to point out their mistakes."

Bass fishing? My boss was now a North Dakotan fisherman? I was still in bed. The only sounds were my rapid breathing and the winter wind whistling outside my window. That near silence was soon shredded by a phone call from Isabelle.

"I knew it! I told you! He's all of nineteen years old, it sounds like. And the business section! Some snot-faced stock market whiz. Why the hell would they hire him for the Style section!" she screamed. But we both knew why. Four words—Yale, *New*, *York*, and *Times*—were enough for them.

"What does a bass fisherman from North Dakota know about gossip or style?" I asked Isabelle. "I bet he shows up in rubber overalls and a bright red patriotic tie."

I was wrong about the overalls. But he did show up in the *Capitolist* office on January 2 in a candy-apple red tie. He was twenty-two years old. His full name was Harold, and he was already married. Married!

On his second day, after he had sent us a ten-page document called "Section changes and expectations," Alison was forced to speak to him. We had spent all fourteen hours of day one communicating by email.

"Marley died," she said, walking up to his desk, already covered in wonky books and stacks of newspapers. Alison's voice was high-pitched and quivering. She stood nervously in front of Hardy, trying to stay professional.

While Rachel had sat with the other editors in the middle of the newsroom, a prime seating spot away from the hallway leading to the front door, management had decided to put Hardy in the back by us. Maybe it was his age, or his salary, which was about half of Rachel's, but he was downgraded to a desk that was only three inches wider than ours. We measured it before he came. It made us feel better for about thirty seconds.

"Marley. Is that your dog?" Hardy asked, not looking up from his keyboard. He was working on her piece for tomorrow's paper; there was so much red it looked like he was editing a piece for Joseph Stalin.

"There's been a death in her *family*," Libby whispered in his direction. "Family. Not family pet."

"Is it a close relative?" he asked, not looking up.

"Yes, she's my aunt and godmother, not my dog," said Alison, taking a step away from Hardy's desk. "She was like a second mother to me." With a desperate face, she looked at Libby for help.

Libby, wearing a winter white pleated dress and Bass penny loafers, shook her head, like an angry boarding school student.

"Ah, sorry about that," said Hardy, standing up but avoiding Alison's eyes. Without another word, he started walking toward the front offices. In his absence we swore like sailors and wished illness and disease on him.

When he came back five minutes later, he was all smiles.

"I checked the employee manual," he reported. "Management approves two hours off for next of next of kin. Why don't you start at seven tomorrow? That will give you time to collect yourself and properly grieve." He looked down at his phone, remembered that he was raised by a human mother and not a pack of wolves, and added, "And I'm very sorry about your aunt."

On our five-minute lunch break that day, Alison screamed about our new boss for four minutes and fifty-nine seconds. The other second was used to say thank you to the sandwich man when he gave us our food. But Julia and I spent a good deal of time on BlackBerry Messenger that afternoon just writing the words "I can't believe he's twenty-two years old."

"If he's the editor of a section at twenty-two, and I'm thirty-one, I think that makes me officially dead," Julia texted.

"When I was twenty-two, I was halfway between intoxicated and insane. I sure wasn't working my way up to the title of senior anything," I wrote back.

"I should probably write my will," wrote Julia. "I want to be cremated. Remember that if I die of natural old age causes in the next week."

When we returned to our desks, I looked over at my colleague, who was skillfully twisting her hair into a silky rope and pretending not to be texting me. She reached up to lower the volume on the TV that was drowning us in MSNBC gobbledygook.

"I have been working in journalism since I was out of college and I'm still not senior anything. I've been here for almost three years, it would have happened by now," she wrote. "The thing with Upton and Cushing is they decide a month into your employment if you're a chosen one or not. If you are, you sprint to the top. But if they think you're not cut from their cloth, then you work with no advancement opportunities for as long as you can stand it. And now I'm thirty-one and I'm going to die soon."

"But you're not old! Thirty-one is not old."

My phone flashed with her next message. "I graduated from UCLA class of 2003, so I am old. This place is like grad school, with less sex and liquor."

She was right about the lack of sex. I had more impure thoughts in church than I did at the *Capitolist*. As soon as you put your thumb on that little soul reader and walked through those thick glass doors, your libido abandoned you for greener pastures.

But as I looked around the room at all the people working as hard as they could, I felt a strange mix of horror and pride that I had been chosen to join these prestigious ranks. It wasn't like Upton and Cushing were actively trying to ruin your life. It was just a pressure cooker. You knew what was expected of you, and you had to deliver or you got axed. And what was expected of you was to work all the time and very quickly. You had to make your job your only priority. This, it turned out, was much worse for the soul than having someone yell at you occasionally, because it was constant, unrelenting fear.

Fear that you wouldn't have enough stories, or that someone would grab your scoop about Shakira's secret meeting with the president and get a quote from the sassy Colombian before your article went live. The inevitable anger you felt when you got barraged with hate mail and when your colleagues looked down at their phones and ran past you rather than saying hi. You were constantly strapped to a computer, and every mistake you made was a public mistake with your name on it. But in my case, the worst part was that at the end of the day, after I had worked my tail off for fourteen hours, my colleagues still deemed me an idiot. Because I worked for the Style section and they covered the White House.

Tucker Cliff, a senior Congress reporter, walked past both of us talking loudly into a Bluetooth headset. My phone flashed with a new message from Julia. "Tucker Cliff. They love him. They've decided he's a lifer," she pointed out. "Olivia Campo. Another lifer. That's just their way. They only want to groom and keep a few of us, but we all have to keep the pace and deal with child editors like Hardy."

Unlike Julia, I tried not to hate Hardy just because he was six years younger than I was. It didn't make me feel great, but it wasn't his fault that they had hired him to supervise a bunch of crones. I wrote him nice emails with lots of exclamation points. I tried to keep my speed Olympic and to stay calm when he edited my pieces to sound like they were written by a man from North Dakota who liked to fly-fish.

During his second week, he emailed me and said that while I was doing a good job, "my output wasn't there."

"Your goal," he wrote, "should be an article every hour."

I reread the line five times, but it really did say that. "An article every hour."

That's when I decided it was okay to hate him. I worked for about fourteen hours a day on average, so he wanted fourteen articles? I wondered how hard it was to get a prescription for speed. I mean, I knew speed was illegal and all, but I bet more people used it recreationally than let on. If I had some, I would just forgo sleep altogether. I would head to the gym, buzz on in to work, roller-skate across the newsroom to save time, and produce Pulitzer Prize-winning four-sentence blurbs about Twitter. And I would do it every hour.

CHAPTER 5

When Hardy had been our editor for a month, I had finally figured out how to make it work.

As the trees outside in the early February snow stood cold and lifeless, I was on autopilot. I shot out of bed at 4:50 A.M. Made instant coffee to save time and started my 5 A.M. to 7 P.M. workday. I worked for two hours like a slug in my bed, got ready in twenty-five minutes, worked and groomed in the hour-long car ride to the office, and then motored on through the day. Sometimes, while spraying dry shampoo on my roots and combing my hair at a red light, I would hear my sister's voice in my head saying, "With limp colorless hair like yours, you need daily blowouts to resemble a human being." But now it was a big day if I used liquid shampoo. After work ended, I would quickly drop by an event, make cocktail party chatter while begging politicians to say something interesting, and then drive my jalopy home. I would try to go to bed before 11 P.M., which usually required two NyQuil with a cheap chardonnay chaser.

It wasn't a recipe for health, but it was a good elixir for success at the *Capitolist*. I was getting used to Hardy's curt, aggressive emails and bookish edits. "This is the Style section," I would remind him when he tried to infect my copy with the terrible plague called "lame." After a while, he started to listen, and we found a way to tolerate each other, fourteen hours a day, six days a week.

Saturday was mine. I had to work Sundays, but from 7 P.M. on Friday to 7 A.M. on Sunday, I got to savor sweet, sweet freedom. Sometimes I spent the night in the city at Elsa's Logan Circle apartment. Other weekends, I convinced Elsa to come back to the town where we had shared our formative years. We would go for trail rides on the ponies I called roommates. We would have dinner at the Red Fox Inn, surrounded by old people in tweed, and then drink brandy out of my mother's nicest glassware on her heated porch.

On the first Friday in February, when Elsa came out to the land of the elderly to keep me company, we strayed slightly off the dirt path to a newly refurbished, very expensive inn named after a dead Confederate general and that had reopened right on the outskirts of town. Throughout our childhood, it was more or less an abandoned property where we took long walks and rode our horses semilegally. But all that had changed. A few years ago, the owners had decided to make actual money and had whipped up a classic country escape for fried city birds. It now had organic everything and a billion sommeliers and all sorts of nonsense like that.

When Elsa and I were growing up in Middleburg, there were small bed-and-breakfasts with historical plaques instead of spas and meditation rooms. Kids rode ponies in tiny Windsor checked jackets and women who filled their calendars with charity polo matches and country club round robins greeted each other in town with warm hugs. About a decade ago, developers realized that the picture-perfect Virginia postcard town where people still woke up on Sunday mornings and fox-hunted was ideal for an outside-the-Beltway getaway. So they started building. But luckily for the town beloved by people who consider jodhpurs daywear, Middleburg is home to a historical society run by retirees with a love of aesthetics and rifles. So not *too* much changed. The new tony hotels were hidden on acres of land and our little streets still looked like the love child of Colonial Williamsburg and Greenwich, Connecticut. Before Christmas, we paraded hunting dogs and horses in our red jackets and white gloves and the rest of the year it was pretty much the same way, minus the ode to St. Nick.

But Goodstone Inn was the new Middleburg. A place that attracted tourists instead of residents with a love of foxhounds and Barbour jackets.

Even though I lived a few miles away, I figured it was a perfect place for us to wrap ourselves in the amazing clothes I had got gratis from *Town & Country* without getting too many odd looks. We would just pretend we were out-of-towners who had come directly to hunt country from Bryant Park.

When Elsa came over, she air-kissed me and bowed before my closet like it was the Sistine Chapel. "Ooooh! Let me wear this," she said after she had thrown open the doors. "This was meant for me. They gave it to you, but they were actually thinking, this dress is made for an artiste!" Elsa said, ripping away a garment bag to reveal a white cashmere YSL dress inspired by Bianca Jagger.

"You're not an artiste. You sell the scribbles of artistes," I replied, helping her slither into the soft dress. "You're really a salesman."

"Which is an art. Trust me," said Elsa from within the dress. "I had to sell a blank canvas that someone had urinated all over. And I did. Don't tell me that's not a skill."

I vaguely remembered all that bathroom art from my years in New York. My guess is that it probably didn't go over very well in Washington.

"There. It's on. But I don't think it will ever come off," she said, trying to electric-slide in the dress. "Can I keep it?"

Oh, what the hell. "Yes, of course," I said. I would have to remember to use it as bait every time I begged her to come to Middleburg.

Since all five feet and three inches of Elsa were dressed as a cashmere snow angel, I decided to wear Hermès orange. Tons of Hermès orange. It was the dead of winter, after all. The world needed color. In New York we would have been gleefully dividing all the free clothes that were being shipped to our office. After a shot of flaming gin and a lot of squinting, this felt almost the same.

Our dinner at the inn was fantastic, and not just because I washed that gin shot down with half a bottle of wine. The food was delicious; it tasted as if it had come directly from the backyard, which, I learned later, it had. So we stayed and ate and loitered. We ended up at the bar, drinking far too many cocktails.

"Do you think my boobs are too big?" asked Elsa, poking at her Victoria's Secret miracle bra. I did.

"I do not," I replied. And that's the intellectual level we maintained the whole night.

Waiters waited on us. Busboys smiled and folded our napkins. I almost, for a few minutes, forgot that I ate most of my meals in the car.

"The art world is fascinating," said Elsa after I complained about how square everyone was at the *List*. "We had a naked sculptor carving President Lincoln out of soy margarine the other day," she bragged. "Over four hundred people came to the gallery to see butter Lincoln. We had to bring them inside in shifts. And you know, it was very cold in there, because of the butter, I mean soy butter. We didn't want it to melt. And they still waited, just because the butter carver was naked. This is such a prudish town. I mean, is it such a big deal to see someone naked?"

I would definitely wait in line to see a naked soy butter carver. "Naked? Yes, very rare here. Doing an activity other than sex while naked? Even more rare. I think you've stumbled upon the next big thing."

Elsa raised her glass to me, slopping half her drink onto the bar.

"So who bought the butter president anyway?" I asked. "I assume with a line out the door you sold it."

"Yeah, of course. You're going to love this one. We sold it to PETA. You know, the People for the Ethical Treatment of Animals."

"Ha! That's awesome. And makes perfect sense."

She looked down at her vibrating phone and leapt off the bar stool.

"I have to take this call. It's Ai Weiwei," she declared, leaving me to Google what an Ai Weiwei was. I wanted artists in my inner circle. Sculptors, dancers, mimes. I was starting to feel very one-dimensional. The bar was pretty full, considering where we were. But hotel rates around Washington fell in the dead of winter. These, I supposed, were the penny-pinchers who didn't mind romantic getaways in subzero weather if it meant off-season rates.

Sitting alone at the bar, I asked the very attentive bartender for something to read while I waited for Elsa to finish her call from Beijing. He handed me a hotel brochure, which was not exactly what I was looking for, but once I saw that there were actual historic houses for rent on the property that cost over one thousand dollars a night, I was more intrigued. Some looked ready to welcome home General Lee, while others were more French country chic. There was also a fat property pig that

snorted around and self-boarding stables where you could park
your horse for a mere seventy-five bucks a night.

"A lot of men," whispered Elsa after she returned from taking the call. She inched down her neckline and smiled at no one
in particular.

The odd thing about alcohol is the way it warps time. What
seemed like minutes of screaming "remember in high school
when you lit your hair on fire with a homemade bong!" was actually hours. Soon we were two of six patrons facing down an
impatient bartender. Elsa waved for the bill, and I watched the
other patrons get the hint and prepare to go. Two women who
couldn't stop talking about spa products nodded for the check.
A tall older man with a stern face and helmet hair headed for the
door, phone glued to his ear.

As he walked slowly past me, weaving through the vacated
bar stools, I caught part of his conversation.

"No, no, don't worry. I'm not asking you to come here. I'll
meet you. Of course I'll meet you," he said. He moved back
the sleeve of his wool blazer and looked at his watch. It looked
expensive. Or at least big and shiny. "I'll be there in ten minutes," he said in a sweeter voice. Then a pause, followed by,
"Olivia, you're breaking up. Are you there? Are you on your
way? Olivia?" He looked at his phone to see if it had cut off
and then flipped it closed.

That's when I hit myself in the jaw with a light thwap to
make sure I wasn't having alcohol-induced hallucinations.

As he walked calmly out of the restaurant, it took the power
of seven hundred imaginary men to keep me in my seat. And not
only did I stay in my seat, I attempted to continue acting normal
so that Elsa, a girl who knew me very well, would not think
I had morphed into a paranoid schizophrenic. Which maybe I
had. Or maybe I was just very drunk.

He had definitely said "Olivia." I was positive. And he was in Middleburg when he said it. But Olivia was not such an unusual name. Plenty of people were named Olivia. It's not like her name was Pig Girl or Hiddeldedee or something truly unique. And if it was the *Capitolist* Olivia he was talking to, so what? Maybe that man was her husband? Or father? Distant uncle? Chauffeur? As my mind raced through fifty different scenarios, I calmly asked Elsa about the weather forecast.

Clearly I should be in movies, because Elsa did not say one word about my peculiar blend of paranoia and enthusiasm for meteorology. Instead she said, "Should we ask your mom to pick us up?" when I fell down the slate steps on the way to the parking lot.

Yes, we should. If someone had pulled me over and asked me to take a Breathalyzer, the thing would have gone up in flames. But I wasn't feeling very sensible. "I promise I'll drive slow," I said, slurring every single word, even *I*. "Plus, this is a Volvo," I said, rapping on the hood. "They use them as humvees in Sweden." That was a total lie. But Elsa played along, probably because she was so drunk she was legally blind.

The next day we did not go horseback riding. We sat in bed until dusk and watched nine hours of *My First Home* on TLC, taking swigs of Pepto-Bismol and gasping at the incredibly low price of property in Wisconsin. What I should have been doing was driving around town trying to find the man who knew someone named Olivia, but my limbs weren't working. Instead I just thought about it until I decided that it really wasn't worth thinking about. No one had tipped me off about the Bay of Pigs. I had just heard someone say someone else's name.

By Sunday, when I crawled in to work to man the desk just in case some breaking Style news happened, I had rejoined the world of sobriety. I was ready to pop out some punchy headlines. I wrote about a portly former congressman sunbathing on a rock in Mykonos. I worked on a slide show of Michelle Obama's shoes. I propped my head on a large University of Texas mug to keep from falling asleep. It was not my mug, but I was working on Sunday and germs were the least of my problems.

I looked up at the flat-screen TV over my desk, the one that always had to be on CNN. Every inch of me wanted to change it to the Lifetime Movie Network, but I was almost positive we did not get that channel at the office. If we did get it and I dared to watch, it was probably rigged so some alarm would go off, and I would be shot with a Taser and turned to dust. So I tried to watch CNN. The hosts were talking to a panel of distinguished guests about something incredibly boring. I listened for a few minutes, trying to figure out what it was. Money. Angry people. Lots of blame-game-playing. Ah, the debt ceiling. How fascinating. I needed some toothpicks to prop my eyelids open.

It was getting very heated, and the main camera focused tightly on the guests as they shared their thoughts. I looked down to check the emails that kept flashing into my Outlook, but someone caught my eye.

There, on my screen talking to Candy Crowley, was the man I had seen Friday night. The man who said "Olivia" into his phone with affectionate authority. I had been completely blitzed, but that was definitely him. He had a strong Roman profile and a chin that jutted out like a rolling hill and thick dark hair graying at the temples. Like an older version of Julius Caesar with twenty more pounds on him.

I looked at the bottom of the screen where the names of the guests ran under their talking heads. Nothing. But when he flashed on again, his name and title scrolled under him. I was looking at the face of Hoyt Stanton, the junior senator from Arizona.

CHAPTER 6

There is some information you need to know and some you don't want to know. "Adrienne, your parents are actually flesh-eating coneheads" would fall into the "don't want to know" category. "Adrienne, is that you? It's the Virginia lottery calling. You've won ten thousand buckets of pure gold!" would be categorized under the "need to know immediately" category.

I deemed "Olivia Campo may or may not be slapping the pony with the junior senator from Arizona" to be "don't want to know" information. This was the wrong instinct, because I was a gossip columnist and that was definitely glorified gossip, but I still didn't want to know. Because what if she was? And what if I found out and reported it and the senator from Arizona had me killed? I was far too young to be bugged, stalked, and murdered. I had never been to Bora Bora or finished *In Search of Lost Time* or run naked around the Washington Monument or gone skiing with Karl Lagerfeld. I had so much living to do.

I was, of course, jumping to conclusions. I had seen Olivia skulking around a pretentious ghost town at midnight. Not a red flag. Maybe a pink flag. Then I had seen Hoyt Stanton, a United States senator, say the name Olivia into a telephone while leaving a swanky hotel bar in the same pretentious ghost town. Another pink flag. I decided to look up his family history to see if there were any Olivias floating around his Wikipedia page. None. His wife's name was Charlotte, his sister Mary-Clare, and out of his six kids—three biological and three adopted—only two were girls, Danielle and Daisy. My mind was spinning with possibilities, and they all seemed to lead to the bedroom.

"You seem distracted," my mother said after dinner *en famille* the next Saturday night. She held on to my freshly highlighted ponytail as I finished the dishes in her hand-carved soapstone sink. "It's not like you, you're usually so vivacious. And you just seem a little defeated."

I think I had become immune to 5-hour Energy shots and extra-strength Excedrin migraine. I needed a new legal upper. Worse, my new obsession with Olivia and Senator Hoyt Stanton was exhausting me. I felt like two little incidents had suddenly stamped every corner of my mind with the words "what if?" I had never seen them together. Never even in the same room together. I didn't know if Olivia Campo was on the other end of his phone call. But I couldn't shake the feeling. Middleburg was too small for coincidences.

"I'm just thinking about a few of the people from work," I answered my mother. I reached for a handful of candy from a bowl on the counter.

"I think you just ate soap," she said. She was right. I had ingested a full teaspoon of lavender-scented Palmolive rather than after-dinner mints, but I was too tired to spit it out.

"You need to stop thinking about work and start thinking about yourself," she said. "You never go out anymore unless it's for your job. You spend your weekends moping around this tiny old person's town, and even your horse looks depressed. You were never like this in New York. Remember all those pictures of you in New York Social Diary and *Gotham* magazine? And you made that 40 Under 40 list, remember? That's the girl I know." She kissed me loudly on the cheek, grabbed my tired shoulders, and told me I looked hunchbacked.

I wanted to remind my mom that in New York, my job started at 10 A.M. and not 5 A.M. That the *Town & Country* editors encouraged us to go out, not to become cave dwellers with female facial hair and lots of Twitter followers. Instead, I just said, "I'm still getting my legs under me."

Braiding my hair, she secured the end with a rubber band meant for vegetables and used a step stool to take a seat on the slightly damp counter. My mom went to Wellesley, too. She loved it. She's on the board now and goes up every other month to help advance the elite education of women. I think she started loving me more when I decided to go there.

"I had lunch with Vivian McLean yesterday, and she told me the most fascinating piece of information. There is a single man living in Middleburg. Not divorced, not a widower, just single and under forty. Dark hair. *Cute.*"

He was definitely going to be either a riding instructor or a horse breeder.

"He's a riding instructor," she said.

"I can't date a riding instructor!" I groaned. "He will announce that he's either bisexual or gay-curious by the time we order a first course. Then he'll want to borrow my clothes."

My mother shook her head and denied that the men in the horse world were almost always same-sex-oriented.

"You should make his acquaintance!" she pressed. "I see thirty in your very near future. When I was thirty, I had already given birth to your sister."

"Well, that was a sound decision," I said, chipping off my zebra-striped gel nail polish with a salad fork. Once, when I was seven, my mother caught me checking my sister's head for horns. Before she could pull me away, I was positive I had found the little nubs where they had been sawed off.

As she reshelved cookbooks and worried about her tired old celibate daughter, I sat on a bench whittled by the British a century ago and watched the fire in the kitchen fireplace start to die down.

"It's a small town. You're going to run into him anyway," said my mom, picking a stray thread off her Max Mara pants. "You might as well just meet him now. And Vivian didn't mention anything about—"

"Vivian McLean's husband dresses as Princess Diana every Halloween!" I interrupted. "Princess Diana from the 1980s at that. I don't think she's a good judge." I shivered, thinking about a man in a gold lamé dress and shoulder pads handing me Snickers bars all through my childhood.

"Well, metrosexuals are all the rage. I read it in *New York* magazine. I don't think you should be so closed-minded. I've always thought you were meant to be with a man in jodhpurs."

My mother actually looked hurt, and I felt a touch guilty. The woman just wanted to play Episcopalian Yenta. But a man in jodhpurs? I might as well frequent a leather bar in Tribeca to find my soul mate. I took my mother's scheme to marry me off to Elton John as my cue to retire to the animal quarters.

Julia was right. We were old. I had a working automobile and didn't have to travel by horse. Maybe I should move out of Middleburg to Logan Circle. I could probably afford to live in a basement with ferocious rodents and several roommates. It would be humbling, but I currently lived with my parents. Par-ents! I felt like a forty-year-old Sicilian spinster forced to can spaghetti sauce all day to earn my room and board. Finally, my frustrated parents would marry me off to a grizzled widower. "We have to get you out of the house!" they would declare as I presented him with a dozen cans of Ragu old-world style and my child-bearing hips. Realistically, my situation was even worse. With my job, I would never have time to meet a grizzled widower.

The Saturday after my mother tried to set me up with a gay man, Elsa called to beg me to come to her gallery on Fourteenth Street for an opening with too many people and not enough wine. I declined. I had trouble going out these days if I couldn't find an angle to write a piece for the *List*. Who needed a social life? Or single men to meet? I was too tired to talk after most days anyway, so my future partner would have to have a fetish for girls with bags under their eyes and BlackBerrys glued to their faces. In case it came down to him, I hoped this was what Vivian McLean's homosexual riding instructor was looking for in a bride.

With the joy of a work-free night ahead of me and a feast of lite beer and candy at my disposal, I opened the drawers of my white dresser and rearranged my sweaters, folding them all in seven moves like the girls who had run the *Town & Country* closet did. I emailed an ex-boyfriend from my magazine days (now probably married to a Russian supermodel, I speculated) and then I replaced all of my beech-wood shoe trees with new hand-carved cedar shoe trees that I had ordered with Amazon's handy one-click service while conducting a phone interview last week. I felt like a domestic anorexic, trying to bring order to my chaotic life by making everything look nice.

Three hours later, still pumped up from wet-dry Swiffering every corner of the apartment and wrapping all my silverware in velvet pouches, I put on a pair of old muddy paddock boots, my thick winter riding coat, earmuffs, and gloves and headed downstairs to see if my horse, Jasper, was asleep. Horses are like *Capitolist* workers, only dozing for about three hours a night, so he was most likely awake.

When I was a kid, my mom made me put my arm in a chest-
nut mare's mouth to prove her contention that horses were
gentle as kittens and I didn't need to be afraid. The horse bit
me and I had to get a tetanus shot. But I got over my fear and
spent many summer nights with my head on one of our horse's
stomachs while it was lying down in its stalls. Payton used to
say that I was going to die, squished by a thousand pounds of
animal flesh. She said that if I died, she wouldn't care at all, and
that she had already had a draftsman come up with plans to turn
my bedroom into a nightclub. But I was never squished.

When I walked through the powder-coated fir doors, I saw
that I wouldn't get to listen to an animal's rhythmic heartbeat
tonight. All ten horses were still standing. Some were drowsy,
with their heads falling below their withers, but Jasper was wide
awake. The barn was flooded with moonlight, and I didn't have
to turn on a single lamp to throw a bridle on Jasper and lead him
out to pasture.

A few years after I was born, my dad, who grew up on a
horse farm outside Charlottesville, Virginia, decided to take a
break from his big job lobbying for Boeing and Lockheed to
get back to his roots and raise horses in Middleburg. Much to
everyone's surprise, he never went back to K Street full-time.

While Payton had very successfully devoted her life to horses,
like my dad, the hundreds of thousands of dollars he had spent
on my young riding career had resulted in me pulling my horse
out at midnight while drinking a Bud Light Lime. I finished my
beer, put the empty aluminum bottle on a fence post to pick up
later, and pulled myself onto Jasper's bare back. My arms shook
and he moved a few feet, leaving me in a defeated pile. But my
second try got me on.

Riding bareback was hard. Saddles have been around since
800 B.C.; why exactly was I not using one? When Jasper got

into a slow trot, I leaned my face against his loose mane, held on, and remembered why.

I had no plans to leave the riding ring or to do more than a few loops around in the moonlight, but as soon as I saw the faint outline of the Blue Ridge Mountains jutting up in the light, I knew where I had to go. I just couldn't get there easily on a horse.

From my parents' house, it was possible, with a lot of illegal trespassing on property owned by the rich and angry, to take Snake Hill Road to the Goodstone Inn. That's where I had seen the senator say Olivia's name in the bar, and that could have been where she was going to or coming from the Thursday night I had seen her on the road—there was nothing nice open in Middleburg at that hour except hotels.

I hadn't thought of it until now, but Goodstone screamed, "Welcome, adulterers with discerning taste!" The staff was practically invisible, and along with a few hotel rooms there were those cozy cabins sprinkled around the sprawling property. If the senator were staying in one, Olivia wouldn't even have to walk through the lobby of the hotel to meet him. She could just drive straight up the hill with the flower beds and the organic vegetable garden, park next to his cabin, and join him there, totally unseen. It was a perfect place for enjoying life and lies, getting away and getting it on, undisturbed by indiscreet staff and inquisitive guests. If you had seven hundred dollars a night to spend, that is, which Stanton definitely did. Wikipedia had enlightened me to the fact that he was not one of those lawmakers who slept on a cot in his office to pinch pennies. Stanton came from a family of politicians and entrepreneurs with plenty of money.

I knew the area around Goodstone very well. The hotel had been remodeled only a few years ago. Before there was nothing but the stone carriage house, and we used to ride our horses on the empty hills and watch the sun set over the rolling mountains. The owner didn't care if we trespassed back then, mostly because he couldn't see us. But even in its new form, the property still had 250 acres around it, now dotted with luxury accommodations.

I jumped off Jasper's smooth back, took his bridle off, and climbed into my old reliable car. The radio started loudly blaring a love songs and dedications show, which I silenced immediately with my fist. I got back out of the Volvo to wipe some frost off the windshield with my coat sleeve, looked up at my parents' dark house, and hopped back in before the car iced up again. After ten minutes of driving on land more suited to an ATV than a station wagon, I could see the low stone fence that surrounded the sprawling estate. Thanks to that drunken night at Goodstone with Elsa, I had a decent sense of the property's houses. Of the hotel's five cottages, I deemed the antebellum Spring House and the colonial-style Manor House too big for two. Maybe Olivia and Stanton had a four-bedroom minimum for their sexual escapades, but that sounded a little nuts, almost as nuts as my driving a Volvo to a remote hotel to see if my colleague was naked and upside down. Scanning the area from inside my now warm car, I set my sights on the brown and white Dutch Cottage, the French Farm Cottage, and the red Bull Barn.

I parked the Volvo and walked the remaining hundred yards to the stone fence. I gripped my keys tightly in my left hand as the freezing cold air of late February burned my lungs. I needed to put my suspicions to rest so I could reclaim my sanity and devote every brain cell to becoming a star *Capitolist* reporter.

But what exactly was my plan? The cottages I wanted to see were, according to the brochure I had read at the bar, a ten-minute walk, on private property, from the main house. And all

I had come up with if I got caught was to say that I was just arriving. So what if it was almost 1 A.M., I smelled like horse, and was on foot with no bags? It would cost me a minimum of four hundred dollars just to check in, but who would arrest a paying guest? I could say I had just walked on in and was traveling light.

Trying to look confident and not like a trespasser on a mission, I headed to the Dutch Cottage first. All the lights were off, and there were no cars out front. On nervous legs, I walked about four hundred yards to the French Cottage. Before I got very close, I could tell that there was at least one light on. I felt elated. It could be them. But when I got closer, I saw that the car parked outside had Massachusetts plates. Unless Olivia had decided to head north and canoodle with Senator Scott Brown, a much sexier choice, I doubted that she was inside.

I prayed that the rolling hills weren't also covered in surveillance cameras, and walked over to my last option. I reminded myself that there was a huge chance they were not there. I had never seen them at the inn together, and the senator probably had to return to his home state and put on the good-husband act sometimes. Or, even worse, they could have been in one of the private rooms inside the main carriage house, which meant I was screwed. Short of breaking and entering, I would never see them there. Outside, on these farm hills, I wasn't really breaking or entering anything. Wasn't it really all God's country, regardless of ownership? I decided that was my Plan B argument. Religious zealot out for a stroll.

I stopped in my lawbreaking tracks when I got close to the Bull Barn. Parked outside the brick red building was the white BMW 650i Coupe I had seen Olivia reclining on weeks ago. It was the same car, I was sure. It had Washington, D.C., plates and the outside was meticulously clean.

Crouching down by the wooden fence surrounding the house, I waited. I didn't know exactly what for, just something. But ten minutes later, nothing had happened. I was too scared to approach the house. I had read Senator Stanton's bio, and the odds of his having a large gun were 100 to 0. What if he went insane and shot me in the face? Or what if Olivia just took a fire poker and beat me to death and then tossed my body into a ravine? There were clearly no cameras out here, or I would already be in lockup at the Loudoun County jail.

So instead of walking to the house, I crawled quietly over to the car. It gleamed in the light of the full moon, as did, presumably, my skulking, shuddering body.

The front seats were pristine. Not a Styrofoam cup or gum wrapper to be seen. But the light beige leather-back seats were a mess. There were clothes piled up, a red knit throw blanket, an old-fashioned picnic basket, and a few books scattered around. I saw the collected works of Muriel Spark and felt immediately violated. I loved Muriel Spark, and I didn't think her work belonged in a car that most likely housed Senator Stanton and Olivia's adventures in oral sex. There were also some boring-looking hardcover biographies. I was trying to read the titles without getting too close to the car when I saw something so identifying that there could no longer be any doubt that it was either Stanton's or Olivia's car. Under Doris Kearns Goodwin's *Team of Rivals* was the neck string of a *Capitolist* entry pass. I couldn't see the badge, which was trapped under the book, but I saw the navy blue satin lanyard, stamped with the paper's logo, that we were all required to wear when we were in the building.

I had changed mine to Hermès orange leather the first week, and Isabelle had ripped it off my neck like it was a venomous cobra. "You can't do that!" she warned. "You won't be seen as a team player. Everyone wears the *Capitolist* lanyard. You have to, or they'll immediately judge you and you'll get stuck covering holiday parties at the Office of Waste Management. Take my word for it," she had said gravely. "I once used one I had from the Olympics, and Julia made me throw it away. She saved me." Afraid of getting the boot for individual expression, I had switched back immediately.

Olivia had never been as stupid as me or Isabelle, I was sure, and like the rest of us she was never spotted without her identifying badge and *Capitolist* noose. I was surprised she wasn't wearing it to sleep, or whatever she was doing in the house just twenty-five feet in front of me.

I backed away carefully until I was, I hoped, out of earshot and then ran half a mile back to my car. I felt like a cartoon character with no knees. Riding boots, which I had stupidly forgotten to change out of, have absolutely no give, which is great on a horse and bad if you need to sprint a mile. Finally I had to bend down to loosen the laces. While I was crunched over, I saw the lights of a car coming down the road.

I immediately threw myself to the ground, which was hard and frozen. Winter, it turned out, was the wrong time for dilettante espionage. There was no foliage to hide behind. Luckily, the car drove past me, and I watched its lights move up the hill to the Bull Barn. As soon as it rounded the bend, I took off running again, jumped the fence, started my car, and headed home. I felt like a suburban mother lost in the woods in her Volvo. I also felt like an idiot. Why was I leaving? I had exactly what I was looking for just a few feet away from me, but when it came down to fight or flight, I had hobbled away in my stiff boots.

I needed time to think. I also needed a mode of transportation with better wheel traction than the Volvo. I had to back up

twice and make two loud attempts to get up the last hill to my
parents' house. When I got close to the house I turned off the
headlights and wheeled the car around to the barn.

Jasper was lying, abandoned, in the outside riding ring. He
looked excited and geared up for Paul Revere's midnight ride
when I approached, but I had to bring him in. I brushed his coat
and thought about what to do next.

It was then that I looked up and saw the camera installed in
the barn. We had put it there to keep an eye on the horses, and if
one was sick, to monitor it through the night. I waved my hand
back and forth in front of it, and the lens moved with me.

I needed a camera.

I lay in bed as the clock crept toward 4 A.M. I was unable
to do anything but sit and chew my nails off thinking about
them, a United States senator on the rise and my evil colleague.
What was I going to do? I couldn't exactly sneak around like
a paparazzi with a telephoto lens, could I? Or *could* I? We ran
pictures of celebs and politicians snapped by paparazzi around
town. What was the difference if I took the photo myself?

As dawn crept up on me, I reached under my bed for the
box of electronics I never had time to use. I found two different iPods, three Flip cameras, a Bose flat stereo, and an alarm
clock shaped like an eagle that a marine had given me after I
hooked up with him in a hotel room during Fleet Week. I think
he had stolen it from the hotel, but whatever. It still worked. I
also had two disposable cameras containing never-printed shots
from the late nineties, a jumble of cords, and one of those giant
roll-up piano mats from the movie *Big*. But no camera. I realized
I hadn't taken anything but a cell-phone picture in the last ten
years.

I needed to quickly seduce a sports photographer and borrow his camera. Or find two grand and buy one. Or rent one!

Could you rent those huge things? Probably. You could rent anything. You could rent people by the hour and have sex with them. Surely I could rent a camera.

Before heading to the office just a few hours later on Sunday morning, I first went to the hotel under the pretense of an early breakfast, just me and the *New York Times* and my cell-phone camera. But the car was gone. I would have to wait until the next weekend. They couldn't possibly skulk out here during the week.

Still, I checked. Every night that week I made the short drive to the east side of the hotel through private property to see if I could spot the car. I had rented a camera from B&H in New York, and with its *National Geographic*-style telephoto lens, I could see almost all the way to Canada. I was pretty sure they wouldn't chance staying in the main house of the hotel, so I concentrated on the five guesthouses. But all week long, I didn't see a single car parked in front of any of the cottages.

Thanks to my nocturnal activities, my brain now had only five hours of sleep a night to run on. I had stopped being able to process things besides basic human needs. My life was now eat, sleep, write, report, drive, lurk around the Goodstone Inn, pet horse, greet parents, repeat. What I wanted it to be was sleep eight hours, have sex with brawny man, write at normal pace, report, drive Ferrari, have someone hand me a videotape of Olivia and the senator having sex, slap them five, win Pulitzer, compete on horse in Olympics, greet parents by phone, repeat. I was very far away from the second scenario.

In my hazy state, I thought I saw a flash of Olivia's red hair around every turn in Middleburg. Every man I saw was the senator until I got close enough to realize that my target was too short, too round, or too something else. Still, I couldn't stop looking for them. After work, I would drive down East Washington

Street and buy a few things from Baker's general store, where I first saw Olivia. Then I would walk past the clothing and antiques shops and pretend to be taking in some air. "Refreshing!" I would exclaim as I did some deep abdominal breathing outside a completely dark, locked store. And then I would walk the main street from the *Chronicle of the Horse* magazine office to the Presbyterian church with the tall white spire. I would, of course, see absolutely nothing of interest. Once, in the early evening, I witnessed a small girl fall off a bike and then eat a slice of turkey that her brother had produced, unwrapped, from his pocket. It had lint on it, but it did make her stop crying. I prayed she wouldn't get Ebola. But that was all that happened. I walked, I loitered, then I would give up, drive home, demand that my mother feed me, and fall asleep for a few hours.

The result was that I was exhausted, getting uglier by the day, and making stupid mistakes in my articles.

"What is this crap?" Hardy asked me as I was drawing a red X on my desk calendar. It was eight o'clock in the morning on the last Monday in February. I had been out looking for the senator and Olivia the night before. He looked down at his printout and read aloud: "Senator Garland and his wife, Lauren, dressed like a John Singer Sargent tableau vivant, perched casually on their leather arm hairs while the *Capitolist* chatted with them."

Oh God. Had I really written that?

"Could you possibly have meant 'arm*chairs*'?" Hardy asked, circling and recircling my idiot typo with his red pen. "Do you know what this shows me?" he asked in his nasal voice as I tried to think up an acceptable excuse.

I dunno. That I sashay around town looking for trouble and sleep for five minutes every night before washing down three espresso shots with a Diet Red Bull every morning?

"That I made a stupid mistake that will never happen again?" I offered.

"Not at all," he replied, rolling up the sleeves of his wrinkly yellow dress shirt. "This shows me that you rely on spell-check rather than your own editing skills."

Was he kidding? Of course I relied on spell-check. If I didn't use spell-check, the word *Massachusetts* would have been spelled *Masachewsettes* all my life. My generation couldn't spell. We texted! And his generation could barely even text. They communicated via Groupons and strange holograms, as far as I could tell.

He sighed and dropped his red pen on my desk. "For you. Use the red pen and attempt to discover your inner editor," he said, moving away. "I know you can do better."

He was right. I could. But I needed to rack up some REM sleep if I was going to write about politicians rather than fore-arm fuzz. The day-to-day of my job had been nudged aside by something out of the ordinary, something that might, despite my assignment to Style, cover me in *Capitolist* glory. A possible affair between Olivia and the senator was a much bigger story than a Kanye West sighting at the White House or a staid couple sitting on armchairs. Why shouldn't I concentrate all my energy on what could be one of the biggest scandals of the year?

I just couldn't get fired or caught in the process.

I needed to relax. I needed something to Zen me out. Something cheap and soul altering that didn't take more than fifteen minutes. That evening, after I finished interviewing a few congressmen about their iPod playlists in the Capitol's Speaker's lobby, and attended a cocktail party saluting congressional pets, I decided to find peace around the domed building. "What a relaxing area!" I exclaimed to no one as I walked down the Capitol's marble steps. I smiled weakly at the stocky security guard who moved the guard rope for me and headed down the south side of the Mall toward the Washington Monument.

It was a beautiful view, one of the best in Washington, but I wasn't in the mood for worshiping buildings named after dead presidents. I had been working in the city for five months but I had barely done anything for myself. Every party I went to I had to cover, every person I met I had to interview. As soon as I crossed in from Virginia, I lived only for the *List*. I felt like seeing something that had nothing to do with the laws of the land, like a zebra, or a trapeze artist, or considering that I could see six different museums from where I was standing, maybe some art. I looked at my watch; it was a few minutes past 7 P.M. All the museums, while gloriously free of charge, would be closed. I slipped on my hat and gloves and pulled my scarf tighter around my neck. In just a few weeks the paths linking all the monuments would be covered in puffy pink cherry blossoms and people enjoying the warmth of spring, but right now, walking around in late February still felt like scurrying on frozen dead earth.

Cutting through the Smithsonian sculpture garden, I walked past a sea of illuminated bronze legs and boobs. "Rodin. Rooooodin!" I rolled the only sculptor's name I could think of off my tongue and walked slowly through the garden of art. When I reached the end of the sculpture walk I took a deep breath and smiled. There! A four-minute walk. I was totally rejuvenated. I was ready to head back toward the Capitol and find my car when two young girls and their mother walked past me holding ice skates. Skating! I didn't realize the skating rink was still open. That would calm my nerves. I wasn't about to risk my life on two steel blades; whoever decided strapping knives to their feet was a good idea anyway? But I still had eleven minutes in my allotted relaxation time to kill. I could watch the kamikaze children go round and round in circles.

Walking to the far side of the rink, I placed my hands on the wall built to keep spectators off the ice and skaters on the ice and was gravely disappointed by the sight of a group of grown men in red ski parkas having a hockey shoot-out. Where were the children? The future Kristi Yamaguchis of tomorrow? Those two little girls I passed were probably crying in despair right now.

I put my hands in my pockets and watched a group of testosterone-crazed guys with hockey sticks screaming out to each other as they slapped a few pucks around. Disappointed, I checked my BlackBerry and readjusted my white cashmere beret. There was one man in a hooded Patagonia parka who was really good. He was making a series of shots from between his legs, finding the goal every time. Applause filled the area and the man next to me started whistling his approval. I turned instinctively and realized that the gentleman in question was not only a skilled whistler but incredibly handsome. Like Hollywood heartthrob handsome. With deep tan skin and thick black hair, he looked like a cross between Andy Garcia and Montgomery Clift. Or a cigar model come to life. Did men in Washington look like this? Non-*Capitolist* employed hockey fans, that is? He clapped his hands, covered in elegant brown leather gloves, together for warmth and smiled at me. I took a small step away from him, afraid that if I was too close I'd do something irrational like lick his beautiful face.

"That's my friend Marty," he said, gesturing toward the really good hockey player. "The Canadian Embassy rented the rink out tonight. Some of them are really bad, but Marty's amazing." Marty hit a puck with his friend's hands covering his eyes and it went smoothly into the goal. Everyone cheered and Marty did a celebratory lap around the rink. "He's also well aware of how amazing he is," my gorgeous hockey fan said with a deep laugh.

It was like hearing an American version of Pavarotti speak.

His voice was a song: Smooth, animated, but manly. God, he would sound amazing reciting our wedding vows. I hadn't seen a man like this since I left New York City, and those had usually been money-grubbing dickheads. But this guy was friendly and hadn't said the words Morgan Stanley! He was also gorgeous and just happened to be talking to sex-starved me. I had to introduce myself. Maybe get an address and some identifying information like his mother's maiden name. No, no. Bad. Overzealous. I had to play it cool.

We watched Marty the Canadian make yet another shot and start pounding his chest in celebration. I clapped, suddenly full of light and optimism and joie de vivre. I loved hockey! What an underrated sport. What was our team in Washington called again? The Penguins? The Geese?

"He is very good!" I replied. I sounded hysterical. And loud. Why was I shouting?

The gorgeous man kindly didn't recoil from my megaphone voice. Instead, with his straight white teeth and perfectly shaped lips, he explained that his friend had played professional hockey in Calgary before retiring and going to work at the Canadian Embassy.

"Of course," I nodded knowingly. "I love Canada. All those lakes and moose." Wait. Was that grammatically correct? Moose? Mooses? Meese?

Perfect Guy laughed, looked deeply into my eyes, and pointed to the rink. "Did you come here to skate? They should be off the rink soon," he said apologetically.

"No," I replied, shaking my head. "I just like to watch. It helps me relax." Slick. I sounded like someone with a neurological disorder.

"Yeah," he replied, putting his glove-covered hands in the pockets of his light gray cashmere overcoat. He turned his head away from me and looked around for his friend, who had left the rink. "I don't skate, either. I'm from the South, so not really our thing down there. I'm actually pretty ready to grab some dinner as soon as Brian Boitano here is finished shaking a leg."

I smiled as warmly as I could. I wanted to give off a vibe of domestic bliss, of homemade cookies and plates full of angel food cake. But maybe that wasn't his thing. I changed my kind smile to a sexy pout. Before I could see his reaction his tall Canadian friend bounced over, having changed his skates for sneakers and smacked my future husband on the back.

"Thanks for waiting, man. I had to get that out of my system. That rink is so oppressively small, it's hard to do anything but slap shots, but the chicks seemed to dig it."

My husband laughed and called his friend pathetic. Funny, too! I was ready to strip off my four layers of clothes for this man. Here and now.

"Cool coat," his Canadian friend said in my general direction. I looked down at my vintage Givenchy coat that I got into a midnight bidding war on eBay for, closed the top button, and said thanks.

"Did you have fun watching the game?" the hockey player asked me. "Enjoy my little performance?" Ew, gross. Marty the Canadian, though also pretty cute, was definitely the kind of guy who watched himself in the mirror during sex. But who was I to judge! I didn't want to exchange saliva with him; I wanted to walk down the aisle to Vivaldi with his gorgeous friend.

"Yeah!" I replied enthusiastically. "I missed the game but I'm glad I caught the end of your shoot-out. Very cool. I need to learn more about hockey. Sport of kings."

My new crush laughed and assured me that I didn't have to lie. Then he put his hand on my actual shoulder and said, "She came to skate and you and your Canadian barbarians ruined her night. You should apologize to her."

I was frozen. Could I casually just grab his hand and slip it into mine for the rest of eternity? Or just maybe place it directly on my boob? Before I could do anything, his hand was back by his side.

I assured Marty that no apology was necessary and that ice hockey was my yet to be unleashed passion. With both men laughing at my bad joke, I got ready to act like a cool, confident, with-it kind of gal and boldly introduce myself, but more of Marty's Canadians joined them and they all started talking about the game. No one was speaking to me or introducing himself so I pulled my BlackBerry out of my coat pocket and started to scroll through my forty-six new messages. This was the moment when the gorgeous guy would break away from the group, put his hand back on my shoulder, and say, "This may sound forward, but will you marry me?"

That didn't happen. The group of hockey players and spectators started walking away, the two men I'd been talking to gave me friendly waves of the hand and said, "Nice meeting you," and I stood there like a jilted bride saying good night under my breath.

By the time I got the words out, the two men had their backs to me. "I didn't catch your name," I added softly, but they were already well out of earshot and I had a tad too much dignity to run after the dark-haired stranger, throw myself at his feet, and beg him to love me physically, mentally, and spiritually.

Who was I kidding. I didn't have time to have a crush on someone. I certainly didn't have time to date. I *had* tried logging on to some soft-core Internet porn site last Friday night but I fell asleep before I had the nerve to push the "Yes, I'm over 18" button. My sex life was pathetic.

CHAPTER 7

Painfully single and with zero weekend social obligations, I finally decided to check into the Goodstone Inn one Saturday afternoon, so that I could stalk the grounds as a paying customer. The hotel couldn't tell me to get lost if I was pitching six hundred dollars their way to be on the property. To pay the hefty overnight fee, I sold two of my *Town & Country* freebie designer bags on eBay, telling myself they were last season, and made my reservation for the blue-and-white-toile-covered Hayloft suite in the main carriage house. I deserved a staycation anyway. Juggling stalking and work had worn me out, and this would be the first time in over five months I didn't have to sleep ten feet above horses.

I was prepared. I had a camera. I had a dog-eared copy of *Photography for Dummies*, and I had a lot of tight black clothing and a pair of gray running shoes. I had also slapped some duct tape on my conscience to keep it from convincing me not to meddle in the affairs of others. That was basically the definition of reporting—meddle, pry, find dirt, report—and I was a reporter. It's no wonder politicians always bitch and moan about the mainstream media. But I was part of it, and I wasn't going to ignore the biggest lead of my extremely short career.

I felt skittish but ready for anything. Except an Olivia sighting.

She had been out of the office almost every day in March, spending all her time traveling with the president or following his every move at the White House, so when I sat down at my desk on Friday morning and saw that she was across the hall, right in front of me, I felt immediately ill.

I was petrified. Was it possible that she knew I lived in Middleburg and was having me watched by a private investigator? I looked at her out of the corner of my dry, tired right eye, but she wasn't paying any attention to me. She was busy reporting, which sounded a lot like screaming "fuck" into the telephone over and over again. Maybe she was a warden before she became a journalist.

"Could she shut the fuck up with her fuck-yous," Isabelle said, looking up at Olivia. "She acts like she's the only person in this newsroom. And every time she screams 'fuck' I'm forced to look up and see her pale, angry little face."

"Wear headphones," said Alison in her signature pinstripes without looking up at us.

"You're wearing headphones, and you can still hear us," said Isabelle. "What she needs to do is shut up. She always talks like that. And you want to know why?"

None of us answered. Everyone else because they didn't really care, and me because I was knocked mute with fear that Olivia could hear us.

"Because that's how the guys talk. That's how Upton talks, and Marcus Isaac, the only person in here with a Pulitzer. Two actually. She's such a pathetic emulator."

"It's not just her," said Libby. "All the women with good salaries here act like men. They curse like men, dress like men, and have banished all pastel colors and emotions."

"Olivia's the worst offender," said Isabelle. Worst offender or not, Olivia certainly didn't sound like a girl who was trying to keep a low profile because she was having a torrid affair with a senator.

Libby nodded, still messaging a source on Gchat. "You're right. She screams like a frat boy all the time but I think she does more TV hits than any other girl in this place. Did you see her on Andrea Mitchell yesterday? She wore all beige. Head to toe. She looked weirdly naked." Libby, like a good East Coast prep, was wearing a party of pastels. "Although she wore that twisty evil sorceress necklace she always has on, too. So, naked except for a symbol of darkness around her chicken neck—good look."

"You know what's sad?" said Isabelle, moving past Olivia's questionable wardrobe choices. "There are barely any female reporters here to look up to and say, 'That's it. I want to be *her*. The reason I'm working this hard is to get *her* job.' I mean, all the senior reporters are guys."

That was true. There were a few senior female editors, not many, about three out of fifteen, but as high-ranking reporters went, there were almost none.

"Olivia's a senior reporter," I pointed out.

"That's the point," said Alison, crossing her thin legs. "Haven't you been listening to us? She's not human. She's a cyborg and you can't actually look up to her."

Julia looked at all of us disapprovingly. "Why are we wasting our breath on her? Could one of you please file something? The page hasn't moved in forty minutes, and you know if five more minutes go by we're going to get a bitchy Hardy email." We all looked over in panic at his empty desk. Lucky for us, he was working from the Capitol that day.

"I have something on Ludacris calling the Tea Party racist," I said quickly.

"And I have something on Kelsey Grammer saying he loves the Tea Party," added Alison.

We all wrote articles in silence, trying to stagger them so that Hardy had a steady flow for the next hour. When I finished my Ludacris piece and sent it off to our child editor, I walked to the bathroom with Isabelle, doing my best not to look in Olivia's direction. I didn't have any hard evidence of her wrongdoing— just my gut and all those pink flags—but I was still afraid she could see suspicion and curiosity painted all over my face.

"I've never even spoken to Olivia," I told Isabelle as we washed our hands. "Actually, she spoke *at* me once, but that doesn't really count."

"You're missing nothing. You haven't forgotten that she stole all my notes and had me banned from CNN for life?"

"That was horrible," I said, remembering Isabelle's flood of tears.

"And for some reason, she's a senior White House reporter even though she's a whopping twenty-eight. She worships herself and has somehow convinced Upton and Cushing to worship her, too. I once saw her reading Machiavelli's *The Prince*, if that tells you anything."

I laughed and squirted a quarter-sized puddle of Purell into each of my hands.

"Why do you know her so well?" I asked quietly when we were back at our desks. If there was one thing Isabelle had zero tolerance for, it was fake niceness. I could string together compliments about terrible people all day, but if Isabelle hated you, she looked right at you and said, "Stop talking, I hate you."

"I don't know her well, but when I first came here they tried us both out on the lobbying beat and we shared an editor. She convinced the editor that I was the worst thing that could happen to lobbying since Jack Abramoff. I was off the beat in two weeks, and she got moved back to the White House beat *and* promoted. Seriously. I heard her tell our editor that I was an incompetent fool who had trouble spelling my own name and should be moved to the Style section. She said 'I can't work with her, and you shouldn't have to, either.'"

I wouldn't have believed it elsewhere, but this was the *List*, where bad-mouthing of colleagues to one's boss was standard.

Isabelle handed me a Diet Coke from the enormous stash she kept in her filing cabinet.

We both kept our eyes on Olivia gripping her phone to her frowny face. "I don't give a shit if this information is embargoed. You said you would embargo it until noon, and now you're saying four P.M.? I have all of it to the copy desk already, and it can't change. You can take it up with Upton if you have a problem." She disconnected her phone call with her index finger and immediately started dialing another number.

Isabelle brushed a few crumbs off her desk. "The thing I never understood about Olivia is how she got here in the first place. She was a metro reporter at a local paper in El Paso. Local paper! I don't get the jump. It's like she went from PTA president to secretary of state in under a week."

"But she's good at her job, isn't she?" I asked.

"Only because she's a ruthless, unrelenting bitch," said Isabelle. "Girls like that are always good at their jobs."

I spent my afternoon writing articles and cowering, trying not to look at Olivia. After four hours, I concluded that she was born without a bladder, since she never got up to go to the bathroom. Her long, stick-straight red hair hung around her head like a curtain of fire. It wasn't yellow red like my mother's shoulder-length bob. It was a hot red. She dressed badly and somewhat seductively at the same time. Her blazer looked cheap, but her shirt fit very snugly and attractively, even if it was badly ironed and fading around the cuffs and collar. And she was always wearing that knotted silver necklace. I was dying to stand up and scream, "Are you having sex with Senator Stanton? Are you, are you, are you?" But of course I didn't. Instead I listened as she yelled, "President's trip to Iraq? Of course I'm covering!" into her phone at a decibel usually reserved for air raids. Finally I turned my computer on its pivot and didn't dare look in her direction for the rest of the afternoon.

I wrote articles. Every hour I shot another piece to Hardy. They were short, and some were terribly boring, but all he seemed to want was quantity so that's what he got. In between my seventh and eighth piece of the day, I allotted myself ten minutes of Google stalking to attempt to find the man from the skating rink. I had nothing on him, but Google knew all, right? I entered "tall, dark hair, gray coat, Canadian Embassy, hockey." I got a series of pictures of toothless hockey players wearing maple leaves. So I tried, "hot hunk, ice skating, brown gloves, thick hair," and got pictures of the fabulously flamboyant Johnny Weir. Our road to matrimonial bliss was not going well. I would just have to go with plan B: find Marty at the Canadian Embassy, call him, and ask him who his hot friend was. There was no way in hell I would actually go through with plan B, but I liked pretending that I was the kind of girl who would do that. Instead, I put my courage elsewhere. I was going to the Goodstone Inn with a camera strapped to my face and I was not going to leave until I had something.

Before I left work that Friday night, Julia shoved a red folder of printouts into my bag. "From my realtor," she said, putting her arm around my shoulders. "He too would like you to join us in the adult world. It's one where we cohabitate with spouses, boyfriends, maybe a friend or two, but not our parents. Try it. You might like it."

I was being property-bullied.

The folder contained pictures and floor plans for apartments, all on Capitol Hill. However much Julia moaned and groaned about the *List*, she lived and played in the land of the wonks. She liked being surrounded by people stamped with RNC and DNC. The men she dated worked in politics, all her friends were high-powered Hill flacks, and she didn't really mind at all. A quick glance at the apartment descriptions she had given me suggested that she didn't mind because she was making way more money than I was. Hired a few months after the paper launched, she had started when they were shelling out the big bucks to bring people in, before the paper was a big name and prestige was the largest part of the compensation package. To bring me in, they just reached under their couch cushions for some change, threw in a 401(k), and called it a day. The only way I could live in Julia's apartments of choice was if I brought five of my closest friends with me. We could each sleep on a yoga mat. It would be charming.

Making sure that the papers didn't fall out everywhere, I hugged Julia good night, thanked her for her help, and pushed the down button to call the elevator. Even though it was well past normal working hours, the garage was still packed with cars. The *Capitolist* had to be one of the only offices in America where the employees didn't rush out when the clock struck 6 P.M. on Friday. Or 7 P.M. It wasn't until eight o'clock that people started to trickle out.

Listening to my heels click on the cement, I walked to the purple section of the garage where I usually parked. It wasn't very close to the elevators, but I didn't exactly drive a car I wanted to show off to my peers.

I was ten cars away from the Volvo when I heard footsteps behind me. Having been raised by two paranoid parents who gave me bear spray before I went to college in one of the wealthiest suburbs in New England, I stopped walking, turned around slowly, and stopped dead. It was Olivia Campo and Justin Cushing. They were walking in stride and smiling. Actual smiles. I didn't know Justin Cushing approved of smiles.

I turned around before I looked creepy but heard her say, "Good night, Justin," and then the sound of him beeping his car open. By the time he started his engine, I realized that Olivia had parked her shiny, perfect automobile in the row behind mine. Why would she park in the purple section? She had a nice car! Everyone at the *List* knew that all the badly paid reporters parked their tin cans in the purple section and the well-paid employees, like Justin Cushing and Olivia, parked their much nicer cars in the green section. I had seen Olivia's car in green before. Was she doing this to toy with my mind? Maybe she really had seen me that night. Maybe now she was going to assassinate me in the parking garage and pop my lifeless body into my trunk.

I could hear the click of her thick, practical heels and was going to jump in my car to make a getaway, but I took three deep breaths like Dr. Phil always suggested and turned around. Olivia was standing next to her white BMW, keys in hand.

"Nice car," I said nervously. She didn't turn around. "Nice car," I said loudly. This time my words echoed through the parking lot. She turned around and faced me, startled to hear my voice.

"A 650i coupe. The most recent model, right?"

Olivia frowned at me but lowered her left hand, which was holding her keys.

"Why do you know that?" she asked with frustration in her voice. "Are you some kind of weird motorhead?"

Was I a what? "No," I replied. "It just says so on the back of your car." Olivia realized I was right and scowled. "Ha!" she said sarcastically, then lifted her keys again and beeped the doors open.

"I'm kidding," I said, smiling and praying I didn't sound like a girl with plans to stalk her that weekend. "My friend has the same one. Drives like a dream."

"Right, well now you really sound like a motorhead," Olivia offered up while opening her door. She looked at my car, a Wellesley College sticker still stuck to the back window, and smirked. "Have a great weekend," she said in a superior voice as she climbed into her car, then started the heavy German engine.

We had spoken. And not just Olivia barking at me. I had started the conversation and momentarily gotten her to feel like a moron. I wasn't sure how I felt—it was a strange mix of nerves, panic, and even a little confidence—but suddenly Olivia seemed less like an unapproachable monarch who ruled the newsroom with a translucent fist and more like a woman, my exact same age, whose career I could potentially ruin.

I threw the folder from Julia in the back of my crappy car, among the empty water bottles, articles that were no longer relevant, and a smorgasbord of beauty products, and jumped in the driver's seat. So my car wasn't made in the last decade. It still got me from point A to point B. "Don't mind that wench," I said to the car, patting the steering wheel, and headed home.

I spent what was left of Friday night studying a map of the inn and comparing it to the Google Earth view. When I felt as if I could confidently crawl around the place in the dead of night, I switched to Googling Senator Stanton. I'd been doing it for weeks now, but every time I entered his name into the search engine, I was sure I would find something that I didn't see before. As usual, there were many photos, with many American flags. Some were with his constituents, others with his wife and handful of children. He had the Internet presence of an upstanding family man and a devoted public citizen. Not one skeleton in his data closet. He hailed from a political family, married his

college sweetheart, and had six children, three of them adopted.
He graduated from Arizona State University and Yale Law and
by all accounts lived a straight and narrow life. His Twitter
account was policy and Bible verses in 140 characters or less.
If you agreed with his politics, there was nothing wrong with
Senator Hoyt Thomas Stanton.

An affair, if he was having one, would signal a major character flaw. He wasn't shipping arms to Iran or embezzling government funds away from elementary education, though, so I
didn't feel a patriotic obligation to report out his story. At this
point, it was mostly just curiosity, especially because it involved
one of my most self-righteous colleagues. And if I was right, it
could break his career and her career, but it would make mine.
I wasn't proud of the fact that bouncing up the *Capitolist* ladder
interested me, but it did. If I was going to put in the same crazy
hours as everyone else, I wanted to feel like I was part of the
team, not riding the bench all season. I wanted Upton to say,
"We'll talk about this at lunch," and walk to my car with Justin
Cushing. A pay raise wouldn't hurt, either.

"You're going hunting?" My father lowered his newspaper on
Saturday morning and looked at me like I was a hot-blooded gun
nut. "Since when do you hunt?"

Getting to the Goodstone should have been easy, but I had
a few hurdles to bounce over going a mile down the road, and a
little white lie was part of it. So I told my dad that I was getting
the guns and going hunting.

My father was kind of like an accidental rich person. He
never cared about making money or having money; he just happened to have a lot because he worked as a big-time lobbyist and
he inherited barrels full from his dad. He wore old jeans, thick

flannel work shirts, and cotton sweaters from L.L. Bean, drove a pickup, bought horses, and used the rest of his cash to keep my mother happy. I hadn't had much time with him since he came back from Argentina, as he was always outside and I was always inside the *Capitolist*, but I liked being able to see him from my window when I got home at night. My dad was the family compass, steady and dependable. He was also eminently practical and not loving my fake hunting excursion.

I had decided I couldn't take my temperamental old Volvo to the Goodstone Inn on Saturday because Olivia had stared it down in the parking garage at *Capitolist* headquarters. My mother's cherry-red SUV was the most unsubtle color on the planet, so I nixed her car, too. My father had a 1967 Mercedes convertible and a Toyota pickup truck. I went with the pickup. It would get me through the mud and might even look like it belonged to a grounds worker.

"When is the last time you fired a gun?" he said, grilling me on my crazy lie. "I took you girls a few times when you were kids. I remember Payton being a very good shot, but you, you decapitated a snowman. Do you remember that? You cried. Payton then ate what was left of the head lying on the ground, and you cried some more. Now you're telling me you're going hunting?"

Oh good Christ, I had forgotten about Payton's decapitated snowman eating. Maybe I should have come up with a different excuse, but I was too far into it now.

"Elsa wants to go," I explained. "She's dating some guy who lobbies for the NRA." This lie was getting worse and worse. Elsa would never date a card-carrying member of the NRA. Her last boyfriend was a sculptor with a heart tattooed on his thumb.

"Doesn't he have a car?" asked my father.

"Of course he does, but no one will pick me up out here, and I don't trust the Volvo to make it up those hills."

My practical dad relented when I made it a safety issue. He ran his left hand through his dark gray hair while he thought about his daughter doing her best Calamity Jane with her artsy friends. Like Payton, my dad was about as athletic as they come. At sixty years old, he was still built like a much younger man, thanks to all his time trying to break his South American horses, but his skin was tan, worn, and a little leathery from the sun. His skin crinkled into deep creases around his green eyes and his mouth twitched slightly under his five-day beard as he imagined me using the wrong end of the gun to chase a charging buck.

"Don't shoot anyone," he finally declared. "It's March. All the fat white men you see will be real, not made of snow." Convinced I was going to both crash his enormous car and shoot either myself or an overweight Caucasian, he walked down to the car with me to show me how the truck brake worked. I loaded my Goyard bag (clothes, computer equipment, camera) into the pickup and gave him room to adjust the driver's seat and mirrors.

"Adrienne, hunting," he muttered as he moved some horse blankets from the passenger seat to the jump seats in the back.

"I'll be fine, Dad," I insisted. "Payton and I used to shoot stuff all the time when you weren't paying attention. I'm actually pretty good." This was also a lie. I was having trouble opening my mouth and saying anything laced with a shred of truth.

"Well, Payton, she's a different story," he said. "I would let her pack heat in a kindergarten classroom. She's a hell of a shot." Like most people who met her, my parents were in awe of Payton. I remember being at a field hockey tournament with her and overhearing my mom and dad saying, "How can one person be so good at everything she does?" They were not talking about me.

"I thought Payton was crazy when she said she was going to

breed racehorses in Argentina with Buck," said my dad, momentarily sidetracked by thoughts of his far-off daughter and her husband. "I said, 'What's wrong with Virginia? We have horses right here. This is the state that created Secretariat. Is a Triple Crown winner not good enough for you?' She could have just moved in with her old mom and dad and helped with our little family business, but she said living at home would be an act so pathet—"

He stopped talking when he saw my face.

"Addy, I'm sorry. I didn't mean to say that."

"No! It's fine," I said brightly. "We didn't all go into lucrative professions like Payton's horse torturing."

"Horse torturing . . ." He laughed under his breath and then looked at me standing awkwardly outside the car door. "Payton did have that spread in the *Robb Report.* Did you see it? Four pages, with pictures and everything."

He looked at me clutching my heart and smiled.

"Oh Addy. The little things like that don't really matter. You're the one with the great career," he said, climbing out of the truck. "You've always worked so hard. Your sister's just doing what she watched me do her whole life."

"But I'm just doing what Mom did!" I countered. "Oh God, that's depressing. You've raised two totally unoriginal children. We're mimics unable to forge our own paths."

My dad laughed a low, rolling baritone laugh. His chuckle was like a good bottle of booze—mellower and better with age.

"I don't think anyone would dare call you two unoriginal. I certainly wouldn't. You and Payton are just a bit different . . . like the sun and the moon." He smiled, clearly happy with his attempt at diplomacy.

"Which one am I?" I asked, climbing into the front seat and buckling the tried and tested seat belt.

My dad flashed me a knowing smile.

"I'm the moon! I knew it. Payton is the lovely hot orb that keeps us all alive and I'm some lump of rock that looks like it's made of molten blubber and doesn't do anything. You're a swell father. Thanks for the pep talk."

"Adrienne," he said, closing the door. "Don't be so dramatic. People are different. Maybe I should have used the no-two-snowflakes-are-alike comparison instead."

I rolled my eyes and waved at him as he yelled some marksmanship advice in my general direction.

It was just after 1 P.M. when I checked into the inn. Before I went to the desk, I drove through the field to see if the white BMW was there. It wasn't. The Bull Barn looked empty. I swerved around the property and drove back down the hill, parking my dad's truck at the far end of the parking lot.

"Brown. Adrienne Brown," I said, handing the young woman at the front desk my driver's license.

"Brown, yes, you're in the Hayloft suite," she said, smiling up at me. As she punched in my credit card information, she looked at my license. "New York City. Did you drive in from there?"

Perfect. I knew I hadn't gotten around to changing my license yet for a reason. If she saw my real address she would most likely ask me if I was Caroline Cleves Brown's daughter, because everyone knew my mother, or she would question my extremely local vacation. Instead I just made small talk about escaping the noise of city living.

"Well, you won't hear a sound out here," she said, handing back my cards. "Total peace and total privacy, that's our motto." Yes, privacy. Unless you had a newspaper reporter with a telephoto lens in her purse checking in with the sole purpose of spying.

"Do you need help with your bag?" she asked, looking at my small tote. "Your room is on the very top floor."

"Oh no. I'll be fine," I said, clutching the bag to my side like it was full of blood diamonds.

"Will you be dining with us tonight?" she asked as she pointed me to the staircase.

"I'm afraid not," I said. "I think I'll try room service. This is more of a getaway trip for me."

"Of course," she said, bowing her head. "Then here is your key. I hope you enjoy your stay."

I hoped I would, too.

I had chosen the Hayloft suite for one reason, and it wasn't because it was a favorite with honeymooners, as the website advertised. It happened to have a huge private terrace overlooking the entire property, including the dirt road that led to the Bull Barn. My plan was to spend the day on the terrace with my fingers crossed for a white BMW to drive up the road.

I sprinted up to the room, dropped my bag on a small pouf of an armchair, and opened the door onto the roof terrace. It was huge. I could have thrown a kegger on it. And, more important, I could see the road that swerved toward the little red barn. The cabin itself was hidden behind a hill, but if any car was headed that way, I would be able to spot it before it rounded the bend. I settled in.

One black SUV, one blue sports car, and two silver sedans drove onto the grounds between 2 and 7 P.M. None headed toward the Bull Barn, and I was starting to freeze. Late March in Virginia was not quite spring and when you sit outside for hours, it feels more like January. I was ready to give up, order ten waffles for dinner, and watch myself grow cellulite, but just as the sun was setting, I heard the rumbling of another car. It wasn't the white BMW I had grown used to checking around every corner for, but it was on the road that went to the Bull Barn. I quickly pulled my camera up to my eye and zoomed in on a dark blue SUV. Just before it disappeared down the road, I saw that it was a Ford Explorer with Arizona plates.

It had to be him, I told myself. My palms started to clam up. I had no idea what kind of car he drove, but how many tourists from Arizona drove to the Goodstone Inn? And yes, it was absolutely stupid to drive your own car if you were having an affair and didn't want to get caught, but lawmakers having affairs did stupid things all the time. Weiner and the twit pics? Bathroom foot tapping? Driving your own car was nothing compared to the idiotic behavior of many of our other esteemed leaders.

On the roof with my camera in my lap, I considered possibilities. If that navy blue Ford Explorer was the senator's, then Olivia could be in it. Or she could be driving up later that night in her own swanky car. Or he could be alone. Or even with his wife. I decided to sit and wait for her white car until the sun set. I couldn't go crawling around the place until it was dark anyway, so until then, I would just sit outside with an eight-pound camera glued to my right eye.

My phone buzzed with a text message. Birds made annoyingly happy cawing noises. And I just sat on a wooden chaise longue trying to figure out what to do next. I needed it to be pitch black out. Then I would dare to creep out toward the Bull Barn. If anyone asked, I would be taking a midnight stroll. I could pretend to be a nature photographer captivated by nightscapes. Plus, I had my get-out-of-jail-free card: the expensive room key.

As I sat on the terrace with my heavy camera hoisted up, I wondered about other people's sex lives. When did old people have sex? If I was going to catch Stanton and Olivia in the act, would I have to do it before he passed out at 10 P.M.? I often passed out before 10 P.M., and I was still in my twenties. God, I wanted a sex life. I wanted to have sex with ice-skating guy eight times in one day. I wanted us to have to wear water pouches filled with electrolytes while we did it just to keep from fainting. But I couldn't muster up the courage to call his Canadian friend so I wasn't even allowed to think about it.

I needed to calm down. I called downstairs for a bottle of not-too-expensive sparkling wine, and when it came up I stuck my hand and a five-dollar bill out a crack in the door. "Please leave it outside, I'm not presentable," I said, handing the anonymous hotel staffer the tip. I popped the cork off the cool bottle and immediately downed a third of it, no glass necessary. Drinking Prosecco out of a bottle: how elegant. I should be the one having an affair.

I flopped back on the wooden chair and looked at my text messages. There was one from my father asking if I had shot anyone. "No," I texted back. "You can stop worrying." Then I checked my BlackBerry. I ignored the note from Hardy reminding me that my Sunday shift started at 8 A.M. I was most likely going to work that shift with no sleep and, considering the size of my first sip of Prosecco, an insane hangover.

By 10 P.M. all the world was dark. Well, the world surrounding the Goodstone Inn, anyway. The dirt roads out to the guesthouses were completely unlit. My plan was to put my camera and a few Cliff bars in a running backpack that I had brought and walk toward the Bull Barn. I didn't have to get too close to it, considering I had rented the Bentley of cameras, but I did need something to hide behind. And all I could think of from my strolls around the place, and the informational brochure I read in the bar, were a few short trees and a large muddy pig.

It was go time.

Once outside, instead of walking, I ran. I tried to make my legs slow down, but it was so dark, I figured no one could see me anyway. So I kept running, I ran over the hill where the car had disappeared and threw myself underneath a pine tree. I felt ridiculous. I was dressed like a poor man's version of Lara Croft: Tomb Raider. But what choice did I have? It's not like Richard Nixon just walked over and professed wrongdoing to those *Washington Post* boys. Good reporters had to dig, right? This was when I wanted a real editor instead of a twenty-two-year-old who was only good at slave-driving. I wanted someone I could email and ask, "cool or uncool to be hiding under a pine tree with a telephoto lens pointed at the hotel room of a United States senator?" But I had no one to ask. If anyone at the *Capitolist* found out I was spying on the nocturnal activities of one of Upton's favorite reporters, they would find a way to rally behind her. I was not a chosen one in the office; Olivia was.

I crouched on the ground and peered into the darkness. I was already elbow deep in their mess; I wasn't going to wade out now.

Lying on my belly like a sloth, I took the camera out of my backpack, wrapped the thick rubber strap around my neck, pointed it toward the room, and looked through the viewfinder. Through one of the only uncurtained windows I could see wooden walls and a stone fireplace with a thick wrought-iron railing next to it. For the next hour, that's all I saw. A family of ants was feasting on the skin I had left exposed, and I had sap dripping down my ankle. I felt like a CIA agent stuck at Girl Scout camp.

Fifteen more minutes went by, then thirty. I remained motionless even as the chill of the dirt crept through my shirt to my stomach. I kept the camera lens high and my eye against the viewfinder and listened to the minutes tick by on my big men's watch. Half an hour. Then an hour. I stared through the lens at the empty room, learning every crease in the couch and crevice in the wall. It felt like an exercise in hopelessness.

Just past midnight, Senator Stanton walked through the room with the wooden walls. Right after him came Olivia.

I was right.

I had been right about so few things in my life! I wasn't right about men, ever. Moving back to Middleburg felt all wrong most of the time, and my *Capitolist* gig seemed like a never-ending mistake. Until this moment.

Though there was just enough moonlight for me to see my hands in front of me, and maybe for someone walking in the fields to see my silhouette, a camera flash would have torn through the dark countryside like lightning. I would have to shoot without flash.

I looked through the viewfinder again. They were standing in the living room, talking, laughing. My right index finger shook with hesitation and then pressed down the shutter. As it flicked open and closed six times, I felt my entire life changing. Olivia wasn't exactly naked doing the reverse cowgirl, but they were in a hotel room together. I doubted they were going to spend the night playing Wii tennis.

He got a fire started, and then they were out of my sight. For what felt like hours, all I could see were his penny-loafer-covered feet up on a coffee table. I was not going to make the front page of any newspaper with pictures of senatorial feet. Even a picture of Olivia and Stanton sharing a bed and sleeping next to each other wasn't enough to make the kind of claim I was now sure was true. I needed skin, sweat, lust. I needed porn.

There was a light on in the back of the little red house; eventually I realized it had to be the bedroom. That was where I needed to point my camera if I wanted to capture anything the least bit incriminating. Otherwise it would be all hot toddies in the living room, and only *Better Homes and Gardens* would want my exclusive.

A few minutes past midnight, the senator's feet disappeared from the table, and I steeled myself to abandon my relatively hidden position and dart into the open field on the bedroom side of the house. A small group of birds flew above me in no particular formation, black streaks in the moonlight. The lights of the hotel's large main house glowed faintly in the distance; they felt very far away.

On my knees in the field of short wild grass, I felt completely visible, as if I were naked in Times Square, screaming for attention. But there were no eyes on me. The only attention I was getting was from my own conscience, screeching questions about how I went from sitting third row at fashion shows to crouching in a dark field late at night trying to take pictures of a senator having sex with my colleague.

I lifted the camera to my eye again. As the auto zoom whirled the world into focus, I saw a dark-stained oak dresser and, next to it, a bed with a carved headboard and a plaid quilt. There was a patterned rug on the floor and a small green plant on a heavy wooden end table. But there were no people.

I waited, the moisture from the earth soaking my thin black pants. I was much closer to the house now. I didn't need to lift the camera until I saw people moving in the room. So I stayed pinned to the ground, trying to look like part of the scenery. I looked at my watch again: 1 A.M. and still not a sign of life in the back of the house.

Just before 1:30 A.M., they walked past the window. They went too fast for me to lift my camera in time. With steady hands, I brought it up to my eye, not letting my nerves take over, preparing for their next pass. When they walked past the window together again, I should have been ready. But instead of continuing past, Olivia turned to look out of the window, pushing back the curtains and putting her elbows on the sill. I put my face to the ground in panic and dropped the camera. It was too dark, I told myself. There was no way. If you weren't looking for me, you couldn't see me. The light from inside would have made it impossible.

When I dared to look up again, she was still standing at the window.

She looked content. Peaceful. Totally different than she did at work. Her hair was tousled, not hanging static and lifeless around her face, and she was wrapped in a thick white robe. She was holding a drink and periodically turning her head around to say something. I looked through the viewfinder at her face. It was bare and scrubbed clean. She looked nothing like the girl who would happily escort you to the edge of a cliff if it meant she could have the lead in the paper.

When I looked at her face again—soft and smiling—I thought about the first time I heard Stanton's voice in the bar in Middleburg. His voice sounded concerned, sweet, loving even. He had certainly fallen for her, and looking at her here, now, her feelings for him weren't far behind.

I saw Senator Stanton move in behind her and put his arms around her neck. He was still wearing a buttoned-up work shirt. Without breathing, I started clicking the shutter release button again.

Together, they stood motionless for a few minutes. Their age gap was noticeable, and even kind of gross. But they looked like two normal people in love.

Or maybe just lust.

He pressed himself up against her body, and she half turned her head, looked up, and started to laugh. He laughed, too, his dark brown hair unmoving, his eyes filled with joy. I shot that, too. I sucked their privacy into my lens with every snap. He was kissing her neck while she kept smiling and saying things I could only imagine. Then, almost roughly, he turned her toward him. He leaned her back until her head was touching the window screen and started kissing her. Still holding my breath, I clicked and clicked, praying they couldn't hear the noise of the shutter.

He pulled her away from the window and pushed her playfully, presumably onto the bed. Just like that, they were out of my line of sight. I cursed under my breath and let the camera hang around my neck. My arms were shaking from nervousness, guilt, excitement, and the weight of the long, heavy telephoto lens.

I waited twenty minutes for them to come back to the window, but no one came. Creeping on all fours through the grass, my camera in the bag again, I made my way around to the glass double doors that opened into the bedroom. They were covered in gauzy white curtains, moving slightly in the breeze. Maybe, if I timed it just right, I could snap while they moved and get something.

Stomach to the grass, I got out the camera and started snapping. I was afraid to check the photos in the camera's LCD screen, for fear of the bright light shining through the darkness. With every rustle of the curtain, I took pictures in the largest format I could. Somewhere in those images, there had to be something I could zoom into.

And then I saw flesh, just for a second, and clicked as fast as I could, like an aerial photographer trying to beat the clouds.

It was almost three o'clock in the morning when their bedroom light turned off. The rest, if more was happening, would be off the record. I got up to leave, but I was almost sure I had it. I put my camera back in the bag on top of my press pass, strapped it all tightly to my body, and started running. My legs moved quickly, muscle memory guiding them through the field. Everything felt disconnected. My body and mind, what I had just done, it was all so far away from who I used to be and what I had been raised to do. But I made it to the parking lot, where I jumped into my father's truck. A change of clothes and a more normal-looking bag were awaiting me there. I couldn't exactly walk into the hotel in the middle of the night dressed like a ninja. I might as well just write the word *sketchy* on my forehead. So I slipped on nice jeans, a more formal coat, and a pair of gold ballerina flats, to make it look like I had been out for a night on the town, and shoved the camera and backpack into a battered Louis Vuitton bag with a zipper. I brushed my hair, put on lipstick, and jumped out of the Toyota truck looking very little like the girl who had stepped into it five minutes before.

I nodded to the night guard at the front desk and took the stairs up to the Hayloft suite two at a time, closing the door behind me and locking it while my lungs caught up with the rest of me. Rushing to the laptop I had left lying on the bed underneath the blue and white slanted ceiling, I attached a wire to the camera, labeled the photos "The Bull Barn," and uploaded them. I password-protected the file, emailed it to myself, and downloaded it onto an external hard drive. Even if the entire state of Virginia was suddenly firebombed, these photos would exist somewhere.

I poured the rest of the bottle of Prosecco into a water glass and slurped the warm wine into my cold body. Fortified, I pulled up Photoshop and got ready to zoom into the dark images.

Thanks to the light inside the house, they were much clearer than I had expected. I pulled up the series of shots I took with the curtains blowing, and even without zooming in, they spelled career ruin. The senator was lying in bed with a sheet wrapped around parts of him. But not the right parts. Olivia, completely naked except for the small necklace she always wore, was next to him. He had his face on her breasts, her neck, her ears.

I clicked through the pictures again and again on my laptop. I was a voyeur, the kind of reporter everyone hated, sitting alone in Middleburg looking at the annihilation of their professional, and probably personal, lives.

I resaved the images five different ways and shut down my computer. I pulled the covers over me and held the silver laptop to my chest. I fell asleep hugging a thousand-dollar machine filled with ruin.

CHAPTER 8

I had always hated starting Monday mornings with a sleep debt, but that's how it was every week at the *Capitolist*. You could do nothing all weekend but pop Ambiens and clock sixteen hours of REM a night, and you would still wake up on Monday feeling exhausted. It was like chasing a hundred-pound Kenyan man in a marathon. Knock yourself out: you could never catch up.

And if there was ever a week where I wanted to start off shiny as the North Star, it was this one. It was White House Correspondents' Dinner week.

Attendees dubbed the dinner "Washington prom," and society journalists called it "hell week." What sounded like one night of handshakes and forced conversation was actually twenty-five parties in six days. The twenty-four-hour news cycle and the national obsession with celebrity had turned the "dinner" into a weeklong A-list circus. Hundreds of politicians turned out. Handfuls of celebrities flew in. Media outlets tried to one-up each other with famous guests. The president got roasted and then got his turn to bash the press. Comedians, cynics, critics, and crashers all exchanged business cards, and a million flashbulbs went off to record it all. Everyone drank heavily for a week, either to celebrate or to cope.

It should have been fun. Or at least that's what I thought

when I was told we would be covering it. "Oh, fun!" I yelped. My colleagues looked at me like I was cheering over a pelvic exam. "It's hell," said Libby. "You have to work twenty-four-hour days for the entire week. And then you get zero comp time."

"But I thought it started Thursday?"

"The good parties start Thursday. The bad parties start Tuesday," said Libby, as if it were as obvious as pairing peanut butter and jelly. "And we have to cover those, too." Her mouth already starting to twitch in frustration. "I can't believe I'm doing this again. I swore I would only cover this shitfest once, and here I am, back for a third. God, get me out of here." She pulled a small rubber bear out of her Kate Spade bag and started squeezing it. "Don't judge my stress bear," she said curtly when she caught me eyeing it.

"It sounds really fun," I said as she headed back to her desk. It also sounded like the one place I was sure to see both Olivia and Senator Stanton. Not having an intimate tête-à-tête, I imagined, but at least in the same building. I hadn't glimpsed them together since the night I saw them enacting May-December passion at Goodstone and while I had amazing pictures, I needed the story to go along with them. And I knew there had to be a story. I wasn't about to publish the photos and let someone else get the scoop; I wanted my hands on the whole thing.

Scurrying up to us like a man whose pants had caught fire, Hardy said, "Everyone, executive conference room, now. Let's work out all the details of this week. People are expecting a lot from us, and we're going to exceed all expectations. We're going to cover everything, from the moment the first door is opened on Tuesday to the last mimosa at Sunday brunch. Game faces go on now. Right now. Say goodbye to that grin, Adrienne Brown. Let's move."

"This from a man who defines 'party' as two people and a bottle of O'Doul's," grumbled Julia as we followed Hardy.

The five of us grabbed our *Capitolist*-stamped pens and note-pads and followed Hardy to the glass-walled room, a squad of well-groomed females on a mission. We blended into the newsroom like transvestites at the Iowa State Fair. I smiled at two grimacing energy reporters as we headed down the long hallway with the smooth blue rug. They looked like they had just drunk a combination of poison and frustration.

"Why are you so nice to them?" Julia hissed at me.

"I don't know. I don't want them to hate me."

She laughed and put her arm around my shoulders. "Haven't you learned not to care about anyone but the girls in our section yet?"

Hardy was waiting outside the room as a meeting finished up. It was the White House team's weekly rundown, and Olivia and her cascade of red hair were sitting right in the middle. A self-important smirk hovered on her pale face. No Olivia sightings for days and now she was around every bend. Well she could smirk all she wanted, I had Olivia porn on my hard drive.

I slowed down, no longer nervous at the sight of her, but she didn't even notice us. She looked aggravated, as usual. She was taking notes in a weathered spiral notebook with a Montblanc fountain pen, the fluorescent lights dancing off its slender form.

"Does Olivia come from money?" I whispered to Julia as we watched her put away her drugstore notebook and very expensive writing implement.

"I don't know. Some, I guess. I think her dad's a dentist in Texas. If you haven't noticed, she has really good teeth. I bet they're all fake. Probably made of marble." The reporters, considered the best in the newsroom, gathered their things and

stomped to the door, while we, with our shiny hair and signifi-
cantly lower BMIs, just stood there and watched.

"Why do you ask?" said Julia, uncapping her chewed-up Bic
pen with her teeth.

"Because that was a Montblanc skeleton pen she was writing
with. They only made three hundred and thirty-three total, and
they cost about fifty grand."

"You lie!" hissed Julia, pressing her nose up to the glass so
she could get a better look. "You have to be wrong."

"I'm not. My boss at *Town & Country* had one. He wore it on
a platinum chain around his neck. But he wasn't stupid enough
to *write* with the thing. It's like making your to-do list with a
Mercedes."

Our curious eyes followed Olivia and her five-figure pen out
of the room. She and the other White House reporters marched
like soldiers back to their desk, oozing a fierce pride. The fact
that they had White House hard passes around their necks was
as coveted in Washington as a Harry Winston necklace was in
New York.

"Get in the room, ladies." Hardy cut our curiosity short. It
was time to talk about the party of the year.

Assigning events, Hardy got to me last. He said, "Adrienne. You have Quinn Gillespie on Tuesday; *Washington Life* on
Wednesday; MSNBC and Fox News on Thursday; *Capitol File*
and the *Atlantic* on Friday; red carpet, the pre-parties, the dinner, the Funny or Die party, and *Vanity Fair* party on Saturday;
and the McLaughlin brunch on Sunday."

He ran his short fingers through the black sponge he called
hair, looked at my stunned face and the shocked faces around
me, and announced, "Well, that's about everything. Oh, and of
course we will still start the page at five A.M. like we always do.
That can't change just because we have a few things to attend to

in the evenings. And don't forget, we have the paper pages to fill, too. I'll have a little additional editorial help here, but with five of you on the street, you should be absolutely fine." He stared at us—five women who woke up before the sun did, curled our eyelashes, read hundreds of pages, glued our faces to Twitter, and managed to write articles we didn't mind having our names attached to. He shook his head, put his arms out like a baseball umpire, and said, "Adjourned."

"You have *Vanity Fair*," said Alison as we walked back to our desks. "That's the best one. I covered it last year, and Sting tried to hook-up with me in the bathroom."

"Why were you with Sting in the bathroom? Drugs?" I asked. Drug addiction would actually explain a lot about Alison.

"Are you crazy? I was trying to get a quote."

"In the bathroom?"

"Sure. What the hell."

Wonderful. Noted. Follow all celebrities at all times, even into bathrooms or basements, into torture chambers or off of cliffs.

When I got back to my desk, one of the paper's videographers was waiting for me, spinning around in my high-backed mesh desk chair. He was assigned to be my red carpet cameraman so that we could co-post our clips on E!'s website.

"Okay, so what's the deal. What time do we have to be there on Saturday?" I asked him as he rapped his fingers on my desk to show he was annoyed with my five-second tardiness.

Simon was the youngest of the young video guys. He smiled and said, "Noon."

"Noon! How can that be? Doesn't the event start at seven P.M.?" I asked. He must have spent his morning drinking cough syrup.

"Yes. But if we want to get any interviews at all, we have to claim our space in the front row on the red carpet at noon." He touched some swirly-whirly device on the small camera he was holding and looked up again. He eyed my Phillip Lim dress and Giuseppe Zanotti platform gladiator heels and said, "You should probably wear comfortable shoes. But you'll be on camera, too, so, well, up to you."

On camera? Comfortable shoes? Those words went together like "North Korea. Luxury vacation." I was going to wear the highest, most expensive shoes I could find. If I had to kick them off and hang out barefoot in a pit of videographers all day, so be it.

As the workday neared an end, I was tasked with the mindless assignment of rounding up our daily tweets. This basically entailed searching the terms "President Obama," "Barack Obama," "Michelle Obama" over and over again on Twitter until my eyes started to twitch from the repetition of 140-character babble.

I scrolled and scrolled through Twitter feeds, my eyes watering from the screen and repetitive motion. My concentration was broken when I heard Olivia and a senior lobbying reporter, Brian Harrington, walking to the back area where we sat. They chatted loudly as they came toward us, not caring if they broke the newsroom hush.

Olivia spoke loudly and clearly, inspiring Brian to burst out laughing. Her beige suit, worn over a pink tank top, looked like it could use dry cleaning, and her heels were scuffed on the toe. But it didn't matter. Olivia could dress like a Hare Krishna and her presence would still command respect.

"Hi, Julia," Olivia condescended as she walked quickly past.

Julia smiled and didn't respond. "I hate that girl," she growled to me when the two of them were out of earshot. Olivia had walked up to Upton, who was standing by the water cooler on our end of the newsroom, and was leaning in toward him to show just how close she had his ear. Brian just stood next to both of them, not minding that he was being completely ignored.

"Can I ask you a weird question?" I said to Julia, who was already back to pounding out copy.

"My favorite kind."

"Is she married?" I asked, trying to look like I was just asking out of the blue. "Because I can't imagine anyone marrying her." Since I had seen her bedding Stanton, I had wondered whether she was just having sex with a married man, or whether she, too, was having an affair. She didn't seem married to me. I had never seen her wear a ring, and she just didn't give off the air of settled domesticity. But I had zoomed in on the necklace she always wore, and was wearing that night in Middleburg. It was a Celtic eternity knot. It seemed like something a not very fashion savvy husband or boyfriend—or United States senator—might give her to profess his eternal love. It was disgusting to think that Olivia was lusting after Stanton, even wearing a necklace he gave her, but it was possible.

"Definitely not," replied Julia. "I don't think I've ever heard about her dating anyone even. Nothing like that. She just lives to serve the *Capitolist* army."

"Are you sure?" I asked. Julia paused and thought about it. "I'm sure," she said finally. "Are you asking because of that weird pen?" She held up her pink Tory Burch pencil and waved it in my face.

"Yeah, I guess."

"It had to be a knockoff or something," said Julia, going back to marking up a book she was reviewing with her loopy writing. "Maybe something she picked up on a press trip to China. She dresses in rags. There's no way she's writing with a pen that cost more than my car."

"But maybe she just does that so she looks like a journal- ist. You know, people in this town take you more seriously if you look like crap," I suggested. It was true. If I wore badly cut suits instead of my usual Parisian prêt-à-porter, I would prob- ably have more Hill cronies. I just couldn't get myself to do it. Polyester gave my soul hives.

"I don't think she has any significant money," said Julia. "She doesn't walk around here with an heiress vibe."

"But what about her car?" I asked, not letting it go. "Have you seen what she drives? That's an eighty-thousand-dollar BMW she spins around in."

"Yeah, maybe she murdered someone for it," said Julia. She looked totally serious. "Or maybe Upton gave it to her for rack- ing up a bazillion Web hits in one day. Who knows how Olivia lives her life; all I know is that I don't want to be a part of it."

I did want to be a part of it. At least enough to understand it before splashing her intimate moments on television screens across the globe. Olivia might have gunned down some yuppie for her wheels, but it seemed more likely that Stanton bought them for her. I doubted she was stupid enough to accept lavish gifts from her illicit lover, but considering the photos I had on my computer, maybe she was.

CHAPTER 9

The week soon launched us through town like note-taking, party-going Adderall addicts. We curled our hair, waxed our everythings, wore cocktail dress after cocktail dress, made excited small talk with everyone who had vocal cords, chased celebrities, begged for quotes without looking like we were begging, kissed up to bouncers, had PR girls kiss up to us, and recorded all of it before passing out for a few hours of sleep. "A few" as in "three."

By the time Saturday rolled around, I felt like I had fought in the front lines of the Crimean War and lost. I had covered so many parties that I no longer could discern famous people from unfamous people. At the Quinn Gillespie party I asked a guy refilling an ice bucket for a quote. He looked at me like I was on acid and said, "Brrr."

But Saturday was D-Day. I had to be upbeat and spunky and celebrity-friendly and ready to stay up all night long. By 9 A.M. I was in D.C. with my dress in my trunk and my exhausted body in a chair at the Red Door salon. "I need everything done," I told the woman at the front desk. "Exfoliate my eyes, dye my hair, tattoo my eyebrows, I don't care. Just make sure it will all last from now until five A.M."

She handed me some cucumber water and led me to the inner

sanctum of the salon, where women got naked and had aestheti-
cians pluck, prod, and remold them until they were ready to face
the world again.

"Coffee?" asked a woman in white scrubs as I looked longingly at a silver urn. "Triple espresso, three Splenda, no cream.
And I really appreciate it," I said before curling back into the
fetal position. My hair looked like yarn and my eyes were blood-
shot and dry. I felt as sexually appealing as a cactus.

My attempt to have a caffeine drip while re-creating my time
in the womb didn't last long. Three hours later I was on the red
carpet at the Washington Hilton in jeans and a sweater with the
hair and makeup of a Las Vegas showgirl. My dress was steamed
and hanging from someone's camera light, but I was waiting
five hours to slap myself together in a public restroom. For now,
I just had to sit like a yogi front and center on the red carpet, behind a rope, so no one dared take our space. I didn't pee, I didn't
take a leisurely walk. I just sat, caffeinated and dehydrated, until
5 P.M. rolled around.

"Lie down in our space!" I hissed at Simon. "Don't let anyone
take it. I have to change."

He lay on his back with his knees bent and his camera on
his chest while the TV crew from *Entertainment Tonight* glared
at him. "Don't try to take an inch of our floor space, Mr. Hollywood," I heard Simon warning as I walked to the bathroom.

I threw my jeans on the floor, apologized to some poor tourist woman who walked in and saw me creeping around in my
underwear, and zipped up a dress so fantastic that my last editor
had allowed me to wear it to the Met Ball. It was so not Washington. It was not what a reporter should ever wear, anywhere,
but I didn't care. I felt like a cross between Marilyn Monroe and
the girl who was painted gold in that Bond movie.

"That's an interesting dress. It looks heavy," said Simon when I came back outfitted and roaring to go.

"It is! It's woven with real gold. Real gold! John Galliano gave it to my former colleague during the Paris couture show, but she didn't want it. Can you imagine. I mean people used to wear armor. What's a little gold? It's not that heavy."

It actually weighed about fifteen pounds and felt as if you had a dumbbell tied to each shoulder, but it was worth it. It's not like Catherine the Great complained that her coronation gown was seven feet across the rump.

"People wore armor to prevent long iron spears from stabbing them in the heart. Why do you need to wear a precious metal?" said Simon, still inspecting my amazing dress. He touched it and screamed. "It's cold, too! Why are you wearing that?"

Why was I wearing this? Because it was a ten-thousand-dollar dress stitched together by the supple hands of John Galliano and a herd of magical Italian grandmothers!

"Just . . . I dunno. It was a gift," I mumbled.

Ten minutes later, I was sweating from the weight of my dress. Simon had me shoved against the red velvet rope with a microphone, and we were elbowing reporters trying to encroach on our space. "Back off, *Washington Post* girl," Simon threatened as we heard the front door open and watched the first famous guest walk in. It was six o'clock. It would be nine hours of reporting and stalking and filing stories before I could slump into my Volvo and drive home.

Lincoln Town Car after Lincoln Town Car pulled up to the front of the hotel. Each one spat a polished and prepped celebrity out into a wave of oohs and aahs and camera bulbs. Rockers, aging rockers, starlets, cinema icons: they all walked the carpet,

popping their hips for the press and blessing the rows of salivating reporters with their presence, if they felt like it. Some
refused to come near us, all hungry and roped off like zoo animals. Others walked slowly down the line, giving everybody the
sound bite their editors were harassing them for.

"What are you wearing?" I called out politely. Nothing. Kate
Hudson completely ignored me. I raised my voice a bit. "Kate!
Kate! Who made your dress?" I tried, a little louder.

"Get her over here!" hissed Simon. Well, sheesh, it's not like
he was helping very much. I needed a fishing rod to nab these
people. If I could just reel them in with precision and a worm it
would be so much easier. "You have to be more aggressive!" he
chided me. "We'll never get anyone if you keep whispering like
that."

So I stopped with the indoor voice. When Matthew McCo-
naughey walked through the door, I whooped and hollered at
him.

"Are you a fan of President Obama's?" I asked as he smiled
for Simon's lens. "I don't talk politics. Sorry, darlin'," he said,
grinning and crossing his brawny arms as the cameras flashed.

Really? No politics at the White House Correspondents'
Dinner, where the president is appearing. Fine, make my job
just a little more difficult. Perhaps you'd like to fling sulfuric
acid in my face.

After we nabbed five interviews, thanks to our precious
front-and-center red carpet space, Simon suggested we give it
up and start chasing celebrities around the building.

"File that story," he said, watching me pound out words on
the miniature BlackBerry keyboard as fast as I could. "Then let's
get the good stuff where no one is around us to eavesdrop. I
saw that *Washington Post* reporter write down your Jessica Alba
quote word for word."

We packed up our journalist junk and headed into the crowd. As soon as we began moving, it was obvious that my feet were most definitely broken. I tried to wiggle my toes. Nothing. Clearly, I would have to have them pieced together by scientists tomorrow. "Is this a bone? Or part of a pencil?" they would ask as they picked at the appendages I once called feet.

"Can you move any faster?" said Simon, watching me trying to walk in Louboutin platforms and a metal dress. Ignoring my death glare, he hoisted his camera up on his shoulder and waited for me to catch up. "Adrienne. We need at least four more celebrity interviews or we won't have enough footage for a ten-minute montage. I need you to find someone." He scanned the crowd. "There's Ben Affleck!" He pointed to a speck of a person all the way across the room, surrounded by a gaggle of guests.

"I think that's actually Congressman Aaron Schock."

"No way! That's Ben Affleck. Go run and see. I'm right behind you with the camera rolling. Go, go!"

"Ben! Ben! *Ben!*" I screamed, running toward him like a stalker who has a future of solitary confinement and newspaper clippings to look forward to.

The tall, frowning actor didn't even turn around. Like a man in deep meditation, he completely ignored my screeching.

"Hi, Ben!" I said, pushing aside a ruddy-faced rod of a man. "My name is Adrienne Brown. I'm a reporter for the *Capitolist*. We're just thrilled you came down to D.C. for this important event."

"Mr. Affleck is not doing interviews right now," said the thin man.

"I'm with the *Capitolist*," I responded, giving him a "know what I mean?" smile. "Would Mr. Affleck have time for just one quick on-camera comment?" I flashed the media credentials around my neck to prove that I worked for the esteemed publication.

"I'm afraid he does not," replied the handler. "He's not doing any interviews. Just here to enjoy the evening."

Not doing any interviews? Why would he fly to D.C. and flaunt his famousness if he was not doing any interviews? I knew his causes. Sudan, the African Diaspora, child hunger, Canadian strip clubs. I could speak his language. But Ben Affleck just stood there ignoring me, perfectly still, perfectly mum. I looked up at his face with my best girl in need of a kidney expression. He didn't crack a smile. He just looked at me like I was a talking worm with a notepad and then turned away.

I left my pride on the floor and headed back toward the rope line with Simon in tow.

"Why are we leaving? They were about to say yes," said Simon, pouting and switching off his camera's fluorescent light.

"His agent told me to go out back and hang myself," I replied, skulking toward the press pool. "He offered me his shoelace. Do you really think it would be a good idea to keep trying?"

"I do. I do," said Simon, shaking his head up and down.

Before we got back to the media rope, one of the security men spotted us and approached us angrily. "Get out of here and back behind the media rope. If I see you off the rope again I'm going to kick your bony ass out forever," he said, expectorating in my face. One frown from Simon and the spitting man declared, "Really, video boy? You're both out of here." Out of Simon's skinny, sweaty hands, the bouncer grabbed his huge video camera like it was grandma's rinky-dink Polaroid.

Won-der-ful. This would be easy to explain. "Me? Oh sure, I'm fine. Just lounging here in prison. Making friends fast. No, no. Not Lisbon. *Prison.* Also, Simon and I managed to lose a fifteen-thousand-dollar video camera to a man who looked like he ate human skulls for Sunday brunch."

This was not going as planned. I had a big fat *Capitolist* name tag with my picture on it dangling from my neck. This was supposed to be my entrée to everything. Instead, Simon and I found ourselves slipping the bouncer a fifty to give us the camera back and promised to stay behind the rope at all times.

That lasted for about ten minutes. "I'm going to take the camera and get some B-roll in the pre-parties. You take this Flip cam and get some more interviews," said Simon. "If we have any chance of getting on E!, we need more. Get more!" He handed me a camera the size of a credit card and ran off to capture famous people shoving canapés down their throats. I turned it on, held it up, and pressed record to make sure there was still time left on the tiny device. No one wanted to talk into a camera the size of a cube of cheese. It wasn't great for the ego.

Leaning against a large marble pillar, I panned slowly across the room, happy not to be chasing anyone or worrying about racking up celebrity interviews. I felt like a documentary filmmaker, blending into the background, rather than a journalist stomping through the human jungle.

I was ready to turn the camera off and resume the hunt for fame when my lens caught a group of *Capitolist* reporters. Isabelle, with her rippling muscles and pretty blond hair, was one of them. I lifted my hand to wave at her, until I saw that standing in the middle of the group of four was Olivia. Why was Isabelle talking to Olivia?

I was too far away to capture any of their audio, but I zoomed in on Olivia's face to watch her as she spoke. With her fiery hair curled and arranged high on her head like a Jane Austen heroine's, she looked softer, less ready to take out a Glock and threaten someone's life if she wasn't chosen for White House duty. Her fair skin glowed pink; she looked much better out of the harsh fluorescent lights of the newsroom. As she spoke animatedly, letting her ethereal forest green dress swish around her, you could almost imagine her having friends, warm blood, the ability to smile. She was talking assuredly to Isabelle and the other two. None of them was drinking; they seemed to occupy a tiny invisible box of personal space.

I watched my colleagues, transformed into night owls. Through the tiny viewfinder, I watched Olivia nod and frown, obviously talking in her barking, masculine way despite her softened appearance.

After a few minutes of spying, a tall, lithe man with dark hair walked over to the group. He was gorgeous. He was familiar, too. I zoomed in on his face, telling myself there was absolutely no way, he couldn't be. But he was! He was the guy from the museum ice-skating rink. The dreamboat with the enchanting whistle and Canadian friends! He was here. Delivered to me by a higher power! And as luck would have it, I was wearing John Galliano. I could have seen this guy when I looked my worst, but the great powers that be had decided for us to meet at a black-tie event. It was fate.

He immediately started speaking to Isabelle, which made sense. Why shouldn't this Adonis talk to the Olympian. Maybe that's who he was, one of Isabelle's Olympic Village buddies or her latest sports world conquest. He said he didn't skate, but he was tall and lean, maybe a skier? The only men Isabelle cared about were adrenaline junkies. I carefully looked at his face to see if I recognized him not just from the Smithsonian skating rink, but also from the podium.

Olivia barked at the other two *Capitolist* girls in their polyester gowns while Isabelle spoke quietly to the gorgeous man—my gorgeous man—with perfect skin the color of hazelnut mousse.

Not blinded by lust like I was, Isabelle turned away from him to greet someone else. He moved aside and looked around the room until his eyes fell on me. This was one of those moments,

I could feel it. This was the story we would tell our photogenic children during Christmas dinner every year.

I dropped the camera down to my side, shut it off, and walked over to the group. I waited for him to rush toward me and to start casually caressing my face and nibbling my ears, but speedy Isabelle got to me first.

"Hi, Adrienne. Wow! I love your dress," she said sweetly as she approached me. She made me turn around so she could see it from all angles. It really was movable art. My gorgeous man just stood there politely while I fought every impulse to start slow dancing with him, and when Isabelle had stopped swirling in her navy gown, and me in my gold, she remembered her manners and looked at my Latin He-man apologetically.

"Oh! I'm sorry," she said, swinging her head around. "I'm so rude. Adrienne," she said, motioning to me, "this is Sandro Pena, Olivia's husband."

The coy smile of recognition I had been rehearsing froze, half assembled on my face. All the air seemed to leave the room and I was left choking on reality. The man I wanted, the man I had been lusting after was married.

To Olivia.

I was positive that I was about to faint directly into the potted plant next to me. My head was light, and my stomach was doing triple axels. I felt just the way I did after Virginia Millbank kicked a fluorescent yellow soccer ball directly into my gut in the tenth grade. But somehow, I managed to stay upright, rearranging my dry mouth into a fake pageant queen smile as I took in Isabelle's words.

I heard Isabelle laugh and say my name, but it sounded so muffled and distant. I finally noticed that Olivia's husband was holding his hand out, waiting for me to shake it. I apologized and put my hand in his.

As soon as our skin touched, I felt my body relax. I could have left my hand in his forever. Up and down our hands went, clasped together, once, twice, before he released mine from his perfect grasp.

And just like that, everything had changed.

"Shall we be going." Olivia's commanding voice pierced through the heavy hush of my love at second sight. She gave me a disapproving look, one she must have learned in executioner training, put her hand on her husband's broad shoulder, just like he had put his on mine, and turned away, leaving me with Isabelle and our two colleagues.

"Cute, isn't he," said Isabelle when we broke away. "I didn't know she was married. She's so mean, I always figured she was single. I guess some men just like bitchy women." She laughed and waved to a friend from MSNBC.

"I think most of them do," I said in a whisper. He didn't even look like he remembered me. I was probably just one of hundreds of blond girls who hit on him at skating rinks. The only gorgeous guy in Washington, the only one I'd been excited about in ages was married. To her! To that horrible red-haired cheater!

I excused myself awkwardly, saying I was still on the celeb hunt, and ran up the escalator steps, or tried to run up the steps, which security had just opened. I started looking everywhere for Julia, who was soon heading into the ballroom to cover the president's remarks. I scuttled around for ten minutes, starting to feel very hot and teary, but finally found her finishing an interview with David Axelrod. She held her palm up as she finished typing on her BlackBerry and then gave me a hug.

"I don't feel great, Julia," I said as she wiped my sweaty brow with her bare hand.

"Are you okay?" she asked. She was wearing a red silk dress, magically free of sweat stains, and had her hair back in a chic black chignon. Her dark eyes squinted at me with concern.

What was I supposed to say to that? Should I tell her that Olivia Campo did in fact have a husband, and that I had fallen for him at an ice-skating rink last month, but that God had hand-delivered him to me, and that now, after one handshake, I was desperately in love with him? Or should I just confess everything about Olivia and the senator and ask Julia to casually slip the news and my phone number to Olivia's husband?

"I think I'm just tired," I said instead as she started moving the curled blond strands of my hair back into place.

"I know. This is such a horrible week. Curt Blye from War-rington Communications came up to me before I talked to Axel-rod and bit my ear. He actually bit it, like Mike Tyson. He said, 'Your face kind of looks like a baby's butt. But in a cute way,' and then bit my ear. People here are so fucked up," said Julia, touch-ing the dimple in her chin cautiously.

"Who is Curt Blye?" I asked.

"You know him. He's that short guy who always wears green plaid. Like he's just poised and ready in case Santa Claus needs an understudy. He works for War Com."

I looked at Julia blankly.

"They represent very rich criminals with a loud message and a lot of money. Basically, if Lucky Luciano lived today and was looking for a reputation makeover, he would give them a call."

"I'm sorry," I said, looking at her face. "You really don't look like a butt. You're very pretty."

Julia hugged me again and adjusted the straps of my dress.

"Rob Lowe. Mr. Rob Lowe. Announcing Rob Lowe," a PR girl from the Bloomberg party said mechanically as she passed us.

"Crap! Come on!" said Julia, grabbing my hand and running us directly into the pre-party with a nod of her well-known head.

"I'm going to ask him about the orgy in '88. Do you think he'll hit me with a shoe or something?" I asked her.

"No, you definitely should. Even if he doesn't comment, you can spin it into him avoiding orgy questions." Julia registered my lack of speed and frowned. "Can't you move any faster? I'm about to shove you on a beverage cart and wheel you around."

That sounded awesome. "Go ahead of me," I told her. "I'll catch up."

Julia sprinted ahead to catch Mr. Brat Pack, and I shuffled along at my porcupine pace, trying to keep her in my line of sight. I looked around the tented patio area. Lots of people. Most of them old, all of them chatting animatedly. Everyone looked important, in that Washington way, and all of them loved looking important in that Washington way.

And then, because of one panoramic look around the room, I lost Julia. Her red dress had been just ahead of me, but the crowd absorbed her. I wasn't in the mood to chase after her. I wasn't in the mood to do anything but think about Olivia and her gorgeous husband and the fact that they were married and that the senator, whom she was sleeping with, had to be nearby.

I didn't chase after Rob Lowe, and I didn't look for Simon and his video camera. I knew we had more than enough footage for a good video, and I had enough reporting for three stories. We had stopped the live blog of the red carpet arrivals, and seating for dinner had not yet begun.

Instead, like a Civil War soldier marching directly into the line of fire, I went off to find Olivia and her husband.

The Washington Hilton was a mess of rooms and floors and, of course, men all wearing the exact same outfit. Tuxedos swarmed everywhere. I was certain I saw Mr. Olivia Campo on the ground floor near a bank of escalators, but the man in question turned out to be too pale. Olivia's husband had dark skin and wavy black hair. He looked Central American or South American. Sandro Pena. I said it a few times softly, just to hear the vowels roll off my glossed lips. It sounded like a name from somewhere well below the Rio Grande. I thought back to our shared moment on the Mall. I should have confessed my love to him then. I could have played dumb; I didn't know he was married. He was wearing brown leather gloves when we met at the rink. What was I supposed to do, rip them off to confirm his married status?

It was on the second floor of the hotel, where smaller pre-parties were being held in a row of conference rooms, that I finally saw Sandro. He was holding a glass of red wine, standing in a crowd near the Reuters party. His hand was on the small of his wife's back, and they were both turned away from me. A few feet ahead of him were George Stephanopoulos and his blond actress wife.

I kept walking. Ten feet away, then five, and then suddenly they were right in front of me. Keeping as quiet as I could, I leaned toward Sandro's back, almost letting the tuxedo cloth touch my face. He smelled like musky cologne and maleness and alcohol and every other mineral that existed on earth. That was it: he smelled like the earth. I could picture him meeting me at the church altar, whisking me away to honeymoon in Madagascar and fathering my children.

His deep voice broke my reverie. "Let's get out of here, go to the dinner," he said to his wife. "I'd like to just sit down next to you and get away from this crowd. I haven't seen you in so long." He ran his hand up and down her lower back as he talked, touching her with the intimate affection of a married man. She gazed up at him lovingly, smiled, and put her arms around his neck. He laughed and kissed her on the top of her head.

I backed away, now terrified that they would see me, and took the escalator downstairs, clutching the rubber handrail until my fingernails left marks.

I was having a lot of trouble thinking about my job. I was supposed to be hog-tying celebrities and coercing snappy quotes out of them, but all I could think about was Sandro's face and the fact that he was with Olivia. How could she cheat on him? He was gorgeous and clearly crazy in love with her. Why would she ever get close to Stanton, risking her marriage in the process—when her husband looked and acted like the ideal man? I wanted someone to kiss me on the head in public and beg to spend alone time with me. Didn't every woman deserve a man who smelled amazing and liked hockey and wore a tux better than James Bond? Olivia had all that and was willing to ruin it all so she could have sex with an old man! She was soulless.

I stood outside the closed doors leading into the main ballroom and gripped the doorknob. I was an idiot who had given up her glitzy New York job, moved to a barn in Middleburg, and gotten mixed up in something messy. And it had just gotten even messier.

The dinner started and finished in a blur. Julia and Isabelle were writing the main story about the dinner remarks and I was tasked with feeding them color from the dining room. In a daze I emailed, "Sen. Prescott ate four dinner rolls, Michelle Kwan said dress was given to her by Vera Wang, Melania Trump said her husband's legs are his best feature. Called them 'beautiful.'" People laughed, people drank, and I just kept working, stuck in a state between shock, anger, and puppy love. And then half an hour before the crowd filed out, it was time for me to get myself together and beat them to the after-parties so I could cover their glamorous arrivals.

CHAPTER 10

I had filed six stories from the dinner at the Hilton and made seven videos with Simon. I was now allergic to famous people and standing upright. I wanted to crawl into my car, take off all my clothes, and fall asleep in the peaceful company of Olivia Campo's husband. But I couldn't. I still had to cover the *Vanity Fair* after party at the French ambassador's sprawling stone residence, the most exclusive soirée of the night.

I jumped out of a cab and got as close as I could to the red carpet set up in the foyer. I was ready to attack. As soon as the overpaid celebrities made it the ten blocks from the hotel to the party, I would start screaming questions about the president.

My scream was more like a hoarse whisper.

After two hours of collecting celebrity quotes while stuck behind a velvet rope, I was exhausted, my feet felt fractured in eight places, and I was still far from calling it a night. I needed some air.

Behind the French ambassador's residence was a huge patio extending into a dark, forested yard. I walked out onto the terrace and looked at my watch: 2 A.M. I had to drive back to Middleburg and file my nightly wrap-up piece, but I wanted three minutes to take in the atmosphere without having to interview anyone. I was at a French manor in a Galliano dress and fate had thrown me into the same room as the man who took my breath away. There were a handful of pesky details that turned the fairy tale into a horror movie, but I was choosing to temporarily ignore them.

I walked down the slate steps and onto the soft, dewy grass. My heels sank right into it. To avoid falling over, I slipped off my shoes and leaned my body against the stone wall.

In a few short hours my brain had gone from obsessing over Olivia and the senator to being consumed by Sandro, Olivia, and the senator. I couldn't believe he was married to her. Of all the men in the world, she had to be married to the beautiful hockey fan. I took out the Flip camera and watched my footage of Sandro on mute. I watched as he spoke to Isabelle, nodding politely and laughing at her jokes. His face was smooth, but slightly square around the jaw. He had a small widow's peak and bright, easy expressions. He was perfect.

The feeling of grass on my flat feet and Sandro's gorgeous image had brought me close to nirvana when I heard a voice I recognized. From where, I wasn't sure. I leaned my head back against the wall until it started to hurt. When the voice got closer, not louder, I realized it was from the movie where that guy saws off his own arm. It was James Franco. Most definitely. That confused, intellectual stoner voice was one of a kind. I peered around the wall to confirm. Franco was in the far corner of the terrace, near my hiding spot, talking to Walter Birnbaum, a former aide to the president who had just gotten the governor of New York reelected.

It was a perfect D.C.-meets-Hollywood moment. One that begged for me to walk up there, obnoxiously interrupt their conversation, and ask for something on the record.

As I sat down on the grass to strap on my shoes, I heard Franco's voice again.

"I'm done with it. I'm done sucking at the teat of phony power. I want to do something real. That's why I'm jumping into the Los Angeles mayoral race."

"Are you really?" asked Birnbaum with excitement in his voice. People in Washington are simply mesmerized by Hollywood stars. They find them as fascinating as talking dogs.

"I'm dead serious," said Franco. "It feels right. I plan to announce my exploratory committee in late May."

Was he really dead serious? I craned my neck around the wall to make sure Franco's face looked serious and not like he had just dropped PCP. I mean, this was the man who chose to teach a college class on himself.

"I want you to help get me elected, Walt," he said. He looked soberish. Sober enough to be quoted. I pushed record on my BlackBerry, which had never left my hand.

"Do you really? Shouldn't you talk to a few people first?" said Birnbaum. I was ready to throw my phone and hit that naysayer on the head. Who was he to dissuade Franco? The actor's mind was made up! He wanted to change the course of history. Let the skinny man soar. Plus, think of all the articles I could write. I would become a Franco campaign expert and Upton would just waltz up to my desk all the time and casually ask me what time we were having lunch with our buddy Mayor Franco. One P.M., I would reply before I reminded him that Catherine Zeta-Jones was also lunching with us. Then I would smirk at Olivia and ask if her husband was free to join us, too.

"I have talked to people," said Franco. "I've talked to plenty of trusted, quiet people and I've made up my mind. I want to put my money where my heart is. Think about it," he said to Birnbaum, placing his hand on the latter's shoulder. God, where was my undercover video crew when I needed them? Why did everything have to be so by the book at the *Capitolist*?

"I don't have to think about it. I'll do it. If you're serious," the wonk replied. He looked down at Franco's glass. "Is that"—he leaned over and sniffed the drink—"absinthe you're drinking?" The glass was filled with two inches of a light green liquid. Oh crap. Could you quote a man drinking illegal Czech liquor?

"It is. It is. I always have a little with me. Fly the stuff in from Prague. Really gets the job done," Franco confirmed with a masculine chuckle. "But don't think I'm going all Toulouse Lautrec on you here. I'm not going to paint some tart in pantaloons doing the cancan. I'm serious about what I said. And I'm holding you to your 'yes.'"

Oh, that was so quotable. The man was sober as a judge! He was talking about French artists. I could tell his mind was crystal clear. I pushed stop on my recorder and typed out "HUGE SCOOP" in an email. I sent it directly to Hardy, followed by "James Franco is leaving Hollywood. Dropping out of acting. Has plans to run for mayor of Los Angeles. Asked Walter Birnbaum, THE Walter Birnbaum to advise him. Is announcing exploratory committee in May. Said this while drinking absinthe, which he had flown in from Prague, but swore he was serious. The two discussed alone in the backyard of the French ambassador's residence at the *Vanity Fair* party. I have the murmurings recorded on my BlackBerry. I hid behind a wall and listened. Filing NOW."

"Send! Send, send, send, send," I willed my phone as I waited for the stupid check mark to appear on the screen.

"How positive are you. Scale 1 to 100," Hardy wrote back immediately.

"100. I have it all recorded. 110. Filing now."

"Fine." He wrote back. "You better not be wrong. If you are wrong, Upton will can you. Will put up immediately. Will ask to have in F2 on home page. File now."

F2! The second lead on the website's main page. It wasn't the top space, but it was the next best thing. I'd take it.

I wanted to ask Franco to elaborate on the record, but if I approached him, he would probably get his rep to keep me from running it. I decided to skip a direct comment, file from the car, and then head for home.

I walked around the side of the wall to try to find a way into the house without looking like I'd been eavesdropping, but I found myself looking directly at a wall of the Chinese Embassy next door.

Crap. I forgot how close the two massive buildings were. I was going to disappear into thin air like that peaceful flower protester in Tiananmen Square. Entire websites would be dedicated to my whereabouts. I was going to be known as the disappearing girl in the golden dress.

Instead, thanks to the annoyance that is the modern security camera, a French assistant came out and escorted the poor confused reporter back into the house through a side door after advising her to wear shoes. I thanked the assistant for his hospitality and slipped out the double doors without any trouble.

The piece went up just before four. By eight the next morning, after I had been asleep for two hours and had to cover a brunch at noon, my BlackBerry started to ring.

"Adrienne, it's Jenny from media team," an excited voice screamed in my ear. "Amazing piece." She caught her breath and kept talking. "Because of it, Franco released a statement of intent this morning! You were totally right. Hardy emailed you twice about it, but you didn't respond."

I looked at my phone and opened the first email from Hardy, which had come two hours ago. It read, "You were right. Which is good, because if you were wrong, you would be seeking other employment right now. Good job."

Good job. Wow. I had never seen those words in a *Capitolist* email to me.

"Adrienne, Adrienne, are you listening to me?" said Jenny, more businesslike now. I wasn't, because I was so tired I had just hallucinated that a pig wearing a beret was talking to me. "Adrienne, CNN wants you. They'll send a car. Ten minutes on the Franco stuff. Can you do it?"

"Uh, yeah," I said, rattling off my address.

"You live *where*?" Jenny dropped the phone in shock. I heard it bang on her desk, followed by a slew of curses. "Oh, Jesus, sorry, I . . . I didn't know people actually lived there. I'll tell them to drive fast. Okay, they just texted back, they're on their way now. After CNN, you have a really quick C-SPAN hit and then a pretape for the CBS *Early Show* for Monday. I know you have the McLaughlin brunch at noon, so they'll drop you off there. How does that sound?"

"Err . . . fine?" I replied, scanning the floor for something to wear and ripping the cap off a 5-hour Energy drink. I spilled half of it on the floor, which meant I only got two and a half hours of energy. I would have to supplement by eating espresso beans and a scoop of sugar-free sugar.

"I know you're tired, but you really can't say no," said Jenny. "It's CNN. The car will be there in precisely forty-three minutes. The driver just wrote. Okay, that's all, bye."

The rest of the morning was a tornado of sound bites and pancake makeup. I talked animatedly at a black wall in the CNN cubicle in Northeast Washington, and somehow that translated into a live television appearance. The host kept pronouncing my name Alien. Alien Brown. But I was too tired to correct him. At the *Early Show* studio I tried to sound as upbeat as possible, which was possible thanks only to three Excedrin and a diet Mountain Dew, which I stole from their break room. Then I found myself wandering around the Hay-Adams hotel with a notepad in my hand, trying to cover the very last party of the week that would never end.

This, I told myself, was just a tiny taste of the exhausting whirlwind I would experience if I decided to go public with the Olivia/Senator Stanton story. I would be making media rounds in the back of town cars for months. But I would never be just another reporter with a byline no one could connect with a face. And no one would call me Alien Brown.

Walking out onto the terrace space called Top of the Hay, I was trembling. I was interviewing Dennis Quaid, and the room started to spin like a carousel. Of course, I wasn't in a room, I was on an outdoor terrace overlooking the White House. But all of a sudden, that started spinning, too. As soon as Quaid finished his sound bite, I excused myself and lunged at a waiter with a tray of orange juice. "Sorry, but if you don't mind, I'll take two," I murmured. I pushed my way inside and found a bathroom.

Sitting on the floor of the handicap stall, I drank both glasses of juice and started to file my report from the floor. It was terribly boring, but I didn't care. The quotes were right and there were going to be tons of photos to brighten up the blandness of my copy.

Then I put my head on the toilet seat and threw up. Along with the orange juice, my body was rejecting weeks of fear, exhaustion, frustration, obsession, and panic. I dabbed my face with a wad of paper towels and tried to collect myself. I put lipstick on my chapped, pale lips and walked out of the room with a forced smile on my face.

I was about to walk downstairs when I remembered that I had come into D.C. by town car. Though I probably would have driven myself into a ravine if I had tried to operate a car, I was an idiot for accepting that ride. Now I had no way to get home. So, like a stranded fifteen-year-old, I called my father and begged him to come pick me up. He said yes and told me to sit tight. I ran back to the bathroom to be sick again.

Shakier than before, I cut through the south terrace to the service elevator that would take me down to the back of Off the Record, the famous bar in the basement of the hotel. I wanted to avoid small talk, celebrities, any conversation at all. But when the doors of the elevator opened into the bar, which I thought would be empty given the hour, I was confronted with a packed house. There was yet another Correspondents' weekend brunch taking place in the popular watering hole.

The mere sight of the crowd weakened me. I plopped onto a red padded banquette. My breath was short; I was exhausted. I needed the weekend sprint to end. I must have looked pretty rough around the edges, because the man whose table I had collapsed next to pushed his glass of water toward me, along with a napkin. I thanked him, touched my upper lip, and realized it was covered in beads of sweat. Embarrassed, I quickly wiped it off and explained that I was just a bit under the weather.

"Drink the water," he urged. "I promise it's untouched." I didn't care if it was toilet water. It looked cold, and I was tempted to dump it on my head. I drank half of it, thanked him, stood up, and said I needed to be outside.

"Here," he said, standing and moving around the table to me. "Let me help you out. There are too many people in here. It's the overflow from the *National Journal* brunch up the road. It's not a good idea to be stuck in a basement with this group if you're not feeling well."

I let him take my arm and lead me up the back stairs and across the street to a bench in front of St. John's Church. The White House was to our left, and the flow of traffic into the stone hotel in front of us was still heavy.

"Thank you, I really appreciate it," I said, sitting down. I was ready to fall asleep for a week on a city bench. As he stood over me, I smiled again and said, "You were so nice to walk me out, but you don't have to stay. Don't feel obliged. You should go back to the party, I'm really okay."

"But what if I'd like to stay?" he asked.

I looked up at him through my haze of fatigue. Nice blue eyes. Decent suit. Blond hair full of curls. He looked like a cherub with Tea Party tendencies. Not terrible, not the best I'd ever seen. But who was I to be picky these days. I lived in the sticks and worked every daylight hour and plenty of the dark ones, too. I didn't have time to meet men, at least ones who were not married to Olivia Campo. I should probably jump on this one before succumbing to a sexual destiny of online chat rooms and anime porn.

I asked him to sit down and join me. His name was James Reddenhurst. He did communications for the Republican National Committee. And when he asked me if I would have dinner with him next Saturday, I said yes, just to see the look on his face when I gave him my address.

It took my father an hour to get downtown, and by the time he found me, I was a puddle of sweat in a linen sundress with a soggy notepad, a tape recorder, and tears in my bloodshot eyes. James shook my father's hand, helped me into his car, and watched us drive away, his number safely entered into my phone.

"I can't do this job," I whispered in my dad's general direction as I buckled my seat belt. "I'm so tired. I just want to curl up and die."

"You know," said my father, not taking his eyes off the road, "you don't have to work there. No one is forcing you to. You could always apply to other newspapers."

I shook my heavy head. "I can't leave now. Everything's

finally starting to go well. I was on TV this morning. I broke a big story. This is what I moved back home to do and it's a really important job."

My dad shook his head in agreement and we drove in silence until we passed the big blue highway sign that said "Virginia is for lovers."

When we turned off the highway, my dad put his hand on my arm and said, "I hate to do this to you, Addy. I know you're tired. But I need to stop by the vet's on the way back and get some medicine for Jasper's eye. The IV doesn't seem to be doing the trick. We're going to try another approach."

"Who's Jasper?" I asked, laying my head on the glove compartment.

"Your horse," answered my dad.

Right, right. That Jasper. I shook my head yes as his blue Mercedes glided home. I wanted animals and fresh air and people who would never grace the cover of *US Weekly* or *Congressional Quarterly*. I fell asleep in the warm, purring car while my father dealt with the vet. I didn't wake up until Monday morning.

When I finally opened my eyes, still feeling like half a human, I had an email from Upton's assistant in my inbox.

"Please come by Upton's office at 10 A.M.," it read. I scanned it four times, but it really didn't say anything else.

When I drove in, shivering from caffeine detox, I put Visine in my eyes and followed his assistant into his office. I hated the fact that every editor's office at the *List* had glass walls. That meant that every single employee could watch the higher-ups chew you out. From time to time, you also got to watch as some dorky reporter got applauded for some dorky reporter behavior, like breaking news courtesy of a little direct Eritrean-to-English translation in the middle of the night. But that wasn't as fun.

Upton's door opened, and he slammed it absentmindedly behind him as he walked quickly toward his desk.

He looked at me and declared, "You are here. Good." He stammered slightly as he sat down across from me. His chair was large and mesh, and his unruly blond hair stuck to the back. I had gazed at Upton's office from a few feet away, afraid to get any closer, but I'd never been inside it before. Dozens of awards, diplomas, and newspaper clippings adorned the walls around him. A shelf of books that he had written stood firmly below the awards and pictures of him with every living president served as bookends. The only lighthearted touch was a framed caricature of him holding a red pen, done by one of the paper's illustrators.

"Good morning, Mark," I said, trying to sound casual and brilliant at the same time.

"Is it still morning?" he said, looking at his Seiko. "I feel like I've been awake for days." He shuffled some papers, opened and closed a folder, and then leaned back in his chair with a book in his hand.

He flipped through it and moved his lips as he read a few pages. Perhaps he had only asked me to come in to observe him as he read. Weirder things had happened inside these walls. I was about to ask if he wanted me to get him some coffee, or a bookmark, when he slammed the book down like a fiery preacher.

"The reason I asked you in here is because . . ." His voice trailed off. He took the closed book off his glass desk and placed it on his lap. It was Nancy Reagan's biography. "Adrienne, this place is a meritocracy. One of the true meritocracies left in the media business. If you don't do a good job, you don't work here, if you do a great job, we say thank you. So, I wanted to just say, this morning . . . I—I—I wanted to say good job."

I almost fell off my chair and combusted at the same time. First a congrats from despicable Hardy, and now this.

"We got lots of traffic from your scoop. Drudge linked it, the Hollywood sites went nuts over it, and the morning shows liked you," he said, twisting his thin lips into an awkward smile and looking to the right of my head.

"You still have a lot to learn. A lot," he declared, just in case I was actually feeling good about myself. "Your reporting instincts are weak. Your research techniques, I hear from Hardy, are sophomoric at best, and you spend way too much time commuting in and out of the city. You really need to consider moving." He checked to make sure I was frowning now. I was.

"That said, you're a good writer." He looked at me. I looked at him. No one smiled. But inside, I was doing the Macarena. The great *Capitolist* ruler just told me I was Carl Bernstein in a dress. "Now, go and write." He gestured to the door. I stood up, thanked him for his time, and ran for the safe corner of the Style section.

Before I could download our conversation on Julia, Hardy yelled at me from his desk.

"Adrienne. There you are. I've been looking around for you everywhere." That was an obvious lie because everyone could see clear as day that I was in Upton's office.

"I only count three posts so far from you today. Did you hear me? Three. Is someone asleep at the keyboard?"

I looked at his smug face in panic. Had I only done three pieces? I looked at the clock. It was 10:18 A.M. I had usually filed at least four by then. With all the White House Correspondents' writing yesterday, I was a little behind.

I looked at Julia in alarm. "Here, write about this," she texted me, sending a link to a piece in the *Hollywood Reporter* about George Clooney's declaration that he never wanted to be president because he liked having casual sex too much. "It's not groundbreaking, but it should shut him up."

I mouthed, "Thank God for you," and started speed-reading the article before I got axed.

After I pounded out three short pieces in a row, I leaned back in my chair and looked around the newsroom. Every person had their head down, typing out stories or reading other people's copy. Newsrooms usually buzzed, but this was like a crypt. People didn't take breaks or talk to their neighbors. There was no banter with a colleague across the room. Instead, there was just hunger and guilt. Hunger because everyone there was cut from the same motivated cloth, and guilt because no one wanted to be caught doing anything but working.

As I refreshed the Style page to make sure my last piece was formatted correctly, I saw Emily Baumgarten, another White House reporter, and Olivia walking down the hall together. Olivia was no longer just Olivia "having sex with a senator" to me. She was Olivia "cheating on a man I loved." I had touched her husband's hand, breathed him in, and thought about him every free moment I had. In my eyes, her transgression had become much worse.

I watched her take her seat at her desk and begin cursing at people on the phone. She didn't seem like the kind of girl her handsome husband would go for, and her husband didn't seem like the kind of man she would handpick to be her mate for life. A girl with an ego like that never went for the genteel Ken doll. She went for the bigger fish. She went for the senator.

My boyfriend in college, brown-haired, blue-eyed Brady Keller, was my introduction to the genteel Ken doll. He was from Raleigh, North Carolina, and majored in environmental studies at Harvard. Together, we did New Englandy things like wearing scarves and mittens and reading poetry under trees.

He wrote me a note every day on paper that he aged himself. I asked him once if this just meant leaving it out in the rain and running it over with his car, but he promised me there was more to it than that.

Brady was the perfect college boyfriend. He was cute, he threw a football skillfully around the quad, he wore a peacoat, he was adept at memorizing Shakespeare, and he had about 3 percent body fat despite his love of keg parties.

After Wellesley, I forgot all about nice boys from the South and discovered a different breed of man: the investment banker. Lots of money, no free time, not all that attractive if you got rid of the expensive clothes, a close personal friendship with every worthwhile maître d' in town, and the owner of a really good Manhattan apartment. That was the kind of man I imagined Olivia Campo married to: someone as pompous and gruff as she was, with a bank account to catapult her to the top. But I had been wrong before.

Julia had gone out and brought us all sandwiches. Hardy thought it was best if only one of us abandoned the production line at a time. When she placed my turkey and sprouts on my desk, she let out a few tsk-tsks and turned my head away from the TV.

"You're watching C-SPAN? Don't tell me you're becoming that girl," she chided.

There were different levels of wonk at the *Capitolist*. We were all forced to watch CNN and Fox News and MSNBC, but when you caught yourself watching C-SPAN and enjoying it, it meant you had officially bathed in the Kool-Aid. I was watching C-SPAN because it was my only legal entrée into the life of Senator Stanton. He was a bigwig on the Judiciary Committee and usually let out eloquent bursts about immigration and homeland security. I was going to have to figure out how to stream it on my computer. Julia would become suspicious if I suddenly found a passion for the most boring channel on television.

My television watching stopped short when the girl responsible for my new C-SPAN habit started chatting with Upton at her desk.

"What do you have in the works?" he asked loudly.

Without looking for notes, Olivia perked up and said, "I've got half a dozen leads—as in paper leads—going right now." She lifted her dry unmanicured hand and started ticking off her treasure box of stories on her small fingers. "There's some talk that Gorham pulled in shady donor funds for POTUS so clearly looking into that. Got great sources in Anchorage." She did? She had great sources in Anchorage? Like who? Retired Iditarod champs? While I sat shocked and a little jealous, she kept clicking down her list. "Then there's all that border fence nonsense that the president is speaking out on—great stuff coming from Texas reps—then there's the pushback on his health care bill, some stuff with the shakedown in the East Wing, and some little crap followup thing on foster care that POTUS is gearing up to sign. I did two articles on it already, but might as well make it a hat trick. Oh, and I've got twenty with Hillary on Friday."

Twenty minutes with Hillary Clinton? Twenty? I wanted just one minute with Hillary. Mike, who sat next to Olivia and whose press trip she had stolen a few months ago, was sitting there trying not to strangle his skinny, ass-kissing colleague. I understood Mike's frustration. Why did Upton have these cozy little desk-sides with Olivia? She wasn't an editor or even the highest ranking White House reporter. She was just the loudest.

I wanted to stand up and scream at Upton to stop slapping all of Olivia's copy on page one because the big story he was looking for was right in front of him and I had it. Olivia may have sources in Anchorage, but I had pictures of her having sex with a United States senator. Even if Upton barely knew my name right now, I could soon have the entire country looking at a picture of Olivia Campo's ass.

I didn't know how often Stanton was looking at Olivia's ass, which—along with her severe lack of ethics—had been bothering me ever since I found out she was married to Sandro. Did they just get together a few times, check the "I slept with a senator / I had sex with a girl half my age" boxes and move on? Or was this something that was going to last? Even break up their marriages. Olivia was absolutely nuts to risk her powerful job and perfect husband for Hoyt Stanton, but maybe she was mentally ill. I needed to find out more.

"Let's go bigger than you think on that foster care legislation," said Upton, breaking my train of thought. "We need some more warm fuzzy stuff because Mike's doing some depressing piece on the president's response to Syria and I could use a picture of a smiling child somewhere close to his." Olivia rolled her eyes, didn't bother to look at Mike, who was now a lovely shade of plum, and promised Upton she'd try.

I went over her long list of stories in my head, trying to see if I could spin any into Style-worthy topics. How was she perusing all those stories? And when did she even get the time to cultivate sources? My five sources all lived in the lower forty-eight. Pushing aside my feelings of inferiority, I stopped short at her comment about "border fence nonsense." Senator Stanton was always talking about his support for the border fence on C-SPAN. He was from Arizona and he was championing the controversial bill. And Olivia was from Texas, where they also rallied behind it. I quickly minimized my Web browser on my computer and Googled Stanton, border fence, Olivia Campo. I got ten hits at the top of the page. She had written about it before, especially about the president's opposition to the bill, but she had quotes from Stanton—the long, good quotes you got from an in-person interview. I wondered where, exactly, those interviews had been conducted.

When I woke up painfully early on Saturday morning, I ducked into my parents' house to poke around for their superior coffee. My mother was in the living room, sitting in the middle of an enormous ottoman, trying to twist herself into a complicated yoga posture. I curled myself on the sofa away from her old-people gymnastics.

"Did you ever just get so tired that you felt like you would never catch up on sleep again? Like there was some tipping point and you had let the pendulum swing past it, and now your life would be nothing but chaos and forced labor?" I asked, shifting positions on the couch.

"Well, to be honest with you, no." She unraveled herself, headed to the kitchen, and motioned for me to follow. I sat in a tall rush-seat chair and watched as she tended a pot of tea.

"I danced with Hugh Hefner at the Playboy mansion and expensed the whole trip when I was a journalist. It was fun. It wasn't this eternal flame of mediocre copy and no joy that you have to keep up."

"*Mediocre* seems like the wrong word," I said, crumpling up a mint leaf and putting it in my nose. It felt like a green bug, but I saw it as a cheap alternative to aromatherapy.

"Well, it's not going to be your best. You're moving too fast. And you're not on drugs like Jack Kerouac and company." She turned and looked at my bloodshot eyes squinting at her. "Or are you?" she asked. "I wouldn't judge you too harshly. You can tell me these things."

I loved how my mother claimed to be fine with potential

annoyances such as drug addiction as long as she knew they weren't true. In reality, she would have flipped out and threatened to do an honor killing. When she found a six-pack of Zima in my closet in high school, she cried and said I had disgraced the family name. Then again, maybe she was just disappointed in my crappy choice of alcoholic beverages. If there had been a case of Château Margaux under my pile of cardigans instead, she might have saluted my sophisticated palate.

"I'm not on drugs," I assured her. She took a seat and crossed her freckled legs. I got my freckled legs from her. "I'm just so tired," I said. And with that statement, the tears started to pour down my face. Curled up on the high chair, I cried like you can only do with your mother. It felt good.

When she finished smoothing down my hair and wiped the rivers of mascara off my face with a perfectly folded linen napkin, I was happy that I was home. I didn't care that I had given up New York and free haute couture and seven hours of sleep a night. I had someone to wipe off my puffy, tired face. I would have preferred if it was Sandro Pena, but for now, I was happy to have my mom.

I was still leaning against her when my father walked through the kitchen with his reading glasses on his head.

"Adrienne. Your sister sent new pictures. Come and have a look." He didn't comment on the fact that I was a tear-stained mess, which I kind of appreciated. I gave my face a final wipe and followed him.

In a nook on the landing between the first and second floors, I sat next to my dad on a wide cashmere sofa as he pulled up a slide show on his black, rubber-coated laptop. The first picture was of Payton standing in front of a palatial white house. Not tacky, but not exactly understated—which was basically how most people would describe my sister, too.

"Look, here she is on the top of her new Range Rover." He opened a photo of my sister sitting in a white dress on the roof of the car. "The whole roof rolls back like the top of a tuna can for better views. They had it customized." He clicked the arrow, and the next bright picture filled the screen.

Payton's hair was curled and golden blond, her skin was evenly tanned, and she still had the same haughty look on her face. There was no denying that she looked absolutely gorgeous against the backdrop of South America. Then I remembered the time she convinced me to eat trash on Christmas morning, and I hated her all over again.

"Doesn't she look like Grace Kelly?" my father said, going to the next shot.

I could still hear her voice. "On Christmas, we all eat out of the trash as a way of remembering the starving children of the world," she said, handing me an apple core covered in hamburger remains. She grinned and clapped her hands while I ate it, then told everyone I ever met for the next five years that I ate trash. Years later, when I was vacationing in Thailand, I bought an enormous knife, which I told the vendor was to cut off my sister's tongue. He gave me a discount.

I looked at her picture again. "Grace Kelly? Without the crown or the talent," I replied.

"Oh, Adrienne. You two were always fighting," said my dad, pointing out the obvious. I rested my chin on his gray head. It smelled like old man pomade and the comfort of home. "Are you still mad because she was always trying to kill you when you were younger?"

"Younger? She put a live raccoon in my bed on my eighteenth birthday. You had to call pest control."

"That was pretty creative, you have to admit," he said, chuckling proudly. "She always had a really funny side to her. That great dark humor, like Woody Allen. I don't know why she had to up and move to Argentina, but I guess Buck had grand plans." This again. The way my father talked, I was pretty sure I would wake up one morning and my entire family would be living in Argentina without me.

"Here's one of her and Buck," said my dad, smiling with pride. Buck was lifting Payton up like he was about to carry her over the threshold. "She's lucky to have found love so young. It seems to get harder when you get older."

I was about to ask him if he'd like to offer me some cash so I could freeze my eggs and tattoo the word *spinster* on my arm, when he pulled up a close-up shot of Buck's smiling face and my mood softened.

My sister's husband's name was actually Tim Johnston, but everyone called him Buck. He was a linebacker for the University of Michigan in the late nineties, and in his first ever game wearing blue and gold, he was thrown out in the second quarter for kicking the Michigan State quarterback in the gut. Hence Buck Johnston. The name stuck, and even though fifteen years had passed since his freshman fall, his weight and ability to crush things had stuck, too.

From the second we met, I preferred Buck to my sister. He never put live animals in my room. My sister was born to inflict cruel and unusual punishment, whereas Buck got that all out of his system by bashing wide receivers in college. Their future children were going to have a hoot of a good time.

"Assure me again that we're related," I said to my father as we looked at a picture of Payton and Buck staring down a family of ocelots.

"I'm afraid that's the dirty truth," he said, setting the photos to slide-show mode. "But she's off living her life now, and you've given yours up to come back here. She's the adventurer, and you're our little homebody."

Screw my mom drying my tears—I had to move. I had to start pushing drugs on the side and save up the rent money. Or maybe I could covertly sell a horse on eBay. How did one ship a horse? Was there a flat rate? Whatever, I would figure it out.

Unable to bear the slideshow, I looked at my phone. I had missed two calls from James, the man who had escorted me out of the Hay-Adams when I was sick. Having been preoccupied by dreams of a toothy Latin American man who had promised his mind, body, and soul to my despicable, adulterous colleague, I had forgotten that I was going out with James that night. But when I saw his name on my phone, a slight shiver ran down my spine, reminding me that I was still a sexual being, despite the *Capitolist*'s best efforts to kill off my libido. I kissed my father on the cheek and headed back to my animal quarters.

It was a beautiful May day and the air was getting warmer; I no longer had to run between the barn and the house. Instead, I just walked lazily and let the too-long grass get my feet wet.

"You buzzed?" I said as sexily as I could when James picked up the phone.

"I did. Am I still seeing you tonight? You sent me your address when I begged for it but nothing else. Maybe you just want me to mail you a letter? Anyway, I hope I am seeing you," he said. In the background I could hear traffic. A fire truck roared by, and then there was the syncopated sound of chanting, a group protesting something or other. "Sorry about the noise," he said. "I'm driving around Dupont Circle with all the windows down. Liberals, everywhere. I hope you can hear me. Are we still on for tonight?"

"Do you mind picking me up?" I asked sweetly.

He laughed loudly over the sounds of the city. "You mean do I mind driving for two hours before we even get to the restaurant? Because you live on some plantation?"

"Something like that . . ."

"For you, of course I don't. I'll just pack some flares and an emergency meal."

"Comedy is not your strong suit," I said, laughing despite my best effort not to.

By 7 P.M., my hair was curled, my eyes were brightened with some black-market potion I bought online in Canada, and my underwear was small and French. I went out and sat in the hammock by the fenced-in pasture to wait for him. The sun was starting to set and Jasper and two other white horses were busying themselves with the art of doing nothing. I was pretending to watch them when James's car pulled up the drive.

"Why hello there! You didn't tell me that we're practically neighbors," he said, stepping out of his car in a dark beige suit jacket and jeans.

"Sorry, did it take long?" I asked.

"Thirty-eight minutes. I drove fast."

Thirty-eight minutes? He drove at Autobahn speed.

Looking around at the gas lampposts and the white horses grazing near the barn, he whistled like a man looking up a girl's skirt. "This sure is beautiful."

"Well, it's not mine. It's my parents'. But I did grow up here. And now I just squat in a room above the barn."

"Your parents still live here?" he asked. His golden curls made him look much younger than I imagined he was.

"Sure, they're in the house, in the kitchen. Want to say hi? You already met my father, after all."

He looked at me square in the face and said, "I absolutely do."

"Nah. Another time," I said, grabbing his hand and heading toward his silver Porsche SUV.

"Can you see out these windows?" I asked as he opened the door for me. They looked like they had blackout screens taped inside just in case there was a German air raid.

"I had them darkened a bit," he said, closing my door and heading to the driver's side. "Lots of prying eyes in this city." He looked out the window just as Jasper started to trot toward the back hill. "I mean, in the city. The one we now have to drive thirty-eight minutes to get to."

As we exited the town of Middleburg, past the small white sign that read "population 976," James started squinting at the even, hilly road.

"It's hard to see with this sun setting in my eyes," he said, putting on a pair of brown Ray-Bans and pulling the eyeshade down.

"That's the thing about Middleburg," I said as we passed yard after yard of perfect horse fence. "You can actually see the sun."

"But you can't do anything," he replied. "Who cares if you can see the sun? It's no fun to enjoy nature in nature. Unless you're a big hippie, like you." He laughed and put his hand on my thigh, then quickly removed it before I could do it for him.

We stopped at the red light by the gas station with the Pegasus wings. The radio was playing an old Billy Joel song, and I realized that I was kind of excited to be going on my first real date since I had moved home seven months ago. Starting to feel more at ease, I looked out James's deeply tinted window to watch the last of the sun disappear behind the Chrysalis winery on the hill. I saw the trees trimmed low to show off the stone buildings and the faint outlines of the rows of grapes. It was only there by the gas station that the road was four lanes wide. We pulled up as the light turned yellow, and James came to a smooth stop. As he fiddled with the radio, a white BMW pulled up next to us. As it came to a halt, I looked down at the two people inside, already sure of who I would see.

Senator Stanton and Olivia Campo. He was driving. When she turned to him, I could see that she was very upset—and not in the cold, aggressive way she was in the newsroom. Her arms were moving, and she seemed to be trying to keep out of his reach. He grabbed her face in his hands and gave her a kiss, and she pushed him away forcefully. He sat stunned while she hit him on the shoulder and opened her mouth wide to yell. Despite her anger, she looked vulnerable—an emotion I didn't think she had in her repertoire. When the light turned green, they had their heads together, and I heard a pickup truck honk impatiently behind them as James drove us toward the city. Looking in the rearview mirror, I watched as the white car turned right and climbed the hill toward the Goodstone Inn.

I couldn't make small talk after that. I sat in the front seat, quiet and still, trying to guess what they could be fighting like that about. Maybe they were ending things. Could Sandro have found out that his wife wasn't tailing the president to China every weekend, but was actually the senator's wanton woman instead? Could he have said, "Olivia. It's him or me. Make a choice or I'm running off with Adrienne Brown." That last part was unlikely, but suddenly I began wondering if things could have gone south for Olivia and Stanton and what that would mean for my exposé.

During dinner with James at the Source, I was a nervous mess. I tried to make conversation, but I kept talking about horses because it was one of the only things I could babble about without much thought. I gave James an anatomy lesson, even drawing a foal on a cloth napkin along with arrows and technical phrases. I told him I had a passion for animal husbandry. At the end of the night, he tucked the drawing into his blazer pocket, like it was a totally normal first date memento.

James, I decided, despite looking like a Fragonard cherub with a Ralph Lauren charge card, was a very nice guy. Medium height, medium build, blue eyes, a firm dimple in his left cheek. He was a little proud, a lot pompous, and way too Washington for me to swoon over, but he was good company, even for a girl in a neurotic state. And the lovely part was, he didn't know me at all, so he couldn't even ask me if I was acting weird. Which I was.

When we walked out to his car, brought up from Pennsylvania Avenue by a valet in a red jacket, it became clear to both of us that I was fairly drunk. He suggested a bar, and when I declined, he suggested some Vitaminwater and an aspirin at his house. To that, I stupidly said yes.

We drove through the straight grid of Washington streets with the windows down. He lent me his arm as we walked into his town house near Eastern Market. It had a window box full of flowers that I was sure he hadn't planted himself.

"How about a martini?" he said, walking to his oak and marble kitchen, which seemed to illuminate magically when he entered.

"Didn't I say water and aspirin?" I replied, my head still spinning.

I waited in the living room while he opened bottles and filled crystal glasses with ice. There were absolutely no personal photos in his apartment. There were three large, colorful abstract paintings, which looked expensive and bland. In New York I went on a date with a Flemish man who spent his weekends painting enormous vaginas on canvas, so boring art didn't bother me too much.

"Did you do these?" I asked as he effortlessly fished a few olives out of a Whole Foods container with a tiny cocktail fork.

"No," he replied. "My decorator chose them. Xavier dos Santos."

Of course. I was actually mad at myself for not recognizing the style. Heaps of beige, reclaimed oak furniture, heavy marble tables, and red, colorful art. He decorated dozens of Washington apartments and houses in the same expensive, flavorless style.

"Before you judge me too heavily, I'm single," James pointed out defensively, after catching the sour look on my face. "And I don't really like to spend my weekends buying lampshades. So I hired Xavier. He's fast, and he doesn't care about my opinion, so that worked out well for me."

I wasn't judging. I lived in a barn.

"Come. Try the Noguchi chair. I just got it." He came over from the kitchen, sat in it, and motioned to his knee.

"Don't take this the wrong way," I said, walking closer to him. "But how do you have all this money? You're a press flack."

He started laughing like I'd just asked him the exact measure of his genitals. "Wow, you really did just move here from New York, didn't you. That is such a New York question."

"It is not!" I protested. "It's a safety question. Maybe you launder money on the side. Maybe you're busy scamming the elderly."

"It's neither of those, I promise," he said, running his hand over the smooth wood of the expensive chair. "I worked for Goldman Sachs for ten years. I guess I was pretty good at it."

An ex-banker in Washington? Quite the rarity.

"Why on earth would you leave that job?" I asked, looking around his apartment. "Didn't you take an eighty percent pay cut to work for the RNC?"

"More like ninety. It hurt," he admitted. "But I wanted to do something a little more meaningful with my life. Ten years on Wall Street and I felt a little bit soulless. Plus, I was sick of those petty New York girls." He flashed me a perfect smile. "So I came down here and worked for Senator Estes for two years and then got this gig. But don't worry," he said, reaching up for my hand. "I'm not broke yet."

He tried to pull me down to the chair, but I pulled away and said, "I'll sit in it if you stand up."

"But that wouldn't be fun," he said, rubbing his knees.

"Have you ever been convicted of sexual harassment?" I asked, fishing the olive out of my glass and popping it and its vodka-soaked insides into my mouth. James had handed me both a Vitaminwater and a martini, which was a disgusting combination, but I was too drunk to care. Plus, the martini came with a side of marble-shaped ice cubes. In my state I found them fascinating and started rolling them around on his impeccable hardwood floors.

"Not recently," he said, smiling.

"Well, that's reassuring."

The two sips of vodka martini were a mistake. I was feeling awfully woozy. I was still speaking, but I had no idea what I was saying. James's face looked like a bowl of pudding painted by Cubists. I felt sick and sleepy, and then, somehow, the world just went away.

When I came to, I was lying in a luxuriously fluffy bed with white sheets and thick down comforters up to my neck. The temperature felt like winter in Juneau, and long curtains hung over the windows. Was I in James's house? It didn't look a thing like it.

Magically, my cell phone was on the nightstand. I grabbed it and called him.

"Good morning, sunshine!" he laughed into the phone. "Yes, you are, you definitely are," he assured me when I asked if I was in his apartment. "You're in the guest room, fully clothed, as you might have noticed. I am such a gentleman."

Oh God. I must have passed out. That was the only explanation. I probably fell on the floor and drooled all over my face and he took a video and it was now on YouTube and I was going to get fired.

But actually, when James explained what had happened, the reality was worse.

"You talked to my mother," he said, laughing. "It wasn't really your fault. My parents just moved to the West Coast and she can't keep the time difference straight. She called, I answered, and you grabbed the phone from me, but she woke me up with a message for you this morning." I conversed with his mother! I needed to check myself into AA for a day. I wondered if they had speed courses for working professionals.

"Did I really? I didn't. I'm so sorry . . . did I really talk to your mother?" I stuttered.

"Did you ever. She says hello. She also sends her regards to Caroline and Winston-who-went-to-Princeton. Mind if I ask who they are?"

"Those would be my parents," I confessed.

"Of course," said James. "Most memorable date of my life. We should do it again. So, how is next Saturday?"

"Sometimes I'm not great with my liquor," I said, apologizing. "I just don't drink very often anymore with this job. So when I do—"

"You don't need to explain," said James, interrupting. "Like I said, most memorable date of my entire life."

I laughed at the fact that he wasn't having me committed, and I agreed to go out with him again. And then, like the gentleman that he was proving to be, he let me shower and drove me all the way back to Middleburg, with the windows open and a painkiller floating in my stomach.

CHAPTER 11

It's strange to learn about people without being close to them. I felt like I was watching an opera from the wings; I would have preferred the limited view from the cheap seats to all the backstage drama I was privy to now. Olivia, Sandro, and Stanton had been shoved to the back burner while I caught up with *List* work after the Correspondents' Dinner. But now that I had filed some meatier pieces, including an exclusive interview with James Franco on his political agenda, I felt like my job was more secure and Hardy wasn't going to fire me on a whim. I was also starting to understand what it took to inch a little higher at the *List*. Before I broke the Franco piece, most of my colleagues looked down at their phones when I walked past them in the newsroom. Now, they looked straight ahead. Maybe, if I decided to go ahead with the Olivia story, they would actually look at me. Perhaps try out an exotic greeting like "hello."

The senator was easier to stalk than Olivia or Sandro. His life was public knowledge, and so was his job. When I got sick of watching him jabber on C-SPAN, I started looking up his hearing schedule and heading to the Hill so I could listen to him speak in person. The first two times I went, it was just a study in the motions of the man, his physicality, the things that made him tick. But the third time I saw him, he took to the Senate floor for half an hour.

Walking up the long hill, past tourists in comfortable shoes, I flashed my Congress pass to the security guards at the door of the Capitol and put my bag through the X-ray machine. Once it had been established that I was not a threat to national security, my possessions were returned, and I walked through the marble building.

"Pass?" a handsome security guard asked as I opened the door of the press gallery in the Senate chamber. I untangled it from my hair and showed him a picture where I looked like a corpse. "Proceed," he instructed me. I walked toward the front row.

Placed high above the Senate floor, too high for effective heckling or accurate spitballs, the press gallery was occupied, as usual, by a handful of reporters reclining in their horrific outfits, scribbling on creased notepads, and punching furiously away on their BlackBerrys like they were instant-messaging Deep Throat. I recognized a girl from the Associated Press who was wearing a mint green oversize polo shirt with a pair of stained khakis and canvas sneakers. She looked like she was ready to depart for spring break in Orlando. Another girl was in a too-loose skirt suit, huge plastic bubblegum pearls, and a pair of ballerina flats with rubber soles.

That was the thing about female print journalists. Dressing up, grooming, having two angular eyebrows—all frowned upon. It was still that archaic mentality of trying to blend in with the boys. But I refused. I just couldn't look like I dressed out of a "take me" bin.

I took out my writing pad (Nepalese paper encased in a pink ostrich leather cover embossed with a quote from Balzac, in

French) and settled into a dark wooden seat. I was scrolling through news on my BlackBerry, hoping I could file something while I waited, when a reporter from Scripps started barking in my general direction.

In a tone that sounded appropriate for bootleggers and criminals, he hollered, "Hey blondie, you got an extra pen?" I turned to him and pointed at my chest quizzically.

"Yes, you. Do you see any other blondes sitting here? Do you have a pen I could borrow?"

I reached into my bag, walked up the stairs, and handed him my backup. He inspected it like I had just handed him a lit stick of dynamite.

"This is shaped like a tiger," he said, examining the exotic writing utensil.

"It's the only extra one I have," I said with a smile, not mentioning that it was actually a panther, it was made by Cartier, and it cost over a grand. "Nah, I'm gonna break this thing," he said, handing it back. "I'll go inside and grab a Bic." He was getting up to leave when a girl unearthed a pen from her messy, mousy brown ponytail and threw it at him.

"Hey, thanks," he said. She raised her hand in acknowledgment while she continued to type, but she didn't say a thing.

Of course. Who would want to write with an enamel and gold pen when you could scribble with a dandruff-covered white plastic stick? What a sound choice. I looked at the Scripps reporter, silently wished him a lifetime of unhappiness and lice, and watched as senators started to file into the formal room.

Stanton was chairman of the Judiciary Committee and was talking today about immigration and the Freedom Fence Act, which would double the length of the existing border fence between Mexico and the United States. Since hearing Olivia say she was writing about the fence and discovering that she had reported on it in depth in the past, I was beginning to think that it wasn't just the issue that brought them together, it was the issue that was keeping them together. Olivia was from Texas, which is where one hundred miles of the fence would go. He was from Arizona and her perfect husband was definitely from Mexico or Central America. That couldn't be a coincidence.

"I can think of nothing more important than protecting our borders, which will in turn protect our freedoms and our families," Stanton declared once he had the floor. Pacing in front of the Senate president, he paused, lifted his left hand, and dropped it again with the elegance of a symphony conductor. "Terrorism is a very real threat. Those of us who see the fence as nothing but a means to keep out illegal immigrants are asleep at the wheel. It's a safety concern. The way the fence stands right now, it's like a catwalk straight into our country."

There were some chuckles from a few in the room. The senator turned and looked at his colleagues. "The American people deserve to tuck their children in at night without fear. I think, especially, of the Americans living in border towns, in El Paso, in San Diego and San Luis. Democrats say the numbers are already going in the right direction and that we should stop making a fuss. But the pace is too slow."

He opened the bottom button of his gray blazer and straightened his navy and maroon tie. It reminded me of the one my college boyfriend wore to the boat races on the Charles River. Stanton's probably smelled a lot less like beer.

"We need more vehicle barriers," he said, his body straight and tall. "We need more pedestrian fence. Seven hundred miles is nothing. I was in the army with men who could run seven hundred miles in a week."

As Stanton finished his address, I held up my BlackBerry and zoomed in on him with the phone's video camera. His body looked much younger than his years. His tan face was covered with fine lines but showed a youthful vigor as he spoke. I thought about the photos I had of him having sex with Olivia. What would his colleagues, sitting here intimidated now, say when they saw those? All his arguments, all this passion would be reduced to nothing if I decided to splash those photos around the world. Few politicians ever recovered from sex scandals and when physical evidence was involved, it was always game over.

Senators were scrawling notes as Stanton spoke. Senator Dianne Feinstein and her perfect hairdo and well-cut St. John suit looked like she was going to explode. But no one's ire was going to prevent Stanton from finishing his eloquent roar.

The reporter from the *Huffington Post* picked up his phone and called his editor. "I'm running late. I'll be in when this fucker decides to shut up. Do we have a stand-alone immigration page? We do? We have a what page? A wedding page? When did that launch? Okay, well, this asshole isn't proposing to anyone, he's just ranting about the border fence, so I think immigration is a better landing page, don't you? Yeah, it should be the lead. I'll file quick. Have someone get a photo off the AP wire of his fists flying. He's like a prizefighter out here."

Shaking his head at the liberal take on the matter, the reporter from the *Daily Caller* smirked and busied himself with his own reporting.

My own notes were nothing but questions. Before I knew she was married to Sandro, I was convinced that Olivia was sleeping with the senator because she was addicted to power. But now I wasn't so sure. Why would she risk her rapidly rising career and her marriage to gorgeous Sandro? Did she have no morals whatsoever? Couldn't she see how great her life was? Or was it something else? Her awfully expensive car and writing implement were definitely red flags. But a desire for cash seemed too simple. She didn't care about strutting around the world in Manolo Blahniks, she cared about leaping over the competition in her Banana Republic flats.

Maybe Stanton was feeding her scoops while she shook her milk shake in Middleburg, helping to push her to the top of the *Capitolist* ladder. But that would mean that their relationship was serious—that they had seen each other more than a handful of times at the Goodstone. If so, what I witnessed outside the Bull Barn was not just the peak of a short affair, but merely a routine encounter—and Olivia really was a reprehensible human being. Then again, it might be all over now. I had seen them fighting in the car only ten days ago, and I could be obsessing over something that was in the past.

I listened to Stanton's words and thought about all those articles Olivia wrote on immigration. They were detailed and frequently quoted by other reporters trying to catch up to her scoops. It seemed unusual considering she was a White House reporter, not covering Congress.

I tried to imagine how a relationship could start between a senator and a woman in her twenties. Had they met in the Capitol? The White House? Was she already writing an immigration story, having established that as part of her beat, or had all those articles come later? I found it difficult to talk to members of Congress about anything but the task at hand. I couldn't imagine making small talk, or flirting with them. There was something about their demeanor, those intimidating pins on their lapels that screamed, "I am not like you." And in Stanton's case, there was also that whole marriage, family values, six-children thing.

The senator seemed very far away from thoughts of family while he spoke on the floor. I knew he lived alone in a large town house on Capitol Hill when he was not in Arizona. I had easily found the address and walked by it one night when I finished covering a hearing in the Rayburn building. It was brick, painted over with thick white paint, and had a red front door with a brass knocker in the shape of an eagle. Next to the door was a black metal mailbox with a gold pear-shaped latch. It looked like any other handsome house on C Street, but it was the only one I paused in front of. Had Olivia been inside? Had she put her wedding vows down the garbage disposal and kicked off her clothes? Maybe recited the Constitution in a thong? Even more difficult than imagining Olivia doing the Charleston in her birthday suit was imagining this man, currently commanding the Senate floor like it was his living room, going home to a normal house, a normal life. After what I had seen him do with Olivia, I couldn't imagine him with a wife and children. How could he share a bed with someone and fill that elegant white house with lies? But, then again, maybe his wife just stayed in Arizona, happily unaware of it all.

I put down my pen and sat back in my seat to listen to the end of his speech.

He delivered his closing remarks in a lawyerly way, threw his notes on his desk, and stood there while some of the blood drained out of his face. When he looked up at the press gallery he was smiling like his opponent was pinned to the floor, down for the count and gasping for air.

Already behind on my story count for the day, I drove back to the office, sat at my small desk, and refreshed the *Capitolist* home page to see which one of Upton's favorite reporters had the Web lead. Olivia's name popped onto my screen. No surprise there; she had a lead at some point almost every day.

I wasn't surprised to see her name at the top of the site. It was the foster care piece Upton had assigned to her that day.

But I was surprised to see Stanton's name liberally sprinkled throughout the article.

I read and reread. The president was about to pass the Foster Care Empowerment Act, Stanton's brainchild, and Olivia had him quoted all over the piece, talking about his own children, adopted from the foster care system. When, I wondered, had she talked to him about foster care? Between countryside sex sessions? Or did she actually make an appointment with his scheduler and go interview him in his office?

This bill, according to Stanton's quotes, was going to change the lives of thousands of teens. A half-million kids were currently in foster care and two hundred thousand had aged out in the last decade. The Foster Care Empowerment Act would help find permanent families for older kids by promoting relative guardianship and expanding federal support by moving the age limit for funding from eighteen to twenty-one. Senators from both sides of the aisle were applauding his work, and the president was set to formally approve the legislation this summer. I read the piece slowly, making sure to mask Olivia's byline behind my Twitter feed in case Julia glanced at my computer. The piece was actually quite moving. I even had to choke back tears at a line about Martha Brinkley being adopted by her music teacher at age seventeen so she didn't have to deal with being still very much a child but an adult in the eyes of the law. I hated that something Olivia wrote was having this impact on me, but considering I cried during the opening scene of *The Notebook*, I didn't give her too much credit. Upton had asked for warm and fuzzy, and the suck-up had delivered.

I walked out of the office at just past 7 P.M. I was very happy about having an early night and turned down an invitation to have drinks with Isabelle and her glamorous athletic posse, so

I could sit at home and try to sort my jumble of thoughts into something I could understand.

I reached for my keys and checked my BlackBerry to make sure I didn't have to write another article from the parking garage. I didn't. But I did have a message from Hardy telling me I had an important emergency assignment and not to fuck it up. Upton was having a cocktail party in honor of *Capitolist* reporter David Bush's general world domination and I was tasked with covering it. Nothing like covering a party at your editor in chief's house for your own paper. Not awkward at all. I was exhausted and didn't want to do anything but drive straight home and collapse into bed. But I had no choice. I looked at the address and headed toward the highway to drive north to Maryland instead of south to Middleburg.

I couldn't believe that out of all the Style girls I had been handpicked by Hardy to cover our own party. Was that even journalism? Wasn't that just a press release about how great we were with my byline shoved on it? When I texted Isabelle about my demeaning assignment she said that I had to do it because I was the newest one on the team and that she'd covered a party at Upton's last year so it was my turn to deal.

The only plus was that there was a chance Stanton could be there. David Bush wrote about Stanton pretty often and as Julia had pointed out to me when I started, everyone loved David.

It turns out that people not only loved David, they worshipped David. At the entrance to Upton's large, elegant yellow clapboard house was a picture of David shaking hands with the president. On the other side was one of David playing Ping-Pong with the Speaker of the House. Just in case a party guest didn't know that David was the most powerful reporter in town, here was a quick picture show to point out the obvious. How handy.

I walked in the door and gave my name to one of the paper's event planners and then pushed into the house past a secret service agent. That was a good sign. Maybe the Senate majority leader was here and if he was, there was a good chance Stanton was, too. The two voted in a perfect line with each other and everyone said that if Stanton didn't run for president, he would at least be the next majority leader if the Senate stayed in GOP hands.

I didn't recognize anyone in the living room, so I pulled out a notepad and walked over to look at a few family pictures on the mantel. The Uptons looked so normal. I didn't know what I expected. Maybe framed photos of BlackBerrys and *Capitolist* time stamps.

A few minutes of that and I felt even more awkward and out of place. I headed to the backyard, opened the door to the large brick patio, and leaned against a white pillar. Maybe I could just blend in with the pillar. I was suddenly thrilled that I had worn an ecru-colored dress. My mother always said ecru was just white but dirty, but what did she know? It was actually a yuppie version of camouflage. I stood there until two people bumped into me because I clearly was blending in with the pillar, and then I dug up some courage and went to ask a few guests why they loved David Bush.

I checked the Congress info book on my phone to make sure I was approaching the right people and made a beeline for a congressman I recognized from watching too much C-SPAN.

"Congressman Ward. How are you?" I said after weaving through guests on the perfectly manicured lawn. Shoving aside Ward's wife as politely as I could, I stuck out my hand and said, "I'm Adrienne Brown, a reporter for the *Capitolist*. Do you have a few minutes to talk about David Bush?"

"A reporter for the *Capitolist*, are you?" replied the portly lawmaker. Up close, he looked like a scoop of Crisco hired to pen our nation's laws. "Well then you've come to the right place! I hear you people are *throwing* this party."

"Yes!" I replied. "That's just how we roll." I was turning pink. This beach ball with a head was making me blush. I had reached a new low.

Luckily, Ward was also happy to gush about David Bush, and considering that my face was bright red, I kept my eyes on my notepad and wrote it all down.

When I was done talking to Congressman Ward, I walked across the garden toward a large grove of hydrangeas and took a glass of water off the outdoor bar. When I stepped back toward the house, I saw Upton talking to one of the policy editors. It was strange to see him outside of the newsroom, not locked inside his intimidating glass office. He still looked like he was about to jump on his speakerphone and blast the whole party with some news of the *Capitolist* conquering the world.

I got five more sound bites from lawmakers about David, spoke to a few TV reporters about why they loved the king of print, and tried to make my way to the door. I mustered up a weak smile for a few of the editors I recognized from the paper and tried not to bump into the waiters making their way through the crowd in the garden with huge trays of canapés. I almost had a run-in with a man holding shrimp tempura and sat down on a wooden folding chair to steady myself before I was covered in fried Japanese food.

I watched as people came out the back door and into the garden for a few minutes. It really was a beautiful house. It was probably built in the late nineteenth century, but the inside had to have been gutted and updated a few times since. The outside still looked original. I somehow had not expected Upton, the leader of new media, to live in an old house. I saw him more in

a McMansion or a shiny new condo overlooking the Potomac
River. This house, elegant and old, was something I would have
chosen if I made ten times my salary. I shivered at the thought
that we had similar taste in architecture and assured myself that
it was always the wife who chose the real estate.

But the woman now talking to Upton wasn't his wife, whom
I still hadn't caught a glimpse of, but Olivia Campo. What was
she doing here? There were barely any reporters, just a few senior editors. I hadn't expected to see her. Was Upton that obvious with his favoritism?

I watched her talking to him, completely comfortable, like
she was always popping by Upton's house for a cozy chitchat.
She was wearing a dress the color of an overcooked steak. Not
exactly brown, but not quite black. It was drab and badly ironed,
but from a distance, and in the soft porch lights, she looked almost pretty. And calm. Almost like she had the night I photographed her with Stanton. I watched them for a couple more
seconds, but their intimacy started to nauseate me. I didn't have
that kind of editor-reporter relationship with Hardy and I knew
I would never have it with Upton. Julia and Libby sure didn't
and they had been at the *List* for years.

I stood up to leave, crossed the garden, and got caught in a
crowd in the living room. It wasn't until I had been standing
there for a few minutes trying to escape without being rude that
I realized that the man blocking my path was Senator Stanton.

I couldn't believe it. Had he been at this party for hours
and I just hadn't noticed? Was I really that bad of a reporter? I
shouldn't have gotten so caught up examining the nineteenth-
century details of Upton's house. I was crap at my job.

Stanton was tall, a good couple of inches above six feet, and
held himself very straight. Up close, I noticed he had a few
extra pounds in his midsection, but his padding was almost

fully concealed by a well-tailored pinstripe suit jacket. His dark brown hair had a little gray around the temples. Not a white gray that makes one look terribly old and destined to live out a life of backgammon and adult diapers. More like a silvery "you can call me Clooney" kind of gray. And of course, he wore two small gold pins on the left lapel of his jacket. One was a circular gold official Senate pin, and the other, tucked right beneath, was a tiny enamel version of Old Glory. He was talking to a shorter man whom I recognized but couldn't place. He was wearing a seersucker jacket and khakis and drinking something with a handful of mint in it. Now I had no intention of leaving the party. I moved to the side so I was a little farther from Stanton but could still listen to his conversation. I put my notepad back in my bag and pretended to be absolutely enthralled with Upton's ficus plant.

It took a few minutes but finally a woman came up to the man chatting with Stanton and gave him a hug. "Taylor Miles!" she said with a strong drawl. "I knew you'd be here and I have something very important to talk to you about. You can listen, too, Senator Stanton," she said, laughing when she noticed Stanton. "In fact, you *should* listen."

Taylor Miles. He was quoted in an article I read on Stanton's immigration stance. I had just placed a Google alert on the senator regarding all things immigration. I remembered him because I wondered if the reporter had reversed his first and last name by accident. Miles was an Arizona state senator and the founder of the Southern Immigration Reform Foundation, a staunchly right wing group, which had been accused of racist undertones by many critics. But that didn't seem to bother Stanton. He continued to talk to Taylor and the woman with the southern accent about some town hall meeting coming up on the border fence and I continued to eavesdrop while staring at a plant.

After a few more minutes, Stanton said goodbye to Miles and the woman and walked out of the party. I counted quickly to ten and followed after him.

I didn't know exactly what I was going to do. Slide-tackle Stanton and ask him if he was sleeping with Olivia? That didn't seem like a very good idea considering security. Instead I just watched him get into a black town car that was waiting for him and then I quickly got into mine. I started the Volvo and was about to head for home but Stanton's driver didn't seem like he was going anywhere. I could see him in the front seat with the light on, reading a magazine.

He was waiting for Olivia. I put my car back into park, took the key out of the ignition, and turned off the headlights. Only minutes later, Olivia walked confidently down the steps and got in the back of the town car like it was totally empty and idling just for her. As soon as her door closed, the car did a quick U-turn and headed up Connecticut Avenue.

Their affair was still going strong.

I had spoken to no one about Olivia, her amazing husband, or the senator, even though I suspected there was a scandalous story behind their affair. If they stopped seeing each other, I wasn't sure I could keep pursuing. I had already overstepped a few journalistic lines of ethics—I didn't want to pole vault over any others. But the sighting at Upton's had quieted my doubts. And lying in bed that night, my mind racing, I knew I couldn't keep it to myself any longer.

I could only think of one person who had the kind of calculating personality I needed and who was far enough away to confide in.

I took the telephone off my desk, moved to the gingham window seat in the living room, and dialed. I heard the unfamiliar ringtone of another country.

"Hi, Payton, it's me," I said.

"And who is me?" asked a commanding voice. If I had to ap-point one person to lead troops into battle, it would be Payton Brown. She even had a name like a general. Everyone who has ever met Payton is scared of her, and that includes her hulking husband. I think that's what won him over in the first place, actually. He had never been scared of anything before and was just floored that the first person who frightened him was a 115-pound stick of a girl from Middleburg, Virginia.

"Me? Who is me? Hello? Are you still there?" Payton screamed into the phone.

"Payton. Stop yelling. It's your sister," I said, already regret-ting my bright idea.

She laughed like a woman who relishes making homemade bombs. "Of course I knew that already, Addy. You're my one and only sister. Well, that I'm aware of anyway. I once had Dad ready to buy a DNA kit to make sure you were his, but that's beside the point. I was just trying to see if your phone manners had improved at all, and clearly they have not."

My phone voice was what one would describe as perfectly pleasant. But Payton, ever the actress, picks up the phone and announces, "This is Payton Cleves Brown Johnston calling from San Andres de Giles, Argentina, and I hope to speak to Madame Butthead," or whoever it is she's calling.

"It's nice to hear your voice, Addy," she said, sighing as if our conversation was already exhausting her. "Tell me everything. What's going on in that hometown of ours? It really is so quaint that you left New York and your glamorous job to move home with Mom and Dad. But actually, you don't live in the house, do you?"

She made it sound like I lived on a mat outside the back door and answered to the name of Fido.

"I don't," I confirmed. "I'm living in the barn apartment. The one the Hollands used to live in until they had another baby." Payton gave a few "umm-humms" and I heard her tapping away on a computer, clearly sick of our back-and-forth.

"I've stopped showering and I roll myself in horse manure every night. It is so therapeutic. A bit like splashing around in the grotto in Lourdes."

My sister sucked in her breath sharply, paying attention again. "You do *what*!" she screamed.

I collapsed into a pile of laughter. "Payton! I'm kidding! I sleep in a bed, not in a big pile of horse poop. Jesus, you're so uptight."

I could practically hear her spine straightening. "Look, Addy, you called me. Now if you've decided to spend a dollar a minute on long distance just to make fun of me in that horrifically sarcastic tone of yours, then so be it. I'll just be your whipping post."

I felt slightly bad for toying with Payton's robotlike mind. We saw each other so seldom that it was easy to forget that she considered humor a time suck favored by the weak.

"I'm not calling to make fun of you, Payton," I said apologetically. "I'm calling to tell you about something more serious. Something that is making me half insane and that I just need to talk out. I . . . I need your help," I admitted.

That perked her right up. All her life, there has been nothing Payton enjoys more than doling out advice like a sage upon a mountaintop.

"Do you now?" she said shrilly. "This is a first. Well, besides the summer you were almost arrested for smoking pot in Constitution Hall, but we've all forgotten about that little incident, haven't we."

Yes, we had. We had forgotten because I was sixteen years

old and it was a Rusted Root concert and I was wearing a dress that I made out of curtains from a thrift store. I don't remember a thing about it.

"I've stumbled across something pretty big," I said to Payton. "Huge, actually. I found something out that could change the course of my life, other people's lives, too. And I don't feel comfortable thinking about it, let alone talking about it. I certainly can't talk to anyone around here. But you, good old you, will happily tell me if I've gone insane."

Payton laughed with delight. "I'm sure I will declare you unfit to mingle with society. Straitjacket city is in your future."

I don't think she was kidding.

As we sat in our two different hemispheres, I explained to her about Olivia having sex with Stanton and how I shimmied on my belly in the dirt for hours in our hometown to get a picture of them together. I told her I was still sitting on the photos because a) I was a wimp and b) I felt like their relationship was more than just sex. I had evidence, I just didn't fully understand why she was doing it. And then I confessed about Sandro. I told her how I wanted to strip off my clothes and have Sandro's babies and what a whole mess it all was.

"*Mess* does not seem like a strong enough word," said Payton when I came up for air.

I explained how the mess could catapult my career forward. If I wrote about Olivia and Stanton's affair, broke the news, I would dominate the front page of the paper for weeks, months. I could sit across from Chris Matthews on *Hardball* and Anderson Cooper on CNN. I would no longer be filing articles that Upton and Cushing didn't bother to read and I would be a guest at their parties, not the reporter tasked with writing about them. And our parents would sit back and marvel and say, "How can one person be so good at everything she does?" And this time they'd be talking about me.

It scared me that I wanted all that, but I did, and I could certainly admit it to Payton. I was sick of being just another one of the nameless Style girls stuck in the smallest desks in the farthest corner. I worked too hard for that. We all did, but I refused to watch the years tick by, waking up every day before 5 A.M. just to be ignored while someone louder and more aggressive was applauded. Someone like Olivia.

I explained that while I was trying to wrap my head around Stanton's affair, I still had to do my job for fourteen hours a day, so I was moving at a snail's pace on the story. In fact, there basically was no story. Just pictures and lots of speculation. "I can't talk about it with anyone at the paper because it involves one of our star reporters. I'm afraid if I hand it to them now, they'll pass my work off and let someone else finish my scoop, send someone else to do the real investigative work. They say it all the time, the *List* is about the five percent, and I'm not in that five percent. I can see them saying, 'Thank you, you've done your part. Mike Bowles will be taking over from here.'"

"But you have to write it," said Payton in a rare moment of encouragement. "You have photos. They can't take those from you. Maybe you were in the right place at the right time in the beginning, but now you've done the legwork. You really haven't told anyone at work about them?"

"Nope. Like I just said, no one, not even the girls on my section. Just you."

"Right. I didn't really believe you. You have a mouth like Hedda Hopper."

This was completely untrue.

"Well, you're the only one I've told."

"Fine," said Payton, conceding. "It makes sense to me. You don't want any help from your colleagues on the story because you don't want to share the glory with them, either."

"That's not why," I replied after a slight pause. The hesitation in my voice surprised me. "I'm not telling anyone because I don't want it to get out. I don't want Olivia to find out. The *Capitolist* isn't a big place and it's full of people who dig up dirt for a living. It's just too risky."

"Whatever you say," said Payton.

We both sat silently in our corners of the world and waited for the other to start talking.

"There's one more thing that's nagging at me, and it might sound a little nuts, but whatever, don't judge me," I said cautiously after a few seconds.

"I would never do that," Payton replied sweetly.

This was bunk. Payton loved to judge me. When I was in my first pony show, when I was six, she jumped up from the risers and screamed, "Number four forty-eight is disqualified for being fat!" and was then escorted to the parking lot by my father. I weighed forty pounds at the time.

"Well, Olivia's husband, Sandro, is this incredible Mexican guy. Well, I think he's Mexican. Let's say Central American to be safe. Handsome, charismatic. Just the full package. But here she is having an affair with a staunchly anti-immigration, terribly conservative senator from Arizona. I think she first got involved with him because she was reporting on immigration legislation. But then she's married to Sandro. It doesn't seem to add up."

"Why? Don't you remember 'Viva Bush' and all that? She could be a Republican. Plus, she's just having an affair with him, not writing policy. Libidos aren't swayed by voting habits."

"You clearly don't live here," I said, stretching my legs out on the window seat.

I heard Payton clanging dishes around. She mumbled something in Spanish and announced that she would be talking to me from the pool area. "It makes sense to me," she declared. "You're married to a blonde, you cheat with a brunette. Your wife is a tiny gnome, you cheat with a giant. You get what I'm saying. You want what you can't have. If I cheated on Buck, I would probably choose a man who resembled a baby carrot."

"You're going to cheat on Buck?"

"No, you idiot. He would shoot me. Or, alternatively, he could just sit on my head. He's still over two hundred pounds. It's like being married to a whale."

Her theory wasn't a bad one. Olivia had young, hot, and handsome. Now she wanted old, rich, powerful, and old.

"Or maybe her husband knows about her affair," Payton speculated.

"No. Not Sandro," I replied. "He would never stand for something like that. He seems really decent."

"Please," she said. "You don't know him at all. You're just smitten and talking like an idiot."

Of course I was. I had never been more attracted to a man. I had uploaded the video of Sandro at the White House Correspondents' Dinner and now fell asleep to a still image of his face.

"I like this kerfuffle of yours," said Payton. I could hear her lighting a cigarette with a flick of a match. "It's nice to hear that you're finally doing something interesting up there. Mom told me about your job and it sounds mind-numbing. All that tweeting. It's for people with low IQs and ADD. But a scandalous affair, that's much sexier."

"Yeah, *sex* is the right word."

"Was it crazy raunchy stuff?" asked Payton, never the shy one.

"Well, kind of," I said honestly. "But that's not what shocked me. It was their intimacy that freaked me out." As I said it, I realized it was their closeness that was confusing me. "There's something between them. Something pretty intense."

"Gross," said Payton, inhaling a mouthful of tobacco. "Intimacy is highly overrated. Still, keep me posted. And by posted, I don't mean call me on a daily basis. Just send me an email every once in a while. I'll get back to you when I can. If I can. Goodbye now."

"You're acting odd," Julia said to me the next day over our three-minute lunch eaten in front of our black Dell computers. "What's up? Are you interviewing other places?" She leaned over our short Plexiglas desk divider and frowned at me. "Because you're not allowed to leave me."

Julia and I had made a pact when we first became friends about the way we would leave the *Capitolist*. We had no grand plans to dart out of there anytime soon; something about the horrible hours and terrible pay was keeping us in our seats. But we agreed that when we did leave, it had to be within a month of each other.

Probably notified that his employees were having fun by some internal spying system, Hardy came to my desk and stared at the top of my head. "What's with your hair," he asked. It was really more of a statement than a question.

"What's with *your* hair?" I asked, flicking my intricate fishtail braid over my shoulder and looking at his weird spongy curls.

Instead of answering me, he put the glossy proofs of the next day's paper on my desk. "I don't like this sentence," he said, pointing to my third paragraph in a piece about the rapper Common's new book. "It's too late to change it now, design will kill us. But I just wanted you to know that I don't like it."

How sweet. Let's not forget the fact that he edited the piece and could have changed it then. But no. He let it go into design and then publicly announced it was despicable.

"Thanks for pointing it out, Hardy," I said as amicably as I could.

Julia made vomiting sounds as he walked away, then lurched for her ringing phone and eased into a conversation with a source. She twirled the emerald ring on her right hand and typed up a series of short sentences with her left. Her years at the *Capitolist* had made her such an ambidextrous multitasker that she'd probably learned to pee standing up to save time.

I had started checking the 175 news sources on my RSS feed when the newsroom loudspeaker crackled on. Upton, when brought on two years ago, had had his speakerphone wired to the entire floor so that he could boom news to everyone at once when he felt a burning desire to echo in our ears like the voice of God.

"Troops. Let's join in the usual place in five minutes," he said. The newsroom reverberated with murmurs of "why?" An all-editorial meeting usually meant we were tooting our own incredibly well-greased horn for something we'd done. Did we have a new big-name columnist? Did someone break a huge story? Or perhaps the *Wall Street Journal* had bought the *Washington Post* and everyone at the latter had been fired. Another thing we were all asked to celebrate as a group was the failure of other news outlets. So maybe the *Post* had accidentally published porn and we all were going to have a champagne toast in honor of their stupidity.

Sadly, it had nothing to do with adult film. It had to do with a story about a politician's shady trip to Eastern Europe, broken by one of our own.

"And we salute Christine Lewis, who broke the story," said

Upton as all the reporters, producers, editors, and copy editors surrounded him and cheered. We craned our necks to look for the girl being heralded for her investigative skills. She popped up next to Upton with red cheeks and a big smile. "She happened to be online at three A.M. on Saturday when she noticed a tweet from an Albanian underground blogger," said Upton with pride.

While I had to put my hand over my mouth to stop either bile or laughter from exploding out, no one else seemed to be surprised at this Albanian blogger detail. I wanted to scream, "Only perverts and those obeying Singapore Standard Time should be on Twitter at three A.M.!" but I didn't. At the *Capitolist*, what Christine did was not just normal: it was heavily applauded. We should all be looking to the former Eastern Bloc for sources.

Still raising an imaginary glass, Upton kept babbling. "At the rate she's going, Christine could become the next . . ." He paused to think about it and then, letting his mouth spread into a slow smile, said, ". . . the next Olivia Campo!" Everyone around him started clapping encouragingly and I looked around for Olivia—who was now noticeably absent.

"It takes a village called the *Capitolist* to get a story like this done, and you should all be thrilled to be a part of it," Upton concluded, smoothing back his blond mane.

It was really high time for scientists to discover the *Capitolist*. There were great experiments on mind control to be done.

"What was she doing trolling Twitter at three A.M.? What a humongous loser," said Isabelle. She had stayed at her desk to keep writing an article about how to choose a State Dinner menu. "You don't even want to know what I was doing at three A.M.," she said when we sat back down again. "Okay, I'll tell you. I was having sex with a *Wall Street Journal* reporter with mild Asperger's syndrome. There, I said it."

"Was it Charlie Stein?" asked Alison, naming one of the *Journal*'s Washington correspondents.

"Obviously," said Isabelle.

"That's repulsive," said Julia, replying to emails on her Black-Berry while talking.

"Repugnant," added Libby.

"What were you doing?" Isabelle asked Libby with a wounded look.

"I was on a date with that petite man from Fox News. It sucked. We kissed and he called me by the wrong name, twice. But at least I wasn't on Twitter. I really don't envy that girl's job, though," said Libby. "She basically has to squash her blood-shot little eyeballs to a computer every second of the day, and then when she finds breaking White House news, she has to write it up, coherently, in five minutes. I would rather be an un-dertaker."

Libby looked at Christine, all twenty-four years of her, now having a tête-à-tête with Upton. "At my first company barbecue she poured an entire pitcher of Diet Sprite on her lap and she didn't even flinch. She just sat there dripping while bugs landed on her and kept filing a story on her BlackBerry. It was amaz-ing."

"I remember that," said Julia. "I bet she gets an intense raise after this one."

"You think?" said Libby. "I've never gotten a raise."

"None of us have," said Julia, sighing. "We're not supposed to talk about money," she added, looking at me. "It's in our con-tracts. But we all do."

I nodded, pretending the *List* rules were pasted in my wallet like the Ten Commandments.

"But she's definitely going to get a raise. I heard that they're not hiring anyone to fill Nicholas Wiik's old job and that they're just having Christine, Olivia, Mike, Tim, Jason, and the rest of the White House team ramp it up."

"I heard that, too," added Libby.

"I thought Nicholas Wiik still worked here? I saw him kicking the Coke machine last week," I said. Nicholas was one of the only White House reporters familiar with the words *please* and *thank you*. He even apologized when he realized I was behind him during his soda machine attack.

"Yeah, he worked here last week," said Libby. "But they fired him last month. His last day was Friday."

They had fired a White House reporter? Fired? I didn't remember him throwing tomatoes at the president or printing a love letter to North Korea in the paper. What cardinal sin had he committed to get the ax? I asked Libby and she just smiled at me like I was a child trying desperately to shove the square peg through the round hole.

"He didn't *do* anything," she explained. "He just wasn't aggressive enough for the White House beat. Nick never got great scoops and he didn't produce as much as the rest of them, even Christine, and she's the most junior."

"So they fired him?"

"Suggested he leave," said Libby. "They don't like to say 'fired' here. They just tell people this isn't the right place for them and ask them if they're not better suited to another publication, like *Tiger Beat* magazine. Then they suggest they scat within a few weeks. Let's call it fired, without the bad press."

Oh God. That was totally going to happen to me. It was like something out of sorority hazing where the house president, a girl who usually resembled my sister, told a hopeful freshman that she was better suited to the fat girl sorority.

We all looked at Christine Lewis, ten years younger and willing to work harder and longer than Nicholas Wiik.

"You know, that child probably makes double what we do, so she should be on Twitter at three o'clock in the morning," Julia offered, spinning around. "If she wants to sacrifice her one-night-stand years for this machine, that's her choice. I give fifteen hours a day to this place. I'm not working Saturdays."

Libby looked at her and laughed. "You work Saturdays every week! Even when Hardy tells you not to, you work. You hate it, but you love it really."

It was true. She did work every Saturday. And most Sundays. Her BlackBerry had a magenta loop on the back so she could attach it to her hand while she drove.

"You know what he forgot to mention?" said Isabelle, tying back her freshly cut hair. "That it was her birthday on Saturday, too."

"It was not," I said. If I ever had to look at Twitter during the deep dark hours on my day of birth, I think I would call for the executioner. I celebrated my last birthday scantily clad in Punta del Este. I was not going to go from naked bonfires to Twitter trolling in one short year.

"I'm dead serious," said Isabelle. "Our birthdays are two days apart, and last week I asked her what she was doing for hers, which happened to fall on a Saturday. She said, 'Working late looking for 2012 copy.' I said, 'I bet Jason Horowitz can handle that on his own,' and she said, 'I've been doing it straight for thirty days. Why would I stop just because it's the weekend and my birthday?' I mean, why would you stop? Because it's your freaking birthday! At least salute your mother for pushing you out of her loins. She's not doing herself any favors. She should be working on her Match.com profile."

"And what was with the Olivia Campo reference?" I asked Isabelle when Libby and Alison were back at their desks. "Kind of random, no?"

"No way. Upton likes to remind everyone that there's a younger, hungrier, cheaper version of all of us nipping at our heels. Even with Nicholas. They could have kept his firing totally quiet, but they let it leak out little by little." The classic *List* attitude of forcing people to compete internally while living in fear of losing their jobs.

"Upton's been dangling the chief White House correspondent position in front of Olivia for the last year. Maybe he wants her to try harder for it."

"But they would never give that job to Christine," I said incredulously. "She's barely out of college! And Tim Schwartz, who has that job now, is forty."

"Of course they're not going to give it to Christine. Well, probably not. They just like making people nervous, even queen Olivia. The *New York Times* is always trying to poach Tim Schwartz, which everyone knows, except you."

"Right, except me."

Isabelle laughed at my ignorance. "They are. Trust me. Of course, Upton keeps doing whatever it takes to keep Tim but we all know he'll jump sometime soonish. Who wouldn't? It's the *New York Times.*"

"So if he leaves does Olivia get his job?" I asked, trying to sound as disinterested as possible while still keeping Isabelle talking.

"Well, probably," said Isabelle. "But there are plenty of other people here who want it. Mike on the White House team. And obviously Christine. And you know they love having wunderkinds here. They could just pay Tim a ridiculous salary for a few more years and then bump Christine into the job over Olivia's head. I hope they do. She deserves it. Christine's pretty dorky, but at least she's nice."

I couldn't believe it. Did Olivia Campo have to worry about

other reporters nabbing her job? Maybe that's what drove her to start sleeping with Stanton. Maybe she actually lived in a constant state of paranoia and that's why she was so mean.

"God, I love this place. You can just smell the pressure," said Christine, the anointed one, with a grin on her eager little face as she walked away from the last of our colleagues toasting her and moved toward her desk. "There is no newsroom in America as exciting as this one," she said to Tucker Cliff, who was walking with her.

"You're right," he replied, clapping his hands together. The smack of his palms caused us all to look up. "We," he said to Christine, "are on fire."

CHAPTER 12

When Hardy and then Upton had saluted my work on the James Franco story, it was the first time I had ever gotten a pat on the back at the *Capitolist*. Most of the time, the higher-ups only talked to you if you had done something wrong, or as in Nicholas's case, advising you to seek employment elsewhere. You were expected to put your nose to the grindstone and never come up for air, let alone compliments and praise.

But when my first big story broke and I had my hand metaphorically shaken by the top brass, I felt my perspective on the place change. So what if they wanted to use up my youth and energy and spit me out? It's not like they tried to pretend they were anything but a sweatshop. I knew that if I made it over a year, I would come out alive and with a bigger name than I had when I went in. But I began to see that if I decided to go forward with the Olivia story, and if the paper picked me and my scoop over her, my career would be set.

I had never met a woman like Olivia before: one who pushed everyone and everything aside for the sake of success. Girls like her weren't at sisterhood-loving Wellesley, and they certainly weren't at *Town & Country*. She was either going to beat us all or crash and burn. And I had the power to make her burn. If I exposed her affair with Stanton, everyone in the *Capitolist* newsroom would actually know my name. I wouldn't just be the tall blond girl in the back of the room who came from some fashion magazine and smiled too much. I, like Christine, would be the subject of one of Upton's ridiculous staff-wide announcements.

It was the end of spring, which meant Congress was constantly in session, the White House was buzzing and Olivia was almost never in the office. She passed through our building only for reporters' meetings. When she came in, I tried to read her; but as far as I could tell, I was invisible to her.

I had started writing some drafts of what I'd seen that night in Middleburg and the other times I'd spotted Olivia and Stanton together, but I still couldn't fit the pieces of the puzzle together—and now I didn't think I could without Sandro. I'd been avoiding this for the last month—I didn't want to further fuel my obsession. But it was time for the cyber-stalk to begin. I entered his name into Google, took a deep breath, and smacked the return key.

I found a mug shot, which luckily wasn't his. I found a few genealogy trees and decided he was definitely Mexican. And then, after a few days of searching and being thankful to have a LexisNexis account and a telephone with a blocked number function, I saw his name and picture on a committee website for the Organization of American States, a group promoting security, democracy, and human rights with representatives from each of the countries in the Americas. On the site, there was no bio, and there were very few details, but it did disclose that Sandro's next committee meeting was at a Chinatown restaurant called Oyamel on May 30.

I typed the date into my phone and counted down the days.

I had been going to Chinatown with my family since I was old enough to walk. When we were younger and the area had not yet been gentrified, we used to eat at a restaurant called Jun Chen's. It had ducks hanging from the ceiling and smelled like spices and grease. When I was very young and Payton already seemed quite old and was able to command the attention of a whole room, I used to hide under the red and white checkered tablecloths and lean against my father's legs. Everything was different now. I had lived in New York, I had Meryl Streep's cellphone number in my phone, and I had made it back home with my liver intact. In the meantime, Jun Chen's had been replaced by Ann Taylor Loft.

I walked past groups of teenagers shopping along the strip of chain stores and headed to Seventh Street and Oyamel. The hostess told me that the OAS group was currently meeting in the Butterfly Room and that she would be delighted to escort me there. I said I was just going to the bar for a drink, not to worry, and headed alone to the back corner of the restaurant.

I sat there for an hour and a half waiting for the meeting to end, watching people eat and laugh with their significant others. An hour and a half at a bar by yourself translates into becoming rather drunk and distracted. I filed a story sourced entirely from Twitter about a country singer obsessed with Newt Gingrich. She even wrote a song about his full head of hair. I called Elsa and apologized for being a ghost of a friend. She told me she hated me, but was in Miami anyway and forgave my vanishing act. I emailed my mother and suggested our family consume more raw fish. And I texted Payton nothing but a smiley face and didn't bother waiting for a reply.

I was on my third glass of wine and my second order of ceviche when Sandro finally walked out of the restaurant's private room with his OAS colleagues. He looked flawless. Confident and handsome and happy and wearing a suit cut perfectly for his tall frame. I wondered if there was a way I could casually steal his jacket and keep it as a memento of our love. He said a few words to the two men he was with, waved in my direction, and walked over to me.

"It's you. From the White House Correspondents' Dinner. It's good to see you survived the party," he said.

"It's nice to see you again," I replied, trying not to froth at the mouth with sexual energy. Upon closer inspection, his clothes were very classic, very Washington. Creased beige pants, a white shirt tucked in, no tie, and the heavy linen sport jacket that would soon be mine. He wore loafers and had a thin gold wedding band right where it belonged.

"We also met at the skating rink," I said, trying to jog his memory. "You were watching your friend play hockey. You were heading to dinner."

"I remember," he said, smiling. "You looked very wintry, very pretty standing by the rink."

He did? He remembered! And he called me pretty. We were one step closer to engaged.

"Are you having dinner here?" I asked. What I really wanted to ask was "Do you know that your wife is having an affair? With a man twice her age? No? Well she is. And he's a senator. But lucky for you, I'm available." Instead I just looked at him and smiled like a lovestruck idiot.

"No, no, just killing some time before I head home," he said. "I was here for a meeting."

After asking politely if he could join me, he motioned to the bartender to bring him a beer and took the empty seat next to mine.

He took a long sip of Bohemia beer and let out a satisfied sigh. "I needed this," he said with a smile.

We talked about the White House Correspondents' Dinner. We talked about his horrible wife.

"Is she joining you?" I asked innocently. I looked into his handsome face and tried not to lose my cool. He had more stubble than he had had at the dinner. He looked a little tired and extremely sexy. I moved my arm past his and let his shirtsleeve glide across my skin. It felt perfect.

"Oh, no, not Olivia," he said, letting his arm linger next to mine. "She's away for work. She travels a lot. But, sorry, you must know that already."

I nodded and explained that we all got the president's and VP's schedules emailed to us. The article alerts on my BlackBerry had let me know that as the traveling White House pool reporter, she was currently in Ulaanbaatar with the vice president.

"Yes, she does love that about her job," he replied. "I like to travel, too, we just—or I—just have different taste in traveling. I'm from Texas—"

"Are you?" I interrupted him. "I love Texas." This was a lie. I had never been to Texas and knew it only through *Friday Night Lights* reruns and stereotypes. But looking at Sandro, I decided I suddenly loved Texas.

"I'm from the southern part," he explained, "and I've never become much of a city person. But Olivia really wanted to move here. When the *Capitolist* launched, she became obsessed with getting a job there. She always wanted to come work in Washington, ever since we met, but when the *Capitolist* came on the scene, she said it was the only place she would work. I guess she just knew it would be a success; she has a sense about these things. She's really taken to living here, but I still can't get into it. Cities tend to suffocate me a little."

I nodded my head in agreement, though I had actually cried over how much I missed New York at least three times since I'd come home.

"So, what do you do, besides reporting?" Sandro asked me, making easy small talk. "Olivia doesn't do anything but work, so if that's your answer, too, that's okay."

I lust after you. I look at a video I took of you at White House Correspondents' over and over again on my computer. I pause it on your face and try to imagine what you're thinking. What life would be like with you. And then I chase your wife around with a camera. I work on drafts of an eye-opening article starring your naked, cheating spouse. And then I look at your face some more.

"I spend a lot of time with horses," I replied.

"Do you?" he said with laid-back enthusiasm. "I miss animals. I wanted a dog up here, but Olivia nixed that idea. Where do you ride horses?" He took a long sip of beer.

"I ride just outside Washington, in Middleburg, Virginia." I watched his face for any sign of recognition, any knowledge of my hometown and his wife's affair there, but his expression didn't change. "It's a beautiful spot," I continued. "It's like living in the pages of a magazine. I always feel like I'm going to run into Slim Aarons or some descendant of the Kennedys."

"I'm afraid I don't know Mr. Aarons," said Sandro, putting down his nearly empty beer.

"It's okay," I replied. "He's dead anyway."

He laughed at his mistake. "Well, then I guess I'll never get to know him."

Timing my question between well-rehearsed bursts of laughter, I asked him if he worked for the Organization of American States. When he seemed slightly taken aback, I mentioned that there was a sign for the meeting at the front of the restaurant. This was of course another lie. It was a restaurant, not a conference center, but he seemed to believe me.

"I do work for OAS," he said, still looking caught off guard.

"I'm actually from Mexico. I only came to the U.S. for school. With a lot of luck, I ended up in College Station, Texas. Has Olivia mentioned she's from Texas?" he asked.

"I think she has, yes," I said, pretending that Olivia and I had an intimate friendship full of chatter about our girlhood days.

"Olivia and I met down there, in college, and she wasn't much of a city person then, either. But that's all changed now. She's found her calling, and it requires a densely populated area and several telephones. But," he said, wiping his stubbly upper lip, "that woman is amazing. Has been amazing me since day one. She can get anything done. She really can. I just have to show her that doesn't necessarily mean running around chasing the president of the United States."

He was wrong about that. Olivia Campo could not get it all done without chasing the president—and the man many predicted would be the next president.

"She was incredible at A&M. We were very involved in school. Did a lot of international stuff. She helped me navigate that huge place, and we got married during our senior year. That was, let's see . . . that was seven years ago." He smiled like an old man drinking to the memories of youth. "I still think it's funny that she's covering the president," he said. "She always wanted to cover Congress, especially the Senate, but I guess the White House beat is the most prestigious, so she took it. I think her heart is still on the Hill, though. She always said there's far more personality up there by Capitol South than on Pennsylvania Avenue."

I looked up at his square jaw while he motioned for another round of drinks. "Please, let me," he said to the bartender, who added my fourth glass of wine to his tab.

After a long pause, he said, "I like your clothes," looking at my short red sundress, motorcycle boots, and long silk scarf.

"You don't look like you're trying hard to blend in. And why should you." His biceps moved while he spoke. His hair was thick, and I wondered if it felt soft to the touch or just like wires held down by heavy products and gravity.

I wanted to lean over and put my hand on his arms, his legs, everywhere. Maybe it was because my world had shrunk so drastically since I left New York, but I was conscious that I had never been so naturally attracted to someone. Sandro was so uncalculated, so easygoing and charming without knowing he was charming. It was nothing like the lip you got in New York or the careful talk most men delivered here. It was refreshing and I wanted his casual confidence around me all the time. Since I started working at the *List*, most people I met were either pompous or guarded, throwing an "off the record" at the end of every sentence. Hell, even my father said it over breakfast when he called my mother "paranoid and high-strung." But Sandro somehow seemed above all that.

"I like sitting here, talking to you," he said after we were both quiet for a minute. "Olivia is always traveling. I feel like I haven't talked to someone in a while."

In a rush of excitement from his compliment, I moved my leg and ran it slowly against his.

He let it linger for a few seconds and then said, "I'm sorry. I must be in your way." He scooted his stool back, pretending not to notice my blatant come-on, but didn't move his leg off of mine for a few seconds more. God that felt good.

What was I doing? He was married. I was working on ruining his wife's career. I couldn't act like a salivating tween. I moved my legs back under the stool and smiled coolly.

"No problem at all," I said, cutting off his apology. "I like talking to you, too. We should do it again."

"Yes, we should," he replied. He was polite but not overly

flirtatious. But then he leaned forward and ran his right hand through my hair. From my hairline, all the way back, he let his fingers comb slowly through it.

"You had something there," he said, smiling.

Oh my God. How embarrassing. I probably had an entire squid from my ceviche sitting on my head during our whole conversation.

"I did?" I asked, feeling myself turn the color of a ripe tomato. This was clearly punishment for sins in a past life.

He stepped down from the bar stool and left some money on the bar as a tip. "No. Not really. I just felt like doing that. You have very nice hair." While I pinched my thigh to make sure I was alive and not in *The Matrix*, he put his hand on my shoulder like the night we met.

"It was very nice to run into you like this. For the third time," he added with a smile. "Are you staying? Or can I walk you to your car?"

My car. Oh God. Why had I driven my actual car here? Why hadn't I used my monthly salary to rent a Bentley for a few hours, or at least borrowed one of my parents' much nicer cars? Maybe I could just stand next to a fancy parked car with Virginia plates and pretend it was mine. Something built in the latter half of the past decade. But Sandro seemed like the kind of man who tapped the roof after you got in and made sure you made it off safely. I loved him despite his horrible wife; maybe he could love me despite my ancient car?

We left Oyamel and headed down Seventh Street toward my clunker. My scalp, where Sandro had run his hand through my hair, was tingling. I walked close to him. Though my boots had a slight heel, he was still a few inches taller than me and I looked up at him as he talked about his plans to visit his parents the next time Olivia was out of town. I was about to recommend he visit the Goodstone Inn with a large shotgun in hand instead, when we got to my embarrassing car. It was parked right in front of a cute white Mini Cooper and I slowed down in front of it, hoping Sandro would just give me a good-night French kiss, a little butt grope, and run off. But instead, after I admitted to owning the oldest car in the world, he took my keys, opened the door, helped me in, and didn't mention one word about it being built during the early days of Bush 43's administration.

So how did a girl with no manners, skin pigment, or ethics land not only someone who looked like a model and had the carriage of Cary Grant, but also a United States senator? Was Olivia secretly reading *Cosmo*'s "The Secret to Getting Any Guy" articles in the White House bathroom? Was the girl swaddled up in poly-cotton blends actually a tantric sex master?

I wanted to start LexisNexising Sandro and Olivia from a public computer. I didn't trust my laptop—IP addresses were too easy to trace—and work was obviously out of the question. On Monday afternoon, I scheduled time at the Library of Congress. I had no idea how I was going to get out of work for two hours and go to the library. I was going to have to lie. Or pretend someone had sent me a tip that a celebrity was at the library having an academic renaissance and I was going to check it out.

My karma took some major blows after I told Hardy that I was running to Union Station because country singer Martina McBride was doing a whistle-stop tour. She actually was, but I had zero intention of going. My friend John, the best paparazzo in D.C., was covering it and had promised to send me a few sound bites to get me through, no questions asked. So I headed up the stairs of the beautiful marble library, knowing I had precisely one hundred and twenty minutes before I started getting a flood of BlackBerry messages harassing me about my whereabouts.

I walked through the main reading room in the Thomas Jefferson Building, with the half-moon windows and rows of mahogany desks and reference books, and headed toward the newspaper and periodical reading room. The only starting points I had with Sandro, beyond his name, were his studies at Texas A&M, his work at OAS, and his Mexican provenance. Olivia, I figured, must have worked at the college paper.

I knew that she, like me, was twenty-eight, and he must be around the same age, which would put them starting school around 2000.

Texas A&M's newspaper was called the *Battalion*. On a microfilm reader, I searched every masthead since 1998 and never saw Olivia's name. Not even as a contributor. Could she really not have written for her college paper? The girl who took a wrecking ball to her colleagues to come out on top? I had expected to see her name in the editor-in-chief slot. From print, I moved to photos. Maybe she had been photographed as part of an activity? Young Dictators Club? Future Homewreckers of America? Or maybe Sandro had been voted sexiest man in A&M's history?

I started in 1998 again and prepared to look at every sheet of every paper printed for the next six years. Black-and-white photos with long captions shined brightly under the light of the machine. Smiling face after smiling face looked up at me until I was so numb to the unlined faces of youth that I doubted I would be able to recognize my targets.

I needed to put myself back together, let my eyes readjust. I put my bag next to the machine to lay claim to my space and walked toward the stacks to stretch my legs. I was in the music history section. I let my fingers drift on the leather-bound sheet music of Rachmaninov, Benjamin Britten, Clara Schumann. I missed studying. Professional journalism was so focused on quick hits, short bites that could be consumed in mere minutes while waiting for the subway. No one assigned long pieces anymore because no one read them. My college thesis on Edith Wharton's and Henry James's road trips was eighty-five pages long, which now seemed like an impossible amount of pages. I'm sure if anyone at the *List* attempted to write more than two thousand words they were immediately let go for having a poor grasp of the demands of new media. When I left *Town & Country*, I had grand visions of penning articles that would go through five drafts before they went to press, sitting down with my editor for hours to make sure every piece ended with a bon mot. Instead, I typed articles on a BlackBerry and all I did when I reached the last line was cheer.

That was at least a sliver of the reason I was letting the Olivia/Stanton affair consume me: it couldn't be solved in an hour or less and then tweeted about immediately. It was a steady stream of work, of pushing myself to do and think things that were difficult.

I went back to the microfiche machine, flipped through hundreds more photos, and stopped on November 21, 2003. That was the date I finally saw Olivia's picture in the paper. And when I saw the caption, I decided it was worth the wait.

Her hair was shorter then. Just above her shoulders. But she was with Sandro, clutching hands with him and another student. The caption of the photo read, "Olivia Campo, Sandro Pena and Paul Martinez lead students in a march for the Students for Immigration Solidarity Campaign," which Google quickly confirmed was a college branch of a national immigrants' rights organization.

So maybe Olivia was indeed the Mata Hari of a left-wing immigrants' rights group, trying to sway the opposition's policy by giving Stanton access to her naked body. It was possible. But it was also possible that it was just a coincidence. Plenty of Wellesley girls I knew had protested against the World Bank and eaten vegan chicken for every meal in college, and now they worked at Credit Suisse and demanded that their beef be from Kobe. People changed.

The other intriguing article I found was from 2005, the year Sandro and Olivia graduated from A&M. It was their wedding announcement. Maybe in Texas it was normal to get married before graduation, but to my East Coast eyes it looked like time travel. It also would have kept him on U.S. soil.

"Seniors Sandro Pena and Olivia Campo were married on March 29 in the All Faiths Chapel. The couple met during orientation week freshman year in Neeley Hall. The two plan to live in Corpus Christi after graduation." There was no picture, which was good, because I think my heart might have broken if I had seen their wedding day.

I forced myself to go to sleep that night without looking at Sandro's smooth, tan face on my computer screen. And when James texted me and asked me to meet him at Union Station Friday after work, I said yes.

As the workweek came to a close, I walked up Constitution Avenue toward Union Station with confidence. James was a very nice, very normal, and totally single guy. I could like him. I should like him. For some crazy reason, he seemed to like me.

When I arrived, he was already in line for the Old Town Trolley, the green and orange relic that took tourists around the city and pumped out historical information in a dozen different languages. "Look who it is," he said, pulling me over to him by the hand and giving me a kiss on the cheek as if we were about to pose for a prom photo. He was wearing a crisp spring suit and a light green Vineyard Vines tie and looked happy to be standing in what was left of the day's sunshine. He moved a strand of my hair out of my face, pushed my aviator sunglasses down my nose, and said, "I'm glad you said yes."

I laughed, grateful for a moment of levity. I had ignored three calls from James that week and wasn't sure how to proceed. But this was good. He felt easy and friendly and unmarried. "You know, I've never been on one of these things before," I said.

"And why would you have," said James, motioning to the ticket salesman. "You grew up around here. You never had to pay attention to the city."

Five minutes later, we were installed on a small wooden bench, chugging toward the Capitol. I looked at the building with its perfect dome covering an iron frame, and for the first time since I had started working at the *Capitolist*, I saw it through the eyes of a tourist.

"What's it like to work in politics?" I asked James as the historic building disappeared behind us.

"It's fun," he said honestly. "Lots of smart people. I've always been a Republican, so it's nice to have that continuity in life. And you feel like you're making a difference. I like helping to shape our message, fixing misperceptions about us and bringing the attention to our great candidates."

"Never mind, let's not talk about politics," I said, putting my arm on the side of the bench and letting the wind turn my hair into a tangled mess.

"It's not that bad a city, is it," said James.

"No, it's not so bad when you look at it like this," I replied. I turned to smile at him and before I could protest, he took my face in his hands and kissed me. "I like you," he said, still cradling my cheeks in his palms. "I don't know if you like me, since I haven't seen you since our amazing first date and you haven't answered any of my calls until two days ago. But I like you anyway. Thanks for coming with me."

A kiss in a trolley with the Capitol behind us. There were worse things. I let James talk about work and his friends and his summer plans and let my mind clear for a while. I hadn't felt this relaxed since the day I drove down the long stretch of highway from New York to Virginia.

When we got out of the trolley, it was drizzling, and he walked me to my car while holding his suit jacket over my head. He kissed me again and held on to my waist until I smiled, squirmed away, and promised I would see him soon.

The rain stopped by the time I was through the city traffic. The days were getting longer, and it was easier to navigate the two small, hilly roads that led into town. I saw the lights of East Washington Street in the distance and I opened all the car windows and the sunroof and let the wind continue to ruin my hair.

As I drove slowly past the historic gas station on the Middleburg line, I saw someone familiar sitting on the hood of a pale SUV. He motioned with his hands, trying to wave me in, and I laughed when I saw it was James. I did a U-turn on the damp road and pulled my car in next to his.

The gas station was faintly illuminated. I got out and stood in front of him. He stayed where he was, leaning back on his hood and smiling. "I decided I wasn't quite ready for our date to end," he said, pushing himself off the car.

"Are you serious?" I replied, amused and genuinely surprised.

"I thought you needed to know just how patient and persistent I am. You've seen patient; now I'm showing you persistent.

And I figured I could catch you here, since everyone has to stop at this light."

"Late-night gas station stalking is normal to you," I said.

"I'm not gas station stalking. I'm Adrienne stalking. Adrienne who is a very, very slow driver stalking. I thought you might find it charming."

"I don't," I replied. It was a little charming, but I wasn't ready to admit it.

The wind started blowing again. By now, instead of looking chic and polished, I looked like I was auditioning for the musical *Hair*.

"You have very nice hair. I like the way it flies around your face," said James, looking at me standing there in the wind. I had to keep my hands on the hem of my dress to keep it from flying up. Without skipping a beat, he said, "Judging from how you almost never return my messages and have only gone out with me twice since I saved you at the Hay-Adams, I'm getting the vibe that you're not in love with me yet. And I think you should be. I'm a great guy, which you'll realize soon enough."

"I will?"

"Oh yeah. And until then, I thought I would just convince you by being incredibly romantic and driving to your quaint little town. Clearly, it's working. I can tell that I'm wooing you."

"It might be working a little," I said, walking closer. "But take me away from the empty gas station and I might be a little more wooable."

"Okay," he said, reaching for my hand. "Let's go to the Red Fox Inn."

"You know what that is?" I laughed.

"Sure. I've been doing my research. I plan on spending a lot more time out here."

He opened his car door, promising we would come back later for mine, and we headed down the slick road to the stone inn. He had his radio on C-SPAN, but I changed it immediately to the Coffee House station and hummed along to the strum of an acoustic guitar.

James turned to me at the next stop sign. "You should like me," he declared. "I can feel you hesitating. Maybe you think I'm too good-looking for you. Too successful."

He smiled as I raised my eyebrows as high as they could go without causing my forehead to wrinkle.

"But really. Seriously. I'm a very nice guy. Call my sister, she can vouch for me. I never lit her hair on fire or tore off her dolls' heads. I'm a great big brother."

That was more than I could say for my sister, pyro extraordinaire.

"I like you," he said again, looking down into my embarrassed face before he put his foot back on the gas. "A lot. I will do my best to make you ludicrously happy if you just give me a chance."

I turned up Jackson Browne's "Running on Empty," now playing on the radio.

"Okay," I said evenly under Danny Kortchmar's guitar strums.

"Okay?"

"Sure. Why not. I've already kissed you on a tourist trolley. I might as well go out with you a few more times."

When we pulled up to the hotel, we parked on the street outside and he walked around to open my door. He put his hand on the small of my back to help me down and led me out the door and into the hotel.

When he ordered red wine, and I asked for tea, he looked at me with surprise.

"You might not believe me—and considering the one-woman

show I put on in your apartment, I would understand why—but I really am sober most of the time."

"I believe you," he replied. "I know what you do for a living. I doubt you would be good at your job if you were a raging drunk."

No, instead I had the kind of job that turned you into a raging drunk when all was said and done. I imagined that my post-*Capitolist* years would be filled with a wine cooler addiction and lots of Jungian psychoanalysis.

While my mind wandered, James interrupted me with a bash of his fist on the table. "Wait! I know that guy. Seriously, this world is too small. That's Chip Mortimer. He was a fraternity brother of mine at Ole Miss."

I turned around, and we both looked at a man with sunburned cheeks wearing a brown linen shirt. He was built like a brick house.

"Are there really people in the world named Chip?" I asked.

"Sure," said James, like it was right out of the Bible. "You want to meet him? He's a real live person named Chip. You can shake his hand and everything."

"No, I'll pass," I said, motioning to the waiter for more hot water. "I'm not really in a small-talk mood."

"Then what are we doing?" James asked.

"Big talk. Full sentences."

After he came back from exchanging hellos, we ordered our meals and I allowed myself one glass of wine.

"I can't believe Chip is out here," he said to the roll of my eyes.

"It's not *that* far away! It takes more time to drive from the baseball stadium to American University than it does to come out here."

"Depends who's driving," said James. "Man, I miss Chip. He was fun. He was such a slut when he worked on the Hill."

"A slut? Like how?"

"I just mean that he worked for everyone. He worked for Manning, Hart, Getz, Stanton. He's a lobbyist for Pfizer now. I guess their offices are out in Virginia or something."

I let his lineage sink in, the name Stanton ringing in my ear, and reached for my drink.

When we left the restaurant and James took me back to my car, he asked me if I was sober enough to kiss him.

Standing outside of his big, expensive SUV, I said, "I'm sober enough to tightrope walk."

"Good," he said, taking my hand and pulling me toward him. He kissed me and put his arms around me to keep my clothes from flying up in the wind.

"This is perfect, this is absolutely perfect," he said, taking a break from biting my bottom lip.

In the next few minutes, we were back in his car, like high schoolers with no place to go. Our clothes were off, our hands were everywhere. And then, because I didn't want to be obsessed with Sandro Pena anymore, I slept with James.

It was only a five-minute drive home from the gas station. When James kissed me good night and I fought off his offers of trailing my car home, I flew through the quiet streets and parked my car on the graveled drive. I ran inside to call my sister from a landline. I wished I'd confided in someone with a little bit more empathy, but everyone else was too close. Somehow Payton and her unrelenting pessimism and inky heart called my name.

"You again," she said when she picked up the phone. "I can't say I'm surprised. I suppose I'm just going to have to keep my nights free from now on just in case you need a shoulder to whimper upon."

"Payton! Just listen to me," I said, explaining the night's events. "I feel like I'm going to do something stupid. Actually, I just did something pretty stupid. I slept with James, in the back of his car, of all places, and I feel inches away from throwing myself at Sandro."

I heard Payton exhale cigarette smoke into the South American air. She still allowed herself two cigarettes a week when Buck wasn't home to chide her.

"So you had sex. Big deal. People have been doing it since genitals were invented. Nothing to fret about, unless this was the very first time you had sex."

"No, Payton, thank you very much. I've been having sex for a decade."

It actually had been over a decade since Jeff Grant had suggested we take off our clothes and "just do it" at his parents' Christmas party in Middleburg. Like tonight, I had idiotically said yes.

"As for Sandro . . ." Payton interrupted my sexual reminiscing. "Let's not dramatize that, either. I slept with a slew of married men before I started dating Buck," she admitted casually. "One . . . two, maybe three. It won't kill you if you do, too."

She had? Was my sister secretly a dominatrix for hire by the hour? Because with her Machiavellian personality and bra size, she would make a hell of a good one.

"But you were twenty when you met Buck!" I said like a missionary shaking a Bible at a girl in a short skirt.

"We didn't all go to the convent known as Wellesley College," she replied. "I went to school in the city. And I didn't meet Buck until spring break junior year."

She had indeed. She had gone to Columbia and become best friends with some soul-crushing heir to the Hearst fortune and spent a lot of time dancing downtown and making other girls feel inferior and fat. When Payton came back for Christmas after her first semester, the Virginia prep school girl was gone and Manhattan Payton had arrived. She was terrifying. Money in Middleburg meant your parents bought you a Jeep Grand Cherokee for your sixteenth birthday and you had your own horse— pretty darn nice by anyone's standards. Except spoiled New Yorkers. All of a sudden it was dancing on tables with hedge fund managers and Fashion Week wardrobes and having someone's parents send their chauffeur to take you to the Hamptons. I was fifteen years old that August when Payton went to college, still happily singing along to Shania Twain and wearing J. Crew sundresses. By December, she had become a skinny space alien with really nice accessories and I was left even further behind.

But, as is Payton's way, she graduated summa cum laude. Her advisor actually wept in front of my family over her thesis on warhorses. I hated Payton sometimes. Most of the time, actually. It really would have done a lot for my ego if she blurted out that she used to pour hot wax on businessmen's crotches for a hundred bucks an hour.

"You remember Eleanor Hearst, of course," said Payton in her breathy voice. The one she put on when she wanted people to actually like her.

Of course I did. She or some relative of hers was in every issue of *Town & Country*. Once I convinced my friend in the graphics department to Photoshop a large toucan attacking her at a fund-raiser for the Bronx Zoo, but we were too chicken to print it in the end.

"Well, Eleanor ran with this incredibly rich group one summer. They were all from Monaco or something like that. They had long names and great cars, and I slept with one of them. Maybe two. And I learned that an older, powerful, married man can be a real aphrodisiac."

I laughed out loud for probably a minute and a half. "You sound like an idiot. If moneyed geriatrics are such an aphrodisiac then why did you marry Buck? He's gorgeous. And technically younger than you are."

"I know," she said. "I grew up. Grown-ups don't need an aphrodisiac. We need a strong man to kill bugs."

Ah, love. "That's really depressing, Payton. You married a man because he can swat flies."

"Didn't you call for my help? You better be nice to me."

She was right. Payton was most definitely one of Satan's handmaidens, but she had one sterling quality: she could keep a secret.

"I need you to come home," I admitted. "For at least a week or two. I feel like I'm sitting on something big, and I'm too involved to act straight on it. I'm sleeping with James when I really want to be sleeping with Sandro. And those Olivia-screwing-Stanton pictures are still burning a hole in my soul, but I haven't done anything with them yet because now I'm wondering if an immigrants' rights group is pushing her into bed with him. Either way, I think that while she was busy wrinkling the sheets, she fell in love. I'm confused—I need your help."

It was probably the words "I need your help," that did it. Words I hadn't said to my sister since 1998 while hallucinating on a potent mix of THC and magic mushrooms.

To my surprise, Payton said, "I'll think about it. I'm exceptionally busy. But maybe I can come in a few weeks." Before I could thank her, she said, "If I decide to come, you must send a car to pick me up at the airport and you must make sure it doesn't have any air freshener in it. At all. It makes me gag, especially those horrific Christmas-tree-shaped ones. They're more effective at making me retch than a finger down the throat." She laughed, because Payton *would* find bulimia hilarious, and said, "Also, tell Mom and Dad that I refuse to sleep in a barn with my little sister."

CHAPTER 13

Sleeping with James had been a huge mistake. I once had sex with someone so he would stop speaking, so I wasn't worried about my pristine honor, but it still felt like one of my stupider decisions. I wasn't lusting after James—I was watching a video of Sandro almost every night and studying his face, the way he laughed, the way he spoke. But he was married, and James was not. If I had to choose one to sleep with, I guess I'd picked the right one. But it didn't feel that way.

I needed to see Sandro again. The way he had touched my hair at the restaurant was so intimate, such a clear sign that he was interested. But I wanted more than just another round of footsie. If I could talk to him alone again, build some familiarity between us, maybe I could figure out how much he knew about Stanton and Olivia. It was hard to imagine Sandro sleeping with his wife if he was au courant of her weekend activities, but maybe he was familiar with the senator's policies. He might be aware that Olivia spent time with Stanton, might even encourage it, but not know that it was naked time.

I pictured myself alone with Sandro. I could just drop the name Hoyt Stanton and see how he reacted. Maybe he would tell me everything he knew and then caress my neck with his tongue.

Finding him seemed next to impossible. Besides his band of hockey-loving Canadians, I didn't know his friends, hobbies, favorite restaurants, anything. I finally realized that one thing I *could* find out was his address. The *List*'s office manager, Megan, had on her desk a binder containing all of our personal information.

The next day at work I walked up to Megan and prepared to awkwardly camp out at her workstation until I got Olivia's address.

"Oh, hi, Adrienne," Megan said sweetly. She had come to the *List* from a law firm and still seemed very far away from the rat race of journalism. She said "good morning" and "thank you" and other niceties that were generally blacklisted in *List* land.

"Hey!" I said, with far too much excitement. I picked up a squishy toy turtle she had on her desk and started poking at its eyeballs.

"I got that at a National Geographic party. Fun, isn't it," she said.

It *was* kind of fun. I clearly needed some children's toys on my desk. Focus! I put the turtle down and turned to walk away, but quickly spun back around. I hoped my little dance move looked natural; I had just practiced it in the handicap bathroom in front of the full-length mirror.

"Now I remember why I came over here," I said. "My neighbor brought over my paycheck stub yesterday. She said it came to her house. So I just wanted to check to see if you guys have the right address for me."

"Oh, that's weird. Sorry about that," said Megan, reaching for a red binder and opening it on her desk.

I quickly ran up behind her, like this was the most interesting task in the world, and watched as she flipped the pages. Brown, Campo, they were pretty close alphabetically. I thanked all that was holy for making my last name start with a *B* and prayed that our names would be on the same page.

Megan quickly flipped to my listing. There I was. Adrienne Brown, then Jeffrey Butler, then Olivia Campo: 2797 Church Street, NW.

When I came to, I realized Megan was asking me about life in Middleburg.

"Oh, I just love it," I told her. "It's beautiful. Everyone has a horse and a dog and there's lots of tweed. You should come visit sometime."

"But isn't the commute horrible?" she asked.

Yes, the commute was horrible. I was almost fluent in German I spent so much time listening to Rosetta Stone in the car. And D.C. drivers were enraged lunatics with lead feet.

"It's really not that bad," I said, smiling. "I can drive and type at the same time now."

"Oh, sure, of course," she said, putting the binder away.

2797 Church Street. I knew exactly where that was. Church was a small, cute street just a few blocks east of Dupont Circle.

Since Olivia always traveled with the president, whose schedule was emailed to everyone at the *Capitolist* every day, it was easy to keep tabs on her. I knew that POTUS was going to be in Detroit and then Madison for the next two days, so I didn't have to worry about running into her. I could just loiter on the block and wait to see Sandro.

The problem with Church Street, I realized when I got there that night, was that it was entirely residential. I couldn't just sit outside of Starbucks and pretend to be reading instead of stalking. There were houses, and there was a church, and that was it. I was wearing a bright magenta dress that day. If Sandro came outside, he was going to see me: I was like a traffic cone on a gray street. After circling the block six times, I found a parking space on P Street big enough for my submarine of a car and walked over to Church. It was 7:15 P.M. I had no concept of Sandro's hours, but very few jobs in Washington released you before 7 P.M.

I found 2797, a very nice, dark gray, four-story town house with a bright green door. The roof was peaked, unlike the rest of the houses on that road, and there were vertical rows of pretty bay windows.

Olivia was clearly making four times my salary! We were roughly the same age, and she lived here. With a gorgeous husband. It was so unfair. She didn't even appreciate it. She spent her Saturday nights having sex in Middleburg. I spent the majority of my Saturday nights not having sex in Middleburg. What an ingrate.

I walked past the house, trying to look natural. I didn't want to leave the street for fear of missing Sandro, so I went to the church. I was a somewhat practicing Episcopalian. They weren't going to turn me away.

Or maybe they were. The doors were locked. I was being rejected by God. Which made perfect sense, since I was using the church as my cover while I stalked a married man and tried to get information out of him. I sank onto the stone steps to contemplate my poor life choices of late.

"They only have evening service on Thursday, I'm afraid," said a voice behind me. It was a woman with dark hair, graying in the front, and a distinct Brooklyn accent.

"Oh, okay. Thank you," I said, turning around.

The woman, who was forty-five or so, gave me a big smile, probably because I looked like a supercommitted Christian on the verge of a religious breakdown. When she was twenty feet past me, I moved away from the church door and walked down the block. Maybe I could just sit on the stoop of a house and pretend I lived there. If the owner came home, I would just apologize and say I had the wrong address.

I crossed the street and sat on the stairs of a ghastly bright red town house and tried to look natural. All the lights were off in the house, so it had to be empty. I wasn't worried. In my dress, I even kind of blended in with the wall. Maybe no one would notice me.

Just before eight o'clock, when I was starting to get both uncomfortable and paranoid that I was going to get picked up for squatting, I saw Sandro. He was walking in from the north side of the church, and he was alone. He was carrying his suit jacket and wearing gray pants and a pink button-up shirt with the sleeves rolled up. He looked handsome, but tired and certainly not in the mood to receive an unexpected visit from me.

When he was a block away from his elegant house, I walked down the steps of the house across the street and headed up the block toward him. I wanted him to see me, smile, walk over to me. I wanted it all to be natural. We would fall in love organically, and he would leave his cheating wife for me as if it were as inevitable as the ebb and flow of the tide.

But he didn't even notice me. I had to call his name. He looked startled, like I had woken him out of a comforting daydream.

"Adrienne. What are you doing here?" he asked, not sounding particularly happy.

"I . . ." What was I going to say? I had expected him to look a bit more excited. At Oyamel, he had said he liked talking to me, that we should do it again. And he said I was pretty and touched my hair! So here I was, ready and able to conversate and interrogate. Or procreate. Whatever he wanted.

"Do you know that I live on this street?" he asked. He sounded more curious than suspicious. I loved his voice. It was smooth and even and easy.

"Yes, I do. I know that you live here," I admitted. "I was hoping to run into you."

"You were?" he asked, surprised.

"Yes," I admitted, stretching out the word.

"Were you waiting for me?"

"No," I said, trying to make my lie sound convincing. "I wasn't waiting for you. I was just hoping that I would run into you. And here you are."

"Yes, here I am," he said, flashing a minuscule hint of a smile. He looked at his locked front door, then back at me, and said, "Well, why don't you come in."

I was about to step into Olivia and Sandro's house.

As soon as my feet hit the hardwood floor of the entryway, I felt like an intruder. This was Olivia's house. Her marital home! Sure, she was having an affair in Middleburg, but she wasn't getting biblical in my bed. I had no right to intrude on her space, on her life. But when Sandro put his hand on the small of my back and led me into the living room, my common sense decided to wait for me outside.

The wide, airy, light-filled room was full of dark wood furniture and low modern couches. A huge screen print of the Texas plains hung on the wall above a brick fireplace, which was dotted with framed photographs. In a large, thick silver frame, I noticed what must have been Olivia and Sandro's wedding picture and looked quickly away.

I had not gone there to tell Sandro about Olivia's affair—I just wanted to get a feel for how much he knew. But standing in his living room alone with him, I felt morally obligated to blurt out the torrid details. And after glimpsing the big wedding picture, I was starting to feel that any kind of relationship between his wife and Stanton would be news to him. He probably only knew the senator's name from CNN or Olivia's articles. Even if they were both working on immigration reform, I doubted Sandro was acquainted with Olivia's style of work.

If I told him the details, maybe he would leave Olivia on the spot, shoot Stanton in the leg, and run into my waiting arms. That sounded fantastic. But first, he would probably tell his wife that he knew about Stanton, and my entire story would be blown. There would be no big article. No congratulatory handshakes from Upton. No payoff for my months of hard work. Did I really want love—or a chance at love—that badly?

He walked over to me as I weighed my options. His hands were in his pockets, and the top button of his pink dress shirt was undone.

"What do you want to tell me?" he asked. He was close to me now. "Is it about Olivia? Is she okay?"

He smelled like he did that night at the Hilton.

"It is about Olivia," I said. "But it can wait." I said, buying a little time. "How about a drink? A beer? I could use a beer." That part was actually very true.

"Sure," said Sandro, relaxing a little. "I'll get us some beers. Come to the kitchen with me?"

Olivia Campo's kitchen? Of course I would go to Olivia Campo's kitchen. I was pretty sure it was filled with rows of sharp knives to bludgeon Christine Lewis with. But sadly, it was more Martha Stewart than Freddy Krueger. It was all white with pale marble countertops and a turquoise Smeg fridge.

"Cool fridge," I said as Sandro reached for two Coronas. I ignored the picture of them tacked up on the freezer. They were in Mexico City in front of a Diego Rivera mural and looked mighty happy. No, he couldn't know about her and Stanton. I hoped that picture got ripped in two when I broke the news. There was also a small American flag and a picture of Olivia and two older people who must have been her parents, in a large silver frame on the windowsill above the kitchen's double sink. They were all smiling and sitting on the bleachers in Cowboys Stadium in Dallas. It almost looked like a fake backdrop. I knew she was from Texas but I couldn't imagine her ever attending a sporting event. I was sure she considered sports just another opiate for the masses. But here she was, wearing white and blue, smiling with her parents. I tried to look at the picture without obviously looking at the picture and noticed that Olivia's mother had red hair, too, but hers was a nice blondish red, not like Olivia's.

It was confirmed. She had parents. Satan didn't escort her to earth.

I walked to the other end of the kitchen where Sandro was standing, but the sight of a stainless steel Cuisinart mixer side-tracked me. And was that a cookbook on baking cakes and pies? Olivia baked? I would have been less surprised to see a huge pile of cocaine and condoms.

"Olivia bakes?" I asked Sandro, pumping my voice full of fake enthusiasm. "When she has time," replied Sandro, looking at the mixer that had stopped me in my tracks. "Which isn't often. But she likes to; it relaxes her. She makes an amazing passion fruit cheesecake. Hasn't she ever brought any to the office?"

Olivia. Bring baked goods to the office. Maybe if Rachael Ray pointed a gun to her head and forced her to.

"I don't think she ever has," I replied. "I love to bake though," I added, sucking up to Sandro. "You should taste my French frosted cherries jubilee à la mode. Award-winning family rec-ipe." Where did I get that? That was a completely made-up dish. Luckily Sandro didn't present me with a baking tin and a bag of cherries; he just smiled and handed me my beer.

Sandro jumped up to sit on the marble-covered island in the middle of the kitchen and pointed at a stool for me to perch on. I could see his triceps rippling through his shirt. I wanted to die.

I wanted to latch my jaw around his arm muscle like a piranha and never let go.

"Grab a seat," he said, handing me a sliver of lime and then lightly smacking his bottle against mine. "I'm glad you ran into me on purpose. Sorry I was unpleasant earlier. I was just a little surprised to see you and I had a horrible day at work. I couldn't get in touch with Olivia and I'm dealing with something messy in El Salvador. Anyway, I'm rambling. In short, sorry I was rude. I'm glad to see you."

There, better. Now we were on the right track. I would go home and put celebrity wedding planner Mindy Weiss on my speed dial.

"I like what you're wearing," said Sandro as I repositioned my dress so that my butt wasn't touching the counter. "You're always wearing these bright colors when I see you. It's rare for a reporter. And for Washington. You look like you should be on vacation. Ever been to Mexico?"

I had. I went to Cancún for spring break and let a basketball player from the University of Florida do tequila shots off my stomach. But I might save that story for later on in our relationship.

"Not really," I said. "Spring break, but that doesn't count."

"Tourism is tourism," said Sandro, laughing. "But I'm from Mexico City. A highly underrated place."

"If it's such a magical place, then why do so many Mexicans want to come to the U.S.?" I was aware that my question sounded ignorant, but I didn't know how else to bring up immigration, besides idiotically.

Sandro smiled and took a swig of his beer. "Oh, you want to get deep, do you?" he said, laughing. He didn't seem cagey or even offended. Instead, he gave me a speech about family connections and job opportunities, and while he said he sympathized with the border crossers, he didn't say anything scandalous. "In case you're wondering, I'm here legally," he added, winking at me. I melted and quickly asked him about college instead of sliding down the counter to rip off his pants.

Sandro told me what a shock it was to move to Texas when he was eighteen, how jarring it was to go to school with fifty thousand people.

"But then I met Olivia and things got much better," he explained. "She was beautiful, so different from anyone I knew at home and just very opinionated and motivated. A little like she is now, actually."

Gross. That's not what Olivia was like. She was *a lot* opinionated and motivated and unfaithful.

"Are you married?" he asked me after he jumped down from the counter and grabbed two more beers out of the fridge.

"Me? No, no, not close at all," I said nervously. "I'm dating someone, I guess, but, nothing very serious."

He pushed a lime wedge into my second beer with his thumb and handed it to me. When I grabbed it, he didn't let go and I was left grasping his hand while he grinned. We stayed like that for what felt like minutes, until I pulled the beer away and he jumped back on the counter.

"You're very quirky, you know. It's pretty adorable," he said, before taking a swig.

I was quirky? Quirky? Wasn't that how you described girls with funky glasses and thunder thighs? I didn't want to be quirky. I wanted to be seductive and mysterious. Everyone always called Payton seductive and mysterious. Even when she was sixteen. I was twenty-eight and I was still quirky.

"So, what was it you were going to say about Olivia?" said Sandro, scooting over to where I was sitting. "Some workplace gossip?"

"Well, kind of," I said, my heart beating faster. Could I really do this? Was I really going to spill my story and ruin my chances of pole-vaulting to the top of the *List* just so I could make out with Sandro? And who knew if he would even lunge at me with an open mouth. Maybe hearing the worst news of his life wouldn't inspire a make out session.

But I had confirmed what I wanted to confirm. He didn't know about Olivia and Stanton. I was pretty sure of that. And now I had the chance to tell him.

But instead of continuing, I leaned into him and put my face up to his. I looked him in the eyes, closed mine, and fell closer. We were kissing. His lips were on mine, and his hands were on my back. I felt every inch of him against me. His breath, his body, the scruff of his stubbly face. I was completely wrapped up in his arms. He held on to me tightly. His hands moved up and down my back; the right one was in my hair again. We kissed harder, faster, he pulled me in even closer . . .

And then, suddenly, it stopped. He pushed me away from him and dropped his hands to his sides.

"What are you doing?" he said. "You kissed me. Jesus! Why did you kiss me?" And before I had a chance to answer, he shook his head and started walking toward the living room. "You can't be here," he said firmly. "I'm married. Very married. And you know my wife."

"You . . . you! You called me adorable. You held my hand. And the other night at the restaurant, you ran your fingers through my hair!"

"I shouldn't have done that and I'm sorry," said Sandro, pacing nervously. "But I'm married. To your colleague!"

But she's cheating on you.

Now I was absolutely sure that he had no idea what his wife was doing. He wouldn't be reacting this way if he did. I wanted to blow up a photo of Olivia and the senator cavorting naked. What would he say then? Would he pull me back into his arms and kiss me like that again?

"I'm sorry," I said, angry and more embarrassed than I had ever been in my life. I felt like I was standing naked in front of him with "I love you Sandro" tattooed across my chest. "I'm so sorry. You gave me signals; I thought you wanted that. I'm sorry," I said, hesitating in the doorway. But he shut the green door so quickly that it almost clipped my heels.

I ran past the closed church, wishing it were open, rounded the corner, and headed down P Street toward the circle. Couples holding hands stepped to the side for me; young women just getting out of work pretended not to notice my red puffy face and I tried to keep myself from turning into a pathetic puddle of tears.

I slipped into the Kramerbooks store on the edge of the circle and sat down at a bar stool in the adjacent restaurant. I motioned to the bartender for a cup of coffee and let the steaming liquid burn every inch of the inside of my mouth. I didn't deserve to have the lingering taste of Sandro's tongue on my palate. He had tasted incredible. Like mint gum and espresso. But I wasn't allowed to have that. I wasn't allowed to have him. And if I kept up my acts of idiocy, I probably wouldn't have a story, either, because Olivia would cremate me with a Bic lighter.

I picked up my phone and called Elsa. She answered quickly, sounding out of breath.

"Elsa, please don't analyze the question I'm about to ask you. Would you say that I'm of sound mind? I mean, I haven't done too many stupid things in my life, have I?"

"Sure you have," Elsa said, huffing and puffing. She explained that she was on a treadmill at the Ritz-Carlton gym.

"I've never been arrested, committed tax fraud, or slept with a married man," I said. But I had kissed one. I had just kissed a married man. He was partially to blame, but still. I was a worthless individual.

"Well, let's think back on your history of colorful mistakes," said Elsa while her feet smacked the rubber treadmill track. "You nearly drowned while skinny-dipping, you called your mother and said you were going to die the first time you took ecstasy, you lost Wellesley student council president to a girl with green hair, and you jumped off your barn roof with nothing but a pillowcase as a parachute because Payton told you to. And . . . oh! You slept with that frat guy just to make him stop talking."

Elsa was right. I was not of sound mind. I was a true idiot. No wonder I had just thrown myself at Sandro. An entire life history of poor decisions had led me to his perfectly shaped mouth.

When Elsa asked if I needed her to come pick me up, because I sounded "a touch upset," I said no. I was afraid I'd crumble under the soothing hand of friendship and tell her everything, and I still couldn't confide in anyone who lived in the Northern Hemisphere.

I stayed in Kramerbooks for two more hours, drinking so much coffee that I went from petrified and repentant to paranoid, shaky, petrified, and repentant.

When I got home, I showered, brushed my teeth three times, and got ready to not sleep a wink because of the caffeine. I did not pull up the video of Sandro, but when my phone rang and I saw that it was James, not Sandro or his enraged wife, I answered.

James was a perfectly charming thirty-three-year-old man who had set new standards for chivalry every time we were together. I should have thrown myself at him. He would love me despite my clear shortcomings, and he wouldn't have to cheat on his wife to do so. But I wasn't there. I was completely torn up with stupid schoolgirl emotions for Sandro.

So when James asked me if he could see me again soon, told me that he hadn't stopped thinking about that night in the car, I had no choice but to say no.

"I don't think that's a good idea," I said honestly.

"You don't?" he said, taken aback. "Do you feel strange about what happened? Because that doesn't have to happen again."

Really? The man would forgo sex and still hang out with me? He was a saint. A young Republican saint.

"Of course *I* would like it to happen again," he clarified. "It was amazing. A little rushed, I admit, but that was my fault."

I assured him that our backseat copulating had been delightful.

"But if you're not ready, not comfortable, we don't have to. We can wait. I just like you. I miss you and want to see you again, but I'm beginning to think you don't agree."

"It's not that," I said. "That was great. You are great."

"Okay," he said, hesitating. "I'm great, but you don't want to go out with me again."

"I think I'm in love with someone else," I said flatly.

The gushing stopped right there.

"James?" I asked after a long, awkward silence.

"You slept with me while debating whether you're in love with someone else? That's pretty despicable."

It certainly was. My voice quivered, and his rose in anger. Finally he promised not to bother me anymore and hung up the phone.

I went to the bathroom and washed my face, desperately trying to soap away tears and humiliation. I looked at myself in the mirror. I had no idea how I had allowed just eight months at a Washington job to transform me into a terrible person.

CHAPTER 14

One thing the bigwigs at the *Capitolist* loved to do was talk about how awesome the *Capitolist* was. They sent out staff-wide emails that were grammatically correct love letters to themselves and saluted each other like they were all saving the world one very quickly written article at a time. But they were just warm-ups for the *Capitolist*'s fourth anniversary celebration. Forget the Fourth of July—the real red, white, and blue came out for the *List*'s oh so cleverly named "Read, White, and Blue" party held in the middle of June.

Celebrities of print and screen came, and wonks said wonky things. Upton and Cushing gave speeches about the *List*'s dominance over stodgy, tired old media, and the employees got mildly trashed and poked around on their BlackBerrys the entire time.

It was my first *List* anniversary party, but Isabelle, Julia, Libby, and Alison had spent our bathroom break yesterday giving me a minute-to-minute timeline of last year's.

"Rochelle Mitzner danced like she was in a Michael Bolton video. Hands up to the sky and everything. It looked like she was being reborn," said Alison, laughing.

"And Upton had us all raise our glasses and salute ourselves," said Isabelle. "It was so awkward. I saw more humility at the Olympic Games."

"Everyone wears navy. Or black. The occasional dash of olive green. They dress like Goths, but without the flair," said Libby, examining her bright J. McLaughlin skirt in the bathroom mirror.

"And all these people who would never be caught dead wasting their breath on us in the newsroom babble endlessly to us in the cocktail lines, as if they respect our intellects. But they're really just drunk," said Julia. "They still think we're idiots. Don't be fooled."

"I went to Stanford," Alison chimed in, reapplying her lip gloss.

"But you wear Chanel lip gloss," said Julia, "so they don't care."

"Well, that all sounds like a real good time," I said, Purelling my hands.

The good news about the real good time was that it was always held in the Freer and Sackler Galleries, one of the most beautiful buildings in Washington. I loved the courtyard. I loved the ethereal green Thomas Dewing paintings that hung from the walls and Whistler's famous Peacock Room. So what if the building was going to be bursting at the seams with egos? Good art, free booze. I would just chain myself to Julia, Isabelle, Libby, and Alison. I needed a little legitimized frivolity after my smooching idiocy of ten days ago.

Julia assured me that no one brought their spouses to the *List*'s parties because it "humanized" them in the eyes of Upton and Cushing, so I wasn't concerned about seeing Sandro—but I was petrified to see Olivia.

Luckily, it was a big museum and there was an outdoor area so if I paid attention, I could stay out of her way. I was going to have to see her at some point, and it might as well be in a building that I knew better than she did. If she tried to decapitate me with a Chinese butterfly knife, I'd know which way to run. I had to be prepared for anything.

An hour into the evening, I hadn't laid eyes on Olivia. The party, full of *Capitolist* employees and the sources and power players we were courting, spilled over from the inside of the museum onto the stone courtyard, which was covered in heavy black iron tables. Tiny white lights were strung in the trees, and with the right amount of booze, you could almost forget where you were. Until Upton had the mic.

"Hey, team!" His voice bounced off the century-old outer walls. "Four years in, *Capitolist* fever has taken over the city, the nation, and the world!"

With that statement Tucker Cliff actually started to jump up and down in his gray dress shirt as if he had just OD'd on laughing gas.

"*Capitolist* originals, old-timers, and newbies, let's give ourselves a round of applause! Unless you're on deadline, that is, in which case keep typing and stop drinking." The courtyard erupted with laughter and clapping.

When Upton's ode to narcissism was finished, Isabelle and I went inside to look at a collection of Whistler paintings.

We stopped in front of an image of a girl in a periwinkle and pink dress sitting on a bed, reading a book. Isabelle leaned in and read the title: *Pink Note: The Novelette.*

"I remember when I had time to read," she said, looking longingly at the framed image.

"When was that?" I asked.

"Before I decided to become a journalist."

"But you were an Olympian," I pointed out. "Didn't you have to stay in constant motion? Run and jump and lift things every hour of the day?"

Isabelle laughed out loud and covered her mouth out of habit because she was in a museum.

"It's a party," I reminded her. "*The* party. It's okay to laugh."

"Right," she said, laughing again. "I really used to read all the time. I'm a James Joyce addict. I've read every word he ever published. Him and Graham Greene. But now, I never have time to pick up a book. Do you?"

Did I? The last non-work-related things I had read were a health warning on the back of a bottle of Campari and *Photography for Dummies.*

"Sadly, no," I replied.

"It's too bad this job makes you so one-dimensional. If I had time for anything else but work, I might actually like my job," said Isabelle, smiling at me. "I'm glad you came to the paper," she added. "It's nice with you here."

Before I could thank her, she clinked her empty glass against my half-full one and headed outside to the wine bar.

Without Isabelle by my side, I felt very alone in the formal gallery room. I smoothed down my purple dress, the brocade fabric still starched and tight, and tried to look busy. It didn't work. I headed out of the room and into the next, larger gallery room, where the martini bar was located, hoping to find another Style section girl. The room had a few dozen guests walking stiffly around, but none of my preferred colleagues. I pulled my phone out of my clutch and texted Alison. "Where are you?" I asked. "Don't want to be seen drinking a blue martini alone."

"Stay where you are. I'm with Libby. We'll come to you," she texted back, explaining that she had to fetch a source a glass of white wine fermented prior to 1996 before she could join me.

The room with the martini bar was quickly filling up. People were getting drunker and, paradoxically, seeking out stronger booze. Two of those people coming in search of martinis in *Cap-itolist* colors were Olivia Campo and Emily Baumgarten.

It had to happen at some point, I told myself. Even if Olivia knew I kissed her perfect husband, I still had the upper hand. I had photographic evidence of her unthinkable acts. I could ruin her. I had to act cheerful and confident and not start crying. I kept my face locked on the woman in the watercolor across from me.

I imagined Olivia coming over and slashing both the water-color and my face with a pizza cutter. But I stood tall, just like Madame Beaujolais used to scream in ballet class. "The plight of the tall girl is that she wants to bend over like a candy cane. Don't be a candy cane!" she used to trill as she pushed my shoul-ders back with the strength of a wrestler.

Tonight, I would not be a candy cane. Olivia was a tiny girl. Maybe I could beat her down by virtue of my height when she lunged at me with death in her eyes.

She and Emily walked over to a painting next to the one I was in front of. I slid my eyes over at them. They were looking at *Harmony in Green and Rose: The Music Room*, a far more famous painting.

"That little girl looks like you," said Emily, staring at a young girl in the center of the painting. She was all in white, except for shiny black shoes, seated on a couch, reading a book. "Her hair, it's red like yours," she said, pointing out the obvious. I wanted to remind her that Olivia was not eight years old, but Emily was too engaged in Olivia worship to pay attention to me.

"It's a beautiful painting," said Olivia dryly, barely looking at it. "Claustrophobic and flat, but beautiful."

"I spent my childhood with my face in a book, just like that," chirped Emily. "I was always reading. That's why I skipped the fourth and fifth grades. You must have read all the time, too, you do everything so fast."

"When I was a kid, no, not so much," replied Olivia, coolly. "I read a lot later in life."

She expressed her boredom by turning and smiling at me. I was still standing tall as a string, staring like a possessed art student at the watercolor.

"You," said Olivia as flatly as the painting she resembled. I prepared for the worst.

"I haven't seen you in a while. I figured you got fired."

She thought that I got fired! I wanted to pull her hair out strand by strand.

"You're Adrienne Brown," said Emily, looking at me with an expression that could only be described as a frown. "Isn't your mother Caroline Cleves Brown? That heartless gossip columnist?"

"Indeed," I replied, ignoring her rude turn of phrase. "She worked for the *Post* for a long time."

"Must have been fun," chimed in Olivia. "Those softer beats really do seem amusing," she said. "If you like that kind of thing."

"I do happen to like that kind of thing," I replied stiffly. I wanted to choke her and steal her husband away forever.

"What do you two write about?" I asked.

"White House," replied Olivia. "The president of the United States of America."

"Me too," chimed in Emily, "but you already knew that."

"I'm going to grab a drink," I said, ignoring her. "Can I get you two anything?" Arsenic? Drano? Bleach?

"We're fine; thanks though," replied Olivia with her back already turned to me. "I have a plane to catch after this. Air Force One, actually."

Unable to find Alison and Libby, I went outside and told Julia about the awkward encounter.

"Fuck that ho," she said, feeling her hair to make sure it was still smooth and pinned in place despite the evening breeze. "You know, I've been here three months longer than she has. On her first day, Tucker asked her if she was a Style reporter, because she sits near us, and she said, 'Oh no. I'm a real reporter.' I almost stapled her hand to the desk."

My endless wavering about what to do with everything I knew about Olivia—continue to dig, or bury it all?—was now leaning much closer to the former. Why should I care about her? She was horrible. If I took her out with a two-thousand-word article and a few artistic nude shots, her husband would likely be mine for the taking. I just knew there was something he liked about me. In fact, he had said it. I was adorable with cool hair.

I stood in the courtyard with Julia, who had started talking about her latest dating woes. "Stop dating Hill flacks," I advised her.

"Whatever, you're one to talk. I heard you went out with James Reddenhurst."

She did? She'd heard that? Oh fantastic. She probably knew that I had slept with him in a car and then dumped him because I was infatuated with a married man. I hated Washington. It was like a never-ending high school prom.

"What else did you hear?" I asked her.

"That's all. Just that you went out with him. He's really cute. He used to date Senator Kirby's daughter. You know, from Iowa. I think they were engaged. He's a very serious guy. Hot, but serious."

As the night wore on and our colleagues started to head home, I heard my BlackBerry ringing in my bag. Incredibly, it was James. I had missed three calls from him. I scrolled through messages to find one from him that read, "Are you at the *Capitolist* anniversary party? I assume you are. Just wanted to warn you that I am too. I'm not trying to invade your territory, but I escorted Senator Kirby here and was left with very little choice. I'm sorry. I'll try my best not to run into you."

James was here. And he had sent a courteous note to tell me so. I hadn't seen him, but I had also downed three red, white, and blue martinis. He could be anywhere. I took his note and back-to-back warning calls as my hint to leave. I said a quick goodbye to the Style girls, nodded to Hardy, who had his laptop out at a patio table, and escaped out the door toward the Smithsonian castle.

I was parked on Independence Avenue, so I cut through the pretty Haupt garden to get there faster. I slipped into my car still fumbling for my keys in my oversize clutch. It wasn't until I had fished them out that I spotted the masculine hand resting on the gearshift and started to scream.

"I'm sorry, I didn't mean to scare you. The door was open, and I knew it was your car. It's a unique car."

It was Sandro.

"The locks don't really work anymore," I replied, my heart racing with arousal and fear. "They haven't for years."

"I need to talk to you," he said.

His hand was still on the gearshift. I looked down at it, wanting to put my hand over his and feel his skin, his pulse, just like in the kitchen.

"You scared me. Terrified me. But I'm glad you're here," I said. "I want to apologize to you about the other night. I'm so embarrassed. I've never—"

He interrupted. "Olivia knows," he said coolly.

I felt my bottom lip start to tremble in fear.

"I had to tell her. I understand you two work together, and I apologize in advance if that makes things awkward for you, but she is my wife. I've been with her since I was nineteen years old. No one else. And then you come along, and you're all gorgeous with these long legs and this blond hair, and your whole aura is so different. I don't know what happened. I acted like an idiot. And I was lonely. Olivia is always traveling, I'm alone all the time, and I guess I just broke a little. You broke me."

He stopped and looked at me, cleared his throat, and started speaking in a firmer voice. Olivia knew about me, but Sandro knew nothing about his wife.

"You kissed me, but I shouldn't have let you. I shouldn't have held your hand and said all those things to you. I was stupid to invite you in, to even talk to you that night at Oyamel. I was leading you on."

"You weren't!" I said, getting upset. I could feel my eyes fill with tears. "You didn't do anything wrong. I just, I—"

"You made a mistake," he said in a hardened voice. "And so did I, but I couldn't keep something from my wife and make it worse than it is."

I nodded, wiping my eyes, humiliated.

"I assume you're aware of Olivia's character. She isn't exactly an easy woman to please," he said.

That was probably more obvious to me than it was to him.

"She was going to have Upton fire you when I told her. She was going to tell him what you did and declare that she couldn't work in the same building with you. She's absolutely right to think they would pick her over you. They always pick her. She's the one that follows the president. She's the one they're grooming."

The tears falling down my face stung my tired skin.

"I'm sorry to upset you, but she is my *wife*, Adrienne. As captivating as you are, she's my wife. And I asked her not to talk to Upton. I said that instead, I would talk to you. That we could come to an understanding."

"What is our understanding?" I said, looking at his tan, handsome face, hoping it would involve having his arms around me again.

"Our understanding is that within a month, you'll give notice at the *List*. You'll give Olivia room to breathe. You can't expect her to keep working with you. You've made that unrealistic. If you agree, she won't speak to Upton about your character flaws."

"*My* character flaws!" Not to mention your wife's, I barely bit back. I wanted to tell him everything I knew, show him the photos and have him grovel for my forgiveness. "You were the one who touched me and kept handing me beers and said I was adorable. This was a mutual thing, Sandro. You can't just tell me to quit my job! It's *my* job and despite what your horrible wife says, I'm very good at it. The paper has hundreds of employees, not just Olivia fucking Campo!" I hit the side of the car with my hand for emphasis and then let out another yell. I had gone from weepy to hysterical.

"Adrienne?" he asked me after a few seconds of my heavy breathing and grinding teeth.

"Yes," I replied, my voice leaking sarcasm, my eyes fixed on the speedometer. "That's what I'll do, Sandro. I will quit my job. Don't worry about a thing."

I heard the passenger door open, and before I could calm down, try to make more excuses to keep him there, Sandro was gone.

I put my keys in the ignition of my old blue car, but I was too upset to drive. I was also too drunk, and Middleburg felt very far away.

I took a cab home that night, the only sound decision I had made in weeks. As the driver headed down Route 50, I opened the two back windows and let the humidity soak me through. It was Tuesday, June 19. And for the first time since I had seen Olivia and Senator Stanton together, I was now under tremendous pressure to get my story to print. I was not going to be the one quitting my job. Olivia was. The *Capitolist* was all I had left, and now that little red-haired hag wanted to take it away from me.

CHAPTER 15

I wondered what unemployment would be like. Would I just go crazy and start eating pots of jam with my bare hands? Or would I stare at my old byline and cry? That's what Olivia wanted: to knock me out of journalism altogether while she sailed to the top of the field. She wanted—no, demanded—this to happen within the next month. I was screwed—unless I could turn my Stanton story into something solid before Olivia begged Upton to have me sacked. My internal clock suddenly sounded like a gong counting down the days left in my journalism career.

I needed something to save me from slipping into career oblivion. If I couldn't find anything incriminating enough about Olivia's past, I needed something on Stanton. He was a public figure, had been for almost two decades—maybe Olivia wasn't the first woman to grab his attention. Perhaps he had a thing for bitchy journalists. That Friday after work, I drove forty minutes east to George Mason University to use their library. I knew my press pass would let me in, and I was less worried about seeing someone I knew at GMU than at George Washington, Georgetown, or American. Plenty of Washingtonians viewed Virginia as the equivalent of Sheboygan in terms of proximity and sophistication, so I decided to play their game and hide out among my commonwealth brethren.

I parked my car in the busy lot and walked into the Fenwick Library. It had been years since I had been inside a college library, and all those happy memories came rushing over me. I was a devoted library studier in college, always choosing Wellesley's Clapp Library over any other corner of campus. I loved the silence, the palpable energy of expanding intelligence, and the potential to procrastinate in the stacks with your peers.

The problem I was going to have with Stanton was the opposite of the one I had with Olivia and Sandro. There was going to be so much for me to weed through on Stanton that what I was really looking for might stay buried in the mass of information. By now I knew the senator's family like it was my own. His father and older brother were in government, but the family money came from the John F. Stanton & Company meat processing and wholesale business founded by Stanton's father. It wasn't glamorous work, but it sent all three of the Stanton men into public office and helped fund their campaigns. Senator Hoyt Stanton worked as counsel for the company after he got his law degree. He'd had his hands and interests in and out of it his entire career. The plant was located in Maricopa County, Arizona, and according to the website, it was still operational and very lucrative.

I was working backward and when I got to Hoyt Stanton's mid-nineties media clippings on the computer, they were starting to thin out. I switched my efforts to microfiche and as with Olivia and Sandro, that's when my research got interesting.

After two hours of going back month by month, year by year, I started using "John F. Stanton & Company" instead of

"Hoyt Stanton" to narrow down the results. Within ten minutes I found something that had me running to the copier to blow up the text.

> Ajo Cooper News, Western Pima County, 1989—Death announcement for Drew Reader.
>
> Public Safety officials announced Monday that Drew Reader of Ajo had died in a machinery accident at the John F. Stanton & Company meat processing and wholesale plant where Mr. Reader was employed as a custodian. Paramedics and police who arrived quickly on the scene declared his death accidental. His wife, Joanne Reader, and his young daughter, Olivia, survive him. Funeral services will be held at Ajo Calvary Baptist Church at 4:00 in the evening on Sunday.

Olivia. The name leapt out of the page like lightning in a flat midwestern sky. Again, it was just a name, and not a terribly uncommon one. But it was in an obituary that mentioned Stanton's family company. Olivia Reader. *Capitolist* Olivia would have been young in 1989, probably in first grade, like me. But *Capitolist* Olivia had a different last name, and she was from Texas. She had a Lone Star Flag tacked up at her desk.

I circled the girl's name and checked dates against the background information I'd dug up for the company. Hoyt Stanton definitely worked there as a lawyer in 1989. He was a state representative then—not elected to the United States Senate until 1994—but the future senator was routinely mentioned in other articles about the plant at that time. His father was the CEO of the company but Stanton seemed to be running the operation until he left for Washington.

Continuing to look up only the company name, I found a second article that was worth printing and highlighting and hiding away as fast as I could. This one was in the *Arizona Republic,* not some local rag.

> Joanne Reader, the wife of a twenty-nine-year-old man who was killed in a machinery accident at an Ajo, Ariz., meatpacking plant has filed a wrongful death lawsuit against John F. Stanton & Company, which may also be fined by the U.S. Department of Labor in connection with the accident.
>
> The lawsuit, filed by Joanne Reader, claims that unsafe working conditions led to the death of her husband, Drew Reader.
>
> A custodian at the plant, Reader accidentally switched on a meat grinder when cleaning it. The other workers present during the incident were not able to turn off the machine before Reader was sucked into it. The accident occurred on May 3, 1989.
>
> Joanne Reader is seeking wrongful death damages, claiming that the device was not properly locked at the time of cleaning. Hoyt Stanton, the owner's son and a plant manager, is acting as counsel for the company.
>
> The Occupational Safety and Health Administration is looking into possible safety violations at the plant.

Not just death, a tragic, gruesome death. With my stomach beginning to churn nervously, I wiped off my sweaty palms and began a search for everything pertaining to Drew Reader and found a legal document stating that OSHA had not found John F. Stanton & Company negligent, and because of the outcome of the investigation, Joanne Reader was barely awarded any financial compensation for the death of her husband. She had his life insurance, which wasn't very much, and a few other molehills of money from the company, but a decent paycheck was not coming her way.

I couldn't believe it. Her twenty-nine-year-old husband was killed in a meat grinder, and she was awarded a few thousand bucks? That seemed absolutely wrong. Even if it was an accident, shouldn't there have been some kind of accident insurance that assured she wouldn't be left a penniless, grieving single mother?

I looked through stacks of microfiche for another mention of Drew Reader, but after his wrongful death case was dismissed, all mention of him vanished. So I looked just for the name Reader. Maybe Olivia Reader had news hits as she got older? A simple last name search was difficult, though, especially with the generic word *reader* fouling up my results, and I got nothing when I focused solely on her.

I wished I had someone to confide in. I needed a real editor, but especially now that my days could be numbered, turning to anyone at the *Capitolist* without a finished story was too dangerous. Olivia was revered by the editors, and it would take a lot for them to kick her to the curb over me. I would have to wait until later and call Payton when she was back from training her miracle horses.

So I kept looking. My left hand felt heavy from the weight of my lacquer camellia ring, but I kept it on instead of placing it on the table next to me like I usually did when I typed. It was a present from Brady, my college boyfriend. It was pretty, and it reminded me of easier days, but I wondered what he would think if he knew I was still wearing it.

Joanne Reader. When I went to check the printed microfiche index for specifically "Joanne Reader *Arizona Republic*" then "Joanne Reader *Ajo Cooper News*," I saw that there was one more mention of her in an Arizona publication that didn't include her late husband, Drew, or daughter, Olivia.

It was her obituary.

Joanne Reader, still a resident of Ajo, passed away in the spring of 1992. The notice, in the *Ajo Cooper News*, was very short. There was no mention of her husband's death three years earlier, or of a young daughter, or of a funeral or family. It just disclosed that Joanne Reader had "Died after a short illness."

What kind of short illness? Surely the woman didn't pass away from strep throat or the common cold. I picked up my phone, moved to a private study room, and dialed a reliable source of mine, a journalism professor who taught a class on pop culture in media at Syracuse University.

Even though it was Friday night, he picked up. "Ari, it's Adrienne Brown from the *Capitolist*. Thank you for answering. I have a very quick question for you," I said, looking down at the short obit I had just printed. "If a celebrity, or someone, had their cause of death listed in an obit as 'died after a short illness,' would that mean anything? Is that code for overdose or anything like that?"

"No, not overdose exactly," he said. "But it's often a polite journalistic way of saying suicide. That person probably took their own life."

It was a horrific reality if it was true, but the sequence of events made sense. Drew Reader was killed in a terrible accident in 1989, leaving behind his wife and young daughter. A few months later, Reader's death was declared accidental, John F. Stanton & Company paid out a few measly bucks, and Joanne remained broke. I didn't know if she was indigent, but the widow of a deceased custodian was probably not flush with cash.

Then, three years after the death of her husband, with no financial remuneration for her loss, she took her own life.

I understood that the sad story I was piecing together could belong to strangers instead of Olivia Campo. But my heart was steadily beating faster. I had been right when I heard nothing but a first name before, so I had to follow this lead like it was etched in stone. If Olivia Reader was Olivia Campo, then it couldn't be an accident that she had landed in bed with Stanton. I flashed back to what Sandro had said about Olivia's early career ambitions. She now covered the White House, but she had been obsessed with Congress. He had even specified the Senate. To have spent her whole life scheming for a way to get close to Stanton, to then take him down . . . it might have seemed far-fetched for most sane women in their twenties, but I wouldn't put it past Olivia. It would explain why she jumped at the *Capitolist* before it was a big name—she knew she could make it her all-access pass.

I stayed at the college library past midnight. I hadn't found another promising lead since Joanne Reader's obit, though I did find one more article about the court hearing declaring John F. Stanton & Company not at fault. Hoyt Stanton had been present in the court when the decision was made, along with five men who had witnessed Drew's death. I wrote their names down in my notebook and drove home.

The heat of July was bringing the smell of horses up through the floorboards of my barn apartment. I had to ready myself to live with the distinct scent until October. When I walked in, I put all my research on my bedside table and grabbed my landline phone. It was almost three o'clock in the morning in Argentina, but Payton would answer the phone. She never slept at normal hours.

But instead of my sister, an enraged polar bear picked up.

"Buck, it's Adrienne. I'm sorry to wake you. Is Payton there? It's important."

He groaned out a mix of frustration and testosterone and put Payton on the phone.

"Are you insane?" said Payton. "It's ludicrously late. Buck thinks you were just julienned like a potato in a back alley."

"I'm sorry, I really am, but you know you're the only one I'm talking to about this," I said.

"Fine, this better be brilliant. You better sound like you're auditioning for *CSI*."

When I finished telling Payton about the kiss and the Freer and Sandro breaking into my car, she had forgiven me. And when I told her about everything I had found about John F. Stanton & Company and the Readers' deaths, she said, "I'll be on a plane tomorrow morning."

CHAPTER 16

Payton's plane was landing at Dulles Airport at 11 P.M. on Saturday. I was surprisingly excited to see her. I hadn't seen her for over a year, because this past Christmas Payton had refused to fly back to Virginia from her ski trip in the French Alps. My parents, when I had enlightened them about her new visit, were thunderstruck.

"But why is she coming home?" asked my mother. "Is she sick? Does she need first world care?"

"Payton? Coming home just to visit?" my dad said, as if I had just announced that Sputnik was due to land in our backyard. "But why? It's not a holiday. We aren't begging her to. She's just coming home?" My answer was yes, she's just coming home to see me.

To see me . . . and help me untangle my thoughts regarding my bitchy colleague, her husband, a United States senator and two deaths that were probably totally unrelated. Just one of those little, pesky problems you ask your sister for help with. Your typical girl talk.

Payton, with her ability to see the worst in people, would surely help. She would see past the emotion I was now drowning in. In many ways, she was like a less word-savvy, much more attractive version of Olivia: confident and brash and unbiased about mowing down the competition to get her way. Maybe she could analyze Olivia's warped mind for me and then, maybe, I would have the story that would make my career, or at the very least, save my job.

When 10 P.M. rolled around, I wrapped myself in clothing Payton might not declare "garbage with elevated price tags" and headed out to my old clunker.

I was going to send a car service to Dulles Airport to pick her up, because that's what would have made her happy—what she demanded, in fact—but I decided the sisterly thing to do would be to provide my own car service, a beat-up Volvo station wagon. She would love it! Right away, straight off a thirteen-hour plane ride, she could feel the rumble of the highway and sit directly on the red Gatorade stain that was still shining brightly on my passenger's seat. The fact that it remained sticky even after I poured half a box of baking soda on it was fascinating in itself—a real scientific mystery.

I set the scene in my mind as I drove down the almost-empty Dulles Toll Road. Payton would step off the plane, looking fresh as an emperor's rose. When she found me and my homemade sign that read "Welcome home, sister!" she would cringe and try to avoid me while also assessing which of us was skinnier and chicer, with better skin and bouncier hair. And though my journey would have taken thirty minutes and hers almost a full day, she would win in every category.

When she walked through the arrivals gate, she took one look at me and stopped in her tracks.

"You?" she said finally, resuming her strut. "Don't tell me you're moonlighting as a sedan driver to supplement your offensively low income." She let go of her carry-on and walked past me without a hug or smile or any other human display of emotion.

"It's lovely to see you, too," I said as I picked her green Hermès Birkin off the floor. I didn't want to be helpful so much as I just wanted to touch it.

"Oh, shut up. I'm glad to see you. I would just be happier to see you with a man in a jaunty black cap holding the keys to a Mercedes," she finally said, kissing the air around my head.

I grabbed her face like she was a puppy and gave her a wet smacker right on her perfectly blushed cheek.

She frowned, looked me up and down, and said, "You're a child. But I imagine you're thrilled to see me."

"I am. And very appreciative you came. I hope first class wasn't too trying. For our journey home, I've chosen a Swedish automobile," I assured her. "Lots of leg room."

She put her hand over her mouth and posed in a dramatic film noir kind of way. "Oh no. Not that old Volvo. Hasn't that been processed at a junkyard by now, or turned into outsider art?"

"No, no! Running great," I replied. "And parked right outside. Lot D. Come on, let's get your bags."

By the luggage carousel, Payton tapped her foot impatiently. And when her bags came, I started to laugh.

"Payton, are you staying through the new year?"

"I was thinking more like a week. Two, tops. Depends how much I can take. Why do you ask?"

Why? One, because I was her airport chauffeur. Two, because I was her sister who begged her to come home. And three, because she had checked a monogrammed leather steamer trunk as if she were sailing off on the maiden voyage of the *QEII*.

"I bet they thought you were smuggling drugs in this thing," I said, tapping the leather lid.

"Some smelly TSA employee did say something about narcotics, but I ignored him," she replied casually. "He stopped giving me a hard time after I gave him my number. Actually, I gave him your number. His name was Cody something. I don't remember. Sorry in advance if he stalks you."

Why wouldn't you give your sister's number to a TSA employee who clearly cared more about getting laid than the safety and security of his own nation? At times Payton was exactly how I would have imagined Lady Macbeth as an American teenager, only less sensitive.

By the time I had pulled back onto the toll road, Payton was asleep. Twenty minutes later, when I was off the fast roads and stuck going through the stoplights near Middleburg, I got a good look at her face as she lay there reclined way back in her seat. She looked so pleasant, so rational. Nothing like the enraged demon woman I had always thought of her as.

Payton slept in my room that night because we didn't want to go into the main house and wake our parents. She was too exhausted to fuss about having to slumber so close to her sister and animals, but I was prepared for her to fume about it in the morning. Which she did. She took three steam baths in a row inside the house and wouldn't talk to me again until late afternoon, when she broke her silence by calling me the family's rotten egg.

After she had cooled down with the help of a Hendrick's martini at the Red Fox Inn, I convinced her to go riding with me.

Payton was an absolutely terrific rider. After she graduated from Columbia and then Wharton, she said she was going to breed horses, and no one who grew up with her was surprised. The only surprises were that Buck agreed to do it with her and that they moved to remote Argentina to make it happen. Watching her ride around the pasture we spent our childhood trotting in, I saw that she had only gotten better. I felt like a kid on a carousel next to her.

When the heavy humidity of July started to break a little, we dismounted in the north end of the grazing pasture and grabbed the reins of the horses. In our mud-covered paddock boots and sweaty tank tops, we walked next to each other with the horses lazily flanking us.

"Do you remember walking the horses like this when we were little? Because we were scared they would smush us if we were on the outside?" It was something we had done every weekend when we were about twenty years younger, before we learned that we didn't really need each other for company.

"Not really," she replied with her head straight and stern. "Honestly, I don't remember that much about living here. It feels like a long time ago. Washington, Virginia, the whole area was never for me. I wasn't really happy until I went to New York."

"Payton!" I exclaimed. "You're not a hundred years old. Don't tell me that all memories of your childhood are gone. You lived here fourteen years ago."

She sighed and gave the black Arabian she was walking a tug. "I just hate that we were raised in the country when there was such an exciting city nearby. Seems like such a waste. I mean, relatively exciting. It's not all that exciting. But it seemed exciting in high school."

"We went to Washington all the time. It's only an hour away. Mom worked there," I pointed out. My memories of childhood were still crystal clear.

"I just remember my first week at Columbia, feeling very out of place. I was thrilled to be in New York, but I felt like a hillbilly compared to those slick Manhattanites," she said.

"Well, I still feel very out of place here most of the time," I replied unsympathetically.

"Mom said you hate your job," said Payton, her face still expressionless. "She said you detest it, and that you have to start at five and write something every hour, and that you want to drink motor oil at lunch and just off yourself, but that she won't help you because you got yourself into this mess in the first place because you wanted a job with more substance."

My mother thought I wanted to off myself? Yet didn't have plans to intervene? She clearly needed to consult that Spock guide to parenting for a little refresher course.

"It's not that bad," I said, dragging my boots through the grass. "Just all-consuming. The hours are so hard. I don't have any time for life. And the pressure can be intense. I always feel like if I get one fact wrong, one tiny thing, my career will be over. And when you're going so fast and resting so little, the odds of slipping are high. But there are good things, too. The access. Working with smart people. And just proving to yourself that you can do it. Plus, I think people are starting to like me more there. The important people."

"Yeah, well, I could probably eat a live snake if I had to, but you don't see me brunching on a cobra, do you. Some things aren't worth proving."

Ignoring her words, I looked out into the distance of the Blue Ridge Mountains and saw lights flashing in the field.

"Look! Lightning bugs. They're one of my favorite things about summer," I announced.

"I'm aware of your childish affection for the luminescent pests," said Payton, deadpan. She sped up to untack her horse and headed into the house to steam off her grit.

Later that night, lounging in our rambling childhood home, I made us iced teas and Payton tried to give me an outsider's perspective on the latest details I had unearthed at George Mason.

"Well, there's no way that girl is getting in Senator Porno's pants all for the cause of immigration reform," Payton concluded.

Our parents had gone into D.C. to catch the Bolshoi Ballet's much-heralded version of *Spartacus*, and we had taken over their room like ten-year-olds, eating takeout on their bed while *All About Eve* played on the TV in front of us.

"And I don't understand why Sandro told you all that stuff about his past, about being from Mexico and marrying Olivia while still in school. If he was in cahoots with her to change that old man's votes, he wouldn't be talking about his below-the-border pedigree. He would be lying. And I don't think he knows his wife is having an affair, either. He wouldn't be serving as her henchman, delivering threats to you in the front seat of your car if he knew about Stanton."

"Yeah, I agree. I realized after I kissed him that there was no way he knew about Stanton. I don't think he would've pushed me off like that if he did."

Payton smiled and called me a mouth rapist before turning up the volume on the TV with our parents' space station remote control. "You can't get all soft and lovestruck and think about Sandro's reaction," she added, handing me a box of General Tso's chicken. "What matters is that Stanton and Olivia got together, period. Your only story is the affair. And it's a big one."

"Yeah," I confirmed, shoving a broccoli floret down my throat, causing me to start choking. Payton did not move to help me. She just sat there in her head-to-toe Lululemon athletic wear, looking like a yoga advertisement.

After I flung my body over hers to reach the water and save my own life, I clarified, "And I do have photos. Pretty incredible photos."

"Show me," demanded Payton. "I can't believe I haven't asked until now."

I made her leave our parents' comfortable room and follow me out of the house, through the wet grass to the barn, where we flopped on my bed and I flicked on my computer. After entering my password, which was typed in three languages, I showed her what I had. Photo after photo of skin and compromising positions. I had them date and time stamped; I had raw files, huge, duplicable files.

"How have you not run this story already?" asked Payton when she was done scrolling through the images. "You should have already gone to print with this. There could be other people on to her. Who cares about the theories. Print the pictures and say it's just an affair."

"But it's not just an affair!" I said, pulling up the picture of Olivia and Stanton holding each other by the window. "Look at this! There's something behind this."

"You don't have time to figure it out," said Payton. "You're getting fired in twenty-five days."

"I know," I said, feeling time start to crunch in around me. "At first I waited because part of me still felt like it was none of my business. It's just an affair, like any other affair. They weren't jeopardizing national security or anything like that."

"And now you've stomped all over your pathetic ideals?"

"No," I said. "I just think there's a bigger story here, even if Sandro's not involved. Before I knew that Olivia was married, I thought she might be risking her career for lust, or even love. But now I think she has to be trying to sway him on something. Immigration is his big issue, but since Sandro doesn't seem to know anything about it, it could be something with Stanton's family's company."

"But you haven't confirmed that the young Olivia in Arizona is Olivia Campo," Payton reminded me.

"I know. I even looked up the name Olivia online, and out of twenty-five thousand baby names, it's ranked as the fourth most popular for girls. That's pretty damn high. Adrienne was six hundred and ninety-six."

Payton rolled her ice-blue eyes at me, stretched down on my bed like a cat, and collapsed into child's pose. With her head smushed into my duvet, she said, "You have to go to print soon. You could lose all your work if you don't. There are curious reporters all over this town. You just have to be the one to press 'go' first."

She turned onto her back and put her head on my needlepoint pillow, letting her hair tumble around her like a halo. "Besides, you know how these things work, Addy. Once the story gets published, sources will creep out. People will be jumping to talk to you and then all the dirty details will follow. But the reporter who broke the story will forever be associated with it, even if they're not publishing all the intimate details. Think about Watergate. Or the Abu Ghraib scandal. That's how it works."

It was true that someone at Goodstone could be on to them. Or even Stanton's wife. But political spouses turned a blind eye all the time, and I did still believe I was the only reporter who knew.

"Hand me the landline. I have to call Buck. He doesn't know where I am," said Payton, folding herself back into a yoga posture.

"What do you mean he doesn't know where you are," I said, reaching for her head. I should have known better: she successfully bit my hand. She was like a lion cub. They look so cute, but really they want to suck out your eyeballs.

"I told him I was going north for a couple days, but I think he interpreted that as Uruguay, not Virginia. Hand me the phone, will you, Fatty Addy?"

"Here," I said, throwing the phone at her back. I fluffed up the European sham under my head and propped myself onto my left side. I listened as she called Buck, purring into the receiver like an expat Eva Perón. She should give global lessons on how to keep your man in check.

"Buck says hi," said Payton when she hung up. "He told me to be nice to you."

"Sage advice."

"Oh shut up. I'm nicer to you than anyone else in my life. I never see you, so it's pretty easy."

I looked at the clock on my bedside table. It was already past eleven, and I had to turn out a solid performance on Monday just in case Olivia had already told Upton to fire me for my sluttish behavior. Sandro was right when he said that they would pick her over me. They would pick her over almost anyone else at the *List*.

"Payton, I have to go to sleep," I declared, motioning for her and her fat-free body to leave my bed.

She stood up slowly and looked at the computer screen. The photo of Olivia with the senator's arms around her at the window was still enlarged in Photoshop.

"We should spend the weekend in Arizona," said Payton as I saved the image for the millionth time and closed the screen. "The article you found is probably nothing, but it could be something. I bet the men quoted in that article about Joanne Reader seeking damages are still alive. We could try to find them. If they knew Drew so well, they might know his daughter. They might be able to confirm that it's the same Olivia."

"You want to go to Arizona?"

"No, *you* should want to go to Arizona. I'm just willing to go with you and pay for it."

"We can't go there," I responded immediately.

"Why not?"

"For starters, I work on Sundays. It's a six-days-a-week job I've been blessed with. And secondly, that town where the girl in question is from is tiny. I looked it up; it's minuscule. You think if we show up there, and it is the right Olivia, that it won't get back to her? I'll be screwed."

"But what are you now? You think the George Mason microfiche files are going to solve this for you? You need people on the record. If we don't find anything in Arizona, then we go to Texas. We go to A&M and start asking questions there. But you have to start flying. Even Friday feels too late."

I was not sold. I felt like once I started speaking to people, anyone other than Payton, that my story was leaked.

"Well, we definitely can't fly into Phoenix," I said. "It will be on the aviation record, or whatever it's called. It will be something that ties us into all this."

Payton started laughing in her superior way. "You kissed her husband in her house! You hid in the grass and photographed people having sex, with a ten-thousand-dollar camera that you rented! I don't think a plane trip to Phoenix is the thing that's going to blow your cover," she said. "You fell upon something by accident. Then a few more somethings. You already have a good story, but if the ducks line up for you in Arizona or Texas, you will have a great story. If you want to ignore my advice to publish now, then you have to go the rest of the way. Otherwise your forgone hours of sleep and the beautiful *Town & Country* clothes you gave up for this job will all be for naught."

Not a terrible point.

"Think about it," she said. "Something made you stay hot on the trail. Why did you start fussing around with all this anyway? You could have let it go."

"I don't know," I said honestly. "It was just the way Olivia was standing next to that car that night. I knew she was hiding something, and I think natural curiosity kicked in."

"Like you wondered if she was turning tricks for horse owners by the side of the road?"

"I felt something was off, but also, it was the fact that it was *her*. It was strange to see Olivia, who is the essence of a *Capitolist* reporter, so out of context."

"So you started snooping."

"Basically."

"And that brought you to her exceptional-looking husband."

"Unfortunately."

"Why unfortunately!" Payton exclaimed. "You never know with those loyal dog types. He might switch on her when he sees those photos. Most men would."

"I still wonder if I can do it," I admitted. "If I can pull the trigger and change the course of someone's life. Many people's lives. It scares me. I feel like it will haunt me forever."

"Well then, you're in the wrong racket," Payton concluded.

She was probably right. Journalism had become an extreme sport, not for the faint of heart. And I had wanted to be in the thick of it.

"We're going to Arizona," declared Payton. She sounded sure and steady, like a doctor about to perform a liver transplant. "Just switch weekends with someone. Say you'll work both Saturday and Sunday the following week because you need to tend to your ill sister."

It would be very *All the President's Men* of me to hunt down a lead far out of state. It was something I had never expected myself to do. I had never been that type of reporter, nor had the *Capitolist* hired me to be that kind of reporter. But people change.

"Okay," I told Payton. "I'll put the vacation request in. But you have to help me hunt down the men who were in the courtroom that day."

Back at my desk on Monday, my cell phone lit up with a text from Payton. I grabbed it, made sure Hardy was not at his desk to chide me for moving, and walked quickly back to the handicap bathroom, the only one in the building with any privacy.

"I have some terrible news," Payton said when I called. Her voice was as bright and casual as if she were saying "The soup of the day is clam chowder."

"Stanton called you, he's having me killed?"

"No," she replied. "There were five men mentioned in the court article, right? Five witnesses to the accident?"

"Right."

"Well, the first one is dead." Of course he was. "People in small towns really are in such poor health," remarked my sister. "He died of heart disease at the age of fifty-one."

I didn't remind her that we hailed from a town with a population of 976. The difference was that our small town was rich.

"Brilliant. He's dead. Do me a favor and don't call me if you find any more dead people. I won't be able to finish the day, and I still have eight more articles to write."

"Is Olivia there?" asked Payton.

"Thank God, no," I said. "The president is in full fund-raising mode, so she's constantly following him."

"Darn. I wanted to come by and see her. From how you've described her she sounds just hideous. I mean, obviously I've seen pictures of her naked, but it's not the same. I wanted to get that in-person vibe."

That would be just fantastic. Payton and Olivia. It would be like having put Muhammad Ali and Joe Frazier in the ring together without rules.

With the help of headphones, caffeine, and candy, I got through the day. I thought about Olivia, Sandro, and Stanton only about five hundred times, Sandro in particular.

That night in the car while relaying the message about my career ruin, he had said I was gorgeous, with long legs and hair. Actually, that didn't sound so good when I repeated it. Lots of people had long legs and hair. Conan the Barbarian. Frankenstein. But the gorgeous part made up for it. If he knew the truth about Olivia, he would leave her. I knew he would. No man could forgive such a breach of trust. Could he?

I turned off the quiet road and pulled into the long driveway, waiting a few seconds as the gate slowly opened. I spotted Payton in the outdoor horse ring with our father riding Gilt, the mare my dad bought in Argentina before I came home. I parked my car next to my dad's truck, slipped off my work shoes, and grabbed some extra boots from inside the barn.

"Adrienne! Look at your sister. Can you believe how calm that devil of a horse is?" asked my dad when I walked toward him. He was wearing riding clothes and his tall boots were covered in mud.

I couldn't. I didn't even like feeding Gilt because she was the most moody, horrific horse my father had ever bought. But under Payton, she moved like a Triple Crown winner.

I moved to the fence and sat next to my dad. We watched Payton canter around the ring effortlessly, the dark brown horse just starting to break a sweat under her.

"I know your sister is mean as hell," said my dad, "but she can really ride a horse."

"She's not that bad," I said.

"Oh, really? 'Not that bad'? That may be the nicest thing I've ever heard you say about Payton. Twenty-eight years and you finally like your sister. Well I'll be. In that case, I'll leave you to it. Don't let that horse buck her off."

We both looked at Payton and saw we had nothing to worry about. She was like Lance Armstrong on a bicycle. My father walked to the barn to put away the lead rope he was holding, and I watched Payton finish up her ride. When she was done, I let her put Gilt away and waited for her to join me on the fence.

"Let's go in the house," she said. "I'm burning up."

Our boots crunched along the gravel driveway, and I slipped my cardigan off and let the heat hit my skin.

"I thought about Sandro way too much today," I told her as we walked. "It's pathetic; don't think I'm not aware. He wants to get me fired. He thinks it's a swell idea. But I bet he wouldn't think so if he knew what Olivia really did on weekends. I bet she tells him she's out of town. The president of the United States is probably her sex excuse."

"You're obsessed," said Payton, opening the front door and walking in. The screen door closed in my face and I kicked it open with my boot and followed her to the living room. We left our riding boots in a muddy pile by the fireplace and collapsed on our parents' white sofa. A few leftover olives and artichokes were in small ceramic bowls on the coffee table and I grabbed them and started shoving them into my mouth with my dirty hands. I was probably going to contract hoof-and-mouth disease, but what did I care? My life wasn't exactly roses right now anyway.

"Work was awful today," I said, leaning back on the couch. "I had to write an article about this speech Jill Biden gave at four P.M. but I had to be done by the time her speech was finished at four twenty-five P.M. Like how is that possible? Time travel? I finished five minutes after and Hardy said I had the journalistic pace of a Galapagos turtle. A turtle."

"Fascinating," said Payton, dissecting an artichoke and only eating the inside. "Tell me again why you chose a career in journalism? A love of premature wrinkles and stress headaches?"

She took her thin hand and brushed it near my eye while mouthing the words "crow's-feet."

"I don't know why I chose journalism," I answered honestly. "Mom seemed to like it."

"Mom also paid five thousand dollars to meet Gloria Estefan in Miami. Gloria Estefan. She's not of sound mind."

What was wrong with Gloria Estefan? I pushed Payton's hand off my face and stood up to walk out to the barn. I was only a few steps away when I felt something ricochet off the back of my head. It was an olive, thrown by the hand of my own sister. I turned around to yell.

"I wasn't quite done talking to you yet," she said with a smile before I could get a word out. Is that what she did when she wasn't through talking? She threw pickled bar snacks at people's heads? She would make a great addition to the United Nations. Maybe she could throw a cocktail onion at Ban Ki-moon.

"Don't you want to hear about my day?" said Payton, putting her feet on the coffee table. I looked at her tan legs, longer and thinner than mine, and decided I didn't actually want to hear how her day was. I had a brief lapse of judgment in New York a few years back and went out on three dates with a plastic surgeon named Stuart from Franklin Lakes, New Jersey. He told me that while my legs were long and dancerly, it would help if I had lipo on my knees to have my kneezles removed. Kneezles, as in the tiny bit of fat that just hangs around on your kneecap. The relationship didn't last.

"I had a fascinating day," said Payton, stretching one of her legs into the air and then thumping it back onto the table.

"Wad'ya do?" I asked, shoving three olives in my mouth. I chewed them fast and placed the pits delicately into Payton's lap.

"Well I'm not going to tell you if you regurgitate food," she said with a yawn. "Don't be such a child. You're actually very old."

"Fine." I put my head in her lap and smiled as big as I could to display my pink gums.

"I went to the Goodstone Inn," said Payton.

"To the what!" I lifted my head and stared at my sister like she had just said she'd been to Planet Zorbitron. "Why did you go there? What did you do? Why didn't you tell me?"

"Well, I thought about telling you," said Payton, picking up a magazine from the coffee table and flicking to the table of contents. "But then I figured, why bother, and I just headed over."

She started reading an article about the blood type diet and was probably on the second paragraph by the time I ripped the thing out of her hands and demanded some information.

"Payton! Stop being such a heartless cow! Speak! Why were you at the Goodstone?" I asked turning red.

"You're awfully emotional for a WASP," she said, then picked the magazine up off the floor.

Would I really go to prison if I strangled her? Couldn't I just show the police officer the picture from 1987 when she put me in a laundry bag and left me out by the trash? He would let me off then. "Abuse," he would say. "You're off the hook." And he would go off on his merry way to find real criminals.

"Payton! Tell me why you went! What did you do? Did you tell them I stayed there to stalk a United States senator? Talk!" I screamed, my candle burning at both ends and in the middle.

"Well," she said, calmly continuing. "It really is very picturesque, a little provincial, but quaint. I see the appeal. Now if I was going to have an affair—and I'm not saying I am—but if I did, it would have to be in Paris. I just don't think my clothes could come off with another man unless we were in Paris. At the George V. In spring . . . or maybe early fall . . ."

This was the person I had chosen to confide in. This photogenic, horsewoman lunatic. Next time I was just going to call Upton, pass him my notes, and keep writing about Hillary Clinton's hair.

"I went to the Goodstone because I wanted to see the place, for starters." Payton finally put down the magazine and turned toward me. "And then, I figured that while I was there I might as well ask some questions."

She did, did she. Sherlock Holmes in a pair of linen pants. I was ready to scream. I was pretty sure that fire was going to come from my mouth and all of Payton's pretty hair would be singed off, but my father chose that exact moment to walk into the living room and sit down on the other side of the couch. "My lovely daughters," he said, smiling and patting Payton's hand. She smiled at him like a girl who knows she's everyone's favorite. "Are you two tired? How about a game of Trivial Pursuit? Think you can beat Payton now that you have that big-time job, Addy?" he asked, eyeing an antique chest where we kept boring things like board games and photo albums.

"We can't," answered Payton, taking her feet off the coffee table and standing up. "Adrienne has chlamydia. I'm helping her resolve the problem." She took my hand and led me out the door toward the barn.

"Chlamydia! Seriously? That's the first excuse that came into your warped mind?" I yelled as I marched behind her toward the barn. "'Hi, Dad, Adrienne has the clap! Sorry we can't partake in family board game night!'"

"Calm down," said Payton as we headed up the stairs. "He knows I'm kidding. Not all of us are as literal as you." She opened the door to my apartment, which, like my car, was never locked, and made herself comfortable on my bed.

"So as I was saying before you interrupted me with your crazy temper tantrum, I happened to stop by Goodstone. And while I was there, I chatted with a few people."

"A few people . . ." I was standing at the foot of my bed,

watching her recline like a monarch waiting for me to fan her with an ostrich feather.

"Okay, I talked to a few members of the cleaning staff."

I had visions of Payton sitting down with thirty people in a boardroom and handing them all crisp hundred-dollar bills for inside information. I was going to cry. There went all ethics, all journalistic standards.

"I can see that tiny little brain of yours working itself up into a frenzy," said Payton, rolling over onto her side. "It's not like *you* went there and questioned the staff. I did. I'm just your source. I happen to be your sister, but that's never really been proven, so just consider me a source. A really good one, actually. Maybe I should call Wendi Murdoch next."

I flopped down next to Payton and looked at the ceiling. "Fine, source. Then be a source and tell me what you found out."

"They're still there," said Payton, smiling. "Every weekend. They still go there, right to the Bull Barn."

Maybe she wasn't that bad after all. What was a little bribery here and there?

I rolled over to face her. "Seriously? Are you sure?" I asked, forgetting my anger. "I assumed they would have stopped going there by now. I've been too freaked out to go back, now that the staff has seen my face. They can't be stupid enough to keep coming back, right?"

"They are indeed stupid enough," said Payton. "I walked to the horse stable, which is just down the hill from the Bull Barn, and started talking to the two guys mucking the stalls. They were pretty cute, from Winchester they said. And they were very happy to chat with me."

"Did you bribe them?" I asked cautiously. "Or do anything else?"

"Like what, Addy?" Payton rolled her eyes. "You're far too paranoid. All I did was ask a few questions. I was just doing *your* job. One of them told me that he cleans the Bull Barn, too, and that he knocked on the door last weekend to clean it and Stanton and Olivia hadn't checked out yet. He said that an older man and his daughter—with red hair? I offered, and he confirmed—were still there. The same ones that he's seen every week."

"He said daughter?" I asked, concerned that Stanton might actually have a red-haired daughter.

"He was just trying to be proper," said Payton. "He knows they're banging. He also said Stanton had the barn rented out indefinitely. He was told to always have these birch wood logs in the Bull Barn on Fridays, to keep doing it until he was told otherwise. And he hasn't been told otherwise. So, I got all that out of him and then I gave him a hundred bucks."

I knew it. I knew she had bribed him. I was screwed. Or was I screwed? I hadn't bribed him. My unscrupulous sister had. And I couldn't do anything about it now except take the very helpful information and run with it.

CHAPTER 17

Despite Payton's completely unethical behavior, I allowed her to book us a trip to Arizona. Alison, who had Saturday duty, agreed to take my Sunday if I covered both days the following weekend. Hardy moaned and groaned and said he was signing me up to work on Labor Day, but he bought my sister-is-sick lie and approved my time off. I hadn't taken a minute off since I started. My sister, I explained to all the Style girls, was visiting from Argentina and had fallen off a horse and needed some minor surgery on her hip.

"Christopher Reeve fell off his horse in Virginia," said Isabelle. "Did your sister fall at the same place? Maybe it's cursed."

"She didn't," I assured Isabelle. "She fell at home."

"I thought you didn't like your sister," said Libby with suspicion creeping into her voice.

"Well, she's kind of snooty, but she is family," I replied. I sounded like I was lying, I knew I did.

"Horses are demons," said Julia. "You're lucky your sister is alive."

Our parents were under the impression that Payton was treating me to a weekend at the St. Regis in Mexico City. Considering that just last Christmas Payton was still devoting a lot of time and energy to emotional abuse, they were elated by her change of attitude and our sisterly bonding.

"First Payton comes here, all the way here, just to see you. And us, I guess. And now she's taking you on a weekend vacation! What a sister you have, Addy," said my dad on the morning we were set to fly out. "You two are getting so close. I could tell last night."

"Screw last night. Don't forget the time she made me eat garbage. I sure haven't. Never will." I grabbed a bagel and started scooping out the insides with a serrated spoon.

"Again?" said my dad. "More garbage? Should I get the ipecac?"

"No, Dad, not again. She just made me eat trash once. Which I think is one too many times, don't you? And if you really still have ipecac, please throw it away. It's probably fifteen years old."

My dad laughed and poured me a venti coffee in a ceramic Starbucks cup.

"As is that memory of yours," he said. "Payton was a lively kid; you should cut her a break. And she's taking you to the St. Regis. You love the St. Regis. You can have dinner on the roof there, you know. On the helicopter landing pad. Your mother and I did it last year. How about that? Order the tequila-marinated chicken with mole; it's delicious."

Yes, that all sounded absolutely lovely. Too bad we were actually flying to Arizona to go chase meat-processing-plant workers.

"Oh, Mexico, it sounds so simple I just got to go!" My mother came down the stairs singing James Taylor and waving her hands in the air. "I love having you girls together under this roof again. It's like Christmas every day," she said, kissing me on the cheek.

"Except I don't live under this roof," I said. "I live under a roof designed to keep animals warm."

"That's because you're the family's wild animal!" she said,

moving her feet like a bull ready to stampede. "And plus, that way you get privacy. You must be saving millions living here with us rather than in Georgetown, so quit your yapping."

Millions? I didn't even make millions of pennies. The only millions I was going to have were millions of hernias. Millions of mental problems.

"The girls are off to Mexico-co-co-co," sang my mother. I reminded myself to check the linen closet for booze when I got home.

My dad dropped Payton and me off at the airport at 5:30 A.M. This was plenty late for me, but Payton looked like she had been yanked out of bed and forced to do strenuous field labor. She was wearing huge Chanel sunglasses, holding two cups of coffee, carrying a cashmere travel throw, and cursing softly in Spanish.

We shooed our father away before he could catch on that we were checking into the Phoenix flight. Thirty minutes later, we were sitting on the plane.

Safely in the sky and munching on pretzels, I realized that this was the very first time I had ignored my BlackBerry on a workday since I started at the *List*. It was petrifying, yet so liberating. I didn't have to put conversations on hold to check it at five-minute intervals. I didn't have to tell a friend to hold her tears because I had to rewrite an article as fast as I could. All I had to do was breathe.

"Planes are amazing," I said to Payton, who had leaned her head against the wall to try to sleep. She had bought us first-class tickets, even though the haul wasn't very long, which was rather nice. If I had had to pay for the trip, we would be on Greyhound. She didn't respond. For the second time in a week I watched her sleep, feeling closer to her than I had in years. Payton had gotten her way since the forceps gripped her skull. But I had to admit that on this visit, even though she still acted like Mussolini in a Gucci minidress, she had softened. She hadn't poisoned me, or suggested I try base-jumping off our roof. And she had helped me considerably with her willingness to push me down avenues I was so hesitant to pursue.

"Payton," I whispered. She didn't budge. I lifted her sunglasses off her face, and she stared at me like she was about to spit in my face.

"Thank you for coming with me," I said. "For coming home and doing all this with me. I don't know where I would be on this story without you. I definitely wouldn't be on a plane headed to Arizona."

Payton rolled her eyes so far that I could only see the whites, which started shaking from the strain. "Shut up," she said, putting her glasses back on. "I'm not doing this for you," she said groggily. "I'm doing this for me. I can't spend all my time with Buck and horses and our overly attentive staff. Buck has some terrible habits. Like shooting everything in sight or eating twelve eggs at one time. Isn't that disgusting? Twelve eggs, yolks and everything." I looked at her, too accustomed to her attitude to really be upset by her reaction. "I'm not doing you any favors. Coddling you has never been an interest of mine. But meddling in the affairs of others always has been." And those were the last words she spoke on the plane.

When we landed in Phoenix, the air was thick with nervous energy. My nervous energy.

"I shouldn't have had that coffee on the plane," I said to Payton.

She looked me up and down like a man selecting a stripper. "I don't think the caffeine is your problem. *Es la culpabilidad.*"

"Guilt. Yes, that might be it," I said.

"You're not doing anything wrong," said Payton, studying my anxious face. "You haven't done anything but kiss Sandro, which was stupid, but not as bad as sleeping with Senator Stanton."

Right. That was one way to look at it. I hadn't broken too many moral codes. But I still felt like the hangman.

"This is what you do, isn't it? You're a reporter. It says so on that horrible ID you have to wear around your neck."

"But I'm a features writer. I work in Style. I write articles that make people happy, not articles that destroy careers. I don't know what I'm doing here."

"Says who?" replied Payton angrily. "Don't let those old men dictate what you can and can't do. Otherwise, you'll be sitting in the back and people will happily call you mediocre for the rest of your life. You've been letting me do it since birth, and it's pathetic."

"Mediocre" was an upgrade from what she usually called me, which was "unfit to breathe."

"And finally, you make this big move to the *Capitolist*, and now you're going to let those egomaniacal bosses decide what you're capable of accomplishing. Why don't *you* decide?"

I pointed to a dark green Jeep Patriot in the rental lot, clicked the car open, grabbed my sister, and hugged her until I actually thought she was going to throw up on my shoulder.

"You're right, Payton. I appreciate the pep talk. I really do. I haven't felt this empowered since I beat Jessica Van Mark in junior hunters and jumpers in Culpepper fifteen years ago."

"You really should be such a better rider than you are," said Payton, reminding me that hugging her until her insides hurt was not going to change thirty years of unpleasant behavior. "And now that you love me so much," she said, "can we get a more upscale car?"

"No," I said. "We're trying to blend in. We can't exactly cruise around in a DeLorean."

When we got onto the long stretch of Highway 85, we fell silent. I realized that in the last two weeks, Payton and I had

spoken to each other more than we had in the last two years. My
father had told me all through my childhood that Payton was my
only sister so I better learn to like her. It took a few decades, but
I was starting to understand his point.

"So whoever this Drew Reader was, he died in a meatpacking
plant owned by the Stanton family," said Payton, taking notes in
a small book. I looked over at the cover. It was definitely made
of an exotic animal skin. Probably something illegal. Probably
white rhino. "And he had a little girl named Olivia and a wife
who was left almost penniless. The wife offs herself a few years
later, and the girl has no parents left. Probably has to be raised
by grandparents or a smelly aunt or something."

"Well, I'm not sure on the offs-herself part. Let's not jump
the gun and just say she died."

"Okay, fine," said Payton. "Either way, if that Olivia is *the*
Olivia, that's a lot to have happen to you at a young age. You can
see why she would be a little intense."

"Sure," I said. "Maybe not quite as intense as Olivia Campo
is, but yes, the death of both your parents is a lot to handle. But
Olivia isn't such a strange name. It's not Emily or Sarah, but
still. It could be nothing but a coincidence. It probably is."

"The phone call in Middleburg wasn't a coincidence," said
Payton, still scribbling notes. "It probably seemed a little crazy
then, but look how right you were."

We drove past a police car and a yellow road sign that read
"high intensity enforcement area" and both looked at each other
nervously.

"It's definitely possible," I said. "Okay, even if she is the same
person, how does it fit into the immigration scenario? I mean,
look at where we are. She's from a border area, too. She and Sandro were devoted to the cause of immigration reform for years,
and Sandro is certainly still involved. So maybe she decided to

take it to the next level, without telling Sandro she was going to extremes, and she got close to the man pulling the strings on border control legislation."

"Okay," agreed Payton. "But the sex can't be a footnote. That's what this whole thing is about, remember? Hot nights in Middleburg, Virginia."

"Or maybe she just fell for him," I suggested after a few minutes. "Maybe I just haven't been able to see that since I'm salivating over her husband and can't believe she isn't, too."

"Maybe," said Payton.

Tall, thin cactuses lined the sides of the road, and we blasted the air-conditioning to save us from the dry heat outside. Payton's notebook paper fluttered from the burst of air. She took a hair clip out of her purse and pinched the pages together.

"Let's talk about Olivia and the love of your life," said Payton, switching gears. "They got married to keep him in the country, and they stayed in Texas, right?"

"Yes," I said. We passed yet another yellow sign about immigration patrols. "She worked at the *Corpus Christi Caller Times* right after college for two years, so they must have stayed there. And then after that she was at the *El Paso Times* for almost two more years before coming to Washington three months after the *List* was launched."

"El Paso," said Payton, doodling the lone star of Texas onto her notes. "Do you think she was still involved with immigration reform when she lived there?"

"Well," I said, "Sandro worked for a nonprofit immigrants' rights group there called the Border Community for Human Rights. It was a very by-the-book nonprofit, nothing extreme. Olivia could have worked with them, too, or with another group, but she couldn't do it openly. Neutral journalism and all that. I imagine immigration is an especially touchy issue in Texas. She couldn't have been associated with anything publicly. I looked up her work for those papers, and she wrote about immigration, but probably not any more or less than other state reporters in Texas. No red flags."

"Let's just assume that she stayed involved and that Sandro stayed involved," said Payton, scribbling again.

"So eventually she hears about this paper being launched and she lands a job there," I said. "It seems like a pretty big step up from the *El Paso Times*, but there are a few reporters like that at the *List*, people coming from practically nowhere, and it was early days, so I'm not reading into her move too much. She's good at her job, and let's just say the *List* recognized that. So she comes to Washington, a place she's always dreamed of living, with Sandro in tow."

"Okay," said Payton. "And they just happen to live in a huge town house in Dupont?"

"I think they pay her pretty damn well at the *List*. They love her. Like six figures love her, so she could pay for it, even without a lot of help from Sandro."

"What does Sandro do at OAS?"

"I don't know. There's no bio or title listed on the site. Just his name and a few committee assignments."

"And you think he's still involved in immigration reform?"

"In one way or another, yes," I said. "He told me his entire family is still in Mexico."

I stepped on the breaks as a small rodent scurried across the road, and both of our bodies were jerked forward.

"Let's try not to die today," said Payton dryly as she readjusted her seat belt. The GPS signaled that we were only thirty miles away from Ajo. "So where do we go from here," Payton murmured, looking at her notes.

I shook my head and kept on driving. I had no idea.

As the scenery turned from highway to town, Payton pointed out a building coming up on our left.

It was a huge white stucco church. We pulled up next to it and looked at the sign. "Immaculate Conception Catholic Church," read Payton, looking up at the cross on top.

"It's absolutely beautiful," I said. It looked like a building that belonged underneath a sunset in Italy. "I would never have guessed."

Payton tried to stretch her long legs, her black linen shorts creasing slightly as she bent at the waist.

"Okay, now listen to my plan B. Ready?"

"Sure," said Payton, her arms crossed in front of her.

"Plan B. We find nothing here. The Readers are just two people who died very unfortunate deaths. We drive to Corpus Christi, we try finding Olivia and Sandro's former colleagues, but we find nothing there. And while we're down here, Olivia is plotting my demise at the *Capitolist*."

"That plan sounds depressing."

"If that happens, I turn in the affair story, plain and simple, like you said. It's still huge and you're right, it's time."

"It is still huge," said Payton. "*Huge.* You don't really need motive and all that when you have a poster-size color photo of them screwing. More information would just be icing on the cake."

More information—some unethical, terrible motive—would make me feel better about being a meddling whistle-blower.

"You have an amazing story to print," Payton assured me.

"I'm way past it being a story," I said. "This just feels like my life now."

CHAPTER 18

It was early afternoon by the time we left our small motel with a list of destinations to cover. We had found addresses for almost everyone quoted in the court article. Five people had been mentioned by name. Payton had determined that one had died, which left us with four.

"Jeffrey Diaz, Michael O'Brien, Travis Turner, and Manuel Reyes," I said, looking at their names and addresses in Payton's notebook. "And we know for sure these guys are all still alive?" I asked as I turned the car back onto Highway 85.

"No, we don't," she said. We were both already starting to sweat. I looked down at the thermostat in the car. 105 degrees.

"We'll find out soon," said Payton. "It's that kind of town. Everyone knows who's dead."

We were driving to the first house, where we hoped Jeffrey Diaz lived, when I realized I hadn't looked at my BlackBerry since Virginia.

"Oh Jesus, what are you doing!" Payton screamed as I swerved off the road and onto the shoulder like I was a race car driver in need of a tire change.

"I haven't looked at my BlackBerry in hours!" I shouted, almost tearing up. "I could have missed something. I . . . where is it!" I screamed, throwing things out of my bag.

"Calm down," said Payton. "It's Saturday, and they know you're off this weekend. I'm sure no one emailed you."

"You don't get it at all. They don't care if I'm off. If there's a story Hardy feels like I should write, then I'll have to write it, vacation or not."

"That's disturbing," said Payton, grabbing my hairbrush off the floor. "You can't work there anymore. Who wants to live like that?"

She brushed her beautiful frizz-free hair off her tan forehead and frowned. "I hate July," she grumbled. "It's so hot and patriotic."

I looked down at my messages. There was one from Hardy asking me to write about a Twitter feud brewing between Tucker Carlson and Meghan McCain, but his message had come in four hours ago.

"I just . . . I knew it," I said, tears filling my eyes. I wrote Hardy back and apologized for not having my phone on. I wrote that I had been with my sister at her doctor's appointment and that there was no cell-phone use allowed in the sterile clinic.

"Long doctor's appointment," he wrote back immediately. "I had Libby write it. Be back on the grid tomorrow."

I threw the phone onto the floor mat and started driving again. I screamed, "I am so sick of writing about crap!" and started hitting the steering wheel.

Payton grabbed my hands and put hers on the wheel.

"Calm down or pull over," she said, trying to keep the car straight.

"I'll calm down," I said, feeling about as calm as Venus Williams losing the Wimbledon final.

"You're poised to write something that's not crap, so let's go ahead and finish this mess. It's your career to change. Change it."

Instead of screaming some more, I drove us to the address we had for Jeffrey Diaz.

"Eight-eleven West Cholla Avenue," said Payton. "I think it's this one. There, with the cactuses in front." She pointed to a very humble white house behind a chain link fence.

When we pulled up outside, we just sat there and looked at each other.

"You're the reporter," said Payton. "Go report."

Right. I got out of the car like I was about to deliver my own eulogy and opened the unwelcoming gate. At the bright blue door, I balled up my fist and pounded gently. I stood there for two minutes but didn't hear a sound. Payton was watching me from the car. I looked away from her serene face and pounded harder. This time I heard movement inside.

A woman in pink leggings and an oversize T-shirt opened the door and looked at me from behind a screen door.

"Hello, ma'am, I'm sorry to bother you," I said as politely as I could. "My name is Adrienne Brown. I'm a newspaper reporter at the *Capitolist* in Washington, D.C., and I'm looking for Jeffrey Diaz."

The woman gasped, started yelling in Spanish, and then slammed the door in my face. A great beginning. I should clearly start writing my nomination letter for the Pulitzer committee.

I turned around and saw Payton come out of the car and open the aluminum gate. She opened the screen door, banged on the wooden one, and shouted "*Donde está* Jeffrey Diaz!"

I wondered what it felt like to get shot from point-blank range? I imagined it was like having your face lit on fire and then scraped up with sandpaper.

The woman opened the door again, surprisingly less irate. Payton switched tones and started speaking calmly to her.

"Tell her I'm a reporter," I said. "We have to be transparent."

"Shut up, please," said Payton, swinging back into English to chide me.

After about three minutes of back-and-forth, I heard Payton thank her. Then she grabbed my hand and led me back to the car.

"What did she say?" I pressed as soon as our doors closed.

"She said she has no idea where Jeffrey Diaz is. That was his daughter, but she said no one in her family has seen him for ten years. She said that if we found him we should tell him he's a worthless piece of pig shit."

"Fantastic," I replied. "Very helpful information."

"I also asked when he stopped working at the meatpacking plant, and she said he worked there right up until he left. She also said that the slave drivers he worked for pushed him over the edge."

"Really?" I said excitedly. "She called them slave drivers?"

"She said it a little bit more colorfully than that, but that was the gist of it," said Payton.

I made her speak the exact line in Spanish into my tape recorder just in case I needed an offensive quote for later.

"Don't get too excited," said Payton. "Everyone thinks their boss is a slave driver."

I entered the next address in the GPS.

"I'm like Erin Brockovich," I said, adjusting my seat belt and shimmying my poor excuse for boobs up a little higher in my push-up bra. "I'm bringing justice to this one horse town."

"You're like an enormous loser playing with her tiny boobs," said Payton, pushing the car into reverse.

I scowled at her and looked down at the notebook. "Michael O'Brien," I read from Payton's notes. "The GPS says he lives by Organ Pipe Cactus National Monument."

"What is that?" asked Payton, looking suspiciously at the image of a national park that showed up on the small screen.

"What do you think it is? It's a park filled with cactuses that look like organ pipes."

The stop at O'Brien's house went a little smoother than my first attempt. His wife, a plump, smiling woman of about seventy, said it was God's grace that had taken him out of plant work and let him enjoy the outdoors again in his new job at the national park. He was a security guard, protecting the cactuses from vandals and the like.

When we left Payton made the point that cactuses should be able to protect themselves, being, after all, something like naturally occurring medieval spike balls, but I told her to suck it. I had a good feeling about Michael O'Brien.

The organ-pipe cactuses were the biggest cactuses I had ever seen. Many were at least four times my height. I was no cactus connoisseur, but the humongous things were actually terrifying. Payton tried to get me to touch one, "for old times' sake." Instead, I left her to marvel at it and approached a park ranger for information on Michael O'Brien.

"He's in the back," he said, pointing to a vast sweep of dry land where nothing but cactuses and dry shrubs grew.

"In the back of . . ."

"In the back! He's in the back," he pointed again. He turned away to tend to a group of tourists and left me standing like a bewildered idiot.

"He's in the back," I said to Payton as she caught up with me.

O'Brien, as it turns out, was in the back. He was just standing there in his olive-drab uniform, looking confused, guarding a big patch of earth.

"Good Lord, if that's not the personification of dementia, I don't know what is," said Payton, turning back around. "I'll leave you to it."

He was old. He looked eighty, maybe older. He must have

been nearly retired when he was quoted in the paper twenty-two years ago. I wasn't going to let my fear of failure (or the indigenous plants that were pricking my bare legs) keep me from talking to him. I approached him with a smile on my face. When he lifted his face to mine, I saw that he had two different colored eyes. Hepetochromia. I had a cat with the same condition when I was a kid.

"I'm terribly sorry to bother you, sir," I said, sticking out my hand.

"I don't know why," he replied slowly. "That's what I'm here for."

I laughed nervously as he shook my hand. His was very warm from working outside and trembling slightly from old age.

Even though the sun was blinding me, I kept my sunglasses off because I wanted to look trustworthy and approachable. Squinting through the strong desert light, I disclosed that I was a reporter for the *Capitolist* in Washington, D.C., and doing a story on the John F. Stanton & Company meatpacking plant.

"Did you work there?" I asked. "I found an old article written in the early nineties that said you did."

He tipped his wide-brimmed hat up and frowned. "I did work at John F. Stanton's, yes I did. I worked there for forty-three years, in fact. But I like it better here. Why'd ya ask?"

Why did I ask? Oh, no reason. I just wanted to get to the bottom of a death that occurred over twenty years ago, and he was one of four people I had on my list to question. But the first was probably dead or in prison, so it was really down to three.

"I had a friend who worked there," I said. "Well, a friend of a friend really, but someone important to me. Maybe you knew him?"

O'Brien shifted his old legs around a bit and squinted into my squinting eyes. "Maybe I did," he said. "What'd he go by?"

"Well, he went by Drew Reader."

"Did you know Drew Reader? You look too young. He died years ago. Ten years ago."

"Twenty-three, actually. And no, sadly, I never knew him. I just would like to know a little bit more information about him."

"Well, I am afraid that's gonna be real hard, Miss . . ."

"Brown. Adrienne. Just call me . . . Adrienne is fine."

"Well, Adrienne, like I said, Drew Reader died ten years back. You're asking questions 'bout a ghost, I'm afraid."

"Yes," I replied. "But I'm just looking into how exactly he passed away. I know it was reported as an accident. But I'm wondering if the company was negligent. If it should have been declared a wrongful death instead of an accident."

"He fell into the grinder. Got trapped in," said O'Brien. "I believe that was reported."

"Yes, it was."

"He was cleaning during the night shift. He always worked the night shift. I remember because he was real young, and that's always who they made work the late-night hours."

"I know it was a long time ago, but do you remember anything about that night? Did you see it happen?"

"No, I didn't see it. Thank the Lord for that. I don't know if I would be standing here today if I had. I didn't see it, but I heard the screams and I saw . . . well, I saw the result, let's just say."

The result. I could argue that twenty-three years later, the result was still happening. "Do you know who was there that did see him fall? I have some names, but maybe you know other people. Men who were not in the courtroom when John F. Stanton & Company was declared innocent of any negligence or wrongdoing?"

"Who was there now, I don't know. It was so long ago. I think that Mexican Jesus Diaz was with 'em."

"Jeffrey Diaz?" I asked.

"Yeah, that's it," he said, lighting up. "Jeffrey Diaz. He run out of town now, though. I think he was there. Him and a few other guys. All guys who worked that tough late shift. Mine wasn't as late as Drew's, but it overlapped. It was late all the same. Never saw my wife at normal hours. I like things so much better now."

I imagined he did.

"Did you know Drew well?" I asked. "Did you know his wife, Joanne, or his daughter, Olivia? I believe her last name is Campo now. Olivia Campo. She might not live here anymore."

"No. I don't remember any of that. Definitely don't. I just remember him dying too young. It was a shame. But I was much older than those boys. I had a wife and my own family. I kept to myself."

I thanked O'Brien, trying not to show my extreme disappointment, and went to rejoin Payton.

"Better," I said when I found her. She was drinking a Diet Coke, still analyzing the cactus.

"He could form full sentences? Didn't drool on you?"

"Don't be ageist," I said. "He was quite articulate and had two different-color eyes."

"That's terrifying."

"Well, eye color aside, he said that the people who were there when Reader died were Jeffrey Diaz and some other guys."

"Really? We knew that already."

"There had to be others," I said. "There is no way that only five people plus Drew Reader worked on a night shift in a huge plant."

"Well, how many people work there?" asked Payton.

"I don't know," I said. "I guess we could go there and ask."

"Adrienne. It's not exactly the same world it was in Upton

Sinclair's day. We can't go undercover, start chopping up cows, and then write an exposé."

I had thought about interviewing someone from the plant's management who had been there in 1989, but in the end I decided it was too dangerous. If I said I was a newspaper reporter from Washington, they would surely think I was looking into Senator Stanton, and it would get back to him as fast as someone could dial ten numbers. I couldn't ask around.

Payton and I soon realized that what we could do was go there and buy something. Meat. Lots of it.

"I can buy it, and your name won't be anywhere," said Payton once we were headed toward the plant. "My last name isn't even Brown anymore."

Judging from the size of the plant, there had to have been more than five people there when Drew Reader died. The complex was enormous. Odious and enormous.

"Oh look," I said, pointing. "You can see all the cows, just waiting to die."

"Of course you can. Where did you think they would be?"

"I don't know," I replied. "I just didn't think we would have to see them."

"Don't be such a hippie," said Payton, pointing toward a door.

"We shouldn't be here, Payton. It's a bad idea." I stopped talking when my voice started to warble. "I can feel it in my bones."

"Oh shut up," said Payton, not even turning around behind her to see if her only sister was okay. "You don't feel anything in your bones. Only old people feel things in their bones and that's just osteoporosis."

"But Payton, we're probably going to get arrested, or shot. It happens all the time near the border."

This time she turned around.

"Adrienne! We're not crawling under barbed wire in the dead of night with cocaine coming out of our ears. We're just walking to a place of business. You're wearing five-hundred-dollar loafers!" she said, pointing accusingly to my practical Tod's fuchsia driving mocs. "I don't think we're about to get cuffed and printed." When Payton turned back around to lead us into the lion's den I could hear her asking God why she was born into a family of cowards.

"What's our plan exactly?" I asked her, trying to calm down.

"We don't need one. We have money. We're just two women who need a large amount of beef."

Of course. Two women needing a lot of beef. It sounded like the opening line of an award-winning XXX movie.

But there was no one there to take Payton's money that day. The plant was locked, and the only workers we could find were outside with the animals.

"Are you . . . could you maybe help us?" I asked a man who was throwing feed out for the huge brown cows. When he answered in Spanish, Payton took over. I thought their exchange would last about thirty seconds, but five minutes later, I was still standing in the middle of cow death row while Payton babbled on. Finally I heard her thank him, and she grabbed me by the arm and led me back to the car.

"Drew Reader wasn't the only death in that plant," said Payton, hurrying away from the field. "That guy, he wasn't here in '89, obviously, and didn't know anything about Reader's death, but he said just three years ago someone died when a forklift fell on him."

"Oh Jesus, that's terrible."

"I know. He was driving up a ramp, and the forklift tipped and he was crushed by it. Other workers used another forklift to pick up the one crushing him, but it was too late."

"Was this in the news?" I asked. "I didn't see anything about it when I was researching John F. Stanton & Company."

"I don't know," said Payton. "But it doesn't speak very well for the company, these accidental deaths. It's not like they're swimming with sharks. It should be a safe enough working environment. Also, there's five hundred workers here during the week. At least. And about fifty on at night. That's what he said, anyway."

"Did you get a name?"

"I tried. He wouldn't give it to me. These guys aren't stupid, and let's face it, they can't all be legal. It's not the most glamorous job, but it's a job. Why put it in jeopardy by accusing your boss of involuntary manslaughter?"

"Well, if there are fifty people here a night, there had to be more than five in 1989. We should be able to find someone to go on the record."

Payton and I ate zero meat that day. Even she, resident of meat-loving Argentina, ordered a grilled cheese when we stopped in a diner to go through our notes.

"You're aware that we really have nothing from today, right?" said Payton after she had finished eating. "You talked to one old man who was there when Reader died, but you didn't learn anything game-changing. And you can't really peg that other wrongful death against Stanton since it was never widely reported. We learned that there were probably more than five people there when Reader died, but we don't know who they were. And we still know nothing about Olivia Reader and Olivia Campo—if they're the same person or not. I think we should keep looking tomorrow, but Addy, I think you have to finish writing this today. You need to get this out even if the only motive you can come up with is multiple orgasms."

"But what the hell am I supposed to write, Payton?" I said, trying to stay calm. "I don't have enough!"

"You have so much!" said Payton. She was getting angry. "You want more so that you can feel better about writing it. Just get over your moral dilemma and put it down on paper. You're smarter than this. Then you can keep talking to more people here. It's five o'clock in the afternoon, and we leave in twenty-six hours. You don't want to leave here with nothing."

"Then get out of my way!" I screamed. "Just get out of my way. I appreciate your help, but you're not doing anything but making me feel clueless right now."

So Payton stood up, fighting back angry tears, and left with the car keys in her hand.

I only saw Payton cry twice in high school: once when she lost the state field hockey championship to a Catholic school in Richmond and the other time at our grandmother's funeral in Charlottesville. I remember being surprised that Payton had the ability to cry over someone. Well, a dead someone. But here she was crying about me. She actually cared about my career, my future. All my life, I had more bitterness and resentment toward Payton than I had love. But the percentages were changing quickly.

I was alone in a diner in Ajo, Arizona, trying to piece together a story that I still wasn't sure I had the courage to write. I was scared of getting something wrong and ruining my career, which felt like it was just beginning. And I was petrified of printing something about one of the most powerful men in the United States government. What business was it of mine that he was having an affair? So he was a lying sack of shit. So were plenty of other people. And his family company was a death trap. Big deal. Why was it falling on me to tell the whole world about it?

I wanted to burn everything I had and crawl back into my cozy cubicle in New York. People thought I was good at my job up there. I didn't have anything to prove.

It took ten minutes of resting my head against the warm linoleum table and two waitresses asking me if they should call a doctor before I was able to admit to myself that now I did have something to prove. I did want to break this story and make a name for myself. The *Capitolist* had gotten under my skin; it hadn't killed me yet, which must have meant that I was going crazy and that I was stronger. I was a better reporter now and one with a functioning backbone.

"Is that the girl from the cactus park?" A gentle old voice woke me from my haze.

"Well, hi," I said, smiling at Michael O'Brien. "It is. I'm just here working on the article I was telling you about."

"Doesn't look like it's going very well," he said. "Why don't you buy me a cup of coffee instead?"

"Okay," I said, signaling to the waitress for another cup of coffee.

"My shift is over," said O'Brien, smiling. Now that we had escaped the glaring sun, I could see that he had two gaping holes where teeth should have been. "I don't want you to think I'm playing hooky now."

"I wouldn't dare," I said, pushing the little metal pot of cream toward him.

"You still walking around town asking people what happened to Drew Reader all those years ago?"

"Not really," I said. "I only asked one more person since I asked you. I should be asking a whole lot more, but I thought you would be a good person to start with."

O'Brien picked up his cup unsteadily and took a sip, spilling all over the table. His hands, covered in liver spots, put the cup down, and he watched me clean up the mess with some flimsy napkins.

"They always making these cups so heavy," he said. "I don't understand it. They should be thinner."

"I think you're right," I said.

He looked up from his drink and stared right at me. "I think you're right, too," he said.

He did? He thought I was right? About what exactly? I looked around me to make sure I wasn't part of some National Park Police entrapment scheme.

"You do?" I said, my heart racing. "You think I'm right about Drew Reader? His daughter, Olivia?"

"Just slow down now," he said. I helped him transfer his coffee from the thick ceramic mug into a lighter Styrofoam cup. "I just said, I think you're right, and that's all I'm going to say."

I watched him drink from a small plastic water glass, his hands still shaking, and imagined him working in a meat-processing plant for forty-three years. I hoped there was a special, relaxing, machinery-free place in heaven for that man.

"I wish you would say more," I said, my voice tired and strained. "I'm afraid I don't have much to go on right now. Just a hunch and well, a few other things, but mostly a hunch."

"Lot of things start out just a hunch," he replied. "Who else you gonna talk to while you're here?"

"Who else should I talk to?" I asked.

He didn't answer. Just looked off into the distance with a content expression. "You want some pie?" he asked. "We got some real good pie down here." He looked longingly at a rotating glass box full of pies.

No, I didn't want a pie. What I wanted him to do was say, "Olivia was like a daughter to me, here is her photo. It's yours to keep. Make a few copies if you would like."

Instead I said, "Sure, let's have pie."

I wiped off my face, which O'Brien pretended not to notice was burnt and sweaty, and asked the waitress for an entire blueberry pie.

"Where you from again?" O'Brien asked between bites. "You say?"

"I didn't," I replied. "I'm from Virginia. Just outside Washington, D.C. I work up there for a newspaper. A pretty important one."

"It's nice up there?"

"Well . . ." I thought about it for a second. "It is pretty nice. Kind of tough, though. A lot of people want a lot of things only a few can have."

"But that's everywhere, isn't it? Everyone wants money, but not a lot of people can have it."

"That sounds about right."

"You should move down here," he said, eating the pie with a spoon. "It's always warm."

"That must be nice."

He hit at the crust with his spoon, gave up when it wouldn't budge, and started eating it with his hands.

"So, who else you talking to? You never said."

I uncrumpled the piece of paper in my pocket and looked at the name and addresses on it. "Travis Turner," I said. "Do you know him?"

"Sure do," said O'Brien with pie flakes on his mouth. "I went to his funeral just last year."

Wonderful. Absolutely peachy. I had one potential source who was missing and most likely didn't speak English, another who was dead, and my most reliable source was just using me for pie money.

"I'd like to thank you for this pie," said O'Brien, standing up with the help of the table edge.

"It's nothing, really," I said, leaning down and writing my phone number on an unused napkin. "Here." I handed it to him. "If you change your mind and decide you have more to say."

"That ain't happening," he said. "But I will let you walk me to my car. How's that sound?"

"It sounds just fine," I said. I took his arm and walked him out to his Buick LeSabre.

"I'm not worried about you," he said after I helped him with his seat belt. "You'll be all right. I've got a feeling about these kinds of things."

He started to drive away but stopped and rolled down his window.

"Drew Reader's little girl doing okay?" he asked me. "Olivia was it?" His car rumbled from old age.

"That was my question for you," I told him.

"That so? Well, now that you mention it, I guess he did have a daughter."

"Do you know where she is?" I asked. "It would really help me if you did."

"'Fraid not. Just remember her being a sweet little girl. Good luck now." And with that he drove off at a snail's pace.

Standing in front of the dusty diner parking lot, I took out my phone and called Payton.

"Tell me you're calm now and I'll pick you up," she said, as if speaking to an unruly teen.

"I'm calm now," I said. "I'm calm, and I think that Michael O'Brien knew Olivia Reader. He didn't say anything really helpful—like her name now being Campo—but he almost did. He said 'Drew Reader's little girl doing okay?' Which basically translates into 'I knew Drew Reader's daughter, care about her welfare, but haven't seen her in a long time.'"

"Can you get it in so many words?"

"I don't know. Maybe he just needs time. I feel closer."

"You better."

"How about you pick me up and I'll tell you about it," I suggested.

"I will. It's just I drove out a little far to see this Puerto Blanco scenic drive thing, so it might take me a second to get back to you."

"A second?" I asked, trying not to blow up.

"Half an hour. Have some more coffee."

I walked back into the diner, smiled at the waitress, who let me sit in the same table, and ordered a cup of decaf. "I'm a little jittery," I explained when she brought it to me.

"I understand that," she said, placing it in front of me along with a receipt, facedown. "You out here to see the cactuses?" she asked.

"Not specifically," I replied. "But I did go see them today and thought the park was pretty spectacular. That's where I met Michael O'Brien," I said, explaining my earlier rendezvous.

"O'Brien, sure," she said. "He's a good man. He hasn't had the easiest life, but he keeps in good spirits. Comes in here all the time."

"That must be nice," I replied. "I've always liked that about small towns."

"He likes to talk to the customers and check up on his daughter," she said, filling up my almost full cup.

I looked up at her happy face.

"I'm sorry," I apologized. "I didn't realize . . . are you—"

"His daughter? I am," she said. "That's why I know he's such a good man."

Thirty minutes later, when Payton pulled up and honked rudely for me, I reached for the check to pay it, but the waitress put her hand on mine and said, "That's on the house, of course. Thanks for keeping my daddy company like that. He sure loves pie."

"That was no problem at all," I said, crumpling the receipt and putting it in my pocket along with the five-dollar bill I had taken out. "Thank you for the coffee. It was very good." I waved goodbye, walked outside, and shoved Payton into the passenger seat.

"Travis Turner is dead," I said, pulling the seat up an inch.

"Perfect," said Payton. "Now what's your brilliant plan?"

"I have absolutely no idea. We try to find the last one, Manuel Reyes. And then we just start asking questions."

"I have another idea," said Payton. In true Payton fashion, she didn't offer up the idea until I asked her about it twice and screamed that I had three weeks to break this story or I would be out of a job.

"Relax. You have such a neurotic personality," Payton replied.

I took a deep breath and exhaled loudly to show her just how relaxed I was. "Well," said Payton, fiddling with the car's GPS again. "I've once again discovered a delightful little piece to your puzzle. While you were busy having a leisurely coffee, I asked a few more questions and now I have an idea of where we should go."

"What kind of questions?" I asked, spraying the windshield to wipe off the dust. "I thought you went to Puerto Blanco?"

"I did that, too," said Payton, turning up the radio. "You took forever."

"You didn't bribe anyone this time?" I asked. I was pretty sure that every time I turned my back Payton was waving around crisp bills to everyone with working vocal cords.

"No, I did not bribe anyone," said Payton, smiling. I absolutely did not believe her. She probably had a thousand bucks cash in her bra.

"But I did find out where Olivia Reader used to live."

"You did!" I exclaimed, totally not caring if she was throwing her unborn child's college fund at total strangers.

"I did. And it's not far. You want to go there or do you want to have some more intimate chats with useless old people?"

"I want to go there," I replied, pushing the Jeep well over the speed limit.

"You never know," said Payton. "There could be something identifying about the house. Something that tells us that Olivia Reader and Olivia Campo are the same person."

Yes, that would be fantastic, but I seriously doubted that there was a mural of Olivia's face painted on the side of the property.

We drove in silence for a few minutes listening to a classic rock radio station with the air-conditioning blasting so loud we could hear it over the music. The town, which was starting to look more familiar, finally rolled into view and Payton looked down at her notes and instructed me to take a hard right.

"Now left," she said when the road started to thin and the houses got noticeably smaller.

"It's down that road there," said Payton, pointing at a long dirt road with no houses in sight. "Or that's what I was told anyway."

"Who gave you the address?" I asked as I hesitated around the turn. The road looked very long and very private.

"A woman in the Laundromat, actually," said Payton, squinting into the sun as we passed a dog running along the side of the road. "I was just walking past it and realized I had never been inside a Laundromat. I mean, even in college we sent our clothes out. So I walked in and there was this older woman behind the counter and I just asked her if she had known the Readers. I said I was a cousin and I wanted to pay homage to their memory."

"You're going to hell," I said, driving slowly as the car bounced on the uneven road. "You can't lie about dead people."

"This from the night-vision nude photographer," said Payton, laughing. "Plus, you don't seem to mind very much now."

She was right. I didn't mind. I was quite happy to have Payton doing everything that, as a journalist, I really couldn't do. I knew it was wrong to turn a blind eye to her behavior, but I didn't really care at this point. I had my career to save.

Payton continued, "I asked about Olivia Campo but she said she didn't know anyone by the name Campo in Ajo. She said she remembered the Readers, but wouldn't acknowledge the suicide. Just said that the little girl never came back after her mother died. But she was able to describe where they lived."

"Children don't disappear," I said, driving slower and slower.

"They do if they're dead," replied Payton.

I turned the air-conditioning vent away from my face and lowered my window. What we were doing was perfectly normal. I was just following a lead handed out by an old senile woman at a Laundromat. And Payton was making fun of me for getting all my information from senior citizens.

"There it is," said Payton, motioning toward a small gray house in the distance.

"There are cars in front," I said, pointing out the obvious. "We shouldn't go. Someone lives there and they'll probably just shoot us for trespassing." I slowed the car to a halt in front.

"This is probably close enough anyway," said Payton.

We sat motionless, watching the American flag hanging from the top of the porch and waving slightly in the breeze.

The house was small. Very small. Our horse barn was about four times the size. It had light gray wooden siding that looked like it had been repainted every couple of years instead of replaced. Some were sagging a little in the middle while others looked like they were hanging on by one tired, rusty nail. There was a porch and two white plastic chairs on it and a potted plant on the cement stairs leading up to the house. It was tired, bland, colorless, but the flag brought it a little sense of pride and ownership. The inhabitants might be poor, but they were part of the map of America, which I sometimes forgot extended far beyond Washington, D.C.

It was hard to imagine Olivia, who now drove a very expensive BMW and interviewed the president of the United States, living here. If Olivia Campo was actually Olivia Reader, she would have spent her childhood walking out that front door, sitting on that porch, walking down this road. That girl could be the same girl who now verbally spat on her colleagues in one of the most high-powered newsrooms in the country. The grass around the house needed to be cut and there was a rusty shell of an old car in the back. I couldn't imagine Olivia Campo ever running up those stairs. I thought about the elegant home she shared with Sandro. It was a perfect slice of Washington . . . and it looked about one million dollars and a couple of lifetimes away from the little dilapidated ranch we were staring at. Maybe we were sniffing around a cold lead after all.

Still, I couldn't shake an odd sense of recognition. Olivia didn't act like she came from money. Not like Libby or Julia or the girls who surrounded me in my youth. She didn't have the ease of it, the casual confidence. Her energy seemed to come from the pit of her stomach, the kind of steely drive I had always associated with people who were used to pulling themselves up by their bootstraps. I looked at the front door, worried that someone very big and very angry was going to walk out. The only similarity between Olivia Campo's house now was the American flag—there was one in Olivia's kitchen in Washington and there was one hanging here. But there were several million in between, too.

"Let's go," Payton finally said after we had been sitting in the idle car for five minutes. "We get it right? Her life—if it was her life—was shit."

I nodded in agreement and turned the car around.

We spoke to six other people that night, including Manuel Reyes, and they all looked at us like we were crazy. "I'm retired, I golf, I have a new wife, and I sure as hell don't want to talk to you" was what he said when we found him at home. No one else we asked knew Drew Reader, and they certainly didn't know his daughter.

"It happened too long ago," I said when we were back in our motel room. "This is an exercise in pointless questioning."

"Start writing," said Payton as she got into bed. "What you already have is simple, and potentially devastating for them." She was right. I had to finish the piece and get it in print as fast as I could.

Before turning off her bedside lamp, Payton announced, "I'm flying back to Argentina tomorrow morning."

"You're doing what?" I exclaimed. "Why? I need you here."

"No, you don't," said Payton, putting her cashmere throw over the pillow like it was made of mold. "You've got this. And Buck misses me. He said eating a dozen eggs alone isn't all that fun. Isn't that just adorable?"

It was disgusting. Why couldn't he consume a massive amount of cholesterol alone? I needed my sister's help.

"You don't need my help anymore," said Payton. "You did in the beginning, but you have it all in front of you now. You just need to find the pluck to press send."

Payton had plenty of pluck. But instead of lending it to my cause, she rolled over and went to sleep.

So I wrote. I rewrote an earlier draft based on what I knew for sure. This meant leaving out 50 percent of what I found interesting, because it wasn't solid enough, but I told myself that if it didn't all blow up in my face, Upton and Cushing would be salivating over their *Capitolist* mugs for me to keep digging.

Once I saw it all actually typed up, I also realized that Payton was right. It was more than enough to undo Stanton's career, and Olivia's, for that matter. I could pursue the rest later.

I emptied my purse and my pockets before bed, looking for a few dollars for the snack machine out by the small swimming pool. I found the five-dollar bill the waitress wouldn't let me give her and the receipt I had crumpled. Both fell to the ground. I bent to pick them up.

But the receipt wasn't a receipt at all. It was just a piece of white paper with a phone number written on it in thin blue pen. I was surprised I hadn't seen it when I shoved it in my pocket the first time. Had O'Brien written it? His daughter?

I grabbed my personal cell phone off the table and ran outside with the number in my hand: 555-571-8764. That was an Arizona number, I was pretty sure. Maybe O'Brien was ready to talk. I put my money in the snack machine and got a Diet Coke, which I drank straight down before dialing.

I held the phone with two hands as I punched in the number and then pressed it to my cheek, turning the volume all the way up. After four rings, it clicked over to voice mail. The number belonged to a woman named Victoria Zajac.

I immediately hung up. Who was Victoria Zajac? It had not sounded anything like O'Brien's daughter's voice. I immediately looked at my phone and prayed that I had blocked my number. If not, then whoever Victoria Zajac was had everything. She had my name, my number, could find where I worked in five seconds flat. I ran inside and grabbed my BlackBerry and called my other phone. It came in as unknown.

"Oh, thank God," I muttered. "Thank you, Jesus and Buddha and Gaya and Krishna and everyone." I put both phones in my pocket and walked inside. A waitress in Ajo, Arizona, had given me a stranger's phone number. She could certainly have heard my entire conversation with her father. Maybe she knew something he didn't. She would have been much closer in age to Drew Reader. She could have even been a friend.

I Googled the name on my phone, and three women named Victoria Zajac living in Arizona came up on the first ten pages of hits. One was a guide in a tourism company far north by the Utah border, and the other two lived in Phoenix.

The first, based on her work info on LinkedIn, sounded too young. She was just out of college and working for the University of Arizona development office. But the second Phoenix-based Victoria was an architect. She worked for a firm that did a lot of commercial office space. With a few more clicks, I found her title. It had the word *partner* in it. That had to make her older. I wrote down her firm's address and walked back to our room. I had to get some sleep.

When I woke up late the next morning, already sweating, I rolled over and saw that Payton was gone. Instead of her frowning face and perfect blond coif was a note that read:

Good luck. Ship my stuff down when you get home. On a plane, not a boat. I expect it to arrive in fewer than five days. Finish your story and see it through till the end. Stop worrying about Olivia and Stanton. Only worry about Sandro a little. You were always far too agreeable of a person. I'm happy to see you've developed a little more grit. Goodbye now.

For the first time in my life, I was sad Payton was gone.

CHAPTER 19

I didn't know what to do about Victoria Zajac. I needed direction, an editor. Just not my editor.

I decided the only direction I did have was Phoenix.

I checked out of the motel and pulled back onto Highway 85. It was a little cooler that morning. The sky was overcast, and the dark dry July heat didn't knock you down like the humidity in Virginia did. I stopped once, at a small convenience store in Gila Bend, where I leaned against the trunk of the Jeep and drank down a whole liter of water.

The people around me, a pretty even mix of Caucasian and Hispanic, wore old jeans, cowboy boots, and T-shirts with faded slogans on them. Some women wore shorts and flip-flops and led their children by the hand. These were the people who had elected Stanton. Term after term, they had placed an X next to his name. And in just a few days' time, if Upton and Cushing printed my story, I was going to make all these people regret their decision. People who didn't vote for Stanton, the few Democrats among them, might flaunt the fact that they had put their faith elsewhere. But most of them, these everyday Americans who made twenty thousand dollars a year, maybe less, would know that they had voted for a man who didn't have the backbone to resist a girl in her twenties.

When I got to Phoenix, I drove straight to the architecture firm where Victoria worked. I didn't know what I was going to say, but I didn't care. She was a lead and I wasn't going to let it go because I didn't have a clear line of questioning. "Bell & Assoc. Architects" read a brass sign on the side of the door. There was a bell that I rang over and over again, but it wasn't answered. It was, after all, a Sunday in July at an office that kept normal working hours, something I had grown completely un-accustomed to.

I reached for my phone and called the number O'Brien's daughter had given me again. If I couldn't reach Victoria, I thought as the phone rang, I could always drive two hours back to Ajo and try to talk to her. Ask her why she had given me the number of an architect in Phoenix. I probably should have done that before making the trip, but she didn't exactly write the number on my hand. It didn't seem like she'd be willing to talk.

I called Victoria Zajac twenty more times that day from my blocked number. But no one ever answered. My plane back to Washington was at 7 P.M., and it was now five o'clock. I could call her from Washington, I told myself. But I was here now. I felt so close.

Instead of driving to the airport, I drove to a Holiday Inn in downtown Phoenix, gave them my credit card, and checked in. I called the airline, paid a fee, and pushed my flight to the follow-ing night. Then, before I could change my mind, I opened my laptop and wrote an email to Hardy saying I had to take Mon-day off due to personal matters. No one at the *List* ever gave a mere ten hours' notice before taking a day off, and it was hugely frowned upon to miss Mondays, but I sent the email anyway.

Hardy responded within seconds: "Fine." A man of few words, but "Fine" was better than "You're fired." Which was what I would be if I didn't get this story together.

I ate alone at a barbecue joint called Bobby Q that night with my laptop, a very large beer, and a plate of pulled pork. I realized I hadn't eaten a thing since the diner in Ajo yesterday.

I stayed in the restaurant for five hours and wrote. I took an existing draft of my article on nothing but Stanton and Olivia's affair and made it meatier, more honest. I didn't know if the *List* would run my photos. They were pornographic, and we were a newspaper left out on tables in the United States Capitol. So I described what I saw. I pulled up small thumbnails of the photos and wrote what was in them. I wrote about those nights at Goodstone, their heated fighting in the car, Olivia reporting on Stanton for the *List*, the two of them driving away from Upton's party together, the staff at the hotel having a standing order to supply their room with posh firewood—everything I could piece together from months of accidentally and then purposefully trailing them. And then I wrote about what I thought they shared. How she pursued him for a reason—a reason I was still trying to figure out—but how it had become so much more. How it was still going on. I pulled up the picture of them at the window of the Bull Barn and described what I saw: Two individually powerful people, who in that moment only cared about each other.

When I fell asleep late that night in a king-size bed with the TV on, I felt satisfied. Even without a bulletproof motive, I had something substantial, something good. I knew once the story was published the truth would come out. Tiger Woods's pretty Swedish wife just smacked his car with a golf club, a reporter penned a few paragraphs, and blammo! His endorsement deals were in the toilet and dozens of hookers were lining up to write tell-alls.

Because my body was on *Capitolist* time, I was awake on Monday morning well before dawn. I braided my hair, made coffee in the little pot they had in the room, and reread what I had typed up the night before. It still felt solid. I just hoped the *List* would chuck their family values for the sake of a story and run the photos.

At 8 A.M., I started calling Victoria every fifteen minutes. After an hour, I still had nothing. I had her machine message memorized, could have given a lecture in her voice. I wasn't nervous pushing redial anymore, nor did I have anything prepared to say. So at just shy of 10 A.M. when she answered the phone, I sat on my bed dumbstruck, unable to say a word.

"Hello? Hello? This is Victoria Zajac," a pleasant woman's voice said again.

What felt like minutes went by before I remembered how to speak. I was sure I was about to hear the line go dead, but when I started talking, she was still there.

"Victoria Zajac?" I asked nervously.

"Yes, this is Victoria Zajac. Who is this?"

"I'm sorry to bother you," I said, trying to regain some professional composure. "My name is Adrienne Brown, I'm a reporter for the *Capitolist* in Washington, D.C."

"From the *Capitolist* in Washington, D.C. Is that a newspaper?" she asked, sounding much less friendly.

"It is," I said. "I'm calling because a friend of mine thought you might be able to help me with a story I'm writing. Would you have a few minutes to talk to me today? I'm in Phoenix."

"You're in Phoenix and you want to talk to me about a story you're writing."

"That's right," I said. I held the phone with my neck and wiped my hands on my skirt. They were covered in sweat.

"Why do you think I'll be able to help?" she asked. "What is your article about?"

I hesitated. Should I say Stanton's name? The meatpacking plant? O'Brien's daughter?

"Well, it's about a few different things. But mainly it's about a woman named Olivia Reader."

There was a long silence.

"Do you know her?" I asked. "Olivia Reader. She's in her late twenties now."

I could hear Victoria breathing slowly on the other end.

"I suppose you could say I did know her," she said finally. "But that was a long time back. That's who you want to talk to me about? Olivia Reader? You're doing a story just on her? Has she done something wrong?"

Wrong? Well, legally she hadn't really done anything wrong.

"No," I replied. "Not wrong, exactly. Would you have a few minutes to talk to me about her? I could come to you. Maybe have a cup of coffee."

"All right," said Victoria, her voice filled with hesitation. "There's a little café near my office."

That I knew already. I had downed a red-eye there yesterday.

"It's called Lux Central. It's on North Central Avenue. Do you know where that is?"

"I do."

"Okay then, I'll meet you there in thirty minutes. That sound all right?"

That sounded like a gift from God.

"That sounds great," I said. "I'm pretty tall," I added. "I have blond hair in a braid and I'm wearing a yellow dress."

"Okay," she replied. "I'll find you."

In Monday morning Washington traffic, it would have taken me an hour to cover the thirteen miles to the coffee shop. In Phoenix, it took me twenty minutes.

When I got there, I sat down at a white plastic table right in the front. It had become routine for me to drink two shots of espresso first thing in the morning, but I didn't want Victoria

Zajac to think I was a neurotic speed demon. I ordered a cappuccino in a mug, a much friendlier-looking drink.

I drank it slowly and waited. Ten minutes, then fifteen. And just when I was about to call her again, even though she was probably having my number traced by the FBI at this point, a woman stood by my table and smiled.

"Are you Adrienne Brown?" she asked. She was a good five inches shorter than me and a little stout. She looked like she was in her mid-fifties. Her dress was what we would have generously called haute-hippie or bohochic at *Town & Country*, and she wore a pair of red plastic glasses. Architect glasses.

I stood up to shake her hand and offered to buy her a cup of coffee. She said she would have what I was having. I walked to the bar and felt her eyes watching me as I ordered. My appearance had to put her at ease. I was a young woman in a yellow cotton dress. I looked like a Disney character. Surely that was better than an aggressive old man who shoved a tape recorder in her face.

As I waited for her drink to be made, I thought about what I was going to say. At this point I just wanted to confirm that Olivia Reader and Olivia Campo were one and the same. I needed her to talk about the Olivia she knew. Describe her to me physically. Maybe present me with a stack of photographs. Then I could determine if I was chasing an invented lead or not.

I sat down and handed her the coffee. I took out my notebook and a pen not made of enamel and gold and started asking her questions. I should have been nervous. I had been since I had spotted Olivia in Middleburg eight months ago. But surprisingly, I no longer was.

"As I said on the phone, I'm writing an article about Olivia . . . Reader. I was told you might know her."

"Has something happened to her?" asked Victoria, holding her wide mug in her hands.

"No, nothing quite like that," I said. "Nothing bad. I mean, she's fine."

She's fine because I have no idea who she is. Olivia Reader could be dead. Or a junkie. Or part of a girl gang smuggling drugs across the border. What did I know?

"When did you last see Olivia?" I asked.

"It's been a very long time. Years. I want to say something like twenty years. Maybe a little less."

"Was she about eight years old then?" I asked, suddenly filled with adrenaline.

"No, a little older. I would say she was about eleven."

Eleven years old. Twenty years ago Olivia Campo was eight. But she had said maybe a little older. It was in the right ballpark.

"Do you mind if I ask how you knew her? Were you friendly with her parents? The Readers?"

"No." She shook her head and put her mug on a folded paper napkin. "Hot coffee," she said, looking down at it. "I never met her parents. I knew her after they had both died." She looked across the table at me. "You do know how they died?"

"I do. I do know how they died. Absolutely horrible."

"It was. Just one of the saddest stories I ever heard. To lose your father so young and then to see your mother die. That's why when I was approached, I said yes. How could you turn down a girl like that."

"Could you elaborate a little?" I asked, trying to stay calm.

"Olivia . . ." she said, twisting her gold wedding ring around on her left index finger. Her manicure was chipped and her ring was cutting into her skin.

"Well . . . Olivia . . . she lived with me, of course."

My face must have shown too much surprise, because Victoria stopped speaking for a few seconds.

"Did you not know she lived with me?" she said finally. I

stared at her blankly. "You didn't, did you. Maybe I've said too much." She looked down at the table, conflicted, her lined hands tense and intertwined.

"I just don't do that anymore, now that I've gotten remarried. But I don't know what the laws today say about the information of kids who have aged out of the system. Please don't use any of this if it's not by the book," she said, sliding her hands across the table toward me and grabbing my arm tightly.

"Please don't quote me on any of this," she continued, scanning my face. Her voice was suddenly high and unsteady. "I don't know how the system works—everything changed so fast!"

She stood up to go and I reached out my hand and grabbed hers firmly.

The system. And just like that, the front page of the *Capitolist* flashed into my head. Olivia's series on Stanton's Foster Care Empowerment Act, which the president was about to sign. Her name. If she had been in foster care, and then adopted, it would have been changed. That's how Olivia Reader could have become Olivia Campo. That's how she disappeared.

Victoria sat back down and when she released my hand, it was sweaty and cramped.

"You're not doing anything wrong," I said, trying to convince myself as well as her. "Olivia's not . . . she's not in danger or anything like that."

"I don't know what's what anymore. All this," said Victoria, throwing up her hands. "I can't be any help." She put her head in her hands and I reached out and grabbed her right one again, this time to comfort her. Foster care. The legislation Olivia had treated as third-tier news, the cause she had dismissed. Was that it all along? I needed Victoria to say more.

We talked off the record for a few minutes. I got us both more coffee and I promised I wouldn't print a thing Victoria told me if it wasn't by the book. Not that I had any idea where the lines were drawn, but I would figure it out.

"And I don't want my name in anything, anywhere," she pleaded. "I only agreed to talk to you because I wanted to make sure nothing had happened to Olivia. After she left me, she didn't keep in touch. Some do, some don't, you know, it depends on a lot. How well they get on with their new family, their age, how long you had them."

"How long you have them in foster care . . ." I said.

"Yes. In foster care," said Victoria, shifting her weight nervously. "I took about fifteen different girls in after I got divorced in '87. Seemed like the right thing to do, you know. And Olivia, I never had a story as sad as hers, and these girls had some terrible stories."

"I imagine they did," I said, writing as fast as I could.

"Olivia, you know she was the one who found her mother after she shot herself in the head. Left temple. Olivia ran outside screaming. They lived in the middle of nowhere. She had to run half a mile to find someone to call the police."

Suicide. I wrote the word three times and circled it. My source at Syracuse was right.

I imagined Olivia running down the dirt road Payton and I had driven on just two days before. Had the same American flag been there? The car rusting in the yard? Or had her mother made an attempt to mask the face of poverty? I thought about that porch with the plastic chairs, Olivia tumbling out the door, yelling for help, only to realize she was horribly alone.

"And when she came to me," Victoria continued, interrupting my thoughts, "she was such a scared, quiet girl. They had tried her out at a cousin's house, but that hadn't worked. They couldn't feed another mouth, they said, but the social worker on her case told me that it wasn't the money. They just couldn't look at such a frightened kid. And then she was with another foster family. I think they were closer to her hometown, a younger couple living in southern Arizona. But she was taken out pretty quickly. The social worker who brought her to me confirmed there had been . . . abuse." She whispered the word and shook her head.

"How long did she live with you?" I asked, trying to act professional, a nearly impossible task considering I was operating in a state of shock. All these months, I had been looking. I was always searching for the more complicated story, for blackmail, for manipulation. This one seemed much simpler. Much sadder.

"Not very long. Less than a year," said Victoria. "I would say about eight months. She had a few visitors, but well, very few actually. A couple and their daughter from her hometown, and one Mexican woman whose name I'm forgetting." I thought of O'Brien and his daughter telling me the pie was on the house and pushing the receipt into my hand. "No family at all. Luckily, she was adopted pretty quickly. She was a cute kid. And a Caucasian girl. That, sad to say it, helps move things along."

"Cute, right," I said writing it down. "She had red hair back then?" I asked, trying to sound confident. "A few freckles?"

"A million freckles," said Victoria, confirming. "But people grow out of those. I hope she grew out of a lot of other things, too. Like those horrible memories."

I flicked my braid behind my shoulder and put my pen down.

"Do you remember anything else about her?" I asked, trying not to sound desperate.

Victoria sat quietly for a second and then said, "I remember she didn't like to take showers. She only took baths and she always asked me to stay with her until she was finished. I didn't have a lot of time—there were other kids in the house when I had her—but I did it. It was something about the way she asked . . . she didn't usually single herself out like that. And I remember she would never take off this necklace she wore. She never said, but I think it was her mother's—a little silver chain."

A silver necklace? I thought of the one she always wore now. It looked pretty new, though silver aged well. But Victoria only furrowed her brow in confusion when I asked if it was a Celtic eternity knot.

"The people who adopted her, do you remember their name?" I asked instead.

Victoria held her mug again, searching her memory.

"It was so many years ago. I remember them being nice people. Of course, the social workers were in charge of that end, not me, but I met them when they came to pick her up. They seemed like two kind, good people."

"Were they the Campos?" I asked. "He's a dentist in Texas. They still live there. Dr. and Mrs. Campo."

"You know, I think that's it," said Victoria. "Now that you say the name, I'm pretty sure that's it. I remember going over with Olivia what her new name would be. We agreed it wasn't such a bad one."

"Are you pretty sure, or sure?" I asked, scratching my nails deep into my arm under the table.

"I'm sure," said Victoria. "Yes, I'm sure. Olivia Campo. That's what her name is. I hate to admit this, but I haven't thought about her for so long. I had the other girls for much longer. Some for years. Hers was just one of those sad stories that consumes you in the moment, but then just goes away. I guess that's what helped me stay open to foster care for so long. I refused to let the sadness get to me. I just tried to make things good for a little while."

"Well, I think you succeeded at that," I said. "She's a very smart woman. Olivia Campo."

"Is she? Well, that's nice to hear," she said, calming down. I looked at my arm; the nail marks were starting to fade.

We both sat there and finished our drinks. I turned the page on my notepad so she couldn't see the words I had circled and rewritten.

"What are you going to write about her?" asked Victoria after she said she should be on her way.

"I'm not quite sure yet," I replied.

"It's really nothing bad is it?"

"It's nothing that isn't true," I said.

Victoria opened the front door of the coffee shop to let a few college students in. She looked at me before she left and said, "You tell her I said hello. Tell her I've thought about her every now and again and that I always hoped she was doing well."

I assured her I would and gave her my number in case she wanted to talk about anything else. But at this point, I didn't need anything else. Over the span of a twenty-minute conversation, everything had fallen into place.

I took my notebook back out and flipped it open. I now had a connection between Olivia and Stanton that was more than just physical. Olivia's life had been turned upside down and bashed around because of the John F. Stanton & Company. Perhaps Drew Reader's death was the kind of accident that was bound to happen even in a well-run industrial facility, but it sure sounded like the plant could have been more careful. And how often does a deceased janitor's family triumph over a bunch of bigwigs and their legions of lawyers? If Olivia thought Stanton's family was at fault for her father's death, and in turn, her mother's, it would be understandable that she wanted to bring him down. But in the midst of all that, she and Stanton must have found common ground on foster care. Maybe he knew about her past—not his family's involvement in it, but the fact that she was in the system he was trying to reform. Maybe that's what had softened her, and kick-started their affair.

I still had a million questions to answer. But I also had far too many people who knew where I worked and knew I was writing a story about Olivia Campo, aka Reader. I needed it to go to print.

On the plane ride back to Washington, I rewrote my draft and when I was finished writing, I wondered if Sandro knew about Olivia's past. I mentioned that Olivia was married to Sandro Pena, her college sweetheart, originally from Mexico, and now working at the Organization of American States. But I stopped there. Sandro was the one point she could use against me, if she tried to deny or fight the story in any way.

I wrote about Olivia's childhood, her time in foster care, her obsession with coming to Washington and working at the *List*. I scribbled lines about how she had likely harbored anger against Stanton and his family because of what happened to her parents, and how she probably sought out the senator with the intention of bringing him down, but something—emotions, love, lust— got in the way, and was still getting in the way. Their affair was ongoing. I didn't know if the company was actually at fault for her father's death, despite the court ruling from years ago, but that couldn't be solved before I went to print. I also didn't know if Olivia was still trying to ruin Stanton's career, or if their affair had derailed her original intentions. Those questions, as Payton said, would be answered later.

As the plane's overhead lights flicked on, signaling that we were about to land at Washington's Reagan National Airport, I looked down at the page in front of me. I had more than five thousand words and a slide show of digital photos that I had to get out fast. I needed help.

CHAPTER 20

Though Hardy and I exchanged about fifty short, lifeless emails every day, I had spoken to him very little in person and never on the phone.

The *List*'s chosen method of communication was quick impersonal emails. Even when you sat next to someone, you didn't turn your head to speak to them. That was a waste of time and saliva. But now felt like the right time to change all that.

Standing at an empty baggage carousel, away from the crowds waiting for their luggage, I looked up Hardy's number and dialed. His impatient voice came on the line after one ring.

"Hi, Hardy, it's Adrienne Brown," I said after he barked his name.

The phone was silent and I imagined Hardy, emotionless Hardy, in shock that I had called him.

"Hi, Adrienne. Why are you calling? Is something wrong?" he finally managed to spout out.

Wrong? Yes. Many things were wrong. Like how awkward it felt to cry to Hardy for help.

"I'm at Reagan Airport," I admitted. "I lied to you about my sister being hurt. I was actually in Arizona finishing a story I've been working on."

Hardy didn't say anything. I thought he was going to start

screaming or berate me with his own brand of dorky North Dakota insults, but he waited for me to finish.

"Between us, very between us, I stumbled on a little something a few months ago that I was able to confirm and turn into a pretty big something." It felt empowering to say it. And to an editor who might actually help me.

"Okay," said Hardy, still calm.

"It's kind of about Senator Stanton," I continued. "You know, from Arizona. Well, Senator Stanton, it turns out, is having an affair with Olivia Campo. Our Olivia Campo. And I have pictures of them in the act. Pretty damning photos. I can explain how I got them and how this all came about, but maybe just not from the airport."

After a few seconds of silence, Hardy simply said, "Wow." He fell silent again and then finally managed to say, "Adrienne, that's very big stuff. That's huge."

"Yeah, I think it could do some damage," I said.

"I'm glad you called me about it. I would like to help, but honestly, I think it's a little too big for me. For both of us maybe. You should call Upton."

Call Upton? I couldn't think of anything more frightening. Couldn't Hardy call Upton? Wasn't that part of his job description? To protect me from the terrifying editors at the top?

But I couldn't ask Hardy to do that. It would be like asking your big sister to beat up the school bully—which I actually had done twenty-one years ago, but then, Payton wasn't your average big sister. And I was no longer that lame. I had to take the reins on this. It's what I had been doing for months.

I thanked Hardy, who proved to be less of a bloodsucking beast than I thought he was, and promised I'd keep him posted.

I had spoken to Mark Upton three times in my entire life: Once when I interviewed for my job, another time when he saluted me for my scoop on James Franco, and once when he stopped by my desk, observed my glass full of cucumber water, and asked me if it was vodka. When I said no, he held it up to his face and smelled it to see if I was lying. I had a closer relationship with my UPS guy than I did with him.

But Hardy was right: I needed real, seasoned editorial help. I knew that Upton and everyone else at the *List* loved Olivia, but even more than they loved Olivia, they feared having their good name sullied. They would surely fire Olivia as soon as they read my draft, which might take the weight of the article down a few pounds, but it was still a huge story. And they were a newspaper that made money from huge stories.

When I got in a cab at the airport that night, I asked it to go straight past the turn for Route 50 into Middleburg and keep on driving toward Upton's house in Maryland.

We headed up Connecticut Avenue, turned left on Thornapple Street, and stopped in front of the yellow house I had seen Stanton idling in front of while he waited for Olivia. I walked up the granite slab walk, picked up the brass door knocker, and gave a few loud thwacks. I looked down at my watch as I waited for someone to answer. It was 11:17 P.M.

When Upton opened the door, wearing old jeans and a wrinkled work shirt, he looked at me with confusion, clearly unable to place me.

"My name is Adrienne Brown. I work for you."

Still nothing. He stood behind the screen door, just looking at me.

"As a reporter in the Style section for the *Capitolist*. Adrienne Brown."

"Of course, of course," said Upton, putting my name and face together. He leaned over and opened the screen door. "I had trouble placing you outside the newsroom. Adrienne Brown, that's right. Caroline Cleves Brown's daughter. And what are you doing at my house in the middle of the night?"

I was there to play canasta. What did he think I was doing? I was a reporter, he was an editor.

"I need an editor," I said as he let me into the foyer. There was a big wooden staircase in front of me and to my left a formal living room with cream-colored walls.

"I'm sure you have one," said Upton. His straight blond hair was pushed back and looked like it needed to be washed.

"I need a more seasoned editor," I said. "I have a story I think you might be interested in."

He pointed to the living room. He took a wooden captain's chair, and I sat down on the white high-back sofa.

"What's the story? It's got to be pretty good if you're showing up at my door late at night."

"Senator Hoyt Stanton is having an affair with a young woman, and she happens to be your employee."

He looked at me suspiciously.

"Jesus! It's not me," I said. "It's not! I'm disgusted that you would even think that."

He opened his mouth to spout out some excuse, but then he thought against it and pressed his lips together.

A woman in a bathrobe walked halfway down the stairs. "Is everything all right, Mark?" she asked, putting her reading glasses on her head. She looked so sweet and calm, nothing like her husband.

"It's nothing, nothing," he said, barely looking at her. "This is . . . uh, Adrienne. Just one of my reporters. Needs help with something. Go to bed now, don't worry. We'll be at this for a while." He waved her off. "I imagine we will be a while?" he asked me.

"Yes, that's a pretty good assumption," I said. I opened my laptop and opened the article I had finished on the plane. Then I opened the most incriminating photo next to it. "I don't exactly know how to say this, so, I'll just let you read what I wrote. And there are a few photos, too."

I turned the laptop around and gave it to him.

I thought he might react calmly, like a seasoned newspaperman, but instead he screamed. "Are you fucking kidding me? . . . That's the fucking . . . that's Hoyt Stanton."

"It is. And that's Olivia Campo."

He held the laptop closer to his face and stared at the photo. "I don't want to know how you got this picture. Do I?"

"Probably not."

"But you took it? This is your photo?"

"It is," I confirmed, sitting nervously on my hands.

"And you have more than this?"

I told him I had dozens more. And an article, which he then read.

"You're just coming back from Arizona now?" he asked. "This conversation you had, with this woman, this source . . ."

"Victoria Zajac."

"Right. That conversation happened today. All that in Arizona happened this weekend."

"Yes, this weekend. I just landed an hour ago."

"But you've had the pictures for . . ."

"Months. Since February."

"And you didn't come to me? No one? Does Hardy know about this, anyone?"

"I just told him tonight, and he sent me here. No one else at the paper knows. I wasn't certain I wanted to go forward with it."

"And now you are? Because I'm sure you can guess that I would like to."

"Yes," I answered without hesitating. "Now I'm sure I want to go forward."

He went to the kitchen to make coffee, and maybe to calm down. Then he came back and read the story again.

"No one worked with you on this? No one from the Style section?"

"No," I repeated. "I just told Hardy an hour ago. He was the one who suggested I talk to you. But when I was reporting, I just didn't trust anyone. And I wasn't sure I wanted to write it. But I guess I changed my mind."

"I'm glad you did," said Upton, clicking through the photos I had opened for him. After a moment he looked up and said, "To be honest with you, I don't read the Style section."

"Maybe you should start," I suggested.

Upton got on the phone and called Cushing. He explained the story, said I was sitting with him, and sent my piece over to Cushing to read.

I stood up from the couch and looked at the framed pictures of Upton's family. The ones I had stared at during his party. It seemed like years ago.

"Do you remember when you told me that I should move into D.C. and out of Middleburg if I cared about my career?" I asked Upton when he came back with the coffee. I was too tired to ask him for sugar.

"No. I don't."

"Well, you did," I assured him. "And I didn't listen."

"Thank God. Are you going to stay there now?"

"Sure, why not. The nightlife is fascinating."

He sat back down in the wooden chair and picked up my laptop.

"You took these photos in Middleburg, right?" he asked. "But you weren't breaking and entering or anything. You were stay-ing there."

"I was. I paid for it out of pocket. It's a nice hotel. You should go there sometime."

He actually chuckled. Then he put the computer on the coffee table and said Olivia's name. "You know how we regard her at the paper," he said. "I am honestly shocked."

I bet he was.

"That's a hell of a life, though. Her childhood. I wonder if anyone had any idea."

"From what I've learned about her, I don't think so."

"And you think they talked about all this foster care stuff? That bill?"

"I think they did, yes," I replied. "I think she was drawn to him because she wanted answers about her family, maybe even revenge. But I think his work on foster care surprised her, perhaps softened her. Maybe even led her to this." I opened the picture of the two of them at the window, the one I was always going back to.

He asked me if I had the photos backed up and then clicked them closed. Staring at all that flesh, that intimacy was getting awkward.

"You know she's in Jakarta right now. With the president."

I did know that. I had seen the pool report she filed when they landed there.

"I need to tell her we're going to run this. I need to give her a chance to read it and dispute anything if she takes issue with any of your facts. If it were anyone else but an employee . . ."

"So we wait until she comes back."

Upton clasped his hands together and rested his forearms on his knees. His gold wedding ring was thick and outdated.

"No. I don't think so. I think Cushing will agree. We run it Wednesday. Today is Monday, right?" He looked at his watch.

It was 12:23 in the morning and too late to get it in Tuesday's paper.

"We edit it tonight, you and me. Get it to print shape. I run it by everyone I have to run it by at the paper tomorrow. That's really just Cushing, our legal counsel—to make sure we don't have a privacy issue with you surreptitiously taking pictures— and a few others. It won't leak, I promise you that. And then when it's about to print, we run it by Olivia in Jakarta. She could warn Stanton, though. That's my worry. I don't want him to have time to put a media response team in place. So we put it online first. Immediately. As soon as Olivia responds, it goes live."

They were going to blindside her with this while she was in Jakarta with POTUS? Was she even going to be able to get back on the plane home, or would her contract be terminated while she was doing her job stalking the president in Indonesia? I had played various scenarios out in my head countless times. In each, I had imagined Upton meeting with Olivia before printing anything. I was even pretty sure that he was going to make me sit down with her in a barren, soundproof room, with maybe a hidden camera or two, and slowly go over the details. I had plenty of Xanax at home, ready if it ever came to that. But this? I felt terrible. I, we, couldn't do that to her when she was alone in a foreign country.

But as I listened to Upton on the phone, I understood that it was quite obviously out of my hands now. Even if I wanted to push the delete button on everything I'd done, I couldn't. It was no longer my story, it was a *Capitolist* story and they were going to take it as far as they could. I had just happened to write it.

I slept on Upton's couch that night, dozing on and off while he asked me questions about the piece. My hair was sticky from the July heat and Upton's air-conditioning was barely puttering anything out. He got me a fan, took a few calls from Cushing, even put me on the phone. Cushing congratulated my work, my initiative, over and over again. It was the first time I had ever spoken to him.

Tuesday morning I drove in with Upton and he dropped me in front of the tall steel and glass building and drove to the side of the building, down into the parking garage.

Only Upton, Cushing, Hardy, and three other senior editors knew about my piece. Upton told me to spend Tuesday just like I would any other day. I was to write my short Style pieces, smile with my friends, and pretend all was right with the world. When the office started to empty out, usually around 9 P.M., he would call Olivia and we would get the story online.

"How is your sister?" Isabelle asked me when I sat down at my desk.

"Did you have the morning off to take care of her?" said Libby. "I haven't seen a byline from you yet."

Oh God. Of course. This was the first morning since my first day that I hadn't written four pieces before 11 A.M. I was going to have to keep up my terrible lie.

"Payton is doing much better," I said, smiling at both of them. "You're so sweet to ask. It was nothing. She just cracked a few ribs. I was in the hospital with her so I did have to take the morning off. And Hardy actually let me."

They both told me how sorry they were and I cursed myself for lying. When Julia and Alison came back to the *List* office after reporting on the Hill all morning, they also asked after Payton. Why did the Style girls have to be so kind and concerned?

"I told you," said Julia. "It's safer to ride an elephant than it is a horse. It's amazing your sister didn't lose her head."

"It's just horseback riding, not the Reign of Terror," I assured her.

All day, I tried to keep my banter light and fun.

Hardy walked by my desk on his way to an editors meeting and said, "You. You're back. Good."

With the other Style girls, I left the office for our five allotted lunch minutes, emailed about keeping the page moving, and rolled my eyes when Tucker Cliff sprinted by, screaming into his cell phone about Newt Gingrich's latest poll numbers.

At 7 P.M., when reporters started to leave, Julia asked if I was walking down to the garage.

"I'm not," I said. "A friend of mine is meeting me here and we're going for a drink."

Ah, another lie. Why not. I was a regular Stephen Glass.

"Okay," said Julia, smiling. "I'm sure you could use one after your tough weekend." She leaned against my small desk, flicked a pen between her fingers, and said, "I'm glad you're back. I missed you. Christine Lewis and Emily Baumgarten got into this huge fight in the bathroom over who was covering the first family's Martha's Vineyard vacation. Emily actually screamed, 'The people of Edgartown need my brain!' and I didn't even get to talk about it with you. These people are insane."

I rolled my eyes in agreement and gave her a hug goodbye. She headed down to the garage and I sat at my desk waiting for Upton to say it was go time. I didn't hear from him until nine.

His message just said, "come here," so I headed toward his large office with the thick glass wall. Before I opened the door, he put his hand up to stop me and I noticed he was on the phone. I sat down at his assistant's desk and waited for him to finish his call. He didn't stand up, or wave his hands. He didn't pace, as he often did in meetings with the higher-ups. He just sat in his chair and talked on the phone for twenty minutes.

When he finally waved me in and pointed to a black mesh chair, he said, "That was Olivia. She has given her resignation as I recommended she should. We'll have to add that to the story, and then it will go live."

I leaned back in the chair, ready to hear the long, dramatic story about how she cried and denied everything and called me a lying whore with elephantiasis of the ego. But Upton didn't say another word about the call. He just motioned for me to stand up and suggested we finish working in the back conference room.

Sitting at the large rectangular table with twenty leather armchairs around it, I read the article quickly one last time.

SENATOR HOYT STANTON CAUGHT IN AFFAIR
WITH *CAPITOLIST* REPORTER

By Adrienne Brown

Senator Hoyt Stanton, a veteran of the Senate, has been caught in a sex scandal, a *Capitolist* investigation has uncovered.

The married senator from Arizona—elected to the Senate in 1994 on a family values, tough on immigration platform—was photographed in Middleburg, Va., engaging in several intimate acts beginning at 2:35 A.M. on March 24, with Olivia Campo, a senior *Capitolist* White House reporter.

After an eight-month investigation, the *Capitolist* was able to confirm that Sen. Stanton and Campo spent many nights together, over the course of several months, at Middleburg, Va.'s Goodstone Inn in the property's private Bull Barn. In low season, the small house, a luxurious renovated barn with a separate living room, is available for rent from

$715 a night. Rates in the summer can reach $1,000. The *Capitolist* has not yet determined if there was any impropriety with how Sen. Stanton paid for the hotel.

At 12:07 A.M. on March 24, Stanton and Campo were observed together in the living room of the Barn. Sen. Stanton, wearing khaki slacks and a blue dress shirt with the sleeves rolled up, lit a fire in the living room's stone fireplace and put his feet up on a coffee table. The two then carried on an intimate conversation. At 2:35 A.M., they moved to the property's bedroom, where they were unknowingly photographed through an open window while engaging in several sexual acts. Photographs of the senator and the reporter in the Bull Barn's bedroom first show the two embracing in front of an open window. They then moved to the high wooden king-size bed where they engaged in intercourse. The photographs also capture several moments showing the emotional relationship between the pair: the senator smoothing Campo's red hair, holding her hands and hugging her during an intimate conversation in front of an open bedroom window.

The photos were taken from outside the Bull Barn cottage by *Capitolist* reporter Adrienne Brown, a resident of Middleburg, Va., who used personal funds to stay at the Goodstone Inn from March 23 to 24.

When the *Capitolist* obtained the photographs of Sen. Stanton and Campo, the relationship was presumed to be purely sexual. But sources in Arizona confirmed more than a physical connection between the two.

Sen. Stanton divides his time between Washington and Phoenix, Ariz., where his family resides. Campo, who was raised in Texas, is a native of Ajo, Ariz., a small border town that has made headlines for border-related violence and drug arrests.

Campo lived in Ajo until 1993, the year after her mother, Joanne Reader, died. Newspaper reports implied, and sources confirmed, that the cause of death was suicide. Following Reader's death, Campo lived briefly with family before entering the U.S. foster care system. South Texas residents Jesse and Laura Campo adopted her in 1993.

In 1989, three years prior to Joanne Reader's death, her husband and Olivia Campo's father, Drew Reader, was killed in a machinery accident at the John F. Stanton & Company meat processing and wholesale plant. According to a 1989 *Arizona Republic* article, Reader, who was employed as a custodian and worked the overnight shift, accidentally switched on a meat grinder while cleaning it and was sucked inside.

The John F. Stanton & Company meat processing and wholesale plant was founded by Sen. Stanton's father, the late two-term Governor of Arizona, John Farley Stanton, in 1952. Sen. Hoyt Stanton, a former lawyer for the family company, served as counsel at the time of Drew Reader's death.

The Occupational Safety and Health Administration investigated Drew Reader's death in 1989 and declared it accidental. Joanne Reader was awarded $15,000 in financial compensation.

According to a source in Ajo, Arizona, there was another death at John F. Stanton & Company in 2008 that went unreported. The source said a night worker was killed when a forklift fell on him. The *Capitolist* is currently investigating safety standards at the John F. Stanton & Company, including Reader's death and the 2008 accident.

When reached for comment in Jakarta, Indonesia, where she was serving as the White House pool reporter, Campo admitted to the affair and immediately resigned from the

Capitolist. Campo confirmed to the *Capitolist* that the senator was unaware of her personal connection to John F. Stanton & Company.

During his last year as a lawmaker, Sen. Stanton has become a vocal supporter of foster care and the U.S. foster care system, championing significant legislation to better the lives of thousands of American children. The president is expected to sign the Foster Care Empowerment Act, a bill originally introduced by Sen. Stanton, in the next month. Stanton and his wife, Charlotte McBain Stanton, adopted three of their six children from the U.S. foster care system.

Olivia Campo has written extensively on Stanton's foster care legislation for the *Capitolist*. The paper is investigating her work for any ethics violations due to the nature of their relationship and expects the Senate will look into Sen. Stanton's proposed bill.

Stanton, 61, has been married to Charlotte McBain Stanton, 59, since 1973. The two met as undergraduates at Arizona State University and along with six grown children, have two grandchildren. He serves as chairman of the Senate Judiciary Committee and is also a member of the Appropriations Committee and a member of the Health, Education, Labor and Pensions Committee.

Campo, 28, has been married since 2005 to Sandro Pena, 29. The two began dating at Texas A&M and were married during their senior year. Pena is currently employed at the Organization of American States in Washington, D.C.

Until Brown brought news of the affair to the *Capitolist* this week, the paper had no knowledge of Campo's relationship with Sen. Stanton. When reached by phone, Sen. Stanton's office chose not to comment on the story.

"And the photos?" I asked when I finished reading. I was wondering if Olivia's naked body was about to be splashed on our front page.

"We're cropping one," he said. "And we're using one full photo of them together, at the window."

Right. The PG-rated one. The one that showed Olivia's incriminating happy face but looked more like an Edward Hopper painting than a nudie mag.

"We're keeping your language, of course, about all the other ones, as you just saw. The description, the detail. But we can't run those photos. We're . . . not that kind of publication." He looked up at me with a smile. "I admit, that just for a second, I considered it. Running them, that is."

When the story broke online a few minutes later, Olivia had been out of a job for over an hour. Talk of Stanton resigning began immediately.

And so did talk of my success.

Just a few minutes after the story went live, my phone started to ring. Too flustered to answer the majority of the calls, I picked up only the ones that were from my Style section colleagues.

"Five minutes ago I was asleep," said Isabelle. "Then my mother called and said, 'Get to the Internet immediately, Adrienne just wrote a huge story.' Of course, I didn't think it was you, *Capitolist* Adrienne. But it was! It is! You fucking photographed that wench Olivia Campo having sex with Senator Stanton. You suck for not telling us but it's insane that you broke this. It blows my mind. How did you have any time? I mean, I barely have time to shower. It's all so crazy. Who are you? You're not the reporter I thought you were. You're the kind of person who follows people around in hotels at two A.M. in subzero weather. You're like the *National Enquirer*."

After giving Isabelle the three-minute version, I answered a call from Julia.

"How did you do it? Tell me everything. What does Olivia look like butt naked? Does she have any weird moles or a huge tattoo that she hides under her ugly little suits? And why didn't you tell me? I would have happily done a little naked spying with you," Julia pressed.

I laughed, apologized for keeping it all so quiet, and told her I would explain in person tomorrow.

On my way to Upton's, I fielded a joint call from Libby and Alison, who had been covering an event together. Both of them started yelling questions at me. "Did you really follow them around like a paparazzo? I can't believe you saw them screwing. I can't believe you didn't tell us! We're your *Capitolist* family. But whatever. You saw that old lunatic naked and with Olivia Campo. Naked Olivia Campo! Does she have fur? She's actually part dog, right? Like a *Twilight* creature? Weren't you terrified of getting caught? And more importantly, why didn't you tell us anything?"

When I woke up the next morning on Upton's couch, I had a long congratulatory email from Payton, ten voice mails from my parents, three from Elsa that were mostly just screams, and twenty-five more from different media outlets wanting to talk about the story. I checked my inbox and saw that it was over-flowing with more media requests and a lot of hate mail. Before I could start replying, my phone rang again. It was Hardy.

"Good morning. Don't worry too much about the Style section today. Obviously your priorities are elsewhere. We'll be okay without you."

After I thanked him, he said, "Was it a good idea to go to Upton?"

"Yes," I admitted. "He's not that bad."

"And neither are you," said Hardy, managing to not sound condescending. "But I knew that before you broke this story. Some of your other colleagues might be a little surprised that it's your name in the byline, but I'm not."

He didn't wait for my reaction to his compliment. He just hung up and kept on being a very motivated twenty-two-year-old whom I no longer despised.

Stanton scheduled a press conference in Phoenix on Friday, two days after the story broke, not very far from the coffee shop where Victoria had helped me bring my story full circle. I hadn't heard a word from her, and I imagined I wouldn't. Like I promised, I didn't use her name except to Upton in confidence.

"Do you want to travel to Phoenix for the press conference?" Upton asked me the day before Stanton was scheduled to talk to the world. He had, we had, made headlines all over the country. Even the international press was covering the story. Another American political sex scandal, this time with a few soap opera twists.

"Phoenix? What do you think?" Upton repeated. "You could report it for us. Watch him give his resignation. You've certainly earned it."

I suppose I had. The majority of the other *Capitolist* reporters traveled for their jobs. But I was getting to a point where I could no longer formulate sentences. Instead of sitting with the Style girls, I had spent the last forty-eight hours camped in Upton's office as he coached me for media appearances and we planned out potential follow-up articles.

"I don't think so," I said. "I think it could lead to a bit of a media circus if the woman who brought his affair to light was sitting in the room with him."

"We like a media circus around here, if you haven't noticed," said Upton.

"I think I would be happier covering from here. I could co-write with someone in Arizona, if that would be better."

"Whatever you think," said Upton. "Let me know by noon."

I didn't go to Arizona. Christine Lewis did. Instead I stayed in the newsroom for a few more hours, having heaps of praise piled on me by reporters and editors who used to look down at their phones when I walked by them. Just like I wanted, they now looked me square in the eye. A few even hugged me. This was, they all agreed, the biggest story we—and now it was a we—had ever run.

I had media hits all evening. People were requesting sit-down after sit-down with me. "And with Olivia," Jenny from the media team told me when she came to ask me if I could do HLN right after CNN. "But she's not answering her phone. No one from here has talked to her since Upton broke the news to her."

I already knew she wasn't answering her phone. I had tried to call her. I had tried to call Sandro. I wasn't surprised that they were ignoring me and everyone else.

My first media appearance of the ten I had scheduled that night was with Fox News. I put in the earpiece, smoothed down my hair and my conservative red Brooks Brothers dress, and tried not to look exhausted as the blond host fired up and then peppered me with a series of questions.

"What are your thoughts on a possible replacement for Stanton?" she asked. "Many down there in Arizona are saying the governor won't pluck a sitting representative because it would mean a special election for that seat. Who do you think the front-runners are?"

"As far as I know, Stanton hasn't resigned yet," I said.

"But he will. You know as well as I do that he will resign

tomorrow. Let me ask you the question again," she pressed. "Who do you think will fill his seat?"

"Well, the law in Arizona states that Stanton will be replaced by a member of his own party, so we know that it will be a Republican. There are a lot of strong members of the GOP in the House. I do think that's where we'll see the governor looking for a replacement. A similar thing happened when then governor of New York, David Paterson, plucked Kirsten Gillibrand from the House to fill Hillary Clinton's seat. Of course, the circumstances were quite different."

"To say the least."

In my ear a producer's voice told me to wrap up for commercial.

"I just hope that the man or woman the governor chooses can bring ethics, accountability, and honor back to the seat," I said. "I'm sure the people of Arizona and the Arizona Republican Party want the same thing."

As expected, the senator did resign the next day. I watched with Upton from his big office, and he put his hand on my shoulder when Stanton said the magic words. He never referred to Olivia by name. He just called her the young woman he was involved with. He said he was completely unaware of her past ties to his family company and mentioned the court case from 1989. All had been just, he said. He said that he and "the young woman" had found common ground on their passion for foster care reform, a cause he would continue to champion even out of office. But his recent actions were not appropriate for any man, especially not a man representing the great state of Arizona.

So, with his wife, Charlotte, standing next to him and his kids sitting in the audience, he let his once illustrious career go. The tongues that wagged about a future Stanton presidency or vice presidency stopped moving. People who had been hyping him up as the next GOP leader with a chance at the White House distanced themselves from their past comments and Stanton's name started to get wiped from the history books, his past accomplishments now replaced by a sex scandal.

On Saturday, the boiling July day after he resigned, I went to New York to do morning shows. ABC paid for my plane ticket, and I had chauffeurs on either end. On the crisp fall day I drove out of Manhattan last year, I had already been imagining my return as a conquering hero—a journalist of substance and importance who exchanged daily text messages with Nancy Pelosi. My fantasy had almost come true—but I expected it to feel differently. I didn't feel like a conquering hero, or a girl who had done anything to merit a chauffeured ride. I just felt exhausted.

On the way back to Washington, I called Payton from the car. We had been emailing almost hourly since the news broke. She had said she was proud of me, was glad she could be involved in some small way, even if I was the one getting all the fame.

"I saw you on the *Today* show," she said. I told her I could hear the TV still on behind her. "It's my computer, actually," Payton said. "You're my new Internet star."

"It's very weird," I said. "Within five minutes of the story going up, everyone who had been ignoring me or bad-mouthing me since I came in October was suddenly my best friend. I talk to Upton like every hour. He's my editor now. When all this dies down, they want to take me off the Style section. Put me on the investigative team. They say I have a nose for it."

"Wow. That sounds like a good thing. You must want that. You should want that."

"I guess I do. I don't know. I'm so tired right now, I don't even trust myself to drive a car."

"Mom and Dad have been calling me every few hours to talk about you," she said. "They're crazy proud. Like screaming

'That's my baby!' proud. But they claim they've only seen you twice since the story broke. Is that true?"

It was true. I had been home twice to get clothes, but every night since late Monday when everything started, I had been sleeping on Upton's couch. There was just too much to do. Too many television reporters to talk to and Upton's constant stream of questions and research ideas for follow-up articles on Stanton's inner circle and Olivia's motive. There were also safety records to look into at the plant in Arizona and court files to be reexamined. Middleburg, which was the epicenter of everything when I was digging, suddenly felt so far away.

Before I hung up with Payton, she asked the question she knew I was thinking about. "Have you talked to Sandro?"

"I haven't," I replied. "I've tried. I called the only number I could find for him over and over again. There's no voice mail, and he's not picking up. The office manager at the *List* said Olivia isn't answering her phone, either, and that their landline has been disconnected."

"Well, you can't blame them for that," said Payton. "I would be taking a very long vacation right now if I were them."

"Yeah, but I still want to talk to Sandro. Just see how he's doing. I still care about him. And in a weird way, I care about Olivia, too. I tell myself every day that I'm not the bad guy. She had the affair, she betrayed her husband, not me. But I still feel guilty."

"Anyone would," said Payton. "But anyone else would have done the same thing, too."

I wasn't so sure.

Five days had gone by since the senator had stepped down. All the talk now centered around who was going to replace him, but I was still thinking about Olivia. It surprised me how much I wanted to talk to her. Her professional life, the one she had toiled for and cared so much about, was gone. She had been at the *List* much longer than I, put in even crazier hours, and I had knocked that all away with my one lucky strike. Maybe not lucky. I had worked hard for the story, and she was guilty as charged, but I still felt compelled to explain. She had been on top at the *List* and I had been at the bottom; now I was on top and she was at the *very* bottom. I had started to feel like we weren't all that different.

Before I left that night, Upton waved me over to his office and gestured to a chair. "Your pictures," he said. "The naked ones. You know, everyone wants to buy them."

I hadn't even thought about that, but of course they did. They were the stuff of TMZ's pornographic fantasies.

"Legally," he said, "they're yours. You're not a staff photographer, and you weren't shooting them for us."

"Don't worry," I quickly assured him. "I have no interest in selling them. I think enough has been shown already, don't you?" One thing I could do to make everything a little less twisted, at least in my own mind, was to not go public with those photos. I could just wipe my computer and put the hard drive in a bank safe. They could sit there forever, nothing more than an electronic memory.

I stood up to leave and Upton looked at me turning to walk back to the newsroom. "Wait, Adrienne. One more thing."

He waved me over and I sat down again.

"Have you heard who the governor is appointing?" he said frowning, like I should be the one telling him.

"I haven't."

"Well, it's not confirmed yet, but it looks like he's filling Stanton's seat with Taylor Miles."

Taylor Miles. The man I had seen talking to Stanton at Upton's party! The monarch of the anti-immigration movement.

"It sounds like it's going to be announced today," said Upton. "We got a tip from the guy who is going to be his chief of staff. He's a friend of ours. A friend of the paper's, you could say."

"Can I ask who it is?"

"I guess you can," said Upton, putting his feet on his desk and holding two BlackBerrys in his left hand. He flipped them over each other like cards in a deck.

"Off the record. Very off the record, it's James Reddenhurst. Current head of communications for the RNC. Do you know him?"

"You could say I do," I said.

James was going to flack for Taylor Miles. I wondered how long that had been in the works. My guess was about five days. I knew James didn't have the same ideals as Miles, but this was Washington. A big job was a big job, and the rest didn't really matter. I wondered if James would still be mad at me now that I'd been indirectly involved in his promotion.

Before Upton dismissed me, he slipped his feet back onto the floor and put his hands through his slicked-back hair. "Water?" he asked me, reaching for a bottle off his desk. I shook my head no. "I really feel like you're one of the few reporters here who now has this place in their blood," he said after taking a swig. "You're going to do great things. You might need to work a little harder, but you're going to really soar here."

"I already start at five A.M.," I pointed out.

"You do?" he said incredulously. "Why does the Style section start at five? That's crazy. No one ever told me that. How long do you think that's been happening?"

"I don't know," I replied. "About four years."

Upton snorted with laughter and I knew he planned to do

nothing about it. "Well stop worrying about Style. You're going to do bigger things."

"What kinds of things?" I asked. Was I going to out every senator playing dirty on weekends? Was that my new job?

"Well, like I said, you've got to do investigative work," said Upton, looking off into the distance, as if my head was thirty degrees to the left.

"Investigative journalism," I repeated.

"Absolutely," he replied. "You're clearly good at it. You're ruthless. The way you pursued that story and didn't tell a soul. It wasn't the choice you should have made. You should have come straight to me. But you didn't blow it, either. You've got an iron spine, and that's just the kind of thing you need when writing pieces that can throw a U-turn in someone's career. Or in your case, just flat-out ruin it."

I was ruthless? It sounded like he was describing the Craigslist killer. Since when did I have an iron spine? I liked kitschy musicals and the Lifetime network. My favorite sport was ice dancing.

"How's your inbox, by the way?" asked Upton. I could feel dozens of reporters' eyes on me as I sat in that office, just as I had since the story broke. It was the way I used to look at the people who had been in Upton's office before me—with a mix of terror and envy.

"My inbox is overflowing with hate mail," I replied.

"I thought it might be. We've been getting a lot of phone calls for you. Don't worry. We're just taking down names. You don't have to talk to anyone. But if you get a death threat, let us know."

A death threat? Fantastic. I needed to buy a semiautomatic for my purse.

"Think about what I said," Upton reminded me. "I think you have the right personality to really fly here."

I stood up to leave and said, "Some might say I already have."

"Right," said Upton. "That was a hell of a scoop." He looked down at his desk. It was covered in papers and printed out emails and little notes on crumpled Post-its. With a sigh, he looked up again. "Can you close the door on your way out? I don't want to hear the noise. The newsroom is still roaring because of you."

It was silent as ever, but I smiled and walked out, gently shutting the thick glass door as I left.

When I went to the Style area, my desk looked like it belonged to someone else. There was a cardboard box on it that said "Julia" in black Sharpie filled with old newspapers and printouts and a few unopened packages addressed to me from PR flacks. Isabelle was on the Hill but Libby, Alison, and Julia were all sitting quietly, researching and writing articles. No one was on the phone or talking to each other. They had their pretty faces plastered to their computer screens and didn't look up at me when I approached them. When I went to move the box to one side, Julia looked up and muttered, "Sorry. It was under my desk and bugging me so I put it on yours because I didn't think you were sitting here anymore."

"It's fine!" I said, trying to be perky. I slid the box over and turned on my computer, my left elbow smacking into the cardboard.

I typed my very long password to relog into my computer and listened as Libby and Alison started quietly chatting. They were talking about a list of some sort. A guest list. A birthday. Crap. Alison's birthday. I vaguely remembered getting an invite to it when I was busy doing all the TV hits. Had I RSVP'd? I didn't think so. And I certainly hadn't wished Alison a happy birthday.

I walked over to her desk and apologized. She pulled her legs under her chair, her pinstriped skirt tight over her thighs, and smiled at me. "It's okay," she said. "You were super busy. We all went to Café Milano. It was great. Lionel Richie was there and Julia, Isabelle, and Libby bought three bottles of Moët White Star. It's my favorite."

"Oh! That's so cool. I'm really sorry I missed it. Can I take you out to dinner to make it up to you?" I asked.

Alison nodded unenthusiastically. "I'd really like that, thanks," she said with her face turned the other way. No one had told me they had seen Lionel Richie. Or texted me to remind me about Alison's birthday dinner. In fact, I hadn't really talked to any of the Style girls since their phone calls the night the Olivia story broke.

I returned to my desk and typed in silence for ten minutes, looking for a short Style item, something I hadn't been required to do since the Tuesday before the story broke.

"Have you written about Mitt Romney jogging in khakis and loafers?" I asked Julia. Without looking up from her monitor, she answered, "We broke that yesterday. Our photog snapped the picture."

I apologized and kept looking for an item.

After I found something on Debbie Wasserman Schultz's hair care regimen, wrote it up and sent it to Hardy to edit, I saw Upton walking down the hall. It was the very first time since I had been at the *List* that he had ever walked back expressly to talk to us.

But he wasn't coming back to talk to us. He was coming back to talk to me.

"Adrienne," he said, smoothing his hair back. "Chris Matthews wants us on *Hardball* tonight, together. Can you come? We can drive from my house after work. They'll send us a car." I nodded my assent and thanked him again for letting me continuously crash on his couch.

When Upton left, Julia smiled at me and said dryly, "You and Upton have gotten awfully chummy. Sounds like you're in line to be the next Olivia Campo. Little Christine Lewis better watch out."

"Well, I worked with him on the story. The Olivia story. So I guess it was inevitable." I stopped and waited for Julia to respond but she didn't.

"He's a really great editor, but I guess most editors in chief are. I just . . . I'd never worked with him before. I'd barely spoken to him. But now that I know him a little better, I can honestly say that he's a lot nicer than he seems."

It was only after I fell silent that I realized none of the Style girls, my only good friends at the paper, had actually congratulated me on my scoop. They had called me the day of, shrieked about seeing Olivia naked, but what they most wanted to know was why I didn't confide in them. It was a fair question. After Upton's staff-wide email about the story I had gotten plenty of way-to-gos from my *List* colleagues, but not from my friends.

"So is it true you're sleeping on his couch? That's what he meant when he said you could go to the studio together, right?" asked Julia.

"Yup. I am. It's kind of weird, I know, but with all these TV hits, I couldn't do the commute back and forth to Middleburg. It's just . . . I'm so tired. I don't think I've ever been this run-down in my life."

Julia turned away from her screen and looked at my face. I had bags under my eyes, I needed to get my highlights redone, and my lips were cracking from constantly reapplying heavy TV makeup.

"You do look terrible," said Julia. "If you weren't a Style girl, I'd have to make fun of you." She smiled and I sat silent and ugly.

"It was a big story," said Julia quietly, her head bent down at her screen. "All that research you dug up is crazy. You should be proud of yourself."

I was. But it was clear that she and the other Style girls weren't.

"Do you think I shouldn't have written it?" I asked Julia. "Is that what's wrong? Because you don't seem to be that into my presence right now."

Julia laughed like I had accused her of abandonment. "It's not that," she said. "Of course I'm glad you wrote it and I'm glad you're here. We're friends, aren't we? Very good friends. You might say I'm your best friend at the paper," she said to me levelly. "But you still chose not to tell me anything about your major scoop."

"I didn't tell anyone at the paper," I protested. "I was afraid it would get out."

"Listen, Adrienne. I don't want to stomp all over your ac-complishment. It's just . . . you've been here long enough. You know what's wrong with this place, but now you're just happily feeding the fire. More than that, you *are* the fire. You just gave the *List* the biggest story in its history."

Seeing my hurt face, Julia backtracked a little.

"Look, I'm in awe of what you did. It's a huge deal. Everyone was saying Stanton would run for president the next cycle. He could have been elected even. And now look at his career. It's amazing what you did, and don't think I'm not proud of you. I'm just surprised you didn't do it for someone else. We always talk about how much we hate this place, how they treat us like ditzes. The other reporters act like we got naked and screwed the big boss to get in here and don't belong. That's why we're shoved all the way back here." We both looked at the wide hallway separat-ing us from the rest of the newsroom.

"Even Upton admitted to not reading our section," she con-tinued. "And you once said yourself that in all the months you've been here, Justin Cushing never even said hello to you. That's not normal behavior. Other publications wouldn't tolerate it, but here they do. So what do you do when you have the biggest story of the year sitting in your lap? You deliver it directly to Upton. And at his house of all places. You could have used it to land a huge *New York Times* job. I mean, don't you detest this place?"

I hadn't even thought about selling the story to another paper. I would have had to quit the *List* and then I guess I could have dangled the story as bait and parlayed it into a spot at the *Times*, but it had never crossed my mind.

"You hate it, don't you?" asked Julia again.

Did I hate the publication that had just helped slingshot my career higher than I could have alone? I didn't. I recognized that there were some deep flaws in the system, but everyone who worked there knew that. We didn't have shackles on our feet. We had great bylines and great titles and could leave if we wanted to, for, as Julia said, a huge job at the *New York Times* or somewhere else. But we didn't. We stayed. Because, as Elsa had said so many months ago, the *Capitolist* was the place to be right now. I knew that, and Julia, as irate as she was, knew that, too.

When my article broke, I saw what the *List* could give me, instead of me just feeding the beast with nothing in return. I had been on every major television network, interviewed by dozens of other papers, and talked about like I was some sort of seasoned veteran. And it's what I had wanted, but I wasn't going to admit that to Julia.

"Listen. I think I've gotten fifteen hours of sleep this week. I'm not in great shape, and honestly, I really need my friends. I need you," I said, hoping that my voice wouldn't crack.

"You've barely spoken to us these past couple of days," said Julia. "Look, it just won't be the same anymore. You're going to leave the Style section and join what they deem to be a far more important team. And let's be honest, we're the only ones who have ever been nice to you, until now."

That was true. The "until now" part was also accurate.

When Isabelle came back to her desk, she slapped me on the back with just a little too much strength and said, "Good story. Amazing stuff. Who knew a Style girl had it in her."

Before I could answer she was talking to Alison about going on a wine-tasting limo ride the first Saturday in August. Soon they all had their heads down again, pounding out short piece after short piece that Upton wouldn't read.

After an hour searching Twitter and three calls to Congress, Libby stood up and rolled her head in a circle. "Argh, that should hold Hardy for about ten minutes."

She looked at my exhausted, pathetic face and smiled.

"You look tired," she said, throwing a Diet Red Bull in my general direction. I opened the can and drank the whole thing down.

Isabelle watched me. "Remember when I said it was possible to have lunch with Upton and not cry?"

I nodded.

"Well," she said, turning back to look at her computer, "I was right. Not only can you have lunch with him without shedding a tear, you can also sleep over at his house."

Julia laughed before shaking her head apologetically. "It's just too weird."

"It's a bit traitorous, really," Libby chimed in. "It's almost like you've run off to work for Al Qaeda or something."

Al Qaeda! She was equating me breaking news for our place of employment to committing war crimes against my own country?

"I'm kidding, Adrienne," she said, walking over and touching my ghost-white cheek. "Lighten up." She sat on my desk and flicked through my notepad full of scribble and Arizona addresses. "I think we're all just surprised. You not only just kissed *List* editor ass and became one of the chosen ones, you also turned on a colleague. She's horrible—trust me, there's no love lost—but she still works here."

"Worked here," Julia corrected Libby, not bothering to look in my direction.

"Libby, she's a colleague but not like you are," I said, swallowing back tears. "She murdered Isabelle's TV career, she did everything in her power to keep Mike from moving up on the White House beat, she told the higher-ups that Julia was a moron within only weeks of starting—she's terrible. I only did exactly what she would have done."

"Yeah," said Alison from her desk. "But since when do you want to be like Olivia Campo?"

I excused myself, walked to the quiet area by the bank of elevators where I had wiped Isabelle's tears so many months ago, and cried alone. No one came after me.

Later that day I watched Isabelle, Libby, and Alison stand up to walk to Starbucks together, and they didn't pause at my desk. After a few more minutes, Julia got up to join them. I just sat and stared at my empty section, trying to cover the page alone. At 3 P.M., I sent Upton and Hardy an email saying I was working from home for the rest of the day, and, surprisingly, Upton wrote me back and told me to take the rest of the day off to prep for a few evening TV appearances. It was the first time I had ever left the newsroom to go home during daylight hours.

I called Payton as I was driving to Middleburg. I hadn't slept in my own bed since the Friday before we flew to Arizona. She listened as I told her about the Style girls snubbing me. "Isabelle and all my friends rejected me for feeding the beast, and Upton called me ruthless," I said.

"Ruthless, no. I wouldn't call you ruthless. But I would call you smart. And hungry. More determined than I ever thought you could be." She took my silence as a cue to keep talking. "As for the Style girls, maybe they've just been there for too long. They've seen too much and have lost perspective. If you had been there for three years rather than nine months, you might have handled things differently. Maybe you would have quit your job and taken the story elsewhere."

No, I didn't think so. I understood the *Capitolist* for what it was. But to Payton, I just said "maybe."

"I'm proud of you," she repeated. "There were times when I didn't think you had the balls to go through with publishing the story and the attention it would bring you. But look at you. You just decapitated two people's careers. Not bad for the little sister."

I hung up the phone and drove toward the old gas station where James had surprised me and past Baker's store, where I had first spotted Olivia. That all seemed so long ago. I thought of myself huddled in my car looking curiously at her as she leaned back on her expensive BMW in her red down coat. I knew nothing about Olivia then. I didn't even know she was married. And now I had been in her home, had seen the house she grew up in, had kissed her husband. What if I hadn't been restless that night? Would I ever have put the pieces of her affair with Stanton together? Call it luck, or fate, I was glad it had happened. And I was happy that after nine months of putting in my dues at the *Capitolist*, I was no longer the nervous girl afraid to get branded envelopes from the supply closet. Isabelle was right. I could have lunch with Upton without shedding a tear. I could also sit in his glass office and listen to him laud my abilities without feeling unworthy.

I drove slowly up to the gate, letting the sensors take a moment to register my car. It was the first time I had ever arrived home from the *List* during daylight hours. It was almost August now and everything moved slower. I loved the long summer days in Virginia, the way people lived outdoors and just relaxed, even me.

Three horses were grazing in the field behind the barn when I pulled up next to it. I got out of the car and walked over to the fence to call Jasper over. More interested in eating than in greeting me, he ignored my whistles and I gave up and turned the corner to climb up the barn stairs to my little refuge. My heels sunk into the worn wood and I pushed my weight against the unlocked door and smiled at the rows of family pictures on the wall and an old blanket in a pile on the floor. After being stuck in the city for a week sleeping on a couch, I was very happy to be home. I kicked off my shoes, changed into shorts and flip-flops, and collapsed on the sofa. I closed my eyes. The world was quiet and still, something I hadn't felt in a long time.

I must have fallen asleep for a few minutes because when my BlackBerry rang, I was jolted awake, my neck cracking loudly as I straightened my head. I missed the call but it started ringing again, right away. I looked down at the blocked number on the caller ID. Not many people called my work phone from blocked numbers except the White House. Suddenly reality came sprinting back. I still had a job. I couldn't just spend my days napping now that I broke the Stanton story. I had to keep going, keep breaking news, writing bigger articles, and proving myself to be ruthless, just like Upton said. I picked up the phone and tried to sound like I hadn't just woken up.

"Adrienne," said a voice I instantly recognized. "I need to see you."

CHAPTER 21

Sandro. I was listening to him breathe. I didn't know what to say. I wanted to ask him a million questions, bury my face in his arms. But I could barely respond.

"Let's meet at the Goodstone Inn," he said after I managed a weak hello. "I'd like to see it. I've never been and clearly, I've been missing out."

"You're calling me because you want to see the hotel . . ." I repeated softly.

"And because I want to talk. There's a lot I have to say to you."

A lot to say? He was going to leave her. I knew it. But the Goodstone? Could I really meet Sandro there? What was he going to do, walk around the Bull Barn screaming with rage while I twiddled my thumbs hoping for him to ravage me? The Goodstone was a bad idea. We needed to meet somewhere more neutral, like on my bed.

"I don't know if that's a good idea, Sandro," I said hesitantly. "There's just a lot of weird energy there—I don't think that's the best place for us to talk. But if you want to see Middleburg, you could come here. To my house."

"Fine," he said in a monotone voice. "I'll see you in an hour. Text me your address."

The phone went dead. An hour. He was going to be in my house—well, barn—in one hour. How was I going to take myself from looking like a bedraggled lunatic to a silver screen starlet in one hour? I texted him my address, casually mentioned that I happened to live on the second floor of the barn, not the really nice house next to it, ripped off my clothes, ran to my dresser, and grabbed my super-boosting water bra and a teeny pair of underwear that screamed "I'm here for the taking." A quick shower, a cup of dry shampoo, a heavy spray of Insta-Tan, a mélange of three kinds of lip gloss, a set of twenty sit-ups, and a bath of organic perfume later and I looked nearly human. I wasn't going to stop traffic but at least I wasn't a lying adulteress like his wife.

I paced across my bedroom, nervously flicking a pen between my fingers. I had so much to say to him, so many unanswered questions. My mind was racing with apologies and declarations and confusion. I still felt something for Sandro. A lot of something. But as I walked through the room perfumed and covered in fake tanning spray, I admitted to myself that it wasn't the same feeling I'd had before I left for Arizona and wrote the article. Sandro had been such a part of breaking Olivia's story that he now felt less like a part of mine.

I walked to my dresser and strapped on the gold Cartier watch I got for college graduation and looked at the mother of pearl dial. I only had eight minutes until Sandro was scheduled to pull up and I was still pacing in my underwear. Flinging open my closet, I reached for the yellow dress I wore the day I met Victoria Zajac. It had brought me luck then, made me calm and confident when I needed it the most. I prayed the magical sundress would bring it all home again now.

I was ready—insanely nervous, but clothed. Should I go to the window and watch him drive in? Or was that too voyeuristic?

Maybe he would see me and change his mind. No, I would do this properly. I would just let him walk up the stairs to my apartment, pray he wasn't allergic to horses, and open the door.

A quiet little voice in my head was whispering that the whole scenario could go in the opposite direction and that Sandro could walk in with guns blazing and curse the day that I was born, but I chose not to listen to that little voice.

Sandro was five minutes late. Then seven. He wasn't going to come. He'd had a change of heart. I would have to subscribe to *Spinster* magazine and learn how to kill bugs on my own. As I was about to cry off my three coats of mascara, I saw my parents' gate slowly open and a black SUV drive through. It pulled up next to my father's truck and I ran away from the window and stood exactly five paces from the door.

I heard his car door shut and faint footsteps on the wooden stairs. When he finally knocked, I sprinted forward and opened the door, trying to stay calm. I was going to keep my cool; I was not going to jump into his arms or burst into tears.

But the person standing on my stoop with a phone in one hand and keys in another wasn't Sandro. It was Olivia Campo.

I quickly looked past Olivia to see if Sandro was behind her but she put her arm out to stop me and I almost fell against her. She shoved me against the door with her pale hands and my right leg hit the side of it.

"Olivia!" I screamed both at the sight of her and because she had just pushed me, hard, away from her.

She didn't respond, she didn't smile, and she didn't lift her hand up to slap me across the jaw. She just stood there silently. If I looked exhausted, she looked worse. She was even paler than before. The confidence she always radiated had evaporated. All that was left was a worn-out girl with a husband who clearly loved her, not me, and very little else.

Brushing past me, her bony shoulder stabbing my arm, Olivia walked into my living room.

"I came here to tell you you're a selfish bitch," she said with her back to me. She stood in silence as I felt my heart rate speed up. She finally turned around after observing the curated contents of my apartment.

"You look ridiculous, by the way. Is that all for my husband?" she said, gesturing toward my unnatural cleavage.

Before I could answer, she raised her voice and said, "I thought it would be a nice idea to catch you off guard. Give you a tiny taste of how I felt when I answered Upton's call last week. I was in a restaurant with the president in Jakarta, but I doubt he told you that part."

I opened my mouth to confirm that Upton hadn't given me the details of their chat, but she shook her head to silence me.

"You are a selfish, heartless bitch. Just like me." She looked at my made-up face, my straight hair and bright dress, and moved toward me. "That's what you think of me, isn't it?"

I stood there, unable to respond.

"And you didn't get this so-called story about me and Hoyt because you're a good reporter," she added. "You got lucky. You happen to live here. Period."

"Olivia!" I said again. I was still in shock. I didn't know what to say besides her name. I had been waiting for Sandro, I had just spent the past hour thinking about what I would say to him, and now his wife—the woman I had spent months trying to psychoanalyze—was here in my living room.

Olivia's red hair was brushed back and her thin arms were locked by her side. She stared at me expectantly, and when I said nothing, she marched in her flat sandals back outside, stopping on the small wooden landing at the top of the stairs. I followed after her.

"Look at you," she said finally, smiling sarcastically at me. "Adrienne Brown. Style section reporter extraordinaire. No one ever paid much attention to you—any attention to you—in the newsroom so you figured that the way to get some recognition was not through actual work, but by ruining my life."

"That's not what I intended to do!" I said quietly. "I was just—"

She cut me off.

"*You* threw yourself at my husband, *you* spied on me in the middle of the night, *you* photographed *me* having sex! Then you flew to Arizona and asked everyone in my hometown all about me! Then—and this is probably my favorite part—you talked to the very woman the government trusted to protect me when I was eight years old. The rest of your dear readers might not know who your 'anonymous source' was but I certainly do. I lived with Victoria. That woman used to bathe me because I couldn't stand in a shower until I was fifteen years old. Did you know that? Because that's where I found my mother, collapsed in a pool of her own blood. Are you aware of how sick it is, to pry into that world?"

I bit the inside of my lip as she screamed. I had asked Victoria for details, but she hadn't told me that.

"What you did is vile!" Olivia continued. "You should be the one getting slammed by the press, not me."

She hit her little balled-up fist against the wall, took a deep breath, and tried to lower her voice. It quickly rose again.

"And after you finished snooping around like my fucking biographer, you tied it all up in a bow, handed it to Upton, and sat around celebrating while he fired me even though you *knew* I was halfway around the world with no friends or family. When I got home, jobless, with my name smeared beyond recognition, I got to watch you talk about it on national television every chance you got. You sure soaked that up. It was just radiating from your hopeful face. 'Look at me! Someone finally gives a shit about me.' But guess what? They didn't and they don't. They just wanted to hear you talk about the senator. About *me*."

"He's no longer a senator," I murmured, but she didn't hear me.

She lifted her head up higher and looked at my tense face, my grinding teeth. "All you are is a messenger. You're not a reporter. And why you're not crying and groveling for my forgiveness right now, I'm not quite sure. You did hang your own peer without a second thought."

"I don't think you have ever regarded me as your peer, Olivia." My body was tingling. I felt guilt—of course I felt guilt—but then in Arizona, and now on TV, I was just doing my job. She of all people should understand that.

And she would have done the exact same thing.

Olivia was tense and silent, looking off to her left at my parents' big white and green house bathed in late afternoon sun. Now that she wasn't screaming, you could hear the cicadas chirping.

"How long did you know about it?" she said finally. "About us."

"Since March."

Olivia looked up at a small white moth flying near her hair and swatted it away.

"Well, it went on for much longer than that. It had been over a year." She looked at me, standing stiffly, waiting for me to react. "Do you want to take out a notepad or something?" she asked. "I'm sure you'll immediately want to file that tidbit off to your pal Upton."

Over a year? Had they really been coming to Middleburg for that long? It was amazing I was the first to catch them in the act.

"I don't want to write anything down," I said finally.

She put her hands in the pockets of her loose black shorts and gave me a once-over. "Your biggest problem is that you don't understand this town," she declared. "You Style girls just sit back there complaining about how hard you work, but there are thousands of people lining up to take your jobs—as trivial as they are. And hundreds of thousands want mine. If you think Christine Lewis is the only person working a seventy-hour week to get the word *senior* next to her title, you're very naïve. Everyone wants to cover the White House. But very few—"

"You never even wanted to cover the White House!" I countered. "All you wanted was to destroy Stanton."

Olivia's face turned whiter than usual and her tired eyes looked straight through me. "Destroy?" she repeated quietly. "I didn't want to destroy him."

I rolled my eyes and moved toward the railing. I knew better. From the moment she learned the name Hoyt Stanton she was ready to rip it out of the history books.

"You didn't think he killed your father?" I retorted. "That he was responsible for his death?"

Olivia put her hand on the wooden railing and sighed, looking disparagingly at me. "Obviously I did, for years. I hated him, the whole family, for decades." She tilted her head back proudly, her freckled face creasing around her eyes as the sun moved lower in the sky.

"I needed somebody to blame, so I did my research. It was all I thought about, all I did. My parents in Texas tried to put the past behind me and I tried to make them happy. But as soon as I got to college, it turned into an obsession."

No wonder she wasn't writing for the *Battalion*. She was too busy with her own investigative reporting.

"But there's nothing," she said firmly. "Trust me," she said, lowering her eyelids. "If there was anything to find on Hoyt and his family, I would have found it. This is my life we're dealing with, not yours. I'm sure you were betting on finally doing some hard-hitting story now, but please don't insult my intelligence by saying you'll wrap the whole thing up by morning."

I knew it would take me a little more than twelve hours, but I still planned on squeezing something important out of the past. Or maybe Olivia was just going to hand it to me. She had already told me an intimate detail about her mother's death. She seemed ready to talk—or yell—about her relationship with Stanton. Maybe because it was already public knowledge and she was out at the *List* and now Stanton was out of a job, too.

"I already wrote a hard-hitting article," I pointed out. "Maybe you read it?"

Every muscle in her face scowled at me.

"You probably think your article is the best thing to ever get slapped on the front page of the *List*," she said, scratching her nails into the wooden railing next to her. "You're probably having the damn thing framed."

Actually, my mother had already had the front page of the paper framed. It was sitting in my bedroom closet waiting to be hung up somewhere. Upton said that besides the president's election, it was the largest type they had used for a headline in the four years they'd been operating. When I told that to my mother, she'd screamed and driven straight to the overpriced framing shop in Middleburg and had the thing mounted like it was a Gustav Klimt.

"I knew it," said Olivia when I didn't reply right away. "Well, I hope you're enjoying this—really soaking it in—because this is the high point of your career. It's not going to get better than this."

"At least I still have a career," I shot back. "And the paper is printing just fine without you."

Olivia dropped her hand from the railing. "I'm not quite done yet," she replied under her breath.

I wondered if I'd misheard her. Not quite done yet? What the hell was she going to do next?

"You got fired!" I reminded her loudly. "And what self-respecting publication would hire you now?"

Olivia shrugged her thin shoulders and brushed a few stray hairs off the back of her neck. "Yes. I got fired. *You* got me fired. But I've got something that hasn't gone out yet."

My mind began racing. What was she working on? Something with the White House? Dirt on the administration? White House scandals definitely trumped Senate scandals and I had heard Upton trying to reassign one of Olivia's stories on the White House counterterrorism team to Christine. A scandal involving them would be big if Olivia still had her hands in it.

"The Foster Care Empowerment Act," she said softly, smiling at my confused expression. "That was mine. I wrote it."

That fluff piece? I was aware that she had written it. How exactly was she going to save her career with that?

Registering my expression, Olivia repeated herself.

"The act. The Empowerment Act. I wrote it."

I leaned back against the wall, needing something to steady me. The Foster Care Empowerment Act. That was Stanton's bill. How could Olivia write it?

"But that was his cause!" I stuttered. "That was what changed your mind about him."

"You really think he cared about all of that?" said Olivia, wringing her hands in frustration. "About orphaned and abandoned kids? His wife adopted those kids so she would have something to do while he was in Washington. If you believe that self-important, anti-immigration, gun-loving man ran for Senate to pass bills on foster care, you're exceptionally stupid."

"But you don't think that!" I exclaimed, regaining my voice. "I saw your face when you thought nobody was looking. I know your relationship was—"

"Was what, Adrienne?" she said angrily, cutting me off.

I suddenly wished we weren't standing on the small landing. I wanted to be in the city where society forced us to be quiet, civilized. Here in the country, we just screamed.

"Please tell me about the nature of my relationship with Hoyt," she asked bitterly. "I'd love to get some insight from *you*."

It was strange, off-putting even, to hear Olivia call Stanton by his first name. I took a deep breath. "You came to D.C. because you wanted to get close to him," I replied, trying to sound confident. I was not going to let Olivia notice that standing so close to her was making me suffocate. This, all this, was her fault.

"And then when you did, you fell in love with him. You didn't mean to, but you did."

We heard the faint boom of what sounded like thunder and we both looked up at the sky.

"You're wrong," she said, seeming startled from the sudden noise. "I didn't want to get close to him. I needed to."

I let her words sink in as I watched the early evening clouds move faster and faster above us.

"Like I said, I was fixated on him for years," she continued as I lowered my eyes to meet hers. "You understand that, I believe. Obsession?" I thought back to all the nights I watched my White House Correspondents' Dinner footage of Sandro, pausing it on his handsome face as he smiled politely at Isabelle. And the way I pressed my body against his in Olivia's kitchen. How I had gone to his house when I knew Olivia was away, and had kissed him, put my arms around him. Yes, I did understand obsession. And somehow, in these surprising moments, I was starting to understand Olivia, too.

"I hate him," she said. "Real hate. A person like you will never understand that kind of disgust. But that was part of the problem—that level of emotion can turn—and it did. It became something else, something less like loathing and more like . . ."

Her voice trailed off and she looked toward the open door of the apartment, at the furniture inside, the window over the gingham bench and the view of the horse fields.

"What I wanted more than anything was for him to become fixated on *me*. Obsessed with me. He had controlled my entire life—my childhood, college, even this move. He had this inescapable hold over me and I knew the only way I could finally shake it was if I could turn it around. It was my turn."

I stood in silence listening to her. This, then, was how she justified it. Not because he had won her over with his passion for foster care, not even because she had fallen in love. The first time she had seen Stanton, talked to him and finally slept with him, these were the thoughts going through her angry, frustrated mind.

"It worked," she said firmly. "That look on my face—the one you described so inarticulately in your article—wasn't love. That was peace."

"You know I could write a story about this," I said, breaking her out of her so-called peace. "Especially about the fact that you wrote legislation while you were a *Capitolist* employee and having sex with a senator."

"But you won't," said Olivia. She smiled at me presumptuously. "You're nothing like me. You printed the first story because you wanted the *List* to acknowledge your presence. And now you've made your little splash. But you can't handle a beat like this one. You can't smear people's lives and not have it eat away at you. That's why you work for the Style section. It's not because you love writing about celebrities or politicians' wives. It's because you're too scared to do anything else."

Too scared? I had followed her in the middle of the night and photographed her naked with a U.S. senator. If she needed evidence of my backbone, she just needed to turn to page one of every newspaper in the country. She and Stanton had graced them all.

Olivia moved closer to me, her eyes flashing.

"You wanted attention and you found it by bringing me down. But I've already lost everything—my job, Hoyt, my reputation, even my family isn't speaking to me. If you write about the bill—the fact that I birthed it and made Hoyt push it to Pennsylvania Avenue the way I wanted it—you won't hurt me. But you will keep thousands of kids from having better lives. And I know your type. You don't want that on your conscience."

I couldn't believe she was admitting to ghosting Stanton's legislation. Olivia—a journalist and a senator's mistress—had written something that the president was poised to sign in a few weeks. I had to write a follow-up on that. It would be huge.

Olivia turned toward me and gave me her classic newsroom smirk.

"Sometimes in life, Adrienne, it all comes down to motivation." She looked at me, my yellow dress damp around the neck from sweat. "Two people can want the same thing, but the one who's more motivated will get it. When I close my eyes before bed every night, I see my mother shooting herself in the head. I have Technicolor memories of finding her lifeless, bloody body folded over on the shower floor."

She gazed at my parents' beautiful house, the horses, the sprawling green fields, then looked back at me and smiled.

"What, I wonder, motivates you?"

I watched Olivia walk down the steps and climb into Sandro's black car. She drove out the gate and turned left, not toward the Goodstone Inn, but toward home, toward her husband.

Inside my apartment the phone started ringing but I didn't rush inside to get it. Instead, I walked down the wooden barn steps, through the unfenced field, and headed alone toward my parents' house. The world around me made the distinct sounds of summer and the heavy, humid air suddenly felt good against my hot skin. When I was a few yards in front of the house, Jenny from the media team called me for the fifth time that day. I answered my BlackBerry and listened as she said, "Lawrence O'Donnell's bookers want you back on. Tonight. Live. I know you're doing *Hardball*, but it's in the same building. Can you? I already gave them a tentative yes." I gave Jenny a firm no and kept walking.

The Foster Care Empowerment Act, what the pundits had taken to calling Stanton's only redeeming legacy. Olivia had written it, not the senator or his staff or a group of lobbyists— an actual girl who had gone through it, had first been abused, then been cared for, and finally, found her way out. I remembered reading the details of the bill in the newsroom. Hundreds of thousands of kids would get federal funding for three more years of their lives. Right now, the day they turned eighteen, they stopped getting financial support. This bill would extend aid until they turned twenty-one. I thought of myself at eighteen, wearing a pink sundress with boxes of brand-new things, dropped off at Wellesley for my freshman fall by my two adoring parents. They paid hundreds of thousands of dollars for me to go there—my full tuition. And when I moved to New York City after graduation, they paid my rent for the first year, came up to the city, and helped me get settled in. I had depended on them then. And at twenty-eight, living on their property, I still needed their help now. How many kids weren't so lucky?

But this story was huge. If I told Upton he would remind me that I was ruthless—journalism's new pit bull—and we would sit down and put it to press. And for what? The ones who were at fault had already lost their jobs. So Olivia had pushed the bill on Stanton—manipulated him to get what she wanted. Wrote it, even. Once Congress passed it, she probably had Stanton nudging the West Wing staff to make it a priority. Then she had ensured it front-page *List* coverage. But did it matter? It was a good bill. It was an important cause. It had already been approved by both the Senate and the House. Olivia wasn't exactly inviting terrorists onto our shores.

I shook out my hair, pinned my bangs back so they weren't falling into my eyes, and started walking faster. I headed up the long hill, turned left behind the house, took three steps into the woods, and started sweating, my cotton dress sticking to me like medical gauze. I didn't have stealth rubber shoes on, nor did I have a bag filled with camera equipment and a change of clothes. But I started walking toward the Goodstone Inn anyway.

The trees above me were full and green. The only sound I could hear were my feet against the dirt.

I did love Middleburg. It was beautiful and silent and only filled with secrets if you looked for them.

When I got to the stone fence where I had first approached the hotel, that night I saw Olivia's car parked in front of the Bull Barn, I stepped over it easily.

I wanted to walk up to the barn. I felt like I had to see inside the tiny little place that catapulted my career forward. I had never looked at it without being crippled by suspicion and fear.

There was no breeze as I walked toward the little red house. The back of my neck felt wet and stiff.

The scenery reminded me of my childhood. I thought of sitting on the back of Payton's horse, when I was too small to ride on my own. We had trotted together on these same hills, before they became a place for the rich to disappear in style. Everything had been so easy then. Before I understood what my mother did for a living, newspapers were nothing more than recyclable words on a page, good for making papier-mâché and wrapping homemade presents.

I was almost at the top of the hill, the one where the navy Ford Explorer with the Arizona plates had driven up the night I photographed Stanton and Olivia. There was so much space to walk through, so much land. Sandro, the loyal Texan, would have liked it.

It was a shame. The whole thing. So many people got hurt, and the only ones who came out better for it so far were me and the new junior senator from Arizona. The *New York Times* called Taylor Miles the most openly racist politician since Georgia's Lester Maddox. But if the foster care bill became law, perhaps more good could come.

I was still about a hundred yards away from the barn when I spotted someone walking toward me. It was a young man, dressed for the outdoors, not taking a stroll for the sake of walking. He was heading directly to me.

"Can I help you?" he said when he got into earshot. He smiled and kept heading my way. "Are you staying with us?" I looked down at his shirt. It was getting almost too dark to see, but when he got closer, I read his small, elegant brass name tag. Roger Pippin. Goodstone Inn Security.

My article may have left the state of Arizona in the hands of a xenophobic leader, but it had certainly heightened guest protection services at the Goodstone Inn. This guy probably had my mug shot and a Taser in his pocket.

I looked out toward the Bull Barn. There were no lights on inside, no cars parked out front. The sun, minutes from sinking behind the hotel's rolling hills, was spreading its rays on the red walls.

It was a far cry from the Oval Office or the Mayflower hotel, where other political affairs had gone down, but there was no such thing as privacy anymore. Everywhere was the wrong place at the wrong time, even out here in Middleburg.

"I can help show you to your room, if you're staying with us," said the polite Goodstone guard again. He had dark shaggy hair and tan arms. He was stocky, and looked more like a Bard College grad with a love of organic farming than security enforcement. But he clearly didn't want me loitering in the fields in the early evening, looking lost.

"Are you staying in the main house? Or in one of our separate suites?"

Still avoiding his gaze, I watched as the sun finally disappeared below the horizon. In minutes, the sky would be covered in dark pink rays of dying light and the temperature would drop a few degrees. But the humidity would stick. Some things about the idyllic area I had called home for so long never changed.

I smiled at the guard, still waiting patiently for my response, and shook my head slowly back and forth, feeling my hair move against my bare shoulders. "Staying. No," I said. "I'm afraid I won't be staying here after all."

ACKNOWLEDGMENTS

I'm forever indebted to . . .

My brilliant, generous parents. Mom and Dad, without your love and support I would still be in the backyard chatting to an imaginary cat and eating mud. Thanks for buying me books, reading me books, and encouraging me to live, live, live!

My big bro. Ken, your creativity is addictive, and with every word I write I'm just trying to keep up with your production line of great ideas.

Craig Fischer, *l'homme de ma vie.* I can't live without you and this book wouldn't be here without your patience and (manly) cheerleading. I'm so thankful; I might even go to another Nebraska football game . . . and wear flats.

Bridget Wagner Matzie, also known as the best agent a girl could ask for. You're professional and hilarious, and your faith in me over the years has been caviar for the soul.

My editor at Atria, Sarah Cantin. If I could handpick anyone to work with, Sarah, it would be you. From the first time we chatted, I knew how lucky I was. Thank you for your warmth, encouragement, and editing prowess. Every time your name pops up in my inbox, I smile, and every time your edits come my way, I become a better writer.

Judith Curr, Greer Hendricks, Tom Pitoniak, Carole Schwindeller, Diana Franco, Anne Spieth, and the rest of the Atria dream team.

Robin Bellinger for her superb early edits.

My wonderful friends—the Outdoor Ed girls, my Vassar family, the Sisters of the Crisis—you're a hilarious bunch, and I blame you for my future Botox needs.

And lastly, *The List* is very much a book about friendships formed in and around a newsroom. Thanks to my work wife Amie Parnes, Beth Frerking, Stacey Pfarr, Rebecca Frankel, the CLICK girls, the POLITICO crew, the glamorous Washington Life team, and the ITP gals for making the written word so much fun.

THE LIST
Karin Tanabe

A Readers Club Guide

QUESTIONS AND TOPICS FOR DISCUSSION

1. As a group, discuss how you consume political news. What is the first type of source that you turn to—websites? Blogs? Television? Radio? Facebook or Twitter? Did reading *The List* change how you think about the media, particularly the way that American political stories are reported?

2. Despite the intense atmosphere at the *Capitolist*, Adrienne soon discovers, *"The paper chewed employees up and spat them out in a matter of months, sometimes weeks. But the ones who made it past the breaking point loved it beyond all reason."* (28) Why do you think this is? Do you think Adrienne reaches this level of loyalty to it by the end of the novel?

3. On the surface, Adrienne and Payton are very different, but in what ways are they also similar? How do you think Adrienne's relationship with her sister shapes her personality?

4. Discuss the factors that are motivating Adrienne to dig deeper when she first discovers that Olivia and Stanton are having an affair.

5. *"That was the thing about female print journalists. Dressing up, grooming, having two angular eyebrows—all frowned upon. It was still that archaic mentality of trying to blend in with the boys."* (171) Consider the ways that gender politics factor into life at the *Capitolist*. How does the double standard that Adrienne articulates in this quote affect the ways that both she and Olivia approach their jobs?

6. Caroline Cleves Brown, Adrienne's mother, was a newspaper journalist too, but in the heyday of print journalism. Do you think Adrienne has a naïve perspective of the new media world going into *The List* because of her mother's career?

7. What did you make of Sandro? Did you feel that he led Adrienne on? What did you think about the note that their relationship ended on—were you hoping for a different outcome?

8. James Reddenhurst is, on paper, a near perfect man for Adrienne. Why do you think she can't commit to him? Is it because she's infatuated with Sandro, or is it something about James? Would you have picked James over Sandro?

9. Hollywood is fascinated with politics and vice versa. How has new media turned politicians into celebrities, and why are Hollywood actors invited to political events? What does this mean for both the news and politics?

10. Did your feelings toward Olivia evolve over the course of the narrative? Do you divide responsibility for the affair equally between her and Stanton, or do you think that one of them is particularly to blame?

11. If you were in Adrienne's position, would you have published the story about Olivia and Stanton? Why or why not? In general, do you think that the extramarital affairs of politicians should make headlines? Does the fact that Olivia was a reporter, writing about Stanton, make the revelation of their affair seem more newsworthy and less sensational?

12. Did you think the Style girls were justified in their anger that Adrienne didn't share the news of her scoop with them before it went to press?

13. In her final confrontation with Olivia, Adrienne says, *"I felt guilt—of course I felt guilt—but then in Arizona, and now on TV, I was just doing my job. She of all people should understand that. And she would have done the exact same thing."* (357) Do you agree?

14. How did you interpret the end of the novel—what do you think Adrienne was planning to do? What did you think she *should* do?

ENHANCE YOUR BOOK CLUB

1. Imagine that you are casting the movie version of *The List*. Who would play Adrienne and Olivia? What about Stanton, Sandro, or Payton? Share your imaginings with the group.

2. The celebrity-packed White House Correspondents' Dinner plays a major role in Adrienne's time at the *Capitolist*, and over the past few years has become a significant event in Washington, D.C. Who would your dream guest be to interview on the red carpet? As a group, you might look up coverage of the event from years past. Consider visiting Click, *Politico*'s equivalent of the Style section, which author Karin Tanabe once wrote for: http://www.politico.com/blogs/click/.

3. Both the town of Middleburg, and the Goodstone Inn, are real places in Virginia. Check out the actual Bull Barn on the Inn's website: http://goodstone.com/.

4. Many of the places Adrienne visits in Washington, D.C., are real too, including the Smithsonian ice rink, Oyamel restaurant, Kramerbooks, and the Freer and Sackler galleries. If you were writing a fictional book about your hometown, which real places would you include in your story?

5. Adrienne spends lots of time crafting her first-day-of-work outfit and it turns out to be all wrong for Washington. Discuss your biggest fashion faux pas. Were any ever caused by first-day jitters?

6. The pace at *The List* keeps Adrienne from having a social life, sleeping more than five hours a night, or even washing her hair with liquid shampoo. Discuss your craziest jobs ever and what you learned from them.